IN PICARDY'S FIELDS

PREQUEL TO THE RESISTANCE GIRL SERIES

HANNAH BYRON

95100000271804

ISBN eBook: 978-90-832156-0-0
ISBN Paperback: 978-90-830892-0-1
Book Cover Design by Ebooklaunch
Editor: Dorothy Zemach
Website: Hannah Byron

Dedicated to all frontline workers worldwide, whether in 1918 or in 2020.

*And to my great-uncles
William Alexander Westcott &
Jack Westcott, who died in WWI.*

Out beyond ideas of wrongdoing and right-doing, there is a field. I will meet you there.

~ Rumi ~

1

TWO MEN

Agnès

Paris, 20 March 1918

The late afternoon sun set ablaze the upper windows of the operation room in the Lycée Pasteur, creating a golden aureole over the electric lamps that illuminated the wounded soldier on the table and the medical staff around him. There was a concentrated silence in the room, interrupted only by the faint hissing of the Heidbrink anesthetizer gas machine and the short commands Professor Alan Bell issued from behind his surgical mask: *Harmonic scalpel ... retractor... lancet*, which were promptly handed to him by the American nurse at his side.

From the other side of the table, the young assistant doctor Agnès de Saint-Aubin followed the surgeon's swift and practiced hands as he removed the bullet from the patient's neck. There was an intense, steady focus in her blue eyes.

"*Voilà!* Another 5mm bullet from those bloody G98s." For a moment, Dr. Bell studied the round ball between his tweezers before depositing it in a metal tray that the nurse held ready. It clattered, metal hitting metal.

"More oxygen... antiseptics!" The surgeon had already moved to the next stage.

Agnès knew how complicated and dangerous this gunshot wound was. It had hit the young French soldier at high velocity, and the trajectory of the bullet had damaged his nervous system. He was bleeding profusely and was greatly in need of a blood transfusion, which another nurse was hastily preparing. With the strong medicinal odor of the chlorine prickling her nostrils, Agnès let her gaze rest for a moment on the young man's still profile, the roman nose, the dark, almost girlish eyelashes over his closed lids, black locks of matted hair emerging from under his operation cap. He still retained a vague glow of health under his ashen color. How old was he? Seventeen, eighteen? What had he dreamt of achieving in this war? And what would become of him now?

"Stitch him up, Doctor de Saint-Aubin, and when you're done, come and see me in the canteen."

Agnès startled. Her eyes met those of her American professor, and she thought she saw a softening in the steel-gray gaze.

"Of course, Professor Bell, right away." Her words were more straightforward than her voice, but she hastened around the table to take up his position next to the stout nurse. The head surgeon had already removed the white cap from his brown curls and was now snapping off his surgical gloves. With his gaze still on Agnès, he gave his last orders to the nurse.

"Nurse Simpson, assist the new doctor. Make sure you check her multilayer sutures. Nurse Belliard, blood transfusion – now!"

"Yes, Professor Bell," both nurses answered, while Agnès took a deep breath and ceased following the movements of her professor to give all her attention to the young patient on the table. His life; not hers.

She heard him disappear through the swinging doors that flapped for a couple of times before falling still. Agnès took another deep breath, steadying her hands before she said in a subdued voice, "Needle..."

The American nurse, ready to exert a maternal preponderance over this inexperienced doctor, instantly handed her the bent needle and thread. In an upbeat voice, she added, "You'll do all right, Doctor."

This kind nudge gave Agnès the confidence she needed, and she completed the complicated sutures under the older woman's scrutiny, knowing she was doing the best job at stitching she had done so far.

While she was washing her hands at the enamel sink in the kitchen unit next to the operation room, she heard the screeching wheels of the hospital bed as the patient was wheeled to the recovery room. She hoped he would live and convalesce completely but knew his chances were slim. So many had already died under her hands. She reminded herself of the next step in the process; no more thinking of the patient at this point.

She should be proud. She had done well, blocking her emotions during the operation and especially during her own suturing. She was making progress. Professor Bell's lessons were finally sinking in; she was developing a neutral attitude to suffering and complications. Agnès smiled at herself. She could hear him say it in that American tongue of his, pronouncing his r's and long, drawling vowels, an English so exotically different from that of her Oxford English tutor.

"Doctor de Saint-Aubin, there is no difference between a male and a female surgeon. Emotions simply stay out of the operation room. Always."

Drying her hands on the blocked tea towel, she wondered what his reason was for summoning her to the canteen. They had never met outside the lecture room or the operation theater, so Agnès felt uneasy. She was mastering the work; simply doing the job, identical to cutting and stitching dummies during the lectures. Truth was that her stomach still felt queasy after every operation – no matter that Professor Bell had told her she was cut from a special cloth; that female surgeons were going to be the stars of the twentieth century. He had taken it upon himself to personally supervise her surgical progress after she obtained her *Diplôme de l'Etat de docteur en medicine* from l'Université de Sorbonne in the spring of 1914; first at the American Hospital in Paris and now as part of his operation team at the Lycée Pasteur. Nothing pointed to him being dissatisfied with her. So, what now?

She suppressed a sudden thrill that he might ask her out. There had never been anything but a professional contact between them, and he was – of course – almost a decade older than she was, somewhere in his early thirties.

"Silly goose, he's probably married. Although he doesn't wear a wedding band. But who does in the operation room?" As she smoothed her springy blonde hair on top of her head and gave her full lips a dash of coral lipstick, she noticed how pale and tired she looked, with dark rings under her eyes, her face pale from the rationing and working long hours. How would he ever notice her if she looked so mousy? To add some color to her cheeks, she gave them both a soft pinch, and then gazed at her own eyes. They were an intense soft blue; *robin's egg blue,* Papa called them. If only she looked a little darker, more French – which was a ridiculous wish as everyone always complimented her on her pale, elflike look. But the Americans loved the dark-haired French girls. She saw it all around her.

Smoothing the dark-green pleats of her day dress, Agnès hastened through the long corridors of the Lycée Pasteur, originally built as a school for Neuilly-sur-Seine but now temporarily turned into an extension of the American War Hospital because the ongoing war demanded more emergency beds every day. Temporarily? It had been going on for close to four years now, and it only seemed to get worse. Outside in the Lycée's courtyard, the blue vans of the American Ambulance Field Service came and went in parade, with never a lull in the arrival of wounded men from the front. But for today, her day at the operation table was over.

Before entering the canteen, Agnès paused for a moment. Doctor Bell had always been honest with her, so there was no reason to think she had muddled things up. Chin up, she told herself.

The hospital canteen was the only place in the 1600-bed hospital that offered a relatively warm space to relax and recuperate. It was a large, whitewashed room with a high, beamed ceiling and a row of tall alcove windows along the Boulevard d'Inkermann letting in plenty of light during the day. Around the clock, the canteen was a beehive of comings and goings, filled to the ridge with the smoke of hundreds of pipes and cigarettes, the chatter of voices, the clinking of cutlery and the scraping of wooden chairs over the sanded floor-boards. On both sides of the long tables, the electric bulbs above them looming as oversized pearls, a variety of nationalities sat side by side. Medical staff, ambulance drivers, recovering soldiers, they all shared just one goal: to win the war against Imperial Germany.

Agnès saw Alan Bell standing near the soup table, engrossed in animated conversation with one of the pretty American Red Cross nurses. His hand touched her arm lightly at times, and he nodded at her while the brunette gazed up at him, recounting what must have been a funny story as they both laughed heartily. Hesitantly, Agnès approached, not sure whether she should interrupt their conversation, but Alan spotted her and gestured to her to come closer.

"Doctor de Saint-Aubin, come and meet Elsie Gamble. She's from Chicago, like me! We grew up on the same street. Now, isn't that a coincidence?"

Agnès noted how he called the nurse by her first name while addressing her formally, but when she shook the girl's soft white hand, Elsie smiled warmly.

"So nice to meet you, Doctor de Saint-Aubin. I won't tell you all the good things Al's just told me about you." *Wink, wink.* "I'm ever so impressed to meet a female surgeon in the flesh. But right now, I should get my lazy behind out of the way, as my shift's starting in ten minutes."

With an amicable slap to Alan's arm, she moved away. Her round hips swayed slightly under her white nurse's coat, a fact that did not go unnoticed by the soldiers in the room, whose weary faces brightened whenever they caught a glimpse of female beauty. Just like the Americans and Brits liked the French girls, the Frenchmen were infatuated with American nurses, who were known to be ever so care-free and spontaneous.

"Sit over there." Alan pointed to a table in the corner that was slightly less crowded. "I'll get us something. Would you like some soup, or toast with scrambled eggs?"

"Just a café au lait and a biscuit, please."

Alan looked at her with one dark eyebrow raised. "Still not steady on the nerves? I won't insist, but after eight hours at the operation table, you do need to eat a little more than a cookie, Doctor de Saint-Aubin."

"I will, in a minute. But first, coffee. And please, call me Agnès."

She watched him order himself a full plate of beef bourguignon and a large mug of tea. He moved with such ease, such composure, speaking French to the fat cook as if he had lived in her country all his life. It had become second nature to her – minutely studying his expressions and movements – but so far it had only been a logical process of learning from him in the operating theater. As this was the first time seeing him interact with others outside the medical sphere, it was a novelty to her but she studied it all just the same.

He came towards her, balancing his food and her coffee on the metal tray, and she noticed the smile had disappeared from his handsome face.

"I'm ravenous," he announced. "I do have something important to tell you, but could it wait a couple of minutes until I've wolfed this down?"

"Of course." Agnès stirred her coffee, steadying her queasy stomach against the strong smell of beef that wafted her way. She intentionally diverted her attention to other people at their table to stop herself from scrutinizing him. When he had put down his fork and wiped his mouth on the linen napkin, her eyes met his again. She was aware she must have looked puzzled, but she could not read his intentions. He seemed to be struggling with something, and for a moment, her heart thumped in her throat.

"I'll call you Agnès if you agree to call me Alan." His voice had lost the professorial tone, but it was flat and devoid of emotion.

She nodded, waiting.

He took a sip of his tea as if weighing his words. "I wanted to tell you that I'm leaving Lycée Pasteur to move to a base hospital at the front."

She still did not reply, but looked down at her coffee cup to hide her disappointment.

"There are two reasons for this, Agnès. The first is that I want to make a real difference in this war – to give it my all, saving lives where it matters most. And secondly, I want to study the major leaps in medical progress where they really happen. And that's at the front. The war is proving to be a great teacher to us doctors."

With some difficulty, Agnès raised her head again. "Why are you telling me this?"

He gave a short, dry laugh. "I didn't just want to disappear. It didn't seem right. You've been my student for four years, and I've been your practical supervisor for the past year. So, the time is right. You're ready to take over from me. You're a good surgeon, Agnès."

"I want..." she started, but then stopped, diverting her gaze again. An awkward silence crept up between them. "I'd like some scrambled eggs on toast now."

"Good choice." He jumped up, giving her space to collect her thoughts. Although she had seen dozens of Allied surgeons departing to the field hospitals closer to the front, it had not occurred to her that Alan might go as well. After all, he oversaw the entire operating team in Paris. But everything was changing. Maybe he was right. Maybe she wanted to go too, and be where she could make a real difference, help the heavy casualties, save lives on the spot.

Agnès's brain worked hard. It was not the first time she had thought about going closer to the battlefields. When the war started, her father and she had made plans to turn their château near Roye into a field hospital, but the Germans had prevented that by seizing the castle during the First Battle of Picardy in September 1914, and since then, its medieval fate hung unknowingly in the air.

Alan returned with her meal and suggested she take her turn eating while he smoked a cigarette.

Having made her decision to ask him to take her with him, Agnès picked up her knife and fork. "You're not in a hurry?"

He waved his hand, dispersing the smoke. "No, not at all. Got all evening. I planned to take a walk along the Seine. Could do with some relative peace before the real madness starts. Care to come along?"

Agnès smiled. "I'd love to!" She had eaten a few bites and pushed her plate aside. Resting her elbows on the tablecloth, she asked in her quiet voice, "Can I come with you to the front?"

For a moment he seemed baffled, then curtly said "No!" while extinguishing his cigarette in the overfull ashtray with a firm jab.

But Agnès was not that easily pushed aside. "Why not, Alan?" Saying his Christian name was an unusual experience, but it felt invigorating.

He jumped to his feet. "Let's take that walk, and I'll explain why."

From the Lycée Pasteur, they walked along the rue Peronnet in the direction of the Seine. The March sun had already sunk behind the tall buildings, and leaden clouds gathered in the sky signaled rain in the evening. They did not speak, and Agnès was painfully aware of Alan's proximity, the tall man by her side who did his best to curb his big strides so she could keep up with him. He was at least two heads taller than she and walked with that American swagger Agnès so admired in him and his countrymen, as if they still needed to secure their supremacy over the Wild West.

Not knowing what to say but dying to ask questions, she decided to remain quiet as well, telling herself to just enjoy the opportunity of being with him. When they reached the boulevard that ran along the Seine with busy traffic going both ways – taxis, private automobiles, army vehicles, ambulances – Alan turned to her.

"Which way?"

"I live two miles to the left, near the Pont de Puteaux. Would you like to go in that direction for a bit?"

"You live near the Bois de Boulogne?" He sounded surprised, then added with an endearing chuckle, "ah, that's right, you're a Baroness. Had quite forgotten that. Gosh, you Europeans! Truly never met so much old blood before in my life. Every other person I speak to is a Viscount or an Earl of something."

Agnès bit her tongue but decided not to tell him she was not a Baroness by birth but had been adopted. "Would you like to walk along the waterside?" she suggested.

"Sure."

They descended the stone steps and went along the broad pavement, with boats and smaller barges gliding past in the diffuse afternoon light. The green spur of the Île de la Jatte was to their right. Agnès breathed in deeply. She liked taking this route home, close to the river, after a long day in the operation room. There was a fresh breeze in every season here, and the pungent scent of the water, cool as a mountain stream, always livened her senses. The dark water rippled in miniature waves, sloshing against the quay when larger boats passed. Green patches of vegetation drifted by, and silver-finned fish skittered under the surface.

They still walked in silence, each wrapped in their own thoughts. Agnès took regular, precise steps, her arms by her sides, her medical bag clutched in her right hand, while Alan, who walked hatless with his brown locks pushed away from his forehead, had his hands folded at his back.

Just when Agnès wondered if she should break the silence because it was becoming awkward, he said evenly, "Listen, Agnès, I had it all worked out. You've trained under me long enough to lead the team at the Lycée. That was my reason for waiting to go up north – to make sure you'd be ready."

She was baffled by his words, but her heart swelled with pride at this promotion. "Thank you. I honestly didn't know you had so much confidence in me."

"I trained you, remember?" Again, that chuckle she had never heard in the operation room. It made him sound younger, more boyish.

"True." She gave him a shy smile, her eyes catching the last of the evening light.

"So, it would be rather inconvenient if you also decided to leave for the front."

"Doctor Davies could take charge."

Alan seemed to ponder this for a moment. "He might."

"It's not a whim, Alan. I've been considering this ever since the war started." And she told him of the sad circumstances of Château de Saint-Aubin.

He listened attentively but shook his head. "I'm not your father, just your mentor and supervisor, but if I *were* your father, I would simply forbid it." The stern professorial tone was back.

Agnès sighed. "I'm sure my father will be in total agreement with you. But what about the rumors that the Germans are considering a new offensive on the Western Front, now that Russia is no longer in the war? They could take Paris overnight, and I wouldn't be safe here either then."

"Then you could flee south, like everyone else will."

"As long as this wicked war goes on, nobody is safe anywhere," Agnès remarked bitterly.

"But there's a difference between seeking danger and staying relatively safe."

"The same goes for you."

Agnès wondered how it was possible she was talking in this manner to her professor, but somehow their walking together in civilian clothes with the bustle of her own city all around them made her ignore the distance they had always carefully observed. And she could not bear the thought of never working with him again. She was not done learning from him; she wanted more, more than this. So she decided to try one more thing.

"We're almost there. Would you care to come and meet my father, to see how he thinks about this ludicrous plan of mine?" She made it sound as light-hearted as she could.

Alan glanced at his pocket watch and then looked at the sky where the clouds were thickening. "I think I ought to be..."

"Please, Alan."

He glanced at her begging face then shrugged his shoulders in a comical way. "Oh, all right, then. I suppose I owe you something after all this time working together. If you want to fight two men, be my guest. Show us what you're worth." He grinned at her, and for a moment she felt incredibly close to him.

They left the pathway along the Seine at the Pont de Puteaux, and after crossing the Boulevard de la Seine, Agnès directed them to a stately mansion on the waterfront. The dark-green front door read in decorative golden lettering *Baron Maximilien de Saint-Aubin et famille.*

As soon as she opened the door with her latchkey, the house-keeper Madame Petit appeared from the front parlor looking questioningly at Agnès. "You're all right, Miss Agnès? You're very late!"

"Sure, Petipat, everything's fine. This is Professor Bell. Is Papa home?"

The ample-bosomed housekeeper nodded, straightening her massive black dress, and looked, slightly bewildered, from the young girl to the tall American who was standing rather stiffly on the doormat.

"Yes, yes, of course. Do come in, Professor Bell. Welcome." Busying herself with making room for them in the parlor, puffing up cushions and rearranging chairs, she addressed the young Baroness but secretly eyed Alan, giving Agnès inward glee at the effort the elderly woman was making at understanding what was going on.

"The Baron is in his music room, as usual," the housekeeper went on. "He was waiting for you, as he'll be going out tonight. Will you be going out as well, Miss Agnès?"

"No, Petipat, it's been a long day. Afternoon shift tomorrow, but still early bed for me." She glanced up at Alan, wondering what would happen tomorrow. He had not told her if he was leaving straight away.

"Now, I'll go and fetch your father, my girl." Moving as fast as her voluminous body allowed her, the housekeeper proposed before she disappeared in the hallway, "Do make yourselves at home, dears, and tell me what I can get you."

"Would you care for a sherry, Alan? Or maybe something

stronger? My father wisely stocked his cellars before the war. We may run out of potatoes, but we've still got plenty of liquor." She giggled.

"A sherry will be fine, Ma'am," Alan said politely, but as soon as the housekeeper had left, he lifted a quizzical eyebrow. "Petipat?"

"Oh, do sit down." Agnès laughed. "It's just my special name for her. She's been like a mother to me."

"Ah, I see. So, your own mother...?" Agnès nodded and hoped Alan would not probe any further in this sensitive matter, but after a while the silence hung heavily in the room, so she added timidly, "My mother died shortly after giving birth to me. I was raised by my father and Madame Petit, who has been with our family since the beginning of time."

"So sorry to hear that." Alan's brow softened with empathy. "If it's any comfort to you, I also lost my mother, though I have some vague memories of her as I was four at the time. My father remarried soon after, but I've never liked my stepmother, whom I was supposed to call Mother as well, and...well ...it's also influenced the relationship with my father." He stared wistfully at the blunt knives on the wall.

Agnès' kind heart went out to him immediately. "My time to be sorry. At least I've had a doting dad, and of course Petipat who's picked me up more times than I can remember."

The air lifted, and she followed Alan's eyes as they took in the room. She wondered what he would make of it and how different it certainly must be from his American house back home, with the parents to whom he did not feel close.

As all the rooms in the De Saint-Aubin household, this one displayed a mishmash of styles, ranging from conservative classic to quirky exotic, very much like the owner himself. The downstairs parlor mostly held objects from the Baron's many trips to the African continent, so it was generally referred to as 'The African room'; other rooms being labeled 'The West Indies Room' and 'The Aboriginal Room.'

The majority of the furniture consisted of high-backed Louis Quinze chairs and canopies in cream chintz, but the coffee table was a wooden elephant carrying a glass plate on its back, and there were a number of rackety stools, carved antelopes, and naked ebony statues, reminiscent of his expeditions into dark Africa. The floor was carpeted with Persian rugs, but here and there the skin of a lion or a tiger had been thrown on top of them, trophies from his safari trips. Oval ancestor portraits were juxtaposed with spears, knives, and other primitive weaponry. It was chaotic, personal, liberal. Agnès feared it gave her guest quite a glimpse into her unusual background.

In a room upstairs, a violin abruptly stopped playing, and a little later, voices could be heard coming closer. Alan rose to his feet, thereby hitting his head against one of the low-hanging candelabras.

"You're okay?"

He nodded, rubbing the crown of his head. "Damn height. Never seem to get used to it." At that moment, the Baron entered, with Madame Petit on his heels, followed by a maid carrying a tray with glasses and a carafe filled with amber-colored sherry.

Her father, although of modest height, at least compared to Alan, managed – as always – to immediately fill the room with his presence. It was not that Baron Maximilien de Saint-Aubin was a remarkably handsome man, nor very imposing, but there was a quality in his posture, a mixture of what Alan had called 'old blood' and a personal artistic freedom, that made certain no one overlooked him. It was in the way he moved, elastic like a cat yet aristocratic in his uprightness, the elegant movements of his arms derived from a life-long practice as a musician, and the ease with which he carried himself, confident but never completely in tune with protocol and decorum. He had the creaseless olive-colored skin from his Spanish mother and the silver-streaked hair and honey-brown eyes of his late father, the 6th Baron de Saint-Aubin.

His clothing was always of good quality and often had a colorful, eccentric twist. Today he was wearing embroidered Persian *babouches*, simple charcoal flannel trousers with a clear fold in them, and a dark-blue pullover under which the collar of his white chemise, with the invariably colorful silk cravat tucked in.

A broad smile spread over his mustached face as he approached them, and it was typical of the Baron that he first went over to his daughter to plant a kiss on her fair forehead and compliment her on her loveliness before turning on his heels and greeting their guest. Agnès knew why he did this – to make clear that any man who might be interested in her would have to deal with the father first, but it embarrassed her as it was rude to Alan, who after all was her professor. And since she was twenty-three, there was really no reason for him to treat her as a little girl.

"Ahh, Professor Bell! Agnès has told me so much about you. Glad to finally make your acquaintance." He shook Alan's hand cordially and then seated himself in one of the Louis Quinze armchairs, putting one knee over the other and rearranging the flannel crease so it went straight over his knee.

Alan sat back down on the coach. Agnès noticed an uncertainty in him she had not seen before, and she inwardly cursed her father. He made a habit of making other people feel smaller than needed. While the maid handed round glasses, she decided she would come to the point straightaway, so Alan did not need to stay in her house any longer than he probably wanted.

"Papa, Alan... uh... Professor Bell is here for a reason, as you might have guessed." Her father took a contemplative sip from his glass and set it down on the side table before looking up at her.

"Alan?" he asked in mock surprise, "Oh... I see. Yes, of course. You have been working together for so long it is probably appropriate by now." And turning to Alan, he added, "You're American, are you?"

"Yes, sir, originally from Chicago, but I moved to Paris in 1910 after graduating from Harvard Medical School *summa cum laude*."

Ha, Agnès thought, *you know how to deal with my father. You're one up on him.* But she remembered Alan had told her that he wanted to see her fight two men, so before her father could further digress on a topic of Americans versus Europeans, she interrupted.

"Papa, this is not a polite visit. It has a specific purpose. I want to ask your permission for something."

"Fire away, my darling!"

"Alan has decided to leave the American Hospital in Paris to work closer to the front. I want to go too."

The Baron took another sip from his glass, biding his time, and Agnès was curious to see which angle he would take. He cleared his throat and fixing his brown gaze on Alan, calmly remarked, "Noble decision. I'm all for it. Where exactly are you going?"

"I was thinking of the American base hospital no 5. in the Pas de Calais, but I have been invited to several others."

The Baron nodded. "You must have been. With your expertise, they'll be lining up for you. Sad business, this war. Only engineers and doctors seem to benefit from it, making one invention after the other. Still, all these novel ideas will come in useful in peacetime, no doubt." He sighed, and Agnès waited.

"Listen, Professor Bell. I'm not at all involved in warfare. I do my humble bit at the Ministry of Food Supplies and in supporting Clemenceau, that sort of thing, but that's about as far as my knowledge goes. However, my good friend Count Horace de Dragoncourt – Agnès here knows him too – is the French ambassador in London, and he also owns a château near Amiens that has been turned into a Red Cross hospital. His eldest children, slightly older than my girl, are in charge, although they aren't doctors. Just yesterday I received a letter from Horace complaining they are desperately short of surgeons, which isn't surprising, I suppose."

The Baron gave a scornful laugh and took another sip before he continued. "Well... you see... if you're not damned set on going to be with your fellow countrymen at the Pas de Calais, you could consider taking a look at Dragoncourt instead. It would give you the extra bonus of visiting one of the greatest French renaissance chateaus, though, by Deuce, what's left of its splendor is anybody's guess." The Baron's face darkened, and Agnès knew he was thinking of their own castle in Picardy.

Alan asked, "How many beds do they have?"

"My dear chap, I have no idea, but I can find out for you."

This was Agnès's chance to interrupt. "If Alan decides to go to Dragoncourt, would you let me go as well?"

The Baron shifted his legs, placing the other knee on top, and now started studying the crease. When he looked up again, his voice was composed and friendly but held an undertone of alarm. "You're safer here and ... and you know why."

"No, Papa, I am not!" Her voice sounded shrill. "I'm not afraid, and I have nothing to hide!"

The Baron glanced at Alan, who was observing both father and daughter, and he added hastily, "I don't see a way around it, my sweet girl."

Agnès rose, her lips pressed together, lacing her delicate, thin fingers in front of her stomach until her knuckles showed white.

"I'll let Alan out. But you know, Papa, that we intended to turn Château de Saint-Aubin into a frontline hospital before it was seized by the Germans, so I don't understand your objection now." In all honesty, she had to admit she did understand, but what was safe these days? Nothing.

Both men rose as well, Alan carefully avoiding the candelabra. The Baron shook his head wearily. "I would have joined you to at De Saint-Aubin, Agnès darling, but there's no way I could accompany you to Dragoncourt. That's the difference."

Agnès looked hopefully to Alan. Would he come to her rescue? But she saw he would not. She had lost the battle, and with it she had also lost him.

"You'll be okay, Agnès," Alan said consolingly, as they stood on the steps outside her front door. Agnès wrapped her arms around herself, chilled and defeated. Alan looked so distinguished in the city's evening lights, yet so unattainable. She felt like running up to her room to sob on her bed, but she restrained herself.

"Will I see you before you leave?"

"Of course. I won't be leaving until the end of the week. Now cheer up, Doctor de Saint-Aubin, you've got your whole future ahead of you."

"Do I?"

Then he did something he had not done before. He grasped her hand and shook it. With the feel of his capable surgeon hand in hers, so warm and strong, she could not but smile, and he smiled back.

Returning to the sitting room, she found her father hiding behind his newspaper, *Le Petit Parisien.* "Alan will be wondering if we're covering something up," she said bitterly.

"No, he won't. He understands I'm protecting you. And if you ask me, he's doing exactly the same."

"You are... you are always so righteous, Papa, but this is wrong! I want to be where I'm needed most."

"You *are* where you're needed most, *mon enfant!*"

2

PETIPAT

A gnès did not sleep well. Twice she was roused from her restless slumber by the sirens of the air raid warnings. Every Parisian was at high alert these days, especially during the nights, as it was never clear what the sirens meant. They could be a warning that the stealthy, silent German Zeppelins were drifting over the city's rooftops or that the dreaded Gotha bombers were approaching from the north. If the heavy drone of the Gotha engines mixed with the shrill sirens, it meant leaving your warm bed and hurrying down to the cellars as fast as possible.

Agnès switched on her bedside lamp to check the time: 4:15 am. Unwilling to leave her bedroom until it was absolutely necessary, she lay listening for explosions, nearby or further away, but there were none; nor the hasty sirens of the fire brigade sweeping past on the Boulevard. Huddled under the bedclothes, even covering her head, she was grateful that the small de Saint-Aubin household would not be forced to descend into the damp cellar tonight, where she was sure rats were also housed.

They had had their fair share of the bombings in the Département Hauts-de-Seine in the past years. In the winter of 1916, a bomb had fallen on the Île de la Grande Jatte, right beside the tobacco shop at the corner of the bridge. Not only had the shock and the damage been terrible, but the acrid, stinging smell that spread afterwards had been so strong they'd had to keep the windows closed for two days. Many more attacks had followed, bringing chaos, panic, and casualties in their wake.

It had been no surprise to the French that the Imperial Army had focused their air attacks on Paris right from the start of the war; after all, that was what they were after – to force the proud French capital to its knees – but so far they had not succeeded. What they had achieved was that the Parisians swayed daily from patriotic bravado to jittery fear and never came to understand these eerie, secretive attacks that fell from the sky like murderous black snow.

When the final all-clear sounded at the break of day, Agnès fell into a deep sleep. Then at seven, she was wide awake again, and the same thought popped into her mind: she dreaded the night behind and the day ahead. It was clear that if she wanted to do her job properly, she had to get more sleep, so she shut her eyelids again, but it was no use. Her stomach drove her out of bed.

Everything seemed a battle these days, even getting enough food. She tried not to pay too much attention to her rumbling stomach; after all, she was still reasonably fed at the hospital, and her father got extra coupons from his Ministry. But the stress and the bad food were taking their toll on her physique. And now her last joy was to be taken away from her as well: working with Alan.

Agnès resolutely threw the covers away and got up, stretching her stiff limbs, just when Gaël, the maid, knocked on her door.

"Come in."

She watched the timid Breton maid – Petipat's new acquisition from her hometown of Saint Malo – tiptoe into the room.

"Ah, you're already awake, mademoiselle Agnès. Did you sleep well?" The freckled girl, no more than seventeen and as flat-chested and foal-like as a twelve-year old, gave Agnès a furtive glance and quickly pattered across the room to open the curtains and the shutters.

Agnès grumbled a negative response while she sat at her dressing table to brush her wavy hair. The maid turned on her flat, worn shoes, and clasping her thin hands in front of her starched apron, murmured, "The usual breakfast, Miss Agnès?"

"Do I have a choice?"

"Afraid not. I wish I could offer you fresh orange juice and *a petit pain au chocolat*," Gaël apologized.

Agnès was aware of the young girl's awe for her, a doctor at the hospital, a Baron's daughter, and an elegant, sophisticated lady. *If only you knew*, Agnès thought, and reminded herself to be kind to the girl and not take her foul mood out on her.

"Then I'll settle for coffee and bread and butter. Please bring it up to my room." Agnès dismissed the maid with a friendly smile, but Gaël kept standing hesitantly on the threshold.

"Anything else, Gaël?"

"Um...yes... Madame Petit told me she would like to see you before she goes to Les Halles to see if she can get hold of some fresh eggs and vegetables. She doesn't know if she'll be back before you leave for the hospital, and she just wants to see you."

"Okay, no problem. And is my father in?"

"Yes, I think he's still sleeping. Would you like me to let you know when he's awake?"

"No, I'll come down myself after breakfast. I'll see him then."

After Gaël had closed the door, Agnès dressed and seated herself at the windowsill to let the demons of the night disperse and find the courage to face the day. Her room was on the second floor of the house, facing the Boulevard. The water of the Seine was a soupy gray, with here and there a fleck of light, as always moving slowly in the direction of the English Channel.

It had rained heavily in the night, but it was dry now. The cars on the boulevard created iridescent fountains of water when the tires hit the puddles. The air smelled fresh, cool, calm; just what she needed to steady her nerves. The hubbub from the street below filled the room, and she found her strength again in the hooting of cars, the chatter of human voices, and the cooing of a pair of love-sick doves on the rooftop. This was the Paris she loved; the Paris she needed. Agnès stretched and welcomed the new day, whatever it would bring.

Suddenly the dream she'd had just before waking up popped into her memory again and made her frown.

SHE WAS SITTING under the chestnut tree in the garden in Picardy reading a book. It was summer. There was no war, and she was small, maybe eight or nine. But when she wanted to get up and go indoors to see why Petipat was summoning her, the war suddenly broke out, and hundreds and hundreds of pieces of shells fell into the garden, preventing her from reaching the house. She tried to open her mouth, to let the housekeeper know she was trying to make it home but had to stay under the shelter of the tree until the shelling was over – but she had no voice. The skies had turned leaden from a constant shower of iron rain. Petipat called her name again, but now it sounded much closer, and she saw the large figure come towards her, fighting her way through the shelling to bring Agnès her little red rain cape. Before Agnès could warn her that it was not rain but shelling, the house-keeper exploded before her eyes, still calling, Agnès, Agnès where are you?

THE RECOLLECTION of the dream gave Agnès the shivers, and she quickly ate her breakfast and ran down to see that Petipat was okay.

The portly housekeeper was in the front parlor, polishing a set of silver cutlery. She looked up when Agnès rushed in. "*Ho-ho*, young mademoiselle, what's the rush? You'll trip over that dress of yours and break your neck when you come sprinting down the stairs like that."

"I had the most horrible nightmare, Petipat, I dreamt...I dreamt..." Out of breath, Agnès could not go on and just slipped onto the chair next to the housekeeper, close to her fleshy hips, as she had done when she was a little girl.

Instead of asking after her bad experience, Madame Petit observed, "Blasted air raids. They spook the hell out of you. You've always had sensitive ears, Missy. Remember when your Papa bought his first motorcar and you stood with your little hands over your ears, screaming, *Papa, it smells awful, and it's broken already because it does vroom-vroom?*" The memory made them both laugh.

"Don't they worry you, Petipat?"

"Oh, they do, but one gets used to so many bad things in this wretched war. You remember Madame LeGrand, the fishmonger from Les Halles? Her son got injured at Verdun the other week. Poor lad's probably blind and crippled for good at only eighteen, and then they tell her that *he* must be grateful to still be alive." The housekeeper looked disturbed and angry.

Agnès knew the fishmonger was one of her best friends. "It's terrible. Where did they take him?"

"I've got no idea, but I'll ask her later today."

"What's his name?"

"Georges Legrand."

"I'll see if he's with us, and then maybe I can pop around and have a look at him."

"You're such a sweet girl, Agnès." Madame Petit stopped the polishing to let her tired, round eyes rest on her protégé. "Your late Maman would have been so proud of you." It was seldom that Petipat referred to Agnès's mother. Their current unstable life must remind her of the ordeal they had gone through when the young Baroness de Saint-Aubin had died of puerperal fever when Agnès was only three days old. It lay on the tip of her tongue to ask after her mother, but as usual Petipat steered the conversation in the direction that she had chosen.

"So that Professor Bell... he looks like a decent American for once. I didn't recognize him yesterday, but we saw him at your graduation, didn't we? Is he married?"

Agnès had to giggle despite herself. She knew the look the housekeeper was giving her all too well. Alan might be second-choice marriage material, due to being American and most likely without any blue blood running through his veins, but Petipat would never pass up a chance for her pupil.

To prevent further probing questions and upsetting her tender heart, Agnès replied, "He's married, Petipat, so can you stop your matchmaking attempts right here and now." She bit her lip, picking up one of the spoons Petipat had just polished and playfully using it as a mirror. Her cheeks were red.

"Ah, well, I just thought you might fancy him, my dear. And since you never go out and mix with eligible young men, you might as well find one in your doctors' circles. It'd give you both something in common to talk about." She shrugged and continued, "Well, your father isn't up yet, but I guess you can tell me what you both would like for supper. I can't guarantee it'll be available, but one can try."

Agnès knew that Petipat did not need any recommendations about the food she purchased, as they always ate everything they were served, but it was part of her instructions in 'how to raise a proper baroness'; one who knew what to serve for meals and how to compose a shopping list for the servants. Agnès smiled. The real reason was that she wanted Agnès near her during their morning hour together before the housekeeper went on the other highlight of her day: shopping and chatting with her friends at Les Halles.

When Agnès was still home-tutored, she would occasionally be given permission from the stern Oxford-educated Mr. Hickinbottom to go with her to Les Halles. She would hold firmly onto Petipat's hand, with a lollipop in her other hand, skipping from one little patent shoe to the other as Jeanne Petit stood gossiping with her friends.

"I have the day off on Friday. I'd love to go with you to Les Halles, like in the old days," Agnès blurted out.

"You're always welcome, my dear, but why would you? It's not much fun these days. People fighting over the little food there is, and everyone's in a bad mood."

"I just miss doing things with you, Petipat."

"Silly girl. Here, take this spoon and a cloth. Then you'll do something with me."

They sat amiably side by side in the morning sun, making the silver gleam. There was no need to talk anymore. Just being together filled their hearts.

WHEN PETIPAT HAD LEFT for Les Halles, Agnès wandered through the house, a little aimlessly, as she recalled the conversation with Alan and her father. She sighed deeply. It would be so lonely without him. She knew she could never become closer to him than they were now – as colleagues – but he was so much part of her daily life; like her father, like Petipat. Agnès was not someone who gave herself easily, but she was fiercely loyal to the people she loved. Loved? Did she love Alan? The thought disturbed her.

Just as she sat down to read *Le Petit Parisien,* there was an enormous explosion somewhere near the Avenue des Champs-Élysées. Agnès jumped up, alarmed, wondering what that could be in the middle of the day. The blast was so loud it echoed on in waves, putting pressure on her eardrums and making all the windows rattle. Agnès had the presence of mind to quickly close the windows before storming out of the sitting room.

Her father appeared from his quarters, his hair in disarray, tying the sash of his satin morning coat around his waist. "What by Deuce was *that?*"

"I have no idea," Agnès stammered, "but it doesn't sound good. Can't be a German bomb. They wouldn't attack us in the middle of the day. Or would they? Maybe it's a gas leak?"

"What an abominably loud bang! It must be the Krauts! Oh, how I despise the rats!" He raised his fist to the ceiling, as if they were personally hiding there. Gaël peeped around the door, trembling and ashen. At the sight of her frightened face, the Baron composed himself again.

"Don't fret, girl, you'll be safe here as long as you stay indoors. Bring us some coffee – black and strong!"

They had just finished their first cup when the telephone rang. Max went to answer it but held the receiver out to Agnès.

"It's for you. Professor Bell."

Agnès got up, still a little shaky and surprised at this early morning call. "Must be an emergency," she said.

Alan's voice sounded hurried. "Major attack on the Quai de la Seine ten minutes ago. Many people wounded. Some killed. The emergency services on the spot cannot figure out what happened. Nothing flew overhead, and it looks like shelling, not bombing. We'll need all the off-duty staff in the theater. Could you come as well?"

"Of course. I'm just finishing my morning coffee. I'll be there right away."

"I'll send a hospital car to pick you up. Thank you, Agnès."

When she arrived at the Lycée Pasteur and hastily got into her operation gear, she was told by a waiting nurse that a severely wounded lady had just been brought in, that Alan was already removing pieces of shrapnel from her body, and that he'd said the effects of this type of attack looked different from the shell wounds the frontline soldiers showed. Agnès hurried towards the operation room, meanwhile putting on her gloves and cap.

When she entered through the flapping doors, Alan dropped his scalpel and quickly came her way. "I honestly didn't know, or I wouldn't have called you. I'm so sorry." He looked quite upset, which he never was in the operation room. The hairs on the back of Agnès's neck immediately stood up. As only his eyes were visible between his cap and mouthpiece, it was hard to read his expression, but they held more emotion than Agnès had ever seen in them before.

"What is it?" she asked huskily, trying to stay calm.

"I wouldn't mind if you left, Agnès," he said softly. "It's a horrible sight."

But she had already gone over to the table, and there lay, scarcely recognizable, her Petipat. A shock like an electric bolt went through her, and clutching the metal edge of the operation table, she needed all her strength to stay upright. The features of the housekeeper's face were hardly distinguishable; dozens of metal pieces had cut her fleshy face, her nose was almost gone, and her mouth was a gaping hole.

But the parts worst hit were her breast and abdomen. The full force of the shell had hit her there, and the metal parts had dug deep into her white skin, cutting her open like a slaughtered pig. There was blood everywhere – on her clothes that had been ripped apart, on the table, even on the floor. She was still bleeding profusely.

"There's no time to waste. I must continue." Alan had resumed working already. "Do you by any chance know her blood type? She needs a transfusion right away."

Agnès swallowed with difficulty, straightening her back, and forced herself to stay at the table.

"o positive." And then almost by reflex, she ordered, "Nurse, tweezers!" With trembling fingers, she set out to remove the smaller metal parts from what remained of that beloved face, while Alan worked on the housekeeper's vital parts. A nurse busied herself installing the blood transfusion. Suddenly a steely calm came over Agnès. She would save her Petipat if it were the last thing she did. She had to blink once, but then her eyes remained dry and her hands moved as if of their own accord: precise, capable, calm.

One by one, she deposited the metal pieces in the tray, all the while talking softly to the sedated patient, not knowing what came out of her mouth but needing to talk, wanting to comfort the wounded woman and herself. She told her she would be all right, that she loved her and needed her, that she had been the best replacement Maman she could have wished for, that she forgave her scolding and reprimanding because she knew that she'd meant well and that sometimes she had been naughty, although not very often, and that one day she would marry and then Petipat would be there, beaming and red with excitement, and on and on she babbled while Petipat slept and for the first time in her life did not talk back.

Alan looked up briefly from his intense work to study her. "You okay?"

She nodded, babbling on, and not feeling ashamed about that or wondering what he would think. She was beyond caring about the rest of the world. It was only work and Petipat that counted; only that.

She had no idea how long they had been working under the

bright electric lights on the ruined body on the green operation oilcloth or how late it was, but at some point it became clear that they were losing their race against the clock. The housekeeper's breath became shallower by the minute, despite the extra oxygen, and her organs were giving out. But still they kept going, hoping against hope; it was a fight Alan clearly also wanted to win, so they gave it their all. Until the very last minute.

In the sterile silence of the operation room, Alan tossed his scalpel back in the tray and tonelessly observed, "She's gone."

But Agnès could not stop, not until Alan took the tweezers from her shaking hand and grabbed her wrist.

"It's no use, Agnès. Please stop."

His voice attempted to comfort her, but she did not want to be comforted. Not at that moment. She wanted to act, to act and then to take revenge. Her mind was as clear as the cold steel that had killed her Petipat. Life was suddenly so simple and yet so utterly cruel and useless. Freeing herself from his grip, she let her arms drop limply along her exhausted body. She was even too tired to cry. Alan took her by the shoulder and led her to one of the chairs near the wall.

"Sit down for a minute."

"No!" Her voice was toneless but defiant. "I need to phone my father, and then I want to make the preparations to lay her out properly. I'll do that myself."

[Image: image3.jpeg]

IT WAS a bright and sunny spring day when they buried Madame Jeanne Petit at the Cimetière Passy under the watchful eye of the Eiffel Tower – a day she, who as a 15-year old Breton girl had come to the French capital to run the old Baron's household, would have loved and taken maximum advantage of. She would have urged the maids to give the carpets an extra good batting outside, or lured both the old and the young Baron into leaving the sanctuary of their music room for a healthy stroll along the Promenade.

For over forty years, Madame Petit had been the pivot of de Saint-Aubin household, during winters reigning supreme over the mansion in Paris and during summers at their château in Picardy. And after Agnès's mother's tragic death, her role had been extended to 'bringing up the little Miss,' a mission Jeanne Petit had taken up with all the formidable force of her kind heart, often fighting *her cause* with the eccentric father who – in the eyes of the fisherman's daughter – was far too strict one day and too lenient the other.

Agnès, her face pale and white, and dressed entirely in a simple black tailored dress that reached to her ankles, black gloves, and a black fedora hat, had just thrown a small spade of sandy earth onto the oak coffin, saying a last farewell to her beloved Petipat. She stood upright, sensing her own pain but also that of her father. For him it must feel as if losing an older sister. The Baron looked shallow and other-worldly. At moments, Agnès feared he was on the brink of collapse; the devastating news that his right-hand in life had been killed had hit her father so hard, certainly as hard as it had hit her. Agnès stepped around the fresh grave to give her father her arm to leave Cimetière Passy together. She tried to catch his attention from behind her black veil, but the Baron stood rigidly staring at the coffin down below the two heaps of turned-up ground, unwilling to move.

"Have you said your goodbye, Papa?" There was deep concern in her soft voice.

He did not answer. She was not sure he had even heard her. He looked so utterly defeated in a somber black suit, the man who liked to dress in bright colors and approach life tongue-in-cheek. Gone was the happy-go-lucky, quick-witted, problem-evading Papa she was accustomed to. Since the news, three days earlier, he had been incredibly frail and even more erratic in his behavior, drinking heavily and playing his violin until late in the night, refusing food or human contact.

"Papa," she urged again, "please talk to me. Tell me what you're feeling. You scare me when you're like this."

Her words seem to shake him from his stupor.

"Heh? What? Sorry, my darling, I haven't been myself. I'm

surprised myself I'm taking it this hard. She's been... she's been part of my life for as long I can remember. Since Maman left Papa to live openly with the Marquis de Villepin, Jeanne has been the center of our life. I just can't imagine life without her."

It crossed Agnès's mind that he had lost all the people he loved: his father, his wife, his loyal housekeeper. She, Agnès, was the only one he had left, and she vowed to herself that she would never leave him. Not if it were in her power. Gone was the idea to go to the Front with Alan. She would stay with her father. Her path was clear to her now. To divert his gloomy countenance, she did exactly as Petipat would have done: she changed the subject.

As cheerfully as she could muster, she said, "Wasn't it kind of Peti-pat's cousin and niece to come all the way from Saint Malo? It must have been an arduous trip for them in the middle of the war. So sorry they had to leave on the return train, and we couldn't invite them to the house."

The Baron only nodded, but it was at least a sign he had heard her and was coming back to her. Arm in arm they walked away from the grave towards their burgundy-red Peugeot 105 that stood parked on the gravel outside the wrought iron gates of the cemetery. Agnès turned to Gaël and Marie who followed close on their heels, with eyelids swollen from crying. They awaited instructions from her now, instead of from Madame Petit.

"Go home, girls, and prepare a light supper for the Baron and me. Then you can take the rest of the day off." Her voice was friendly and resolute, which made her wonder about herself. Petipat had managed to turn her into the 'young Baroness' after all. But it was too late now for her to witness the fruits of her hard labor.

At the gates, Agnès also exchanged a few words with the priest, a gangly young man who – according to his emotional sermon – had known Madame Petit quite well. That had been a comfort to Agnès, who realized she had never paid much attention to Petipat's personal life. The people who had attended her funeral were a handful of women, Madame Petit's friends from the neighborhood, and of course Madame LeGrand to whom she had been on her way when she was hit by that monstrous new German weapon, the Paris Gun.

As father and daughter were about to step into their Peugeot, with Agnès insisting she would drive, she was confused to see Alan coming their way, holding a small bouquet of pansies.

"Sorry to be so late, sir, Agnès! I came to pay my respects. And to apologize to you. I feel I've failed in my profession." He shook the Baron's hand solemnly and nodded in Agnès's direction. This simple, kind act seemed to revive Max, and he waved away the doctor's apology with some of his former vivacity,

"No need to apologize at all, Professor. Agnès told me how you both fought like lions to save her life. If you couldn't do it, nobody bloody could."

"Thank you, sir." It sounded rather humble from the Sorbonne professor.

"You know what," the Baron said, reviving more by the minute, "let's go for a drink at Au Chien Qui Fume on the rue du Pont Neuf. That was Jeanne Petit's favorite place. Before the war, we used to go there for her birthday. You remember, Agnès?"

Alan looked doubtful, and Agnès did not miss the dark rings of tiredness under his eyes nor the deep lines on his lean, clean-shaven face. She had not been working since the housekeeper's death, which meant even more shifts for him. He had most likely been standing at the operation table since the crack of dawn.

"Do come, Alan," she said softly. "It might be one of the last times I see you before you leave."

"All right, but let me deposit these flowers on her grave first. Oh, and I did come by métro."

"We have the Peugeot waiting." The Baron was smiling now, which lifted the corners of his drooping mustache. "We'll take you home afterwards. No fuss at all."

All the tables of the outdoor café of the corner restaurant with its burgundy-red awnings were occupied, and waiters continuously emerged from inside, balancing full trays of drinks above their heads, shouting "Attention, attention!" It was as if the Parisians had en masse decided to make a resolute stand against the attacks on their city and show the Huns that under no amount of pressure were they willing to give up life as they had always lived it. There was no denying, though, that most of them were dressed in black, also having arrived from the nearby cemetery. Their small ensemble found a table near the window, and the Baron ordered drinks.

"It seems like we're always drinking sherry." It was Agnès's attempt at giving the conversation a light tone. "Well, it *was* Petipat's favorite drink, so here's to her."

"To Petipat!" they said in chorus.

They raised their glasses and drank for a moment in silence, each contemplating the loss of another civilian life, that horrendous by-product of the war that served no purpose at all.

After having taken a large sip, the Baron mused, "I was only three years old when she came to our house. I remember a ruddy-faced girl standing on the doorstep with her clothes in a bulky bundle. For some reason, I still remember her standing there. It must be because she spoke so weirdly, and she smelled of fish. Isn't it strange that I still know that?"

"We do have early memories of things that made an impression on us," Alan observed helpfully.

"It must have been in 1874. I didn't have a tutor yet, so I had plenty of time to hang around Jeanne, as I always called her. It was you, Agnès, you started calling her Petipat. To me she was always Jeanne, and I was Master Max until...until Papa suddenly died in 1890 and I – at the age of twenty-one – was addressed as Baron Max. We both struggled with that transition. I think it's because of Jeanne that I dislike class distinctions. She was really like a sister to me. I even spent a week with her family in Saint Malo during my school holidays. Her father took me fishing on his trawler; we caught cod and haddock. It was one of the biggest adventures of my life, maybe even nicer than trekking through Africa or Australia. Yes, Jeanne was family to us, always steering the house clear of disaster till disaster struck her. It's so unfair." The Baron cleared his throat, as he was wont to do when he was stressed, and then loosened his black cravat with an impatient tug of his hand, took it off, and flung it on the damask tablecloth. This seemed to give him a little more air, but Agnès could see he was close to tears. She felt her own eyes becoming misty as well.

"Listen," he continued with some difficulty, "I'm devastated beyond words, and I've no idea how we're going to survive without her, but there's no replacing her, and I've made up my mind about a couple of things these past days." He placed both his hands on the white damask cloth, the golden signet ring with his family emblem and a large diamond in the corner sparkling in the electric light. "Tough times lead to clear insights." He smiled sadly, but there was warmth in his brown eyes as he turned his gaze to his daughter and from her to the man he had already understood meant a lot to her.

"So, this is how it is: if the war comes to Paris, Paris must come to the war."

"What do you mean, Papa?" Agnès was puzzled; afraid he was losing it.

"It means, my dear, that you will be going to the Dragoncourt hospital at the front. Doctor Bell has agreed to it, too."

"No, Papa!" Agnès shook her head vehemently. "There's *no way* I'm going to leave you! You need me here. I've quite given up the idea." But then she realized what he had been saying, and gazing at Alan, her face became a huge question mark.

Alan avoided her gaze, pretending to be interested in what was going on at the other side of the window; worn-out housewives hurrying to Les Halles with their empty shopping bags flapping against their thighs. As she could not get Alan's attention, she turned to her father again.

"What is this? What do you mean?" she demanded.

"It means, my dear child," the Baron explained, "that I phoned Professor Bell yesterday to ask if he would be willing to stay with you at Dragoncourt for at least a couple of weeks until you've found your feet there. That's what he has agreed to do. I also phoned Horace de Dragoncourt – you know, he's in London with his wife, but according to him, Jacques and Elle would greatly appreciate two experienced surgeons in their hospital château."

"But what about you, Papa?" The sudden change refused to sink in.

Her father put his slender, brown hand over her white one. "Jeanne's death has made me realize that one should not stand in the way of another person's desire. Life is too fickle these days. You know how much you had to fight with me to study medicine instead of getting a degree in literature. You won that fight, and now I understand why. If the war hadn't happened, you'd probably have chosen another path, but your generation now chooses much more tactically."

"Thank you, Papa." Agnès, who had been sitting on the edge of her chair, sank back against the cushion, still confused. "But you haven't answered my question: what about you?" This was between them, no matter what Alan's role in it was.

"I'll be fine, my dear, really I will. I'll probably go to our apartment in Nice for a bit, just to be away from...you know...from it all." He made a vague gesture with his hand. "I'll hire a housekeeper, don't worry. Plenty of women looking for a job these days. By God, I hate this war! I just want to finish my biography on Chopin in peace! Is that too much to ask for? You, on the contrary, my dear brave girl, want to do your patriotic bit, while I just want to get away from this bloody war as far as I can. If that makes me a coward, so be it!" He emptied his glass and ordered another one.

"You're not a coward, Papa!"

The Baron's mustache was going up and down vehemently as he worked his mouth behind it to control his rage and his conflicting emotions. "It doesn't mean you won't be in grave danger, my girl, even more so than everybody else, and you know it. I'll be feeling it in my bones every minute of the night and day, but that's the price I'm willing to pay for this noble folly of yours. I'll come visiting as soon as I can!"

Alan had been quiet during this discussion, but now Agnès felt it was time he explained himself.

"Why?" she demanded.

He looked at her calmly, but behind the calmness she could see other emotions in the steely eyes, things she could not read. Was it care, guilt, or something else?

"When your father phoned me and explained his new take on your work, I decided to say yes. Unless you object to it, of course. I've taken the liberty of phoning Dragoncourt hospital, and they're really understaffed. So, it's up to you."

Agnès's mouth fell open. "Of course," she said, still with some hesitation, but then more firmly, "Of course I'll come with you."

"That's settled then," he said in a flat voice, and Agnès wondered if he was only agreeing to the new plan as a promise to her father. There was no going back on it now, but his attitude did temper her enthusiasm.

"You're sure?" She tried to read the calm, clear gaze but failed.

"Yes," he replied curtly, "but I really should be going now, so if you'll both excuse me..."

Before the Baron could reoffer him a drive home, he was already out the door.

"He'll come around. You'll see," her father said reassuringly. "We're all under a lot of strain. Don't read anything into it, my dear."

"I hope you're right, Father."

3

TO THE FRONT

The entire de Saint-Aubin household had lost its luster now that the scepter-waving matron was gone, and Agnès knew it was a good thing both her father and she would take a break from the oppressive atmosphere that filled the house. It had been eerily silent without Madame Petit's formidable presence, her booming voice at all hours of the day giving orders to the maids and equally bossing around the master and young mistress. Now there were only the two maids left, Gaël and Marie, who crept around the house like frightened mice, clearly lost without the housekeeper's direction.

Every object, every room breathed Petipat's presence, and it made missing her all the harder. Memories flooded Agnès day and night, and she was sure that her father was going through the same. He had been right. Without realizing it until now, Petipat had been *family*; she'd been far more to them than an ordinary housekeeper. It was not just because of the important role she had played; it had been her personality.

I suppose I'll miss her severity most of all, Agnès thought, as her eyes filled with tears. What a good person she was, just because of her firm belief in a strict, unbending view of life, which was actually based on kindness.

Love was an overarching but elusive concept to Agnès; nobody ever talked openly about it in the de Saint-Aubin household, although her father addressed it as an abstract concept or compared it to art. Yet she sensed it everywhere – how Papa had loved her Mama, and then Mama's child, and how she had loved Petipat instead of her Mama with all the loyalty of her loyal little heart. But there had never been kisses or cuddles between them, although Agnès vaguely remembered putting her little arms around her legs and being dragged along and clearly remembered sitting in her broad lap being read nursery rhyme books.

What had been plentiful were half-smiles and jam tarts; and Petipat taking care of all her small needs; of nursing her through her childhood maladies with a cool cloth on her forehead; of stern rubbings with a stiff towel after her bath; of prayers side by side on their knees before bedtime; of doing her school work while the housekeeper darned socks; and of course their weekly walks to the Église Saint-Pierre with her prayer book, dressed in her pink Sunday dress with starched petticoats.

There had been endless squabbles about her meals, her clothes, her manners. Walk, talk, behave as a Baroness! With a capital B! Petipat had been at every bend of the road of Agnès's life. Until now. She could simply not grasp life without her and moaned aloud more than once, "Why didn't I tell you that I loved you, Petipat! I'll do you proud. Maybe not as a Baroness but perhaps as a doctor. I'll save as many lives on the front as I can! I promise."

On the day she and Alan were to leave for Picardy, Agnès came down to the breakfast room and saw her father's valises and violin case standing in the hallway next to her own luggage. So, he was really going to Nice! Her father's violin had been silent for days, which was never a good sign, but today he was sitting upright in the breakfast room, munching a slice of toast while reading his morning paper and looking rather chirpy. Freshly shaven and with his long silver-threaded hair brushed thoroughly, he was already in his traveling outfit, an elegant light-blue gabardine suit with a bright-red waistcoat and a gold-specked cravat. The prospect of a change of scenery seemed to give her father something to look forward to.

Agnès let out a sigh of relief at seeing him this way. "Ah, Papa, our last breakfast together! Isn't it strange? Hopefully not for long." She planted a kiss on his cheek and wrinkled her nose at the lavish splash of cologne he had dabbed on his mustache.

"*Mon ange*," he said, putting down the newspaper, "I hope so too. Let us pray for peace very soon."

While Agnès took her place at the breakfast table, Gaël rushed in, her cheeks red and her apron strings undone, muttering excuses as she poured her a cup of coffee and refilled the Baron's cup.

"I will wait for you to phone *me* instead of the other way around," her father said as he folded his newspaper. "The Dragoncourt telephone will most probably be needed for more urgent matters than calls from an over-worried Papa. However, I will write regularly, and you will write to me too, won't you?"

"Of course, Father, whenever I have the time. I'll phone and I'll write. But please don't worry too much about me. I'll be all right. The Germans won't bomb hospitals. Well, at least, I don't think they will," she added doubtfully.

"Don't count on it, my daughter. These Boches are the most barbarian human beings that have graced the earth since the Dark Ages. I've always hated them but never so much as today. The Prussians with their military bombast most of all!" He looked at her with that furious agitation he always had when he referred to the German nation.

"I know, Papa, and so do I."

They finished their breakfast in silence. Agnès had no idea how to go about saying goodbye to her father without breaking down, but he must have sensed her anguish and came to her rescue.

"My train leaves at ten. I've ordered a taxi to take me to the Gare de Lyon. It will be here any minute. What time is Professor Bell picking you up?"

"About ten-thirty, Papa. So, you'll be leaving first?"

He nodded, dabbing his voluminous salt-and-pepper mustache

with the corner of the white serviette. He sprang to his feet more cheerful than he obviously felt.

"Let's not make a fuss of this temporary farewell, my dear, that would only burden us further." He pressed a quick kiss on her forehead, mumbling "Bless you, my girl," and as Gaël helped him into his overcoat, the taxi driver rang the doorbell, and her father was already out the door. The front door clicked shut behind him.

The utter silence of their Paris home enveloped her, the home that had been their haven since her birth. Never without Papa; never without Petipat. She stared at the breadcrumbs on the tablecloth, misty-eyed with tears. What now? It felt as if her whole life had been kicked from underneath her in a matter of days, and she had no idea what awaited her next. Was it all her fault? Had she set this awful train in motion by wanting to go to the Front with Alan, to remain close to him?

But she had little time to consider these heavy questions, as the main reason for her new concern was about to arrive. In the hallway her suitcase stood ready, a yellow leather case with her initials embossed on the front and the corners reinforced with silver rivets on small triangles of the same light-colored leather. It held the simplest and plainest of her clothes, her toiletry necessities, some medical books, and her diary. On top of the suitcase stood a matching hat case, containing the black fedora she usually wore to church. Next to it stood her canvas medics bag, khaki with a red cross, which she had decided would also serve as her handbag, as fancy bags would be useless and inappropriate at the front. Only her purse, her doctor's license, and the French passport with her legal name would make clear who she was.

Alan had said he would stock a hospital truck with as many supplies as they could take – bandages, morphine, operating equipment, and even stretcher beds and crutches – so it seemed wrong to use more space than absolutely necessary. But the urge to travel light was deeper than that. Agnès felt she had to make a clean start with her life. In the last couple of days, with the loss of Petipat uprooting her whole existence, she had felt pushed to the front with a force that overrode her conscious decisions. It was a primal drive, a necessity to take revenge in the only way she could: by saving as many Allied lives as possible, by drowning herself in the war, only the war, and nothing but the war.

She looked around the familiar parlor one more time with a heart heavy with grief. The Baroque clock on the mantelpiece chimed ten, the clear bronze bell always a sign for the housekeeper to emerge from the recesses of the house to check on the Baron's daily needs. But the house remained silent, the maids having withdrawn to the kitchen at the back and her father having taken flight from a house that no longer possessed a soul.

Perched on the chair she had sat on only five days earlier to introduce Alan to her father, Agnès waited, idly smoothing out the creases of her cashmere travel dress with her slender white fingers. Everything had seemed so much simpler that late afternoon. Petipat had been very much alive, and Agnès had resigned herself to staying in Paris to take Alan's place as head of the operation team for the duration of the war. She knew how strongly he had been opposed to her coming with him, but there was nothing she could do about it now. Her life was hanging in limbo, and only a jolt out of that limbo would hopefully make life worthwhile again.

I'll try to stay out of danger at all costs, she promised herself. *I have to. Papa is right, but I'll do it also for Alan's sake.*

At that moment, the doorbell rang, and she opened the front door herself, seeing him standing there, tall and handsome in a new army medical uniform but with an agitated frown creasing his forehead. The engine of the Ford T of the American Field Service was running.

"You're ready?" He sounded stressed, but seeing her expression of uncertainty, he added, "What's wrong?"

"Should I be wearing an army uniform as well?"

"No, that's not needed at the moment," he replied curtly. "Here – let me put your stuff in the truck." He was already passing her to scoop up her luggage, placing both her suitcase and hat box on his shoulder and marching down the steps as if they weighed nothing.

Agnès followed with her medical bag, listening to the front door click shut behind her, her heart sad and wearisome. She did not allow herself to look back.

Before she knew it, they were driving along the Avenue de le Seine, and she was saying goodbye to Paris, not knowing when or if she would ever see it again. The awkward silence that had never existed between them in the lecture room or the operating theater but had been obvious the few times they had met outside their common meeting ground hung in the truck's cabin like a dense fog. Alan was driving with great concentration, braking regularly and then speeding up again, swearing under his breath at the thick Paris traffic. All the while an angry frown remained etched on his countenance.

Agnès felt numb and rattled, so she turned her attention to the window and the familiar sights, saying goodbye to them: the Eiffel Tower, Notre Dame, Sacré Coeur. Battered by bombs, its citizens hungry and grieving too many loved ones, Paris was still relatively intact, at least physically. Where they were heading now, Agnès expected to look entirely different, nothing like the Picardy she knew and loved.

As they came to the north of Paris along the Avenue du Temps des Cerises in the vicinity of Taverny, Alan relaxed a little, his grip on the steering wheel less tense and his face returning to its usual composed self. He lit a Lucky Strike cigarette, inhaled the smoke deeply, and exhaled with a grateful sigh. "Sorry, Agnès, I've been in a foul mood, but it's got nothing to do with you."

"It's okay," she said, glad he'd finally broken the silence. "I've had better days myself."

"Compared to you, I should be ashamed of myself." She did not miss the bitter tone. Was there a tinge of shame? Having no idea what he was hinting at but feeling unsure whether she should ask when he seemed so stressed, she lapsed into silence again. Alan flipped the butt of his cigarette out of the window and looked straight at her. "I'm in a foul mood because my wife left yesterday. Gone to the States."

Agnès gasped. So, he *was* married. She squeezed her hands together in her lap. He was married, but his wife had left him and gone back to America. That seemed a strange thing to do during the war. But then Alan was doing his own thing as well, and these were extraordinary times. What did she know about love and marriage? Maybe his wife had wanted to feel safe, to be with her own family while Alan was at the front. Agnès tried to think of something neutral to say, but it came out before she could help it.

"I had...I had no idea you were married."

"Oh, yes. At least, I think I was."

"To whom?" Agnès expected one of the American nurses.

Alan made an angry gesture. "Suzanne."

"What does she do?"

"She's a painter."

"As a hobby?"

"No, actually, as a career. She actually managed to make somewhat of a name for herself."

"Wait... you don't mean Suzanne Blanchard?"

"The same."

Agnès was stunned. Alan was married to Suzanne Blanchard, the famous Parisian cubist artist who made delicate, airy pastels and had exhibitions at the Musée de l'Orangerie and as far as New York?

"Oh, my goodness, Alan, I had no idea. I've read so much about her in *Le Petit Parisien*. But why has she gone to the States? She's French."

Alan shrugged his shoulders and lit another cigarette. "I'd rather not talk about Suzanne anymore right now, if you don't mind. Let's focus on our expedition to get to that bloody front."

The angry frown was back, and Agnès decided not to push him. Before her rose an image of the dark beauty with short-cropped hair, big mournful eyes, and a Cupid's mouth that invariably held a cigarette. Suzanne Blanchard was not just one of Paris's sought-after artists, she was also known to be a staunch suffragette. Agnès had devoured the scandal around her that had erupted in early 1917 when she had led a campaign for voting rights for French women, hoping France would follow Holland's example. It had all begun so smoothly but had backfired when she started to attack Clemenceau in an open letter in *Le Matin,* calling him a *male chauvinist with retarded morals.*

The elderly French prime minister was immensely popular. He was the only one capable of steering France through the war, and criticism of him was considered close to national treason. When the whole press from conservative to progressive started to attack Blanchard, she had declared she would never involve herself with politics again and only paint.

Agnès studied Alan's profile. Somehow it did not surprise her that he had chosen such an outspoken French woman as his wife. He must have felt her scrutiny because he shot her a gaze with those irresistible steely eyes. "And how have you been coping these past days?"

"It's been hard." She dragged her thoughts away from the realization that Alan was a married man and concentrated on their trip together.

"Anytime you change your mind and want to go back to Paris, let me know, okay?"

"I don't want to go back. Only when the war is over. I've quite made up my mind to help where help is needed most."

"So have I." The earlier tension dispersed, only to be replaced by a new gap between them. She hoped they would at least become friends next to colleagues. She needed him more than ever in her shrinking world.

As they approached the river Le Sausseron at Vallangouard, they encountered the first roadblock with the blue-coated French soldiers, with blue helmets and bayonetted rifles crossed over their breast, standing on guard. It took the young soldiers only a quick glance at the Red Cross truck and their American medical documents adorned with the Rod of Asclepius to shout, "*Allez, allez. Bon voyage!*" and they were on their way again.

"If you want me to do some of the driving, let me know," Agnès offered. "I know this road like the back of my hand, as we used to take it every summer to our château."

"No, I'll be fine as long as you give me directions. But you must tell me that story about your lost castle near Roye!"

"I will, but not today." She turned to studying the latest military map they had obtained from the ambulance drivers in Paris. "Until Chantilly I know the way by heart, but from there, it may prove a bit of a puzzle. We're supposed to head west towards Amiens instead of north to Roye. In the old days, that was the same route, but I don't understand exactly from this map where the current frontlines are. We certainly must avoid the region near Compiègne and Noyon. And I suspect there will be plenty of roadblocks and deviations after Chantilly."

"We'll get there in one piece, don't worry." Alan was obviously more cheerful now he had told her what had been bothering him.

For the next fifty kilometers on their north-bound route, things went relatively smoothly. Alan had to park the truck by the roadside twice to let convoys of trucks filled with English, Canadian, and American soldiers pass by, waving their respective national flags up front. Under the canvas hoods, the soldiers smiled and waved to them, singing songs as if they were off to a party instead of the war. For the rest, nothing much pointed to the battlefields lying ahead of them, although they could see smoke rising skywards in slender gray plumes when they reached the Val d'Oise, and Agnès thought she could hear the vague boom-boom of cannons over the roar of the truck engine.

When they stopped outside Amblainville for a simple lunch of pickled cheese, sandwiches, and ginger beer that Gaël had packed for them, there was birdsong around them in the young foliage, and the tiny corn stalks in the fields gave the impression of a normal spring ahead. The March sun had come out in its full glory, spreading a golden light over Picardy's sloping hills, chasing shadows of elongated light and darkness against the green hillsides. In other circumstances their picnic, as they sat side by side on the army blanket spread on the new grass, would have seemed like a romantic outing, but Agnès felt sad and tired.

Alan looked around the countryside appreciatively. "Never knew Picardy was so pretty. And so close to Paris. For some reason we always went south – you know, the Côte d'Azur, that sort of thing.

Absolute waste to turn these beautiful fields into a battlefield. Who could think?"

Agnès just nodded, the 'we' in his comment making her again acutely aware of his marital state.

Their conversation once again stagnated, so they ate and drank in silence, and she started looking forward to being at Dragoncourt in the presence of Jacques and Elle, whom she had not seen for ten years but who were very hospitable and funny. The prospect of being around other people so that she would not have to be alone with this man, who made her uptight and silent, lifted her spirits. When they got back to operating together again, things would get better; they knew that routine. A personal relationship between them just did not seem to work.

But then again, there might be other surgeons at Dragoncourt, and she might not even see much of him. He was planning to stay for a fortnight or so and then be gone. Just as well. It would give her pained heart the necessary rest. Deep in thought as she was, she was not aware that Alan, who was now lying on his side on the blanket smoking another cigarette, was studying her.

"What about you, Agnès?" He flipped the ash onto the grass. "Do you have anyone special?"

She shook herself from her daydream, blushing that she had been taken off guard. "No," she stammered, "no, I haven't." Glancing furtively at him, she saw that his attention was fixed on her in that intense, scrutinizing way she never understood.

He threw the cigarette stub away and sat upright, stretching his long body. "I can't believe it. You're such a nice girl. Your father couldn't have any trouble finding a good match for you."

She had been sitting with her legs tucked under her, the skirt of her navy dress fanned out around her, and her black hat atop the soft pale-gold hair to protect her from the sun. Absent-mindedly she had been tearing clover leaves from their stems, letting them drop in her lap one by one. She stared down at the tiny green triangles on the dark-blue fabric, observing with sadness how they were already withering.

"I've always put my career first; I know that sounds odd for a woman. Also, I was nineteen when the war started. I know most girls usually have had propositions by that age, but it hadn't happened to me. After my father finally consented to my 'doctor mania,' as he called it, he also told me that marriage would be my own affair – if and when I was ready for it. My father isn't like other fathers; he's actually quite modern, or others would call him eccentric. No, it was actually Petipat who always came up with suitors, this Viscount or that Minister. She could never accept me being a professional woman. To her, working was a coarse business, and certainly unsuitable for someone of my class." Agnès let out a sad little laugh. "Poor Petipat!" Then she halted, realizing she had been telling Alan more than she had intended to, but he didn't seem satisfied yet.

"Do you think you'll ever marry and have a family of your own?"

Abruptly getting up, Agnès brushed the green leaves from her dress and started packing the remainder of their lunch in the wicker basket with impatient movements. "I don't know. Why all these questions? Certainly not as long as this war goes on."

"Sorry, I didn't mean to probe." Alan also got to his feet, and helped fold the blanket and put everything back in the car. "It's just that you're a bit of an enigma to me, Agnès de Saint-Aubin. Beautiful, classy, eligible – but all you do is work. It seems strange for a young Parisian woman. Most of them who can afford it choose to stay at home, and with all the new liberties the war provides, enjoy life as they can with their girlfriends and beaux."

Agnès raised her shoulders and, hopping into the passenger's seat of the truck, remarked, "I guess I've always been a bit on the solemn side, not doing things the way others do them." To her surprise this made Alan grin, the boy-like expression she had seen during their walk along the Seine and her heart ached. *Go away*, she thought, *go to another hospital, let me be!*

The closer they came to Château de Dragoncourt, certainly after Beauvais, the more obvious the signs of war on the east side became. They were stopped along the road three more times by roadblocks, and French or British soldiers with grim faces and heavy-looking machine guns snarled at them instead of giving them a friendly welcome.

"*Présentez vos safe conduits!* Show your passes! *Vous allez où?* Where are you going?"

The same questions over and over again; but as soon as the soldiers found out they were surgeons on the way to help their wounded countrymen near Amiens, weary smiles lit up the haggard faces and the Ford T was let through with as much ceremony as the exhausted men could muster.

They passed abandoned houses, collapsed into a rubble of stones, with bomb craters in the courtyard. Around the ruins, patches of high, stalky grass overgrew red cabbage and leek fields, reminders of once well-kept vegetable gardens that would have fed families through the winter.

After Clermont, along the D916, they drove westwards through deserted villages and hamlets with most of the gray stucco-fronted houses severely damaged, half of the roofs collapsed, leaving a debris of broken red tiles on the pavements, while shreds of once-white lace curtains flapped out of broken windows. Some of the houses had broken-down front doors hanging akimbo. There was not a living human being in sight, only once a solitary white cat with a high arched skinny back scurrying along the stone walls.

"Poor kitty cat," Agnès sighed. "I wish we could take him with us."

"Better not. The people will hopefully return home soon. He'll make sure he stays alive by catching mice."

They passed burnt meadows with blackened tree trunks sticking up, as if they had entered a spooky moon landscape instead of the lush countryside that had once been Picardy. The first graveyards appeared, rows and rows of white crosses, here and there with a tiny bouquet of flowers attached to the cross or lying on the freshly upturned soil.

"So, this is the real thing." Alan gazed around with an astounded look, and giving Agnès a quick glimpse, his eyebrows furrowed, and he said rather worriedly, "Still sure you want to go on?"

"Stop asking!" It sounded firm enough, but at times Agnès

instinctively held her hand over her mouth. Was this what human civilization had come to in the 20th century? How on earth had this happened?

And then suddenly they were diving back into the shade of a long, winding road lined with old plane trees sprouting into fresh green above their army-camouflaged trunks, nature unperturbed by the devastation around it, lush and whole, switching from one extreme to the next.

After they had taken the D920 in the direction of Villers Breton-neux, their final destination, the war came so close it was all-pervading, the rat-tat-tat of the machine guns, the cannon booms, the high, piercing whistling of shells. Then came the acrid smell of burnt materials – it was not clear whether rubber, human flesh, metal, garbage, or a mixture – permeating the truck's cabin through the open windows.

Soon after, the disastrous results on humans themselves became visible. For miles they had not seen a living soul, but now the wounded men appeared everywhere in the fields, with missing arms or legs, bandages around their heads, lying on stretchers, or just deposited on a blanket in the grass with red cross nurses and doctors walking among them, kneeling next to them, doing what they could to spare lives or at least give the dying as much comfort as they could. The moans and cries that rose from the fields were a pitiful litany to the skies above.

"What the devil!" Alan exclaimed, "I never realized it was *this* bad."

Agnès just watched in silence, her eyes wide, hands itching to help but knowing they could do nothing here but drive on and set to work as soon as they reached Dragoncourt.

"Almost there," she announced, and as she said it, she saw the tall castle rise before them as Alan steered the truck around the last bend of the rue Victor Hugo at Cachy. He spotted the castle at the same time and mumbled an astonished "Nom de dieu!" under his breath. Agnès remembered her father telling Alan he would be impressed with Château de Dragoncourt's splendor, but she herself had forgotten how beautiful it was and gasped. It had been at least ten years since she'd last visited her father's friends.

Where their own medieval château in Roye was a sturdy, well-built fortress, Château de Dragoncourt was of refined elegance, a small version of the Loire castles, breathing the best of classic French renaissance architecture. It had been positioned on a flat piece amidst low-sloping green hills, with the forestry around it cut down so it rose proudly out of what had once been meticulous *jardins à la Française*, all symmetry and central perpendicular axes leading from the house.

The closer they came, the more the lack of repair and neglect overshadowed the luster, but it was nevertheless magnificent. The trees, a well-chosen combination of hornbeam, beech, and chestnut, were standing in their original straight lines but now formless and saggy, in desperate need of a good clipping. The ponds were either drained or filled with murky green water, but the white plaster statues and rose arches were still very much intact.

The winged castle, though here and there in lack of paint, seemed so far untouched by the war, with its richly decorated walls of cream-colored stucco and gray-blue slated roofs, a myriad of round turrets and dormer windows, all of which were also adorned. On top of the highest turret an immense Red Cross flag flapped in the wind.

As they entered the driveway with its wide gravel path lined with box hedges that had once been cone-shaped, the real change became apparent. There were wounded men everywhere on the lawns, those who could not walk having been wheeled out in chairs or beds. Nurses with white headbands and red crosses on their white-aproned bosoms walked among the mutilated men like floating angels. Despite the sunshine and the smiling women, there was a dreariness to the scene that struck Agnès more than all the other images so far. Nothing at Dragoncourt would be as it had been before the war.

Apart from the wounded men, there were groups of British soldiers stretched out on the grass in their belted, khaki uniforms, smoking, reading, or playing checkers.

"I hadn't expected so many soldiers here as well," Agnès said, astonished.

"Oh, yes, forgot to tell you. The young Count said on the phone that Dragoncourt also houses a division of the British 4th Army; they occupy one of the wings, the hospital the other." Alan steered the truck cautiously through the people, who were everywhere, even on the driveway. He was looking for a parking spot amidst the many private cars, military vans, and Model T Ford ambulances that stood on the gravel along the front side of the castle when they were overtaken by a black ambulance at high speed, its rubber tires screeching on the gravel. Alan hastily put the truck in the grass next to the path.

"We'll leave it here for the time being. Not much space further on anyway."

As they were still sitting in the car, they saw two women in baggy khaki uniforms with red crosses on their arms hurry out of the ambulance, open the back door, and grab the handlebars of a stretcher with a heavily bleeding man, whom they ran up the steps into the castle.

"That must be Elle, one of the Dragoncourt twins," Agnès said, pointing to the back of a tall, willowy girl with a long braid of copper-brown hair down her back. "She's an ambulance driver now. Gosh, how she's changed. Before the war, she was all about glamor and fun."

"Let's leave everything in the car and announce our arrival first," Alan suggested, while Agnès slipped out of the uncomfortable car seat, stretching her legs after the long, bumpy drive. It was a relief to finally arrive at their destination despite the grim circumstances that were certainly awaiting them.

They walked up the steps to the big double oak doors of the castle that stood ajar. At the platform, they were stopped by a young British sergeant with a kind, round face and the shadow of a dark mustache above his soft boy's lips. The blue eyes under his Royal West Kent Regiment cap had a rather startled look, as if he could not completely grasp where he had landed.

"Papers please," he ordered, and after a quick glance at them, said, before ushering them inside with his gloved hand, "I'm Sergeant Cooper. On behalf of Major Hamilton and the Royal West Kent's 6th battalion, welcome to Château de Dragoncourt, doctors." It sounded rather solemn for his young age.

Agnès took a deep breath, aware she was about to step into the big unknown, but nothing could have prepared her for what they encountered as they entered the large central hall with its high arched ceiling from which fat stucco cherubs and angelic creatures with harps gazed down stoically on the chaos below. Wounded soldiers lay everywhere – on stretchers, blankets, in armchairs, some even on the Persian carpets that were spread out on the black-and-white tiled floor.

All of them were, to various degrees, moaning or crying, and some let out deep, piercing screams while nurses in long-skirted uniforms made their way among them, their quick glances spotting the ones who were suffering the most so they could give them some relief by jabbing a morphine injection into a bloodied arm or leg. Incipient agony was everywhere, and those who were silent fastened their sunken eyes on the newly arrived doctors, a desperate, voiceless begging for release.

The predominant color was not the khaki and blue of the men's uniforms but the dark red of stained blood. It covered everything from the torn flesh to the ripped-up clothes, the furniture, the carpets, the walls. Even the nurses with their once-white aprons and hands were smeared all over. The next thing that struck Agnès and made her gag so badly she had to put a hand over her mouth was the all-pervading stench of festering wounds and decaying human flesh. The impact on her senses was so sudden and so intense it made her sway on her feet, and Alan had to grab her elbow to keep her upright.

"Steady, girl. Keep your chin up." But his own voice faltered, sounding distraught.

She nodded at him, grateful for his support. Alan produced a white handkerchief from his trousers pocket and handed it to her. Putting it over her mouth and smelling his intimate male scent of sandalwood and musk, she felt soothed. Still with a tight grip on her elbow, he directed her around moaning bodies and recently deceased men, around pools of blood and overwrought nurses, to the side of the hall where, between a row of marble pillars, it was a little less crowded.

"We're not in anyone's way here." He let go of her elbow but kept a close watch on her to see if she were standing firmly enough on her own legs.

"I'm okay, thank you." She leaned her back against one of the pillars, welcoming its cool surface. From where they were standing now, they had a good overview of the scene: the nurses and volunteers were carrying the wounded men in a procession to the operation room and wards. Agnès recognized the original maze of corridors that led from the great hall to the rest of the castle and the living quarters.

"I don't think anyone has time to come up to us," she remarked, "but I think I remember where the family quarters used to be in the old days."

"You're right. They're far too busy to notice us. Lead the way, doctor."

They looked at each other for a moment, and with the real horrors of the war now sinking in, the wordless exchange was clear to both. *Let's go for it. Now!*

They made their way along the east corridor among a throng of medics hurrying past with both full and with empty stretchers. Agnès recalled how Count Horace had led her through these passages, and with a shock she realized where they were heading: the opulent dining room, *la grande salle verte,* the castle's bustling center and what it had been turned into. For surely, the former hub of Dragoncourt was now the operating theater.

She was right. They passed by a long row of beds with dozing men awaiting surgery. Without anyone stopping them, Agnès pushed open a broad wooden door, and they walked straight into a huge square room that was now the operation area. Two big lamps shone strong rays of light on the big oval dining table that was covered with a green rubber mat, where at one end two male doctors were bent over a patient with a concentrated frown between their white head caps and mouthpieces. They did not look up, and neither did the two nurses assisting them.

Agnès glanced around the room and saw that the former golden and crystal chandeliers had been tugged high to the ceiling and that in the shadows the olive-green walls still held the gilded-framed pictures of the Dragoncourt ancestors, who for centuries had looked down on people eating lavish meals but were now witnessing completely different scenes. For the rest, nothing much remained of the dining room of the old days. Her quick professional inspection told her that the operation room had all the necessities and supplies – Marie Curie had even delivered one of her X-ray machines – but there certainly was not enough staff.

The atmosphere in the operating room was very calm and organized compared to the chaos in the entrance hall. Order reigned; there were only the usual sounds of the anesthetizer gas machine, the metal clicks of the doctor's equipment, and the short, staccato orders. Those familiar sounds seemed to steady them both. Here one could work; here they had it in their own hands to give a shot at saving lives. Agnès watched Alan taking stock like she was doing and instantly breathed more freely. They were back in the saddle, safe, together.

4

CHÂTEAU DE DRAGONCOURT

A slender, young man, his dark hair in need of a haircut, entered through a door on the other side and walked into the operating theater. He had a clipboard clamped under his arm. Peering around through silver-rimmed spectacles, he saw Agnès and Alan standing in the semi dark, outside the electric light that illuminated the operating table. As he moved in their direction, Agnès saw that his white coat was smeared with old bloodstains. His demeanor was listless, as if he had lost the capacity to take in that what was going on around him, and he just kept moving automatically, one foot in front of the other.

"Hi, Jacques," Agnès whispered, so as not to disturb the operating team.

He looked at her with the same unseeing eyes with which he observed everything around him, but then his mouth curled into a wide grin.

"Agnès!" he whispered back, stretching out his arms as if wishing to embrace her. "Agnès de Saint-Aubin, as I live and breathe!" Because of the sudden flood of relief, they did embrace, and Agnès smelled blood and disinfectant on him, the last scents she would associate with the dashing, sporty Jacques de Dragoncourt.

"Gosh, Jacques," she uttered, her face still against his chest, "where have the years gone?"

He disentangled her from his arms and took another good look at her with more light in his somber countenance.

"We've lost them. We've lost those precious years!" Then Jacques turned to Alan and shook his hand cordially. Putting a finger to his lips, he beckoned them to follow him across the operating room to the door through which he had just entered.

Agnès recognized some of the old, vibrant Jacques as he closed the door after them, "So glad to make your acquaintance, Professor Bell. So humbled that you and Agnès have come to help in this chaos, this absolute chaos, I'm humbled, really humbled!" His voice trailed off again, and the forlorn look momentarily returned to his face; but with some effort he regained his composure.

"We absolutely have to find a quiet place in this madness so I can give you an idea of the hospital and my own role in it – and that of my sister Elle, of course. Please, come this way!"

Jacques led them through a long corridor lined with family portraits until they came to what was called *the garden room*, a place Agnès remembered fondly. Here she had conversed with the old Count about Chopin's piano music over a cup of Darjeeling tea ten years earlier.

She simply had to look at Jacques again. "It's so strange to be here. I could never imagine this beautiful castle being turned into a front-line hospital. But at least this place reminds me of what it once was."

Jacques smiled at her, blowing the straight dark lock that had fallen over his brow away, a gesture she also remembered. "I know this must seem like an out of place spot for a hospital to you. My weary eyes have already become accustomed to it, as it's been this utter madhouse for two years now. But to you, Agnès, it must seem like sacrilege."

"It's horrible. I must admit I hardly recognize the château but for the walls and what hangs on them. However, this room..." Agnès said dreamily, "This room takes me right back in time." It felt as if a strong hand of fate had sent her here. To do what? To change?

Jacques was busying himself putting stacks of papers on the floor as one of the telephones on a side table constantly rang. He ignored it, and it stopped after a couple of rings, so it had probably been picked up somewhere else.

"Do sit down." He gestured to the space he had created on the settee. "You both must be parched after the long drive. Tell me what I can get you – tea, coffee, or a bourbon perhaps?"

Agnès sat down, accepting Jacques' offered coffee, but Alan took his cup and wandered over to the bay window and gazed outside, his back to them. Jacques extended his long legs under the coffee table, and with his hands behind his head, gazed intently at Agnès.

"Heavens, girl, you haven't changed a speck. How come they make girls like you so beautiful?"

"Stop it, you flatterer," Agnès retorted with a half-smile, enjoying the compliment but keenly aware of Alan's presence in the room. She quickly added, "Dear God, I've changed so much. What was I at thirteen? A bookish nymph, afraid of the physical body, socially awkward, and shy as a squirrel?"

"Do admit Elle and I were catalysts in your change, dear Agnès!"

"For sure, you were! Spending time here was certainly a different cup of tea from living with Papa and Petipat." She cringed at the mentioning of that name, and Alan inched closer to her. Agnès braced herself.

"Life here was in the fast lane compared to the slow pace of the Saint-Aubin household." She did not add that an extra charm had been that she'd secretly been smitten with Jacques.

Looking at him now, ten years on, she still remembered every line of his face – the searching oil-slick eyes, the rebellious lock of straight black hair falling across one half of his face. Even the athletic built of the former Eton rower, hiding under a white coat with the red cross on his biceps – it all still seemed to be present. New were the spectacles and the dramatic change from mischievous teenager to a man aged before his years. He was clearly no longer living for sports and girls and parties, but was all grown up and serious; something the young Jacques would have scorned, calling it *yawnsome old age*.

"Ahhh, but I have changed too," he sighed, "it's inescapable, this sad merry-go-round."

With her usual attentiveness, Agnès sensed that under the layers of fatigue and oddly discovered determination, the former Jacques was still present, that complex being with strong passions and wild plans, covering a sensitive and bewildered human being, never sure which direction to take until Elle intercepted him. At the time, he had invariably chosen the direction that was going to be *jolly much fun!* To which degree had he chosen this new self? Or was it still Elle who called the shots?

It did not seem like a good idea to reminisce on her feelings for Jacques right now, with Alan so close, so Agnès turned her attention to the room they were in.

"So, this room is still much as it was before. What's it used for?" Her voice was neutral, interested.

Jacques, who was still studying her, snapped out of his reverie and also gazed around the former bright breakfast room, whose four, high curtain-less windows let in a surplus of light from the terrace and the gardens beyond. In the distance, a golden sun was setting over the rolling hills of Picardy, once a lush farmers' paradise now reduced to a macabre Armageddon.

"Yep, in a sense. We use it as the staff's headquarters and recuperation space. Only changed a few things to make it more practical. Mummy, with her artistic tastes, would die a thousand deaths if she saw it like this, but luckily, she and Papa are in London for as long as Dragoncourt remains a hospital." He pointed to the two long tables along one wall, decked with a white tablecloth and holding two large percolators with coffee, teapots, plates, cups and saucers, and slices of chocolate cake under bell jars. Agnès imagined the disorderly jumble of chairs and stools in a corner around a square table and a large cabinet with more papers sticking out would also leave a deep frown on Countess Virginia's smooth forehead.

They were sitting in the old place, with the formal high-backed chairs with the matching sofa and inlaid coffee table in the middle of the room.

"With all the class differences disappearing like melting snow, we still hang on to this spot," Jacques grinned, patting the chintz covering of his chair. "This is Dragoncourt only! And you of course," he added quickly, "while Papa and Mummy look down on us." He reverently looked up at the two oval portraits hanging over the two fireplaces: Count Horace and Countess Virginia.

Agnès followed his gaze and soon recognized more familiar items. "Oh, I remember the Delft blue tea set. So cute!"

"Yes, and we keep it safely locked in its cabinet. I don't want Mummy to kill me after I've survived this war just because someone broke the handle of one of those monstrosities."

Drinking tea from those beautiful bone china cups...and reading.

"Henry James, *The Wings of a Dove*," Agnès and Jacques cried in unison.

Alan turned on his heels and looked from one to the other as if they had gone mad, but they burst out laughing, and a ripple of relaxation flooded through Agnès. Suddenly she felt okay in this cozy room with the golden light, and for a short while the dark clouds that hung over their lives, the castle, and the whole era temporarily dispersed.

"Can I have another coffee, please? If I may interrupt," Alan interjected, raising one eyebrow. "And can you let me in on your secret?"

"Sorry, Professor Bell, just the book we were both reading at the time. We were both Henry James mad back then. Can't stand the chap's novels these days, so long drawn and fabricated, but that's another matter. Pardon if I thereby accidentally offend your American heart." Jacques chuckled playfully, "Oh, yes, more coffee. On its way! More milk, more sugar?"

"No, it's fine as it is, just two spoons of sugar. And please call me Alan." Alan ignored the reference to his American background.

"Okeydokey!" Jacques seemed to have come alive, all movements and activity, as if suddenly years had been taken from his shoulders, and the once dashing, fun character he had been so easily re-emerged from the rubble.

Agnès felt Alan's penetrating gaze on her as she watched Jacques pouring the coffee and remarked, "This is so strange, Jacques. I was here for such a short while ten years ago, yet I remember every detail of it, and everything about you as well."

Jacques broke into a smile, that ready smile that brightened his whole being, and while blowing the lock of hair from his face, he handed them both another cup of coffee and dropped in the chair opposite her.

"Dearest Agnès, let me tell you that your presence here is a tremendous boost to us. And I'm sure Elle will feel the same. I hope that together we can make this hell more bearable. It might help if we keep remembering how silly and young and innocent we were at the time. God knows, we need some lightness of spirit in this ordeal." And turning to Alan, he added, "And that includes you, Prof…. Alan. Any friend of Agnès's is a friend of the Dragoncourts."

Alan, who had come to sit in the chair next to Agnès, gave him a polite nod and drank his coffee in silence while the two old friends continued to relate old adventures and giggled as teenagers.

But soon Jacques returned to the more serious stuff. "Let me give you a bit of an update on the situation here. As you probably know, we're currently almost on the front line. You've already had a glimpse of the amount of wounded men we get here. It will only increase with the German Spring Offensive just launched, and to make matters worse, the two surgeons operating here now are moving to an American mobile hospital outside Villers. So, your arrival is absolutely heaven-sent. I have a constant request out with the American Hospital of Paris for more surgeons, or even ordinary doctors, but they keep telling me most prefer to stay away from the front, which I totally get."

He smiled sadly. "It's only the brave hearts like you that venture closer. That said, we might have to evacuate from here any day now, as there's no saying the front line on the Amiens side will hold. During dinner tonight, Major Hamilton, the English major who's stationed here with his garrison, will give us a briefing on the military situation."

Alan, who had been paying closer attention to Jacques now he was talking about their work, interrupted him. "Sorry if the question sounds rude, but may I ask you what your position is here? Apart from being the Count de Dragoncourt."

"Nothing rude about that, old chap." Jacques ruffled his dark hair and laughed apologetically. "Good question actually, but I'm not sure I can give you a proper answer. First, I'm the replacement Count. My father, the French ambassador in London, is the real Count De Dragoncourt. And for the rest?" He giggled almost like a girl. "As Agnès here can testify, I used to be absolutely useless when I was young, and I'm afraid I still am. Let's say I'm a sort of Jack-of-all-trades here, or more possibly one could say I'm the spider in the web. I try to make schedules for people and materials, but they usually turn out to be useless by the time they're needed, as everything changes all the time." Jacques cleared his throat. "I think you could best define my job as, everybody asks me everything and I take action upon their requests. And if I'm not in the position to take action, I make sure I deliver the message to a person more authorized." He looked a bit puzzled at his own explanation, but Alan came to his aid.

"Ahh, now I understand. You manage the operation. But you're not a medic?"

"Heavens, no!" Jacques cried, "I've just overcome my daily bouts of fainting whenever I see the color red." All three laughed.

At that moment there was a soft tap on the door.

"Come in," Jacques called, and the white-capped head of a nurse with striking turquoise-blue eyes peeked around the door.

"Sorry to interrupt," she said with a strong Scottish accent, "but I heard that th'new surgeons had arrived, and Doctor Webber and Doctor Martin are absolutely exhausted. An emergency has just been brought in, and I was hopin'...."

Agnès and Alan were already on their feet, and with Jacques on their heels, followed the nurse back to *la grande salle verte.*

"Ai, thank you," she said gratefully. "My name's Bridget McGovern, and I'll show you where everythin' is."

As soon as Alan and Agnès had hoisted themselves into their operating gear, the patient was brought in. He looked extremely young and vulnerable, clad in a long-coated khaki uniform with knee breeches as worn by the Indian army, a Commonwealth participant.

"He's no older than seventeen," Alan remarked bitterly. "How young do they send them nowadays?"

Both the soldier's lower legs had been almost amputated during a mortar shelling, and he had pieces of shrapnel everywhere in his body and face. The turban on his dark-skinned head, once a pristine white, was caked with mud and blood. He was half conscious.

Looking up at them and holding Agnès in his gaze, he whispered, "Revant Chopra Sehgal, 34th Royal Sikh Pioneers." He sighed with relief as Bridget gave him the anesthetics and dozed off.

"I'll see to his legs," Alan commanded. "You start with the shrapnel."

Agnès nodded but her vision was almost blurred by a revisiting of a similar situation a week earlier. Again, this was going to be a race against the clock with very little chance of success. The young Sikh had already lost too much blood, and due to the warm day, the wounds on his legs had started to become infected. But Agnès braced herself and set out retrieving the hundreds of shards from his body, an immense and precise operation that took all her concentration.

As always at the operating table, she lost track of time; only the patient's breathing was her clock. But at some point, briefly looking up, she realized daylight was gone, and it was deep into the evening. Alan was having his own fight, making the amputations complete with the help of Bridget. Only the harsh electric light fell on the boy's brutalized features, and she could see what a handsome young man he had been, with the grace and delicate perfection of the people of North India. His body was lean and slim, with thin but muscled upper legs and arms, and his skin was smooth and dark. His long black hair lay entangled along his shoulders with the unwrapped turban around his head.

Although her hands were steady, she was aware of her emotions as she worked. She was glad that he was not in pain, at least temporarily, but for the first time in her career, she also felt that what she was doing was totally opposed to what her profession had taught her to do – that she had to carry out this insane work on a body that should have been healthy and whole, on a boy who without knowledge of where he was being sent had exchanged the sun-laden golden hills of Punjab for the ghastly conditions of the trenches in Northern France, most likely without knowing a single person.

And if he died, with him the sun would die in a family in Punjab, as it did every day in Liverpool, and in Paris, and in Sydney, and in all these other places where mothers and fathers and wives were waiting for letters from boys like Revant Chopra Sehgal instead of getting the dreaded telegram.

Aware of her anger and frustration, she still worked on without pause, her eyes almost too red and swollen from exhaustion to focus on the scalpel in her hand as she retrieved another large piece of shrapnel from his brow and dabbed the wound with ether. Over and over, almost automatically, her hands did their work.

Suddenly she startled as he blinked and opened his autumn brown eyes to look at her. The gaze seemed steady; not drugged, not dead. Alarmed by her sudden jump, Alan and Bridget came over to see what was happening. The boy made a small movement with his hand, as if trying to stop her.

"Am I hurting you?" she implored, while Alan peered over her shoulder and Bridget went to check the anesthetics.

The boy blinked his beautiful deer-like eyes, and Agnès asked again, "Do you want me...us... to stop?" Her voice choked in her throat as she tried to speak, but she saw how he nodded, the tiniest of movements of his head.

With difficulty, he put the fingers of his brown hand on her surgeon's glove, as if asking her to come closer. Agnès bowed down and brought her face close to the young Punjabi, just in time to hear him whisper in a breaking voice, "Thank you...doctor, you are... an angel ...a beautiful angel. You are ... you are...the balm ...for my soul." Then his head fell sideways, and he was gone.

[Image: image3.jpeg]

WHILE AGNÈS HUNG her head over the grimy bucket, purging the contents of her meager lunch into it, Alan stood next to her, murmuring words of encouragement, his hand resting on her back. Tears ran down Agnès's cheeks when a new convulsion gripped her, and she raged at the thought of another defeat, yet another beautiful person dying under her hands.

"There, there now," Alan kept repeating, "it's okay to be upset. But you can do this. We can do this!"

Physically still feeble but determined not to let herself be discouraged by the recent two failed surgical attempts, Agnès, on Alan's arm for support, entered the dining room in the same navy dress she had worn for traveling. At pre-war Dragoncourt, this would have been unheard of, but she saw that none of the others had cared to change; most were still in their stained uniforms. Two young women, one of whom she recognized as Elle, stood talking in the corner of the room wearing jodhpurs and sturdy boots, with men's braces over their chemises and their sleeves rolled up. If it had not been for their slender waists and female bosoms, they could have passed for men.

This room was unknown to Agnès; she was sure she had not been here on her earlier visits, and it was at a considerable distance from the hospital units, at the far end of the castle's west wing, away from the turmoil. Agnès was glad to leave all that behind her for a couple of hours. There was a lively, animated atmosphere in the dining room, with people chatting, drinking, and smoking, a welcome change from the sounds and smells of war and a distant reminder of the social Dragoncourt in its days of splendor. It looked like it had once been the former servants' quarters, possibly serving as the staff's dining room, adjacent to the main kitchen. It was very basically furnished, with a table offering places for at least twenty people, straight chairs, some storage cupboards.

"Able to manage some food?" Alan asked. "You should at least try."

"I'll try some vegetable soup. And thank you, Alan, for not making a great deal out of my temporary weakness."

"You're no longer my student, Doctor de Saint-Aubin, and you behaved perfectly normal. Felt damn rotten myself." His brow knitted with concern.

At that moment, Elle spotted them. Her gold-flecked hazel eyes lit up as she stabbed her cigarette in the overflowing ashtray and strode over to them, a wide grin on her lovely face.

"Sweetie!" she exclaimed, opening her arms wide to embrace her former friend. "How are you feeling now, my darling? How awful to start your work here like this! Yes, Bridget told me! How bloody awful!" She drew Agnès in a bear hug, and Agnès felt the muscular arms wrap around her, arms that carried stretchers with grown men every day. No wonder Elle was a bundle of wiry muscles. Agnès let herself be enclosed in that tight, warm embrace, and let it soothe her. She remembered Elle always had been the motherly type, and with her current position, it seemed even more so.

"I'm fine," she muttered against Elle's shoulder.

Then releasing Agnès from her embrace but still holding her hand firmly in hers, Elle turned to Alan. Contrary to her brother, she immediately drew him into her circle, open and hospitable as was her character. Her face was turned upwards to him, oval and sweet with its regular features, and a braid like a thick brown rope hanging on her back, almost reaching her waist.

With her warm voice she exclaimed, "Ah, there you are – Agnès's surgeon! I've been so much looking forward to meeting the famous Sorbonne professor. Welcome, Doctor Bell."

Agnès could see from Alan's reaction that he was also feeling better because of Elle's open friendliness.

"Please, it's Alan," he insisted, and jokingly added, "And it's actually the other way around. She here is Alan's surgeon!" He pointed to Agnès, and she saw the boy-like grin she loved so much.

Elle chuckled, winking at Agnès. "I don't care one bit what you call each other! We're just so damn happy to have you here. Now, let me introduce you to the rest of the folk here, although most have already gone to bed. Jacques excused himself. He took over my last ambulance shift to the front." Still holding Agnès by the hand, she went to the head of the table, where a Brit in a green uniform with an impressive row of colored ribbons above the left breast pocket rose to his feet.

"Agnès, Alan – please meet our ray of hope in these troubled times. His official name is Major Gerald Thomas Hamilton, and he's the commander of some illustrious royal battalion from Kent; you know, some modern kind of King Arthur and his knights. But we generally call him Gerry."

Gerry, who had been following the bustle in the room with slight amusement, gave a curt bow and shook their hands. Agnès thought he looked rather young to be the commander of a battalion, but what he lacked in years he certainly had in authority. She sensed that behind that youthful, healthy countenance was a calm and balanced man with a will that would be hard to bend. She instantly liked him.

Sturdy and of average height, Gerald Hamilton shared with other military men that very upright and dignified posture, as if born into his uniform and willing to die in it, should fate demand it. His hair was sandy-colored and bristly, cut very short but still managing to form the beginning of a cowlick at the hairline. Because his eyebrows and mustache were of the same sandy shade as his hair, and his skin had the pale, freckled complexion of the Celtic race, he gave the overall impression of being rather colorless; but his eyes, although also of a pale greenish-blue, were sharp and missed nothing. Agnès supposed they would flash with sudden vehemence should his authority be questioned.

"Countess Elle is actually our ray of hope," the major retorted with a smile. "She's able to make everybody laugh." His voice had a faint East Kent accent that Agnès remembered from her visits with her father to London before the war.

"I'm afraid I'll never rise to the legendary status of King Arthur, try as I might to bring this bloody war to an end. That said, I only command one company of the 6th Battalion, consisting of the eighty men stationed here at Dragoncourt. The rest of the battalion is at the front under the command of Lieutenant-General Reginald Walters."

Agnès thought his modesty became him. Before Elle could drag

Agnès to the next person at the table, the major raised his voice so that the small group in the room stopped talking to listen.

"I had planned a briefing tonight to inform you all on the hazardous frontline situation, but due to the late hour and the absence of many persons involved, I've postponed till tomorrow evening. 20:00 hours sharp. Thank you."

There was only one other man sitting at the table, who had said nothing so far nor shown interest in the chatter around him. He was dressed in civilian clothes and sat bent over a lined notebook, in which he was scribbling hurriedly with long, ink-stained fingers. Elle said loudly, almost in his ear, "And this specimen here is Philip Lane."

"Oh, hello," the young man mumbled, not looking up, his dark-blond head bowed over his notebook as he continued to write at high speed. "Sorry to be a bit preoccupied, but one's got to strike while the iron's hot. 'Tis my daily dose of poetry; left side of the brain having a bit of fun. Do you write poetry yourself?" It was not clear if he was addressing anyone in particular.

"Come on, Phil." Elle gave his shoulder a vehement push so the fountain pen made a wide black scratch across his written page.

"Hell, Elle!" he cried indignantly. "Have you no respect for a starving poet? It was bloody well meant to be a poem for you, you cruel Clytemnestra! You're a man's worst nightmare! It's all ruined now, just like my heart!" But he did screw the top on his gold-inlaid pen and snapped the notebook shut.

"I so wanted to make a dash for her heart before one of these breast-beating, heroic soldiers got a chance," he said sulkily, looking up at Agnès in mock despair. He had deep-set violet eyes, quite extraordinary in color, and apart from the mockery they held another, unreadable expression. Was it pain; genuine heartache? Philip was a finely built man, with the aristocratic features of old English families, well-bred and with that slightly haughty expression of the upper classes, like his voice which unmistakably had that drooling Oxford accent French aristocrats so loved to replicate. Agnès did not know what to make of him as she shook his hand, feeling his grip was rather limp.

When he shook Alan's hand, he said, "You doctors are the real deal in this war, like the military men. Academics like myself are absolutely useless. Altogether obsolete race!" It sounded disillusioned, but Elle gave his shoulder another punch, which extracted an *ouch* from him and a grin.

"Don't be too modest, you old rat!" she protested. "Phil's one of Jacques's Eton pals, and he's proved to be a true gem here at Dragoncourt. He helps with gardening and repairing things. And he regularly drives to Paris for our supplies."

"Yep." Philip nodded. "That's the new me. The Earl of Timberwood & Pottery, at your service."

The last person the newcomers were introduced to was a solemn-looking girl in the same ambulance uniform as Elle, with a distinct golden crucifix around her slender neck and a closed, unsmiling face surrounded by a mass of dark hair. Her face was dominated by her large, soft brown eyes and a prominent nose, while her mouth was rather small, the lips pursed together.

"Meet my friend Marie-Christine Brest," Elle said proudly, putting her arm around the girl. "M-C and I are chums from our finishing school days in Switzerland. M-C's not just an ambulance driver but also a nurse, so she may be assisting you during operations."

M-C gave as friendly a smile as she could, showing a row of tiny white teeth in her small mouth. "Thank you for coming," she said simply. "I hope you settle in soon."

"How long have you been here?" Alan asked.

"Two years. It's been quite a ride, but we hang in here all together." As she said it, she fingered the cross on her breast.

Elle looked from her friend to Agnès. "M-C, I've been thinking. Would it be okay if Agnès shared our quarters with us?"

M-C shot Agnès a quick glance and nodded. "Of course!"

"That's arranged then," Elle concluded. "Jacques has a room prepared for you next to his, Alan. And now – food, everybody!" She clapped her hands.

At that moment Jacques bustled into the room. Taking his place at the dinner table, he looked around appreciatively. "Glad and humbled to see everyone in one piece for another day!"

The rich, herby smell of the *coq au vin* filled the room, and Agnès had a strange but overwhelming sensation of feeling more at home than she had in years.

5

LETTERS FROM HOME

Madeleine

Le Manoir, Switzerland, March 1918

On an early spring morning, Madeleine de Dragoncourt lay sprawled on top of the chintz cover of her single bed staring at the ceiling. Through the open window, a clamor of girls' voices in all different languages rang up from the garden room below. The high-pitched voices suddenly died when someone clapped her hands, and the affected voice of Madame Paul broke through the hush.

"*Allons-y, mes filles*, time for breakfast!"

Madeleine jumped up and, uttering a loud "Crap!" sped downstairs. The last couple of steps before she entered the breakfast room, she slowed down and adopted a very straight posture, making the expression on her face as deadpan as her lively face could muster. It was impossible to completely mask her slightly huffy expression, but she did what she could before pressing the doorknob and striding in, the long auburn tresses of her undone hair trailing behind her. As she had expected, all eyes were on her, especially those of Madame Paul, who was putting on her glasses that always hung on two pearl strings on her bosom to inspect her with both pinkies lifted. The pale blue eyes, the color of celestite, fixed hard on Madeleine, expressing a reproachful disappointment.

"*Bon matin*," Madeleine greeted, aware her French sounded much more polished than the Swiss French accent of the new headmistress of Le Manoir. She made a reverent bow in her direction. "I sincerely apologize for my late arrival, but I accidentally locked myself in the bathroom. That is also the reason I've had *no time* to do my hair." She never knew where her next diversions from the truth would come from, but they popped into her head as easily as the silver trout jumped above the surface of Lake Geneva.

"And pray, how did you come out?" Though on guard against Madeleine's pranks, Madame Paul invariably approached the youngest sprout of de Dragoncourt family in all seriousness, hoping against hope that she was speaking the truth.

Madeleine knew of her position as the headmistress' newest rebellious acquisition in need of straightening out, but so far, she had outsmarted her. "With a hairpin," she replied triumphantly, taking her seat next to her roommate, Carolina Hohenzollern, and eyeing the French toast and bacon and eggs with relish.

"*In my office* after breakfast!" Madeleine mouthed the words as Madame Paul spoke them aloud, evoking subdued giggles from the girls opposite her.

Although she had been at the posh finishing school on Lake Geneva since the end of the summer of 1917, Madeleine had continued to feel like a queer duck among swans and did not under-stand how all the Dragoncourt girls before her had finished their education here with flying colors. Because all the women of her family had been sent to Le Manoir since its establishment in 1851. How had her eldest sister Elle, not against a bit of tomfoolery herself, endured all this table-setting and curtsying? And her own artistic, outspoken Maman, of whom everyone said she was the spitting image? That dull Antoinette, the middle sister, had lapped it all up, there was not a single doubt in Madeleine's mind. Antoinette was Le Manoir incarnated, all style and outward appearance but little substance or spirit.

"Mademoiselle Madeleine, where is your mind?" It sounded sternly from the head of the table.

"Comment? Excusez-moi!"

"Pass the salt to Mademoiselle Chérie and stop daydreaming."

"Yes, Madame." Why was Madame Paul always keeping a beady eye on her? Other girls sometimes looked out of the window, home-sick or in love. She sat up straighter, trying to feign interest in the polite conversation the girls were taught to keep going at the table and the display of correct table manners, but it was all exceedingly boring. Madeleine let out an audible sigh that again kindled some chuckles from her table companions and another scornful look from the Matron.

"If this goes on much longer, I'll go daffy," Madeleine thought in despair. "My God, what a set of birdbrains. If this is the training for my future life, I'd rather be dead."

On her right was Carolina, the gentle, black-haired Romanian princess, who was Madeleine's only bright spot in the otherwise glum yet luxurious circumstances at the school. Sensitive to her friend's fit of unrest, Carolina turned to her and whispered, "Come on, Maddy, we'll have a game of chess later, and I promise I won't let you win." Both girls loved chess and were good at it, though Carolina was much better at it.

Madeleine shot her a grateful smile. "Done deal!"

The day drudged on without any proper highlight for Madeleine. The only small victory was the effortless wrapping of Madame Paul around her little finger when summoned to her office. When Madeleine walked in, a sulking impression on her pretty, young face, Madame Paul raised her gold-rimmed spectacles on the pearl strings and put them on her long nose for close inspection of *la petite Française*, as she called Madeleine. And although *la petite Française* had done everything in her might to make the stern matron of Le Manoir disapprove of her, Madeleine knew she actually liked her and often condoned her many mishaps.

Well, maybe she did not like her personally, but Madame Paul always went on about Paris, and the accomplishment and natural femininity of Parisian ladies. She was quite blind when it came to France and the French. Being a diplomat's daughter, Madeleine made skillful use of this favoritism. If the Swiss matron believed that Madeleine embodied those enviable qualities and served as an example of French sophistication, why not use it to her advantage?

The inspection took a full couple of minutes until Madame Paul asked, "I have been wondering what is bothering you, Mademoiselle Madeleine. Are you unhappy here? Do you perhaps miss your family?"

"Yes, very, very much, Madame." It had not been hard to squeeze out a couple of tears.

"Ahhh... I understand. The war is hard on everyone, but you *are* making great progress... some days."

"You think so, Madame?" Fake smile; tears wiped away with a lace hanky.

"Well... you could try a little harder. And maybe not spend so much time with that Romanian girl, but more... say... with the other French girls?" Madeleine had steered clear from the other Paris clique from the start. They were all the sort Antoinette adored, a stain on their dress or a loose strap of a ballroom shoe being a calamity of world proportion.

Madeleine knew that Carolina was much more sophisticated, intelligent, and spirited than any of these French minxes, but that Madame Paul in her blindness could not see that. Poor Carolina was often in the matron's firing line, even when Madeleine herself was the real culprit.

They had arrived together in September, Madeleine from London, where Count de Dragoncourt was the ambassador for France, and Princess Carolina Hohenzollern from her father's castle near Bucharest. Roommates and both eighteen, they had been inseparable from the beginning, despite their totally different temperaments and backgrounds, much to the displeasure of Madame Paul, who only took the Eastern European royalty for their money but greatly disliked anything or anyone east of the River Rhine.

"But... but," Madeleine objected in her most endearing voice, her amber eyes full of devotion, "Madame always tells us to spread the Gallaecian elegance and style to other civilizations, so it only makes sense I instruct Carolina and not the other French girls."

Madame Paul blinked, unable to contradict that, and once again Madeleine was let off the hook. It felt like an empty victory to Madeleine, though; there was no real challenge or bonus in it.

She entered the room she shared with Carolina on the first floor feeling deflated and irritated. The futility of her existence here at the finishing school seemed in such stark contrast to the war that was raging over Europe that was also impacting her own family. But Madeleine bit her lip. She was doing her family a favor by staying safe. It was the price she had to pay for the time being.

"Maddy, you've got mail!" Carolina exclaimed, waving a thick envelope with a French stamp.

Madeleine raced towards her and tore it from her friend's hand, recognizing the handwriting. "Elle!" she exclaimed, exhilarated. "I've got a letter from Elle! It's impossible!"

"I'll let you read in peace." Carolina was already grabbing her stole and her reading book. "I'll be in the library. Make sure you come and fetch me after you've read it. I want to hear all your news from home!"

Madeleine was already tearing open the letter, and her eyes flew over her eldest sister's ink-filled lines.

CHÂTEAU DE DRAGONCOURT, *1 January 1918*
 Dearest Madeleine,

· · ·

You reading this letter means some form of normality still exists in this world, as the postal services must have functioned. So, I'm going to write this letter in the confidence that it will arrive! Happy 1918! Gosh, we've made it alive through this war for another year! Hurray!

You must think I've forgotten all about my baby sister, but nothing is further from the truth! I would have written you much earlier – actually planned this letter to be for Christmas – but life got in the way. It is unbelievable that we did not celebrate Christmas 1917 together. It must be the first time in the history of de Dragoncourt family. I'm sure of it!

So, this Christmas, whenever I had a moment to myself – which was hardly ever – I reminisced about our family gathering of Christmas 1916 in our house on rue du Faubourg Saint-Honoré in Paris. Do you remember, Antoinette being highly pregnant with Maurice junior and claiming an extra portion of Christmas pudding for her unborn child? Just to get the sixpence, of course. Well, we know that's about the biggest mischief that good little Netty will get in to. But we had a great time, despite the fact that Jacques and I were already involved in running the frontline hospital in Picardy, and Papa and Mummy had to leave the next day for London because it was the only flight available that would take civilians. That week was actually the last break I've had, but more about that later.

How are you, my little Maddy? I can't tell you how relieved I am that you are well and safe in neutral Switzerland, far away from the hell and destruction of the war. I can imagine it's not really your cup of tea, becoming a right little madame to snatch up a rich Duke or Marquis, but at least you'll be able to go riding a lot and you can enjoy some peace and quiet. I thought I'd never say it, but I could do with a bit of Le Manoir myself just now. The idea that my mind would only have to occupy itself with table decorations and new upholstery for the sofa seems like heaven on earth. I'm sorry I keep returning to our situation here. I wanted so much to make this letter light and breezy, as I know you need a happy message, but living in grim circumstances 24 hours a day has affected my brain, I'm afraid. I can't really think of anything but surviving the day.

LET *me tell you about the people who are here at Dragoncourt so you'll know that. Apart from Jacques, I have some good friends around me who help us run the hospital. There is a changing staff of nurses and doctors. We're not really in charge of that. They come and go. Most are from the American Hospital in Paris. There are some dashing surgeons, but no one has any time for romance.*

TALKING ABOUT ROMANCE. *Ha-ha. Do you remember Philip Lane, Jacques' friend from Eton? He arrived some months ago. Not as a soldier – he's got some condition that prevents him from taking up arms, but he wanted to do his bit for the war, so he just traveled over, as Jacques had told him that we're always looking for staff. He claimed there wasn't much lecturing to be done at Oxford anymore since all the students had enlisted. I think he was in the literature department there.*

Phil's all about poems and ancient scripts. Quite a studious person but also very funny. Lately, he's got it in his head that he has a crush on me, but he's so much in the clouds, he wouldn't even know what physical love is. Not that I know, but I've got at least a clue. He doesn't. Anyway, he does all sorts of jobs for us, which is a great help because most of our old staff have left, and I can't blame them. It's not really safe where we are, some 50 kilometers from the Western Front. Phil is great but crazy as a loon.

THEN THERE'S *my friend M-C. You remember her? She and I became best friends at Le Manoir. Only positive thing that happened to me there! Since I knew she was trained as a nurse, I asked her early on to come and help, and she's by my side all the time. We drive the ambulances to the trenches together to transport the wounded back to Dragoncourt, and I really wouldn't know what to do without her. I know a thing or two about nursing myself now, as we often have to perform first aid on the spot. Nursing wouldn't be MY profession, though. I still want to become a racecar driver, and driving these T-Fords at full speed – sometimes even through ditches, ha-ha – certainly enhances my driving skills. If this bloody war would only end, we could pick up our lives where we left off! Anyway, M-C is a very solemn and religious girl, but she has a beautiful soul and works as hard as a boat worker.*

FINALLY, in our immediate team is this Scottish girl – young woman, I should say – also a nurse. Her name is Bridget McGovern. I must say I don't really know how she arrived here, probably via Paris. I'll ask her. We just clicked, she's lovely. Always upbeat under the most horrendous circumstances. You'd like her too!

For a couple of weeks, we've also had a battalion from a British garrison stationed at Dragoncourt. It's for our safety. The major in charge, Gerald Hamilton, is from Kent, so it's lovely to chat with him about England. He knows London like his inside pocket, so we discuss pubs and theaters and stuff. Gerry's a great sport.

YES, my dear sissy, it's these people that make life at Dragoncourt bearable for Jacques and me. Jacques is sort of okay, and he's enclosed a letter for you, so you'd better find out what he has to say.

I will try to phone you one day – if they don't cut our lines – but both the military and the medical men tell us the lines should remain open for emergencies, so I'm reluctant to phone you, although I'd love to hear your voice.

Sweet dear Madeleine, please take heart and realize you're at the best place you can be right now. This war won't go on forever, and then we'll be together again!

WITH ALL MY LOVE,

Your sister Elle XXX

P.S. NETTY TOLD me to let you know Loulou is fine. She doesn't like the animal, but one of their gardeners is taking care of it. So, don't worry about Loulou!

AT FIRST MADELEINE just stared at the letter, not feeling anything. It had been many months since she'd had a sign of life from home, the last letter being from her mother a month after she'd arrived in Switzerland, telling her to be a good girl and that London was preparing for the Christmas season.

This letter from Elle was different, raw and real, and it confused her. It pulled the lid from her concealed emotions; emotions she had not even known she possessed. First came a wave of longing, of belonging, of being once again the Benjamin of the family, the coveted one, the cared-for one, the one they had securely tucked away behind the Alps. But she had a role to play, a pivotal one in her family: she was the funny monkey, the precious little prankster, the one who made them laugh and cheered them up. Then came anger: they had abandoned her, fighting the war without her, thinking her too small, too young, too immature to be part of anything that vast and dangerous. And finally, she felt resolution: this life at finishing school, this preparation for life, was *not* what she wanted; perhaps some time but not this time. Her family needed her; they would not survive without Madeleine in their midst. She was of vital importance to their well-being, even though they believed the opposite. Madeleine sighed deeply as she took out Jacques' shorter letter that was enfolded in Elle's.

For a moment, she pictured the twins, Elle and Jacques, so different and yet so inseparable. Elle was the eldest in everything, although in terms of birth they only differed by ten minutes. Elle, soft and sweet as she looked and behaved, actually had a fiery side, which had come out at the age of fifteen when she'd announced she wanted to be like Dorothy Levitt, the first woman racing driver, and had ordered Papa to buy her a De Dion-Bouton as well. Madeleine had been exhilarated when Elle raced them between Paris and Picardy and tried to break her record every time. With fondness she remembered how Elle had taught her to drive and not to be anxious or uncertain at the steering wheel.

Jacques was more difficult to fathom but equally loved by Madeleine. She thought Papa had been too firm with him, saying he needed a proper education as the next Count de Dragoncourt, so he had been away a lot, at Eton and Oxford. Madeleine had felt for him because he did not seem to enjoy his life away from the family and certainly away from Elle. He liked social gatherings, not stuffy books, and of course sports. Madeleine with her surplus of energy had loved the endless games of tennis and long stretches on horseback. She had even taken up rowing with him.

Slowly she enfolded Jacques' letter.

DEAR MAD-MADDY,

Elle told me to write to you although you know I can't properly put two words together. I miss you, I miss fun in life, I miss the good times we had. Life is no fun at all at the moment, and I have no idea when this is going to stop.

Sometimes I try to remember life when it was normal and we were a family, but this bastard of a war has been going on for so long that my brain only thinks war, war, war. Sorry to be such a spoilsport, blame it on Elle. That's a lame joke, I know.

DON'T FORGET *that I love you and that I hope you're having a great time exploring the Alps and having fancy tea parties. I wish your finishing stuff was over and this bloody war too, and we could all go motoring again to the Pyrenees or sailing in Antibes.*

Take care, my Mad-Maddy, and think of your brother from time to time.

JACQUES

THAT NIGHT MADELEINE cried herself to sleep, and not even Carolina could comfort her.

6

ESCAPE

The next day, Madeleine was in a foul mood. She had slept very badly and felt more imprisoned in her golden Swiss cage than ever before.

"This is out and out boring! Even an ant would fall on its back and die if it had to do this!"

Narrowing her beautiful feline eyes, she tossed the embroidered Léron napkin on the table and flung herself in a chair. Carolina, who had been helping Madeleine folding the napkins and putting them in neat stacks so they could be stored in the linen cupboard, stared at her friend in dismay.

"Maddy, get up at once! If Madame Paul sees you like this, sprawled on a chair in the middle of the morning, you'll be in trouble."

"Carolina dear, whoever cares about napkins at a time like this has completely lost his wits! Look at us. Filling our days curtseying and arranging table linen when there's a war going on. You know what? I'm leaving!"

"You can't. Madame Paul won't allow it. You haven't finished the training," Carolina said in her heavily accented Romanian English.

But Madeleine nodded vigorously, making her flaming auburn hair dance. "You watch me! I'm done with this place!"

As Madeleine watched Carolina pick up the napkin she had cast aside and flatten the square piece of cloth on the smooth surface of the mahogany table before folding it in precise squares, she contemplated fishing a Gold Flake cigarette from the pocket of her linen dress and lighting it in the school's dining room but decided against it, as even to her that seemed a tad too bellicose. As little as she cared for her own reputation, she was fond of Carolina and did not want to endanger her friend's position any further. But that her situation was unbearable, and a cigarette would have been very welcome, there was no doubt.

At that moment, the broad double oak doors swung open, and through them strode Mme Paul Vierret in all her self-importance. Invariably dressed in dark-blue taffeta, her ash-blonde bun stylishly rolled to one side and coiling like a snake at the nape of her neck, the headmistress was not older than thirty-five but seemed older because of the way she dressed and moved. She stared fixedly at Madeleine, who was rising slowly to her feet, swaying from one side to the other and holding a hand in front of her mouth while she steadied herself with the other on the arm rest.

"Pardon, Madame Paul, I almost fainted and am so poorly right now. May I be excused to lie down, please?" Her voice sounded as weak as a wet paper bag, and she let her eyes roll upwards in a dramatic way. Madeleine was aware of Carolina's surprised gaze on her, and she dared not look in the direction of her friend for fear of collapsing in a fit of giggles. Those expensive drama classes at the London theater were now paying off!

Madame Paul raised her gold-rimmed spectacles on the string of pearls and put them on, inspecting her closely.

"Okay, lie down and rest. I'll have Nurse sent up to your room to check on you. Carolina, you finish the work and then set the table for the waitressing lesson that starts at eleven."

Before Madeleine left the room, she managed to give her friend an apologetic glance for leaving her with all the work, but as she climbed the stairs to her room, she felt greatly relieved. In the bedroom, a long, narrow room with a pretty postcard view of Lake Geneva from the bay window, Madeleine threw herself on her bed with only one thought: how to get out of Le Manoir as fast as her nimble feet could run. She had read Elle's and Jacques' letters at least a dozen times, and it had all become clear to her. They missed her and she missed them. And then there was Loulou to think of, her little monkey, who missed her too. The sense of being needed in this world gave Madeleine energy. But now to act, and to act fast.

Since her arrival, she had thought the lessons in etiquette and good housekeeping an insult to her intelligence and the idea that these would land her the best options in marriage debilitating. Now Elle's letter confirmed that she had also disliked it here. That left only chubby, easy-going Antoinette eagerly lapping it all up in the run-up to her marriage to Monsieur Maurice Martin. And for what purpose? The man was just a commoner from Rouen, whose lack of blue blood was only compensated by his weighty purse.

"That's not fair." Madeleine corrected her own trail of thoughts. "In their own way, Netty and Maurice are happy. It's just not the life I want; at least not now!"

Her head clear now, she fully realized that it was not just the silly lessons, it was the uselessness of living in a neutral place while the rest of Europe bowed its head under the assault of a gruesome war. This had been so depressing; it had seeped her energy until she was on the brink of falling ill physically. Yet she had no idea how to change her situation; how to escape from it.

Her parents would never allow her to leave before she had finished the course next summer, hoping that by then the war would be over. And Madeleine knew too well what that meant. The end of the course and the end of the war would invariably lead to the same outcome for her: being paraded around society until the most suitable aristocrat snapped her up and subsequently hid her in his castle in the countryside with a string of kids while he went gallivanting with friends and mistresses.

"No, thank you! Sod off," she cried aloud.

There was a light tap on the door, and Nurse walked in, looking alarmed.

"Sorry, I was waving a mosquito away that had landed on my arm."

"Fool someone else, Mademoiselle. There are no mosquitos in March!"

Madeleine thought it wise not to react any further and held herself limp while the nurse, her face prim and disapproving under her starched white cap, took her temperature and checked her tongue and pushed firm hands on her stomach.

When the nurse was gone, having prescribed hot tea and dry biscuits and a couple of hours of rest, Madeleine continued her mental quest for escape. It was clear she would have to run away, but as she had no money of her own and was underage, this was easier said than done. She wished she had an ally to confide in, but here at this snooty finishing school, both staff and girls seemed only bent on living by the rules. There was no one to help her. And then there was the war going on. How could one travel? She had no idea.

Madeleine decided she would just pack her suitcase and sneak away, walk the five miles to the station, and board a train back into France. Bluntly, confidently. She emptied her purse on the bed and grimaced. With a bit of luck, it would just be enough to buy a train ticket to Versailles, where she would ask Antoinette for some extra cash, pick up Loulou, and be gone again. But as Madeleine would have left Le Manoir prematurely and without permission from their parents, it was unlikely that law-abiding Netty would be willing to help, rather than making a big scene out of it, phoning Papa in London, and urging Maurice to drive Maddy straight back to Switzerland.

But it was a risk worth taking, and it was her best option. If the plan worked, she would go straight home to Château de Drag-oncourt, help Elle and Jacques, carry their burden with them, and prove to them she too could throw her weight behind the war effort. Jacques and Elle would probably be less difficult to convince. There was plenty she could do, she was sure of it, although she had no idea what. She was no longer a baby. At eighteen, she was perfectly capable of standing on her own two feet and making mature decisions.

A dozen times at least, Madeleine was on the brink of letting Carolina in on her plan, but she decided against it every time. It was a hard decision because she felt so alone and had so many doubts what to do and how to do it. But it was better not to compromise sweet Carolina. If Caro did not know where Madeleine was, Madame Paul could not hold it against her dear friend. She would write her straight after her arrival. And after the war, they would meet up and laugh about it all.

She carefully selected some of her clothes and personal belongings and put them in her smaller suitcase, leaving the big trunk, her hat case, and enough of her things lying around the room that Carolina would not immediately become alarmed when she came up to change for dinner. To demonstrate her good behavior, Madeleine descended the stairs for lunch and declared herself quite revived and able to take part in the afternoon lessons.

She did not miss Madame Paul looking at her suspiciously, so despite her big appetite, she dutifully nibbled on a dry biscuit and sipped the herb tea the nurse had subscribed, eyeing the others with envy as they tucked into delicious smelling pork cutlets with cream and mushroom sauce. It got even worse when home-made apple pie with thick vanilla custard passed under her nose, with her mouth watering and her eyes feasting, but the promise to herself that she would be out of the place that same night steeled her will.

Madeleine's biggest hurdle was how she could disappear before nightfall and before Carolina and the rest of Le Manoir went to bed. Since she had to be at the station before nine, there was no waiting for the house to fall into silence. The first precaution she had taken was to hide her suitcase in a deserted shed behind the stables, where she could easily pick it up and get back to the road leading into Lausanne.

The afternoon went smoothly, and although at times Madeleine's heart pounded in her throat, she made it through the lessons and afterwards dove into a good dinner, again pretending she did not notice Madame Paul's scrutiny. She even managed to save some bread and cheese to take on her the trip and stole an apple from the fruit basket on the side table. The girls were supposed to do another hour and a half of studying after dinner, but if the weather was nice, they were allowed to go for a walk along the lake.

"Come on, Maddy, don't be a spoilsport." Carolina was tugging on her sleeve as Madeleine made her way to the library. She gave her friend a quick peck on the cheek, knowing it was the last time she would see her, but excused herself,

"I really have to do my homework, Caro. I missed most of the morning lessons, as you know. I'm sorry." Carolina's dark eyebrows raised quizzically as she stared at her. This was a first – Madeleine de Dragoncourt caring about studying the sequence of silverware and glasses. But as the other girls were calling her to come along, Caroline skipped away, calling a hurried "See you later."

Madeleine watched the slender back in the crimson floral dress disappear around the corner, and a lump filled in her throat. Out of her life walked the only person she had loved here, whom she was going to miss and who she knew would be worried sick about her. She was again tempted to leave Carolina a small note, but recovered herself with a firm *No*. She could not risk being intercepted at the station.

As soon as the chatter of the girls was no longer audible, and Madeleine was sure Madame Paul had retreated to her office for her evening coffee and paperwork, she dressed in the dark brown dress, the only drab article she possessed, and tiptoed down the stairs and out the back door. She paused for a moment, listening attentively and spying around her. There was no one in the courtyard.

The gardeners had stored their tools and gone home, and the horse boys were busy in the stables brushing the Arabian mares. She could hear them talking with each other, but they seemed quite busy and preoccupied. Dusk was approaching fast; the sun, bright and deep red, was about to dip behind the Savoy Alps on the other side of the lake, coloring the water in a velvety surface of deep purple.

Madeleine could see the silhouettes of the girls moving along the waterside like a cluster of protected shorebirds. The sky was almost cloudless; only three elongated slithers of slate-gray clouds lazily traversed the darkening sky. It promised to be a clear but cold night. She would have to hurry to reach the warm station and be gone.

When she was convinced no one would enter the courtyard, Madeleine made herself small as a cat, and creeping along the stone garden wall that still radiated the warmth of the day, she managed to reach the shed where her suitcase and coat were waiting. She let out a sigh of relief. So far, her plan was working. Now she would go straight through the arboretum, protected by the rows of trees, to reach the back gate that led to the road. From there she would follow a maze of small streets to get to the main road to the city center. Staying as close as possible to the walled side of the street, she prayed her dark coat and suitcase would blend in and that no prying eyes would notice her.

There were hardly any people in the streets, and only the occasional motor car rumbled past, not identifying her as an escapee from Le Manoir. Halfway to the station, she checked the little clock hanging around her neck. A quarter to nine. This rather stressed her, as she would have to run to make it to the night train in time. Speeding up, she quickly became out of breath. Sweat trickled down her back, and her suitcase became heavier by the minute. But she was not ready to give up yet. If she missed that train, all was lost.

Why did dinner have to go on for so long? she fumed inwardly, meanwhile cursing her impractical shoes that were hurting her toes. But she finally made it to the station, the black fingers on the huge white clock pointing three minutes to nine.

She stormed towards the ticket office and, gasping for breath, exclaimed quite unfemininely, "Quickly, sir, one single fare to Paris!"

The fat ticket seller on the other side of the glass panel watched her indolently, and scratching his bristly head under his cap, drawled in his slow Swiss accent, "No need to rush, Miss, the train's delayed by a good ten minutes."

Madeleine took another deep breath. Good; but not good. Her

brain was working overtime. The train had to come soon. Every minute she stayed longer in the station, they might find out at Le Manoir that she was missing and come looking for her. She paid for the ticket and, mumbling a quick "Thank you," made her way to the international platform. To calm her overwrought nerves, she bought herself a *café au lait* and a slice of sponge cake from the stall, anxiously eyeing the bottom of her purse.

When she had finished her coffee and licked up the last crumbs of her extravagance, *le train bleu* rolled into the station as an elongated blue caterpillar. Hissing and puffing, it came to a shrieking stop at her feet. Immediately, a porter in white tunic and blue trousers rushed up to her.

"Number of your sleeper, Miss?" She handed the young man her ticket and followed him and her luggage to carriage number 18. He placed her suitcase in the rack above her seat but did not move away. His head bowed down politely, he waited until she put a franc in his white gloved hand, after which he shuffled away, mumbling a thank you.

Madeleine sank down on the plush chair, and a deep sigh of relief escaped her modest bosom. Only then did she become aware of the hustle and bustle around her. Travelers, both in uniform and civilian clothes, followed by porters loaded with suitcases, were boarding the train on their own, in couples or entire families, moving past or sitting down near her. The usual goodbyes and farewells were exchanged from the platform, relatives waving white handkerchiefs, some teary, some showing dapper smiling faces. Was this the last train to depart from Switzerland? It seemed almost like an exodus.

Watching all the goings on as if in a dream, Madeleine sat motionless in her seat as if buttoned up in a tight cocoon, with only one urgent wish running in every fiber of her body: for the train to start moving, to free her of the terror of seeing Madame Paul's triumphant face appear at the window, dragging her back to Le Manoir, and all would have been for naught. But nothing of the sort happened, and an hour later they were crossing the border and entering France at Mâcon.

As night enveloped her and the lights in the compartments were dimmed to shadowy small pinpricks, she lay down in the narrow cot and let her exhausted body be rolled half unconscious in the swaying carriage. Even in this state of half sleep, she could not yet believe it – that she had actually done it. She was free; free at last.

As the heavy locomotive hissed and sputtered on and the long blue caterpillar slowly crossed nightly France towards Gare de Lyon, Madeleine finally fell into a deep sleep, blissfully oblivious of where she was heading.

AT TEN THAT MORNING, a disheveled Madeleine, her stomach rumbling and her hair and make-up in disarray, pulled the cord of the big brass bell outside her sister's mansion on the Boulevard de la Reine in Versailles. She leaned against one of the marble pillars that supported the Rococo portico to steady herself. One of the Martin maids, clad in an immaculate black dress that stood out stiffly from the waist and reached down to the ankles, opened the glass-paneled door. She gasped, clasping a pudgy white hand over her mouth.

"Ohhh... Mademoiselle Madeleine, praise the Lord. You are safe! Madame Martin was so worried!"

"Yes, I'm here. Now let me in." Madeleine brushed past the baffled maid, clutching her suitcase in her hand.

"Madame is giving Master Maurice Junior his breakfast in the nursery," the young girl cried after her, as Madeleine made straight for the breakfast room.

"Well, inform her I am here, and please tell cook to bring me a big breakfast."

Madeleine was wolfing down a second helping of porridge richly sweetened with golden syrup when her older sister sailed in with a displeased look on her chubby round face. The middle de Dragoncourt daughter was the only fair-haired member of the family, and her diminutive size and soft round curves, inherited from their paternal grandmother, were a sharp contrast to both Elle and Madeleine who were tall, willowy girls like their English mother Countess Virginia. Antoinette's temperament, easy-going, at times even docile, was altogether different as well. Madeleine reckoned that this time, her sister must be really upset because the dissatisfaction showed on her fair face.

"For Heaven's sake, what is going on, Madeleine de Dragoncourt?" Antoinette demanded, her small hands with the many sparkling rings placed firmly on her broad hips.

Madeleine swallowed the last spoonful of hot porridge and thought it wise to wait for her sister to finish the torrent of accusations that would most probably follow before saying anything herself. When nothing came, she looked up from her plate to eye her sister with suspicion.

Antoinette just stood there in her expensive mauve morning dress, her platinum hair done up as if she were going to a party, big emerald earrings dangling from her delicate ear lobes.

Madeleine rose and walked towards her sister with the intention of giving her a kiss, but Antoinette recoiled from her.

"Don't!"

It sounded harsher than Madeleine had ever heard from her sister, and she was briefly caught off balance. She returned slowly to her seat, shrugging.

"Ah, well, if you don't want to greet me, it's up to you, Netty. I'll tell you why I'm here, but please don't keep standing there like that. At least sit down."

Antoinette, her face white under a lavish layer of powder, perched on the edge of one of the breakfast chairs, folding her hands in her lap and waiting with an accusatory look on her face. The same pudgy maid who had opened the front door stuck her head around the corner, but Antoinette waved her away with an impatient gesture.

"Go and do the shopping, Juliette." Turning back to Madeleine, she implored, her blue glance flickering, "I'm still waiting for your explanation."

"There is none," Madeleine replied in a flat voice, "I'm done with Le Manoir. That's all. I'm going home."

"To London?"

"No – to Picardy."

Now Antoinette looked even more sour. "You can't, sister, and you know very well why. The château is right on the front line."

"Jacques and Elle are there." Madeleine played with the sash of her serviette, letting it tickle her palm, her eyelids cast down to not further upset her sister.

"That's a different matter altogether," Antoinette said in a shrill voice. "That's because Papa was asked by Monsieur Clemenceau to turn Dragoncourt into a war hospital. Otherwise none of us would be there right now."

"But they are."

"You are *not* going there, Madeleine. I forbid it. I have phoned Papa, and he's agreed for you to return to London if you really consider it impossible to finish your education at Le Manoir. I was flatly against this decision, as I think you need Le Manoir more than any of us, but you know Papa. He can be far too lenient at times." Antoinette pressed her lips together primly.

"He said what?" Madeleine glanced at her sister from underneath her dark brows. "Heavens, revolution!"

"Don't be so unbearably cynical!" Antoinette snapped. "You'll be on the boat train by tonight."

Madeleine rose to her full five foot nine and exclaimed angrily, "No way!"

Antoinette rose too but had to look up into the face of her taller sister. In the same high-pitched, shrill voice with which she had conducted the entire conversation, she concluded, "Consider the matter decided. Now go and have a bath and change. My dear husband will drive you to the Gare du Nord tonight. I'm going out to help stage a matinee for the wounded in the Palace gardens, so I'll see you tonight before you leave." When she was at the door, she turned one more time and added, "And take that monkey with you. You'll find it in the glass house. One of the gardeners has been taking care of it. I don't want it in the house. It stinks!"

Her petite sister swept out of the room before Madeleine could answer.

"Heck!" She was trapped. Without money, she could not even get to Château de Dragoncourt. What now? For the time being, she would do what Antoinette had suggested, as she felt positively road-weary, and her clothes were crumpled and smelly. She needed time to brew on a new plan for her and Loulou, and what would be a better place than in a steaming hot bath?

The bathroom adjacent to the guest room Madeleine always used when staying with her sister was as luxurious as everything in the Martin household. Lying stretched out in the bathtub filled with warm, scented water, Madeleine closed her eyes. Briefly she did contemplate the idea of just returning to her parents in London, sitting out the war, having some fun. But then she jerked herself upright, so sudden that a big gush of water flooded over the edge of the marble bathtub and splashed onto the parquet floor.

"Nooo!" she cried aloud to herself. "You were done living the easy life. Remember?"

Hurrying out of the bath, she dressed in a soft green cashmere traveling dress, jammed a green felt hat on her lustrous hair, and put on some sturdy walking shoes. She inspected the contents of her suit-case and tossed all the fancy dresses out on her bed. She repacked it with long-sleeved blouses, warm jumpers, slacks, and sensible shoes – all the spare pieces of fabric she could find in her closet at her sister's house. Just one low-cut, emerald green evening dress – in case the war ended, and they could throw a party at Dragoncourt. It was done in minutes.

Snapping the suitcase shut, she dragged it down the stairs to her brother-in-law's office on the ground floor. There she rummaged through the drawers of his enormous desk, and with an *Aha!* retrieved a 1000francs note from a cigar box and put it in her purse.

The house was silent; her nephew and niece were probably taking their afternoon nap, and Antoinette had gone to her charity event. Maurice, who worked for the Ministry of Interior Affairs, was probably at his office in Paris.

Madeleine looked around the opulent office quarters one more time, scanning it quickly. A smile broke over her face when she spotted the keys to Maurice's Renault EU, the family's spare car, which was only used for outings, as the Martins owned at least three more vehicles. Without hesitating, she grabbed the keys, jotted a note that she was only borrowing it and would have someone drive it back from Dragoncourt the next day. She gave the note a kiss and placed it on Maurice's desk.

"Now, Loulou, and then out of this place!"

But for a moment, all Madeleine had eye for was the magnificent dark-green car with its gilded adornments and ochre wheels standing invitingly in the driveway. Its canvas hood was closed, which was just as well, as it would make her less visible. Having placed her suitcase in the trunk of the Renault and giving the gleaming car an appreciative tap, Madeleine swerved around the corner of the house and headed for the greenhouses at the bottom of the large garden. On coming nearer, she heard high, weak shrieks and quickened her pace. Loulou was in pain!

Madeleine swung open the glass door with such vehemence that it rattled the glazing. A tiny black monkey was sitting huddled under an acacia plant, scratching her furry body with her little hands, and whining with pathetic yelps. She looked ratty and underfed.

"Oh, my darling," Madeleine cried out, speeding towards her. "What have they done to you?" She was not sure who grabbed whom first, but Loulou was in her arms, hugging her mistress as tightly as she could, even trying to slip under her coat. Madeleine just stood there, embracing her little friend, tears streaming down her cheeks.

"Oh, my darling, oh my neglected little darling," she kept repeating. "Here – let me have a look at you." She felt the little body, the ribs sticking out, and the fur dirty and knotty. No bones were broken, but the quick, coal-black eyes, usually so full of mischievous light, were lusterless.

"Let's find the blighter who was supposed to take care of you," Madeleine said angrily, but Loulou clamped her little body forcefully against her, and she thought better of it. "He was that bad? Well, let's forget about it then. You don't have to see him anymore. I promise! We'll patch you up at Dragoncourt, okay? I've got food and drink for you in the car, and we'll get you clean clothes when we get there. Why did they leave you naked, when I left your dresses with Antoinette? Bah, they don't care for animals at the Martins'. I wish I had time to see my horses; I hope they've at least been looked after properly. But there's no time to check now. Let's hit the road before Netty comes back and my plan goes to ruins."

Madeleine loved chatting with her monkey again, and although Loulou did not talk back in words, she made content, little noises that showed with her whole being how pleased she was that her mistress was back. Again, Madeleine had to sniff and wipe her hand over her cheeks. She had not come a day too late. Loulou was in a bad state, but her spirit was as strong as ever. Jumping on Madeleine's shoulder, she tried to tip her hat from her head with her dainty little hands.

"You want to give me a kiss, don't you?" Madeleine lifted the hat and felt the wet lips on her cheek.

"Time to brush your teeth, Lous! They haven't done that either. You're a smelly little bundle of love."

The little monkey made a whining sound and jumped onto the hood of the car, staring pensively at her. Big skin-color floppy ears stuck out of the short black pelt, and she made endearing little *chuck-chuck* sounds, grinning widely as she showed her very long, very yellow teeth.

Madeleine grinned back. "They don't make them more adorable than you, my monkey pie. Hop-hop, get into the car. We're going on an adventure."

Loulou rubbed her furless little belly with one hand and winked at Madeleine.

"Yes, food before all else. Now, get in!"

As she reversed the Renault off the gravel pathway and steered it down Boulevard de la Reine, she felt royally pleased with herself. It was a sun-laden afternoon in the middle of a busy and bustling Versailles, when she took to the road with Loulou in the passenger seat who was munching happily on an apple. The light was already returning to the black ape's eyes. At the end of the street, the Royal Palace, stately as a ship under full sail, was ablaze in the afternoon light, as untouched by war and attractive to visitors as it had been for centuries, although the statues in the gardens were wrapped up in gray tarpaulin, and anti-aircraft guns stood on the rooftops pointing to all directions. Passing the gardens of Le Château de Versailles she drove the majestic car north and soon Versailles was behind her.

A not-too-experienced driver and without a map, Madeleine knew an arduous journey lay ahead of her. She would need to get to Amiens before nightfall, but it was at least a five-hour drive. The fuel gauge indicated that the gas was low, and she had left without fuel coupons. Afraid that her ingenious plan would come crashing down on her after all, she started singing *La Madelon* at the top of her lungs.

Quand Madelon vient nous servir à boire
Sous la tonnelle on frôle son jupon
Et chacun lui raconte une histoire
Une histoire à sa façon.

WHILE SINGING, she decided she would have to use all her Le Manoir charm to get some gas and obtain a map. At Cergy, these decisions could no longer be put off. She found a shop where she was able to buy a 5-liter bidon of L'Automobiline without much trouble, and hoped with all her might it would last her to her destination. Maybe she was going to be lucky after all. As she replaced the cap on the tank and was about to step behind the steering wheel again, Loulou drew her attention, and she had to let the little monkey relieve herself behind a deserted building.

"Good girl! Good potty-trained little Loulou!"

Loulou fell asleep, snoring ever so lightly, and the rest of the journey ran much more smoothly than anticipated. They reached Château de Dragoncourt without difficulty by eight that night.

Madeleine felt exhilarated as the dark-green Renault swerved around the last bend, its headlights pointing the way along the tree-lined road. The castle was unlit but for a dimmed light above the entrance door, something quite unthinkable before the war, but she could make out the contours of its massive walls, the windows like large black mirrors and the many turrets pointing upwards. A huge red cross flag was waving its eternal message into the opaque sky.

Along the driveway, she slowed to a walking pace, maneuvering the big car around the many vehicles that stood parked on either side. Loulou awoke, yawned, and put her front paws on the dashboard, stared at the approaching castle with the same mesmerized look as her mistress.

"You like it? It's our new home," Madeleine muttered, and she was again so relieved to have Loulou with her. The presence of her monkey made her feel less alone and more confident she would be able to tackle the family dispute that would certainly erupt upon her arrival.

Near the entrance to the castle, it was remarkably busy despite the evening hour. People were going in and out, ghostlike in the semi dark: military men, nurses and orderlies. A few of them were wounded soldiers, most of them bandaged, missing arms or legs.

Madeleine parked the Renault amidst a cluster of the army vehicles and ambulances and hopped out, exhausted but relieved. What immediately fell on her like a thick, damp cloth was the pungent smell of gunfire, smoke, and decaying flesh that permeated the air. It struck her as nothing so far in this war had been able to do.

Before the war, when they used to arrive at Dragoncourt for the summer vacation, it was the crisp, dewy air of the Picardy fields that had always been such a treat to her, after the long winter months in Paris filled with gasoline and chimney smoke. The first thing she would do as soon as Papa brought the family car to a halt was jump out and fill her lungs to the brim with the fresh air, her way of starting their sultry summer with lots of outdoor activities, tennis, and horse riding, a celebration of her abundance of energy. Now the air was acrid with the suffocating smell of interminable death and woe.

It deflated her earlier exhilaration and made her feel tiny, insignificant in this huge war that was rampaging over her ancestral home. Madeleine swallowed hard so as not to burst out crying. What had happened to the happy place of her youth? Who had done this to them? Taking in the magnitude of the destructive force so close by, she stood on quavering legs until she felt a small paw in hers – Loulou by her side, grinning up at her.

"Oh, you little thing," she sniffed, picking the monkey up. "What a comfort you are. I've missed you so."

Leaving her suitcase in the car to first inspect the lay of the land, Madeleine made her way to the castle's entrance, with Loulou on her shoulder. On one of the stone balustrades of the veranda a broad-shouldered military man sat smoking a pipe. He was silhouetted against the dim light above the entrance, and though Madeleine knew nothing of army ranks, the number of stripes and ribbons on his jacket made her assume he was an important chap.

The man put the smoldering pipe on the balustrade and rose to his feet, blocking her way. He was quite impressive-looking, although not much taller than she was, and she saw he had friendly but watchful eyes and a funny sandy-colored mustache. "A new face around here!" he observed, with the Kent accent so familiar to her from her London days.

Friendly or not, Madeleine instantly realized the blue-green stare missed nothing.

"Madeleine de Dragoncourt," she said, not knowing whether one shook hands with military men or saluted them, so she kept her hands by her side. Loulou hid her little head under the rim of Madeleine's hat, shivering with trepidation.

"One of *them*, then?" He cocked his head in the direction of the entrance.

"If by 'one of them' you mean I'm Jacques and Elle's sister, you are right," Madeleine replied primly.

"That I could tell the moment I saw you approaching. Quite a likeness to Elle!"

Gaining confidence from his pleasant tone, she ventured more boldly, "And with whom do I have the pleasure?"

On this, the soldier saluted with a brief tight movement, stretching the tips of his fingers to his cap. "Major Gerald Hamilton, at your service, ma'am."

"Golly," Madeleine chuckled coyly. "But major, where have you been wounded in this war? You look quite in one piece to me."

At this he laughed heartily. "I'm not wounded, Miss. I'm stationed here at Dragoncourt with my army division. We've been here since last November, to protect the hospital and supply the rest of our battalions at the front."

"Ahhh, I see... oh yes, Elle told me so in her letter. I'd quite forgotten." Madeleine cocked her head flirtatiously to one side. "Then I think I will feel quite safe as long as you are here too, Major Hamilton." She smiled her ready smile at him, revealing cute dimples in her rosy cheeks.

"Are you visiting for the night, Miss Madeleine?" She thought she heard concern in his voice.

"I hope not, dear major. I intend to stay in my own home from now on and help with the war effort." She said it with as much bravado as she could muster.

Major Hamilton cleared his throat, gazing at her intently as if mulling over what he would answer to this. "Ahh... I see. Well, to tell you the truth, we're expecting a new German offensive any day now, and we may not be able to stop it. So, everyone's to be evacuated over the next couple of days. I'm afraid your visit is going to be cut short by these developments."

Madeleine gazed at him as if he were splitting her entire world in two. "But where is everyone going?" she asked incredulously, trying to subdue the panic in her voice.

"Further south, maybe even as far as beyond Paris. Paris may fall too, you know. There's no knowing what the Germans are capable of right now, with fresh supplies arriving from the Eastern Front every day."

"But you can surely fight the stupid *Boches*? The Allied forces have done so for four bloody years. And now with the Americans also putting their weight behind it... At least you could try, couldn't you?"

"Maybe best leave military matters to military men, Miss de Dragoncourt," he said with a dry smile. "Anyway, do you want me to accompany you inside? Can I carry your luggage for you?"

Her military plotting instantly forgotten, she gave him an endearing smile. "Would you, dear major? My suitcase's in the car, and it's ever so heavy."

Gerald Hamilton put his pipe in his breast pocket and walked with her to the car.

"Nice car," he remarked appreciatively, "you've got taste."

Madeleine thought it wise not to inform him about her 'borrowing' the vehicle from her brother-in-law.

Lifting her suitcase as if it were light as a feather, he added, "And what's with the monkey?"

"Oh, that's Loulou, my pet. She's a bit shy and tired from traveling, but she'll be fine in the morning when she's had her bath and is properly dressed again." She took the half-sleeping monkey in her arms, and the little animal curled up against her bosom and fell asleep again.

"Where do you want me to bring this?" Gerald had swung her suitcase on top of his shoulder and was marching it to the front door.

"I'd better go and see my brother and sister first. Do you know where I can find them?"

"If you're lucky, they'll still be in the dining room. They're expecting you, I assume?"

"Of course," Madeleine lied. "So take me to *la grande salle verte*, please."

The major turned on his heels and looked straight at her, his expression quizzical. "I beg your pardon?"

"The green room. The dining room."

"I don't think that's gonna work, miss. That's the operating room nowadays."

Madeleine gazed at him in horror. "It can't be. That's the most magnificent room in our entire château. That would be... like blasphemy!"

"Well, it is what it is, Miss, so don't bite *my* head off. I've got nothing to do with it."

"So, where do we dine now?"

"I don't know what the Dragoncourt rooms were used for before it became a military post and a hospital, but we have our meals right at the end of the west wing. Does that ring a bell?"

"The servants' quarters?" Madeleine was flabbergasted. "I played there in the kitchens when I was a kid, but I've never eaten there."

"Well, the food is jolly good, and it looks like a decent place to me, but I'm no judge of those fancy places, Miss. I'm just a simple squire's son."

Meanwhile passing down the corridor that led to the west wing, Madeleine's mouth fell open with shock.

"Oh, my goodness, my goodness," she kept repeating. "It's changed so much. I hardly recognize my old home."

"I'm sorry, Miss," Gerald said, and his voice sounded sympathetic. "I know it isn't much of a homecoming for you, but the war's changed everything for everyone."

"I'll get used to it." It sounded braver than she felt. "If Jacques and Elle can do this, so can I. But I'm very glad Papa and Mummy can't see it like this. My father would have a stroke on the spot."

They reached the servants' quarters, and Gerald gently dropped her suitcase at her feet. "I'll give you some family time and I've got work to do."

"Thank you, Major," Madeleine said warmly, "and good night to you, sir."

"Good night, miss."

Her clear gaze followed the major as he disappeared through the corridor again. Gosh, he was smashing. She had no idea military men could be so spunky. Tomorrow she had to find out everything about him. With that in mind, Madeleine found herself before the door that led to the servants' rooms.

7

A SURPRISE VISIT

W ith the sleeping monkey in one arm and her suitcase in the other, Madeleine kicked open the door with her foot, but did that so brusquely that it flung open and bounced against the opposite wall. Four heads snapped up in surprise.

It was Elle who cried out first. "Madeleine, for Heaven's sake. What is going on? We've been so worried!"

"Oh, hello to you too. What about 'Welcome home, little sister'?" It came out more sarcastically than she had intended.

Elle rose from her chair and already stood in front of her younger sibling with hands on slender hips, her face dark with fury. "You stole Maurice's car to drive all the way up here? Are you insane?"

At her bitter tone, Madeleine let her chin drop, and her eyes filled with tears. She had been traveling for twenty-four hours, and she was exhausted and afraid. And now she was not welcome here too. Everyone was hostile to her. She tried to look past Elle to Jacques, who was sitting at the table, hoping he would at least come to her rescue, but before her brother could say anything another voice in very lah-di-dah English sounded from the other end of the table.

"Give the damsel a break, Miss bully Elle! That's your sister you're talking to. The girl's been traveling to come and see you, and you give her a welcome like this?"

"Shut up, Phil," Elle raged. "It's none of your business." But she did soften her expression a little and, seeing her little sister's shoulders starting to shake, she added in a friendlier tone, "Come and sit down, Maddy. Let's get some food and drink in you first. But for Heaven's pity, why did you do this? And bring Loulou to this din on top of everything?"

In a small voice, Madeleine sniffled as she sat down on one of the straight servants' chairs, "Loulou couldn't stay with Netty anymore. Look at her. She's all neglected and ill. But don't worry, I'll look after her myself."

Jacques had now risen from his chair and came over to give his little sister a peck on the cheek. "Hi Mad-Maddy, it's good to see you. Did you get our letters?"

She smiled at him through her tears and nodded. She wanted to say that was why she had come – to help them – but suddenly it all became too much for her. Her brother and sister looked so different, so grave and old in their war outfit, and being in this part of the house that used to be servant territory was even more unsettling to her now frail state of mind. Nothing was as it had been before, and it confused her terribly.

Feeling the initial hostility evaporating, she glanced around and saw there were two more people sitting at the long table. The young man who had spoken up for her looked as British as he sounded, and he had the most peculiarly colored eyes. He too came around the table and kissed her hand gallantly.

"Philip Lane, also known as the Earl of Timberwood & Pottery, and from now on your eternal servant, ma'am."

This made her giggle through her tears and she remembered Elle had written that he was funny. She could instantly see he was not Elle's type, so his quest to win her heart was doomed to fail.

The other person at the table was a dark-haired girl in a nursing uniform with a golden crucifix prominently over the red cross on her breast and a mass of dark hair parted in the middle. Madeleine recognized M-C, whom she had seen once before the war. But she had changed a lot since then. M-C used to be chubby but was almost translucently thin now and even more serene than before. She just waved at Madeleine, a brief lifting of her lower arm, and continued to read her Bible.

As in the old days, it was Elle who took control of the situation. As the initial shock of her baby sister's unexpected arrival subsided, she clearly regretted having been so hard on her. Sitting down on the arm of Madeleine's chair, she put her long arm around the thin shoulders that were shivering from all the emotions.

"Here's what we'll do, Maddy. We'll give Netty and Maurice a ring to tell them you and the car have arrived safely. Tomorrow Philip has to get supplies from Paris, so he can drive the car back to Versailles."

"Am I supposed to return from Paris on foot?" Philip whined, pulling a face. "Oh my, my fate as Elle's slave here is becoming more wretched by the day!"

"Don't be silly, Phil," Elle retorted. "We'll arrange some form of return transport for you."

Jacques had already picked up the telephone set and dragged it outside in the corridor on its long, coiled cord. Presently his muffled voice could be heard on the other side of the door.

"Now you eat first and then you'll sleep with me in my room tonight. Okay, pumpkin? Tomorrow morning we'll discuss how to solve this." Elle took off her sister's hat and stroked the tangled mass of auburn hair.

"Thank you, Elle." Madeleine gratefully pressed her face against her sister's rough ambulance uniform. "Can Loulou sleep with us, too?"

"I guess she'll have to."

"Thank you."

Jacques came back into the room as Madeleine and Loulou were already attacking a plate of potatoes with veal and beans.

"Tried to smooth the ruffled feathers a bit," he announced, pushing his spectacles up the bridge of his long nose. "Netty was mainly relieved that Maddy was safe, and Maurice that the car was still in one piece."

He winked at Madeleine, and her hopes went up. At least they had not yet mentioned sending her back to Switzerland or on to London. In her heart of hearts, she felt they secretly were pleased to see her now she was really here. She finished gobbling down her food, yawned, and announced she was ready for bed.

"Off you go, both of you," Elle commanded, and Madeleine would not have had it otherwise. She did not even protest that she wanted to sleep in her own room as she was led up the stairs to the tiny maids' bedrooms. Loulou was wrapped in a blanket and placed in a cardboard box next to Madeleine's bed. The young escapee and her pet slept as soon as their heads hit the pillow.

AWAKENING THE NEXT DAY, Madeleine rubbed her eyes, wondering where she was. She half-opened her eyelids, still drowsy from the deep, dreamless sleep she had fallen into the night before. Although the latticed shutters were shut, yellow sunlight filtered through the slats, sprinkling rays of light over the room, and Madeleine felt her heart beat a little faster. The spartan place she found herself in might be unfamiliar and unlike any bedroom she had ever slept in, but she was home – home at Dragoncourt!

She peered around the narrow bedroom with its two single beds pushed against the walls, the one she was occupying and the other neatly made up with a brown quilt where Elle had slept. For the rest, the room held an antique-looking washstand with a white porcelain ewer, a plain chest with drawers, and two wooden stools. Still rubbing her eyes, she felt something suddenly jump on top of her. Loulou wriggled her little body close, and nestling her furry head on the pillow, gazed adoringly at Madeleine.

"Hello, you!" Madeleine scratched the furry little forehead. Loulou grinned.

Madeleine grinned back. "I'd have to find you one of my dolls' dresses. but I'll first have to find my old bedroom. I haven't got a clue where we are right now, *ma belle*." The size of the room and its furnishing pointed to them being in the servants' quarters, but it was confusing to say the least why Elle was not sleeping in her own bedroom. And why she had not been taken to hers.

"I'll ask them to take us to my rooms today, sweetie. And you and I will get dressed properly. That is, if they let us stay." Madeleine looked doubtful, but Loulou just kept watching her mistress intently.

With Elle gone, Madeleine had no idea how long she had slept or what time it was. There was a lot of noise outside in the castle's court-yard: people shouting at each other, the drills of soldiers, and cars honking. Inside the building the sounds were more diffuse, but it felt as if the whole castle was a beehive, a commotion of organized activity.

Still slightly disoriented but hoping she would be able to find her way back to yesterday's dining room, Madeleine slipped into Elle's dressing gown and slippers. With Loulou on her arm, she peeked around the door. She realized they were on the top floor of the west wing, a long, narrow corridor with doors on either side, where the servants used to sleep; a corridor where she had played hide-and-seek with Antoinette only seven years earlier. It was deserted.

Going back into the room, she quickly dressed in her crumpled travel dress, as her suitcase was nowhere to be seen. Given that the castle was full of strangers and that she had no idea whom she might meet on the stairway, yesterday's dress was her best option. Imagine she should bump into that dashing major and he should see her in a state of half undress. Oh, no! If she wanted to show her worth for the war cause, she should be prepared for action, not romance.

After an unpleasant splash of cold water on her face and a vague attempt at combing her thick tresses with Elle's comb, she and Loulou made their way down the spiraling staircase. At the bottom she found herself right in front of the door to yesterday's dining room, which she furtively opened. It was empty but for Philip, who was sitting at the table scribbling in his notebook.

Looking up, his face broke into a wide smile and he cried cheerily,

"*Ahhh*... hello, my beautiful Countess! What a sight for my weary eyes you are! You're even more adorable in daylight than in the tenebrosity of dusk."

"Hi, Philip," she replied shyly. It was hard to fathom whether he was making fun of her with his over-the-top choice of words. "Where is everybody?"

"Everybody but me, you mean? Oh, they've all been gone eons ago. You see, there's just no way this bloody war will comply with normal office hours." He shook his dark-blond head wearily, pointing to a chair next to him. "But do sit down, milady, and let me serve you some breakfast."

Philip gave Loulou a little pat on the head, "And would the tiny madame also want something to nibble on?"

At this encouragement, Loulou hopped from Madeleine's arm onto Philip's shoulder and went with him to the kitchen. So far, the little creature had seemed quite shy with other people, but she had obviously taken a liking to the quirky Brit. When he came back with a delicious smelling plate of crispy bacon, white beans in tomato sauce, and eggs, Loulou was triumphantly holding a slice of white bread between her little fingers.

"I thought you had to go to Paris?" She hoped her question sounded casual enough. It was still possible they had instructed Philip to take her back to horrible Versailles.

"I was just waiting for the keys to the automobile you so graciously borrowed."

"Oh, sorry. Let me get them now."

"No, eat first. I've got plenty of time. Going to make the most of it now by flirting unabashedly with you now that your chaperones are gone." He winked at her and she giggled.

"I bet you're more interested in Elle. She's much more your type." Madeleine laughed as she attacked the food with relish.

"How do you know that? Are you a clairvoyant as well as an angel? I am pining for Elle night and day, but she's such a sphinx when it comes to matters of the heart. I've put my entire Earldom at her feet, but she just tramples on it. Oh, will you be my accomplice, darling Countess? You will help me win her heart, won't you?"

"I can try," Madeleine said thoughtfully, still munching her breakfast, "but I'll want a favor in return."

"Anything, my angelic middle woman." His peculiar eyes scanned her face with interest.

Madeleine cleared her throat. She had no idea where to start and whether she could trust him, but it seemed the only option she had left.

"You may know I've left my finishing school in Switzerland against the wishes of my parents, and that's what's upset the whole family and why Elle was so angry with me last night. They still see me as a little girl, who had best fill her days with stupid, irrelevant things and be kept as far away from the war as possible. If I refuse to go back to Lausanne, they'll send me to London where my parents are, but... uh... I want to stay here...at Dragoncourt... and be of some use like everybody else." She looked up hopefully at him now that she had his full attention, but her heart sank as she saw his expression fall. Was she about to lose her last possible ally?

"Listen, Madeleine." All the joking was gone now. "Your family is right. No one in their right mind should stay here on the front line unless they have a very good reason. Do you have such a reason?"

While she moved her fork around in the tomato sauce on her plate, she pondered his question. Then she nodded. "I think I have a part to play here, yes. I may have no qualities in nursing or cleaning, but I could be helpful, for example, in cheering up the wounded men. I can sing, I can play the piano... and..." She looked at him with a seductive, catlike glance. "I can be very funny too, certainly together with Loulou when she's pulling her pranks." Then more seriously, "Don't you think it's important to cheer up distressed people in horrible times like these? And no one has time for providing some much-needed cultural outlet. Only I do."

She saw the word *cultural* resonated with him. At least he was considering her suggestion.

"I see your point, Madeleine, surely I do, but I still think it isn't a good idea. Moreover, we'll be leaving Dragoncourt any day now to go to a safer place."

"Well, every day counts, Philip. Plus, when I put my weight behind this, I'm part of the team. I'd be able to go with my family wherever we're evacuated to."

Philip still looked doubtful, taking in all her youthful enthusiasm with his brows raised, but some of his former light-heartedness returned when he said, "And I guess your ladyship wants *me* to plead your case favorably before your brother and sister?"

"Yes, Philip, yes! And I promise I'll talk about you to Elle in such glorious terms she'll fall in love with you head over heels."

Philip laughed, but it was not full out. "Sounds more like we're both battling for a lost cause, fair lady! Anyway, get me those keys *immédiatement* or I'll never get to Paris. I'll consider the pros and cons of our plans while roaming the French lanes. Tonight, we will hold council, you and I. Just make sure you're not evicted before that time."

"I promise!"

With a little more confidence that she might have an ally on her side, Madeleine set out to roam the castle with Loulou on her arm but whichever corner she took, she found all the nostalgic memories from the playfield of her youth completely destroyed.

She had been thirteen the last time the family had vacationed at Dragoncourt for the summer, a spindly teenager with arms and legs too long, devouring stacks of romantic novels and with a crush on the garden boy, whom she spied on from her bedroom window. With his muscled arms and strong back showing a triangle of perspiration on his shirt as he clipped the hedgerow bushes, she had pined for a kiss from him. Even the pining had been sweet because Dragoncourt had been a merry, light, and happy place, and her life just a string of garden parties, balls, and musical events; a living, throbbing place where she, the baby, had been safe and pampered and very much adored.

How different and foreign this Dragoncourt felt: grim, lusterless, without music or joy. The people she passed in the corridors all looked preoccupied and stressed, and no one seemed to think of stopping to ask himself: *Where is my life going?*

Madeleine felt as if the weight of the walls came crashing down on her, as if all the pain and all the fighting that was taking place right at that moment both inside and outside the castle imploded in her frail body, and for a moment, she staggered and swayed on her legs. She had to steady herself against the wall and breathe deeply. Loulou gazed at her somberly, seeming to feel the oppressing heaviness too. She clung to her mistress's neck with her little arms as if wanting to seek cover.

Strengthening her resolve, Madeleine made an effort to calm both herself and the monkey. She could not afford to become overwhelmed by the magnitude of the situation in which she and her family found themselves. She had to be strong; to fight her own fight with this devil of a war. For all of them. *Where there is no joy, I will bring joy.* The thought was so clear she did not even know if she had spoken it out aloud. She started to move forward, and though she did not know where precisely she was heading, she went up to the first floor where in former days her bedroom had been. She would start her exploration there.

"Let's see if we can find you a pink frock. That will cheer you up," she said to Loulou, clinging as much to her as she to her favored pet.

The monkey understood her perfectly and let go of her tight grip on Madeleine's neck to nestle in her arm again. But when they had climbed the spiral staircase to the first floor and went along the narrow corridor from the servants' rooms to the main body of the castle where the family quarters used to be, she was stopped by a young soldier on guard, inspecting her sternly from under his cap with the emblem of a staggering horse pinned up front.

"Where are you going, miss?"

She smiled kindly at him, remembering she wanted to be everybody's sunshine. "Hi there! I just wanted to go to my room. It's over there." She pointed to the end of the landing.

"Sorry, miss. Those rooms are reserved for the wounded."

This puzzled Madeleine. "But soldier, are you telling me that there are men sleeping in my private chambers?"

For some reason, the young man thought that funny, but he tried hard not to smile, keeping his clean-shaven jaws as clenched as possible. "It may have been your bedroom before the war, miss, but it is so no longer."

"And, mister soldier, do you by any chance know where they have put my belongings, or are you telling me the men are not just sleeping in my bed but also playing with my doll house?"

The muscles under his firm cheeks twitched, but he could not stop himself from snickering. Madeleine giggled too.

"I wouldn't know, miss. Maybe you can ask Major Hamilton? He's in charge of the operation."

"Oh, I know *him*," she retorted with a wink, "but mister soldier, as you seem to know little about what you are guarding, you most likely also can't tell me the whereabouts of your boss."

"But I can, miss. I'm not the total ninnyhammer you may think me. Major Hamilton is in the officers' room on the ground floor, but he's in a staff meeting right now." His young round face flushed as she questioned his capability.

"Don't worry, mister soldier," Madeleine replied in a light tone. "I'm as confused as you are in this place, so please enlighten me: where is what you call 'the officers' room'?"

"It's the library... uh... the former library, miss. And it's Sergeant Cooper, miss."

"It's Miss Madeleine, Sergeant Cooper, and Loulou the rabble-rouser." Madeleine smiled at him mischievously, and Loulou gave the amazed soldier a peck on the cheek before hopping back on Madeleine's shoulder.

She turned on her heels and walked away with her shoulders straight and her head high. This little conversation had lifted her spirits. His gaze was on her as she retreated, and feeling how she had temporarily made him forget his somber mood, she was happy. She could do this.

Later that day, Madeleine was sitting with Loulou, dressed in a pink frock with a hole cut in it for her tail, at the dinner table. She felt triumphant. The day had been a string of adventurous activities from exploring the castle to singing an aria in the main ward with all the wounded men instantly infatuated with her but most importantly with Major Hamilton having shown his appreciation of her efforts to bring some joy. Now it was a matter of winning over Jacques and Elle. Madeleine impatiently awaited Philip's return to put their mutual plan into operation. Night was already falling, so it meant they were not going to send her away tonight. She had won another day.

It surprised her that hardly any conversation took place during dinner. This would have been considered very rude in the old days, but the other seven people that sat around the long table spooned their food, a meat casserole with cabbage, in silence, apparently relishing the warm food and the moment's calm in their crazed lives. Madeleine studied them in detail as was her habit and was particularly taken in by the blonde woman opposite her, who had been introduced to her as Doctor Agnès de Saint-Aubin.

She vaguely remembered stories about Agnès visiting the Château with her Baron father when she was much younger, but Madeleine had never met her. In no way she would have guessed that the frail-looking young woman was a doctor, despite the blood-smeared doctor's coat she was wearing; she was more like a fairy from a children's book; like Tinker Bell stepping out of *Peter Pan* into real life. She had tiny yellow curls whirling around her slender neck, a mass of hair the color of ripe corn on top of her head, and the cleverest blue eyes Madeleine had ever seen. A fine face, with high cheekbones and the skin so smooth it looked like soft cream, in which nature had penciled arched eyebrows in light brown, then below those lovely eyes a straight classical nose and beautiful lips, the lower lip slightly fuller. The chin was delicate and pointed. The only drawback to her intense beauty were dark rings of tiredness below her eyes. Her expression was one of fatigue as well, but she sat very upright and composed.

Madeleine could see she was struggling with her food, forcing herself to eat but not enjoying it. Everything about Agnès de Saint-

Aubin intrigued her. She had never met a female doctor before and would in no way have expected to encounter one here at the front line in her family's castle. With her feminine intuition, she sensed Agnès was interested in the tall American surgeon at her left, but that he was preoccupied and not picking up the little hints. Madeleine simply could not stop looking at Agnès, and at some point, her object of interest must have noticed her stare as she raised those lovely eyes and smiled at Madeleine. Madeleine smiled back.

The doctor put down her cutlery, and after dabbing the corners of her mouth with a napkin, said, "That monkey has fleas and is under-nourished. Did you know that?" The voice was kind and melodious, that of a well-bred Parisian lady.

"Yes, I know. She's been away from me for a while, and the people didn't take good care of her. What can I do about it?"

"I might have something for the fleas. And I could give her a general examination after dinner, if you want, although I'm not a vet."

"Oh, would you? Thank you!"

Just when Madeleine thought a more animated conversation would come to pass around the table, the sandy-haired Major Hamilton drew all attention to himself by tapping his water glass. For Madeleine this was the first briefing on the situation, and drew herself up, not wanting to miss one word.

Before Gerald began his monologue, he looked around the table, briefly catching her eye. For a moment he seemed to hesitate, and only Madeleine knew why. But he restored himself and said, "Latest news from GHQ in Montreuil. Jacques, can you make sure Philip is informed on his return from Paris?"

Jacques nodded in the major's direction but seemed more inter-ested in the rice pudding with cherry sauce in front of him, attacking it with relish.

The major continued. "With the enemy on our doorstep, the emergency evacuation of the wounded will be put in motion tomor-row. The ambulances we have at our disposal will transport the men to Paris, where they'll be spread among the hospitals in the city. Departure's at noon. This part of the evacuation must be completed by the end of the afternoon. The ambulance drivers and nurses will be escorted by twenty of my men, led by Lieutenant David Brown. They'll stay in Paris until further order. Only those too weak to be transported will stay at Dragoncourt, some thirty patients."

Hamilton's gaze rested briefly on Agnès and Alan, and then on Bridget and M-C, who sat clustered together at one end of the table. The four nodded gravely.

After having lit a fresh pipe, the major continued, "The day after tomorrow, all non-military staff, except for a bare minimum of medics, is to leave for Amiens. I hope we'll have the time to carry out this part of the plan, but it's a race against the clock. The Germans are extremely near." Gerald looked stern and resolute.

Madeleine felt her heart thump in her throat. She had heard the booms of the cannons and the rat-tat-tat of the machine guns coming closer during the day, and the acrid stench that permeated the air had become still denser, but she had believed that the Allied forces were so much stronger than the Germans that they would hold the lines.

This sounded like capitulation, and just when she had gathered the courage to help with the fight. It threatened to temper her enthusiasm, but soon she was mesmerized again by all that was happening. As long as she was not sent back to Paris, she could go with her family to Amiens. Her clear gaze never left the major's handsome warrior face. For sure, he alone seemed capable of wringing the wretched necks of these *Boches*.

But she heard him say, "I have but one wish, and that is that the enemy will have the decency to spare Château de Dragoncourt and those who have to stay behind, as it is very clearly marked as a war hospital. However, we cannot count on it. The latest military situation is alarming, to say the least. And all the stories we have heard from Belgium do not point to us dealing with a dignified or even civilized adversary." He sighed before tugging firmly on his pipe and exhaling a twirl of caramel-scented smoke. The inside of the dark brown pipe sparked a deep orange-red glow.

"We had anticipated this new German offensive, which started three days ago on March 21, but not its devastating force. The towns of Bapaume, Perrone, Ham, and Roye have already fallen and are once again in German hands. The strategy is clearly to break through the Allied lines in this part of France and then try to outflank the British forces that hold the front from the Somme River to the English Channel."

"They haven't been able to do that for almost four years," Jacques interrupted. "What makes you think, Major, that they would succeed now? The Germans must be as exhausted by this trench war as the Allies."

Gerald sighed deeply and shook his head. "It's somehow different this time, Jacques. It must be the fresh forces coming from the Eastern Front, and they know we're eagerly awaiting the arrival of American troops. This is their time to strike. I'm afraid they'll try anything to bring the French to their knees and force them to appeal for an Armistice."

"There certainly was a lot of panic at the front today, and twice as many casualties," Elle observed, and M-C nodded. "Both ambulance drivers looked even more weary than usual."

Gerald waited patiently before resuming his briefing. "To put up as much resistance as they can, the Allied armies are concentrating all their main forces in this area, the passages to the Channel ports, and the rail junction of Amiens. These places are of vital importance to us. If we lose them, defeat is almost certain. So, General Haig has ordered our troops to leave strategically worthless ground, the parts that have already lain barren for years due to the endless fighting, and only defend those lightly. Hardly any civilians live in these areas anyway, but as you all know, we are here on the edge of that war zone. We're the so-called fringe in between."

Once again, he looked around the table, a concerned frown between his light eyebrows, his attention settling once again on Madeleine. She nodded, showing him she was listening and sympathized.

Gerald Hamilton took another puff on his pipe. "GHQ expects the German generals are planning more of those short-and-fast offensives, both further north in Belgium and to the south at Aisne and Champagne-Marne. We have to brace ourselves for these attacks until American reinforcements arrive. That will boost the morale of our Commonwealth and French armies. I tell you the Americans *are* the decisive power in this war. There's no doubt about that. The rest of the forces have suffered too much and are stretched to their absolute limits."

At this moment, Philip burst into the room, shouting, "Holy moly, what a journey, the Huns on my heels this whole woebegone odyssey!" But seeing he was interrupting the major's briefing, he mumbled an *Oh sorry, old chap* and sat down to his dinner, winking at Madeleine as he started his meal.

Madeleine could not help but think that although this man was absolutely crackers, he was the most alive of them all. And like her, he seemed determined to make the best out of a poor situation. But she had little time to muse about Philip, as the major – after a quick disapproving look in Philip's direction – continued his somber soliloquy.

"Let me spend a few more words on the emergency evacuation plan for the day after tomorrow. With a small group, I want to test this plan tomorrow after the medical transport is on its way. In the event we're taken by surprise, I think it's best to be as prepared as we can be. Jacques has already shown me the secret eight-mile tunnel that leads from the castle all the way to Blangy-Tronville on the Somme." Gerald paused for a moment and an almost imperceptible smile showed under his mustache.

"I know it's not the time and place to deviate much from the peril we're facing, but as I love a bit of history myself and as it might be handy information for you as well, Jacques will explain the origins of the tunnel – why it was constructed in the first place."

He gestured to Jacques who clearly had not been counting on making any contribution and was just about to help himself to a second serving of the pudding, so he muttered a distracted, "Oh... okay, my fellow, give me a sec." Blowing the mane of dark hair from his brow was his habit when he felt troubled or unsure of himself, he peered around through his round spectacles, and Madeleine could tell his mind was not on the remote history of their forefathers.

"If you don't mind, Gerry, I'll just give a short version." Not waiting for an answer, he continued with a sigh, "Louis de Dragoncourt, the first Dragoncourt Count, had the tunnel constructed in the sixteenth century, soon after he had the castle itself built. Louis was a member of the Bourbon family and a leader of the Protestant party, so he chose the symbol of a white dragon, in line with the French court. Our coat of arms hangs in *la grande salle verte*, if you feel inclined to inspect it.

"At the time, Château de Dragoncourt was one of the strongholds of the religious wars that pestered France, so two impressive gatehouses and an underground jail with an intricate locking system were built. There was also a need for an escape route, which resulted in the underground tunnel. You can imagine what kind of a slave labor went into that. But despite the blood, sweat, and tears, it might be our ticket to freedom today." He ended looking sour and lit a cigarette.

Major Hamilton thanked him, and as everybody was ready to rise from the table, he quickly added, "So, we'll inspect it, including materials, such as stretcher beds and supplies, at 16:00 hours. I'll make a list of participants and leave it on the breakfast table. I bid you all good night."

Madeleine rose as well, still mulling everything over in her head. Neither Elle nor Jacques had suggested she returned to Paris with the medical convoy. Her adventure might not be over yet. It sounded all so fascinating and fun, but as she watched the rest of the company rising from their chairs with hanging shoulders, she wondered what was wrong with them.

Her consultation with Philip would have to wait because he was still eating, and she had not had a chance to talk to Elle about him. As long as her fate was unsure, she would rather avoid Elle and Jacques as much as possible. Time for a bit of action on her own.

After dinner Madeleine went in search of Agnès, who took the time to examine Loulou.

"She's quite healthy, just underweight and she's suffering from the fleas. Look, she's scratched herself open, here in her armpits and groin. I have this tar-like ointment you can wash her with. Just make sure you give her a bath afterwards, as it's foul-smelling. But it will kill the fleas. Repeat it next week."

Madeleine thanked her wholeheartedly and would have loved to chat a little longer with the beautiful, mysterious doctor, but Agnès excused herself, saying she still had to look in on a number of her patients.

Not knowing what to do with the rest of her evening, and secretly hoping she would bump into the handsome major again – smoking that delicious smelling pipe – Madeleine took Loulou outside, but she was taken aback by the deafening roar of the approaching war and the acrid smell it brought in its wake.

The major was not outside; there were only the two guards at the entrance, who looked strained, holding both hands on their guns as if ready to shoot but when they saw it was the funny, flirtatious Madeleine with her monkey, they relaxed and followed her admiringly with their eyes.

One of the two shouted to her, "Don't go strolling outside, Miss Madeleine. It's way too dangerous out there."

She fluffed her abundant locks endearingly, retorting, "I won't, dear soldiers. Just one ciggie. I promise I'll stay on the driveway, and I'll be back before you know it."

"You'd better, miss, or we'll have to come and fetch you," the other soldier shouted.

Madeleine giggled. "I'll yell if I need your help, but don't bet on it. Loulou and I are quite capable of looking after ourselves."

Despite the threatening atmosphere, being outside was a change from the stifling atmosphere of fear and dread that hung over every room in the castle. It was true, Madeleine mused, that they were in grave danger, and she had no idea where they would be tomorrow. The parking area in front of the castle was extremely busy: medics and orderlies were loading supplies and stock into military vehicles, most of them with a large red cross on their khaki canvas hood. In one special truck also sporting a red cross, she saw valuable assets being loaded that had been in the Dragoncourt castle for centuries, packed in crates or wrapped in bed linens. This surprised her, but she supposed it was by order of Elle and Jacques.

Madeleine sauntered down the driveway in the direction of the main road but made sure she stayed in sight of the castle. She felt confused, as she lit a Gold Flake cigarette and inhaled deeply. Everything had moved so fast, from the stiff routine in Lausanne to the utter chaos at Dragoncourt. She exhaled. Maybe her family had been right not wanting her here; to spare her this nightmare, this hell on earth that had once been the happiest place of her youth. Perhaps it was too much for her. Loulou clung to her as usual, frightened by the booms and the cracking of shells.

"Better take you back indoors, *ma petite,* no rest for the wicked here." She sighed, extinguishing her cigarette under the heel of her shoe. There was an unexpected lull in the noise, which made Madeleine wonder if the fighting parties had perhaps decided to call it a day. Enjoying the relative quiet her eardrums were given, she sank down on a stone bench under a box tree, still deep in thought and absently stroking the little monkey's back.

Then Loulou raised her ears and was all attentiveness.

"What is it?" Madeleine whispered, straining her own ears. She heard something. A soft moaning; a human voice, very nearby. *Oh, no,* was her imminent thought, *A wounded soldier. I must find him. Now I can do my bit and show them.*

She got up cautiously and stealthily moved in the direction from where the groaning came. Loulou, sensing the situation began whining nervously herself.

"It's okay, sweetie," Madeleine shushed, but she did not feel very at ease herself. She gasped, clamping her hand over her mouth to refrain from screaming out. By the side of the road lay a German soldier – motionless, but certainly not dead. He was looking straight at her, with dark eyes deep in their sockets. Her thoughts raced. She was unarmed, and all she could think was *Run!*

She was about to turn and run inside before he might get up or snatch her ankle. Find the guards, or better Major Hamilton, who would take care of this Boche. Shoot him on the spot or put a knife in his body; whatever.

But as she turned to race away, the soldier called out to her in English. "Miss, it's not what you think. I'm not a German soldier! I'm a British spy in a German uniform. I was gathering information behind the lines, but I got shot accidentally."

His English was good. It sounded authentic; but Madeleine was not convinced. Yet she did not move away and asked, "What's wrong with you?"

"I got shot in the leg. I knew Château de Dragoncourt was a hospital, so I was trying to reach it, but I was in too much pain. So, I was resting here for a bit when I heard you. Could you help me, please?"

"How do I know for certain you're not a German?"

"I can show you my papers." He produced the tag from under his coat, and Madeleine peered at it. It read *Charles Green, 9th Scottish Division, 26th Brigade, Infantry, G/5489.*

"You don't sound Scottish," she said, doubtful.

"I know. I'm not. But I joined the division because my parents used to live in Edinburgh. I grew up on the English side of the border."

"Okay," Madeleine uttered, half-convinced. "It sounds strange, but then this war is strange, isn't it? I'll get some help."

"Thank you, miss." He smiled at her, his white teeth flashing in the dark.

She ran back to the castle and was glad to find Gerald smoking his pipe in his usual place on the balustrade.

"Ger... I mean, Major Hamilton," she exclaimed, panting for breath, "I've found a wounded soldier in German uniform near the road, but he says he's a British spy. Could that be possible?"

Hamilton looked at her closely. "Did he speak English? Strong accent?"

Madeleine shook her head and started, "Still..." but the major interrupted her.

"Leave it with me. We'll approach him with caution. It happens a

lot these days – spies putting on uniforms of dead Germans to infil-
trate behind the lines. And if his English is good, he's probably one of
them. I'll ask some specific questions, see if he knows the answers."

"If you think so."

"We'll keep him well-guarded, don't worry."

Gerald hopped off the balustrade and ordered two of his men to
go and collect a stretcher. He told them not to be astonished that the
wounded man was wearing a German uniform and that he would
deal with the soldier himself.

Madeleine stayed on their heels, not wanting to miss any part of
this, feeling quite safe in the company of broad-shouldered, well-
armed Gerry and his lieutenants. During the major's brief interroga-
tion, she constantly eyed the spy with intense concentration, her
eyebrows furrowed.

Hamilton decided that the man was one of many British spies in
enemy clothes because he knew his answers, so he could safely be
brought in and looked after.

Madeleine followed the stretcher as a bloodhound hunting a
trace but was told in no unclear words that she was forbidden to
enter the operating room into which the soldiers marched. This
brought an abrupt end to her first contribution in a war-related event
and displeased her greatly, but there was no other option than to turn
around and go to the kitchen for a cup of tea before she went up to
her bedroom. Climbing the stairs a little later with Loulou in the
crook of her arm, she was satisfied with herself that she had brought
a wounded soldier to safety.

She sat down on the bed with the faded quilt in the unadorned
bedroom she shared with Elle and tried to calm her inner turmoil at
all the confusing events of the day. Loulou, as usual, sensed her
mistress's confusion and tried to comfort her by kissing her cheeks
with her wet monkey lips.

"Oh, my sweetie," Madeleine sighed, "the war is so bloody close.
It makes me edgy." She lovingly scratched the top of the black-haired
head. Loulou's gaze seemed to convey she understood her mistress,
and she made little cooing noises as if to comfort her.

The door opened, and Elle entered, or more precisely, stumbled across the threshold. Her happiness at her sister's much-needed company was dampened when Madeleine saw the state her sister was in. She looked beyond exhausted – her clothes and hands were smeared with blood and her thick braid was in disarray around a face white as a doll, in which the brown eyes looked enormous, their gold flecks extinguished.

Madeleine ran to her aid, glad to take her mind off the pressing matters she had been pondering. "Here, let me help you get off those heavy boots!"

Elle sank in an armchair, her arms and legs sprawled. With difficulty, Madeleine eased the mud-caked boots off Elle's swollen ankles. On removing her socks to warm her feet, she saw Elle's toes were a bloodless, chalky white.

Quickly putting the woolen socks back on, Madeleine said, "You're frozen. Let me run you a bath."

"Thank you, darling, but I think I'm too wasted. I need to sleep." Elle placed her bloody hands over her tired brow and took a shallow breath. "All I need is a stiff cognac to knock me out for the night. Tomorrow's another day."

"You can't sleep like this, dirty and drained," Madeleine protested. "A bath together with your cognac will do wonders. I'm going to see to both."

Elle dropped her hands, and her face broke into a jaded smile. She did not object, though.

Madeleine was already busying herself, turning open the big brass taps on the enamel bath in the adjoining bathroom, thanking her father aloud for having put in this luxury before the war even for the servants. While the steaming water rose, she poured her sister a large Cognac Pradelle from the tumbler next to Elle's bed and declared everything ready.

"I've even added some scented herbs that I found in the bathroom cabinet," she said proudly. "Pity I couldn't find any bubbles, but there's a bar of lavender soap." She helped Elle out of her sturdy uniform and washed-out undergarments and into the bath. Sinking back in the hot tub, Madeleine saw tears well up in Elle's eyes, and it took them both by surprise.

"This is so good, Maddy, thank you so much." Elle took a large sip of her cognac and lay back, closing her eyelids. Madeleine sat down in a wicker chair, smoking and studying her sister. Her face was so frail and bony, with blue veins running down her temples and her eye sockets a murky brown, showing the years of accumulating stress and overfatigue. Her alabaster shoulders looked gawky, with the collarbones protruding and her breasts lying like small lifeless pears against her rib cage. Her skin was saggy, as if too loose, despite her thinness.

Nothing was left of the vivacious Elle in her yellow ballroom dress who had opened the dance on her eighteenth birthday with their Papa, a yellow ribbon around her crowning glory of walnut-colored hair, glittering diamonds in her ears and on her fingers. That girl had vanished. At twenty-five, Elle was aged, all the luster of her youth gone. Madeleine wondered if her sister would ever be able to feel alive again, really alive as she had been at eighteen; whether she would still be able to love and not only hate and survive the next day. Perhaps love Philip? Something good needed to happen in her life instead of only dread and blood and tiredness.

Elle opened one eye and saw her sister's scrutiny. "We haven't even talked about your presence here, Mads." She sat upright in the bath, folding her arms around her wet knees. "I've just been so busy. Have you and Jacques talked?"

Madeleine shook her head, slowly, pensively. "It's too late now anyway, Elle. I'll leave with you. It wouldn't be safe to go anywhere on my own in these circumstances."

Later, lying side by side on the narrow beds in the dark, with Loulou tucked in Madeleine's old cot by her side, she listened to Elle's even breathing and felt grateful for the day, for her sister's presence, for the fact that the whole family was still alive, while this cruel war was tearing so many other families apart. In a way they were lucky – Papa and Mummy safe in London, Netty with her family in Versailles, and she was together with Elle and Jacques, whom she loved best. Sleep evaded Madeleine as she listened to the ever-present drone of the war, which was marginally quieter for the night but still there, always there, in the occasional crack of a mortar or the drumming of an airplane overhead.

Her thoughts dwelled on all the young and not-so-young men lying out there in the damp trenches, all nationalities, in different uniforms but with the same hardships and the same hopes: to survive and get back to their loved ones, hopefully unscratched. Why all this fighting over a strip of land and someone's damned honor? Did anyone still remember the assassination of a minor Austro-Hungarian royal that had been the cause of all this? No! It was sheer ludicrousness. And she wanted to stop it, but how?

Madeleine found no answers. Still listening to Elle's deep, regular breathing, she turned her never-ending thoughts to the next day. She was looking forward to inspecting the tunnel to Blangy-Tronville with Gerry and his men – anything that contained action and adventure but also that might lead to answers. And really walking through it would be like being a 16th century Protestant clergyman fleeing Catholic pursuers, wearing a gray cassock with the symbol of the White Dragon stealthily stitched on the coarse habit underneath.

As far as she knew none of her siblings had ever been inside. She only knew the wooden door at the end of one of the less important sculleries. Why this tunnel had never piqued her interest before puzzled her. In the old days, it would have been a great hiding place for Netty and her. But then again, Antoinette would probably have been too scared to enter the dark cavern or afraid to stain her lace dress on the dirt walls. It would be great to explore it under the safe protection of the broad-shouldered, muscled Gerald Hamilton. And with her thoughts on the Major, his sandy mustache and his lovely, ocean-colored eyes, Madeleine finally fell asleep.

8

THE NET TIGHTENS

Agnès

Château de Dragoncourt, 1 April 1918

Having scrubbed the dried blood from her hands and forearms, Agnès peered in the mirror above the wash-stand, and with a tired gesture, brushed a strand of springy hair away off her forehead. The face that stared back at her was more like a faint appearance from the one she remembered only a couple of weeks earlier at the Lycée Pasteur in Paris. That face, though tired, had been alive; tired but hopeful. This face, this woman she hardly recognized. The blue eyes look dead and lusterless, and the light hair was dry and stringy and hung in dirty ringlets around her temples and in her neck. The skin had a sallow, grayish shine and was too tight over the jaw bones that stuck out; her lips, usually so full and red, were a thin, compressed line. This image scared her, so she looked away, busying herself to get out of her operating apron.

It had been another unremitting day at the operating table without a break, with more men dying under her hands than staying alive. She let out a sad sigh and wondered once again if she should have listened to her father and Alan and stayed in Paris, done her bit there; maybe she was not cut out of this cloth after all, maybe it was all too much for a young, inexperienced surgeon, maybe she was falling apart under the pressure of extended focused attention during long working hours. She was only a slip of a girl, after all, at five foot three, not powerfully built; and though her mind was strong, her body was giving clear signals that she was at the end of her tether. Was this only a man's job?

In the operating room next door, she heard the subdued voices of Alan and Bridget discussing the first signs of gangrene in a pilot's right leg. Amputation to prevent its continuation, or give it a chance with Thomas splints? Automatically she wanted to go back in and give her opinion: "Yes, splints – remember the Canadian soldier last week? A similar situation, and we saved his life and his leg!" But she bit her tongue, remembering that Alan had told her Bridget and he would battle on without her and that she should rest.

For once Agnès had not protested, since she felt so frazzled that she was running the risk of making mistakes. Her eyelids had refused to stay open, and her hands had been trembling without her being able to stop them. But the thought of the beautiful young Frenchman in his light-blue uniform, with severe burns all over his body and both his legs broken, his condition so critical that he too was in that familiar race against the clock, almost made her push open the door to the operating room again and jump right in.

But she slowly shook her head at herself. "Give in, girl. There's nothing you can do for him right now that Alan and Bridget aren't doing." Dropping her operating clothes in the dirty laundry bin, she told herself she should grab a hot cup of tea and something to eat before her head hit the pillow, so she slowly made her way through the long corridor to the garden room, hoping Jacques had left the teapot in the cozy and some sandwiches.

At that moment, she heard the familiar shuffling behind her and saw another stretcher being brought in. Seeing that the patient was in a German uniform, her eyes, despite their weariness, grew large in alarm. She stopped the two British soldiers who were carrying the injured man, and she immediately noted the soldier was not in grave danger. The young man with strawberry blond hair and weak bluish eyes with black rings around the pupils was gazing at her with what she thought was a degree of cockiness.

"What's going on here? There's a German hospital on the other side of the front. He doesn't belong here. This is French territory." Her voice was acid.

"He says he's British, Doctor, that his name is Charles Green," one of Gerald's young sergeants stammered. "So can we bring him in?"

"Put him down here for a moment. Let me ask him a couple of questions," Agnès ordered. But her mind was racing. Should she address him in German, in French, or in English? Then she checked herself. She was safe. What was she thinking?

The soldiers put the stretcher down, but the young sergeant who had spoken before addressed her timidly. "But ma'am... uh... Doctor de Saint-Aubin, Major Hamilton has already questioned him, and he says it's okay. That he's British, and the uniform's just a cover-up."

"Now does he?" Agnès still looked suspiciously at the blond man, but with a sigh she said, "Well, all right, in that case, bring him in. I'll check the wound. But I'm going to have a cup of tea first. He's got nothing major wrong with him. In the meantime, ask Nurse Brest to give him a painkiller. I'll be back in ten minutes."

It did dawn on her that Alan was going to be livid with her for attending to a minor wound like this and not going straight to bed as she had promised, but Agnès could not help being intrigued by the arrival of this man, and somehow the mystery gave her new energy. She still held the gaze of the man on the stretcher, who was following the interaction between the soldiers and the doctor with great interest. He had not spoken a word in any language yet, so it remained a mystery who he was and how he had ended up at Dragoncourt. She would have time to ask all those questions when she had a quick look at his shot wound, and then she'd leave the rest of his treatment to one of the nurses. Ten more minutes, at the most, she would tell Alan.

Agnès opened the door to the garden room and saw that the

lights were dimmed, but that Madeleine was sitting in the corner playing and talking with Loulou.

"Hi, I've just come in for a cup of tea and something to eat. Do you know if there's anything left?" She felt slightly awkward in the presence of this glamorous sister of Jacques and Elle, who always looked as if she had just stepped out of a magazine, while she, Agnès, felt old and dirty, with not a shred of femininity left in her.

But Madeleine seemed delighted to see her and immediately leapt from her armchair. "Do sit down, Doctor. Let me get something for you. You must be exhausted." She swung the little animal around her neck and busied herself with the teapot, babbling on: "Loulou is already scratching herself a lot less, thanks to your ointment. She doesn't like the smell, though, and neither do I, but I told her that it's doctor's orders."

"Thank you," Agnès replied, taking the teacup and letting her worn-out body sink into one of the comfy armchairs. "I *am* exhausted and wanted to go to bed after my tea, but they've just brought in a man in a German uniform. I have to check on him in a minute."

Madeleine swung around and faced Agnès, squinting. "Gerald says he's a British spy. I found him in the grass near the drive. Scared the wits out of me. But it's just like something from the novels, isn't it?"

Agnès smiled. "I don't know. It's been ages since I had time to read. Gosh, I miss it so much!"

"I know, I love reading too! I had all the time in the world to read in Switz..." She bit her lip, realizing Agnès probably was not interested in the life of a spoiled upper-class girl at this time in her life, so she quickly added, "But what's much more important right now is that I look after you. Would you like me to make you something? Sandwiches, heat some soup?"

"Would you? Grand. I've hardly had time for dinner, and Alan keeps telling me to eat more. I'm honestly trying to, but whatever I eat, I seem to burn it instantly."

Madeleine had swiftly gone to the kitchen next door and called,

"Those long hours standing at the operating table, no doubt! Would ham and cheese do, and some pickles?"

"Anything you can lay your hands on."

Madeleine soon returned with a plate laden with thin slices of bread, from which chunks of cheese and a thick slice of ham stuck out. While Agnès ate slowly, Madeleine sat down opposite her, observing her every move while sipping a glass of red wine. Loulou was sitting on her shoulder, mimicking Agnès as she ate. The girls laughed, and Loulou grinned with satisfaction.

"I admire you so much, Doctor. I wish I could be you!"

This observation made Agnès look up from her plate, and swallowing the last bite in her mouth, she uttered incredulously, "Be me? You're kidding! You must be the only person in the world who wants to be *me*. I certainly don't want to be *me* right now. Oh, and please call me Agnès. I'm fed up hearing doctor this, doctor that all day. I'm not a doctor right now." She smiled wanly, which brightened her lovely, delicate face.

"Oh, I didn't mean it in that way," Madeleine hastened to add. "I understand that your work is horrible right now, and that you're absolutely knackered. It's just that you have such a beautiful profession, certainly at a time like this, keeping men alive who would otherwise die a senseless death. And I was told you're so incredibly good at what you do." The gaze she gave her was so full of admiration that Agnès snickered,

"Good at what I do? The poor men are constantly dying under my hands! Some days more die than that I can save. But who told you that I'm good a doctor? Jacques, I suppose?"

"No, it was Alan. He was full of praise for you. I had a chat with him this afternoon. Looked after him a bit, like I'm looking after you now. He was so kind, and kept saying he would be nowhere without you. Honestly, he kept repeating it so much that I thought he must be in love with you." Madeleine winked at her but stopped her bantering when Agnès blushed.

Curtly she remarked, "He's not in love with me. Alan's married. But it's good to hear he's proud of me. He trained me, you know. He was my professor at the Sorbonne, so it's a great honor to work with him."

"Sorry for my blabbing. I shouldn't," Madeleine said apologetically. "One of my bad habits." She was stroking Loulou's little back, and the monkey closed her eyes and nestled against her. "Would you like some more? Or a glass of wine, perhaps?"

Agnès shook her head. "I still have a job to do, and if I drank alcohol now, I would fall sound asleep on the spot. No, let me check on that new acquisition in the hospital and then I'm off to bed. Thank you for feeding me, Madeleine. That was delicious and very necessary."

"Any time! I really enjoyed talking with you because no matter what you may think of me, I admire you loads."

"Thank you for that too." Agnès was already out of the door, hoisting herself back in her white coat, on her way to the last patient of the day. On entering the operating room, she saw that Alan was just about to leave and surprised at seeing her back. He assumed she wanted to know how the pilot was doing.

"He's stable, but he'll probably need another operation on that shoulder tomorrow. Gave him an extra dose of morphine for the night. I'm off now, and so should you be. I thought you had already left?" He gave her that scrutinizing surgeon look.

"I know, I had, but I'm just going to check quickly on that guy in the German uniform they just brought in, and then I'll turn in."

"Need any help with him?"

Although it was tempting to keep Alan by her side when she had this eerie feeling about a patient in the enemy's uniform, she shook her head. "No, I'll manage. See you tomorrow."

"Yes, it will be our last day here with everybody. Strange, isn't it?"

Agnès smiled sadly. "Yes, very strange. I'd prefer them all to stay here, certainly now we've got our routine. I suppose we too will have to move if it becomes too dangerous?"

"I suppose so. Good night, Agnès. Make sure you get some proper sleep."

"You too, Alan!"

They had brought the German soldier into the smaller operating room, and while Agnès put on her face mask and gloves, she heard Marie-Christine talking to him in a loud, shrill voice, the way Agnès had never heard the reserved nurse before, least of all to a patient. If anyone was soft-spoken, it was M-C. Agnès hastened to the door and peered around it but made sure she stayed out of sight.

M-C was visibly upset, her narrow face red and angry. In her Alsatian-French, which had a slur of German, she was addressing the soldier who was still lying on the stretcher bed that had been placed on the floor. Either he did not understand her rapid French or he was afraid of her, because he was ogling her in a state of alarm. Fingering the large golden crucifix around her neck, M-C seemed to be almost spitting in his face, and her words were certainly not very Christian.

"What the devil are you doing here, you piece of trash, you ugly Hun? What do you think we're doing here at Dragoncourt hospital? Huh? Answer me, you coward!"

But the soldier did not answer, bewildered by the tiny, dark-haired fury standing over him.

"Lost your tongue? Well, let me refresh your memory: we patch up men here that you and your lot hack to pieces. And now you have the nerve to show up here with a scratch on your leg?" M-C was gasping for breath.

Agnès deliberated stepping in, but her curiosity about how the soldier would respond to M-C's torrent of accusations kept her hidden in the shadows.

While M-C caught her breath, the soldier finally interjected in correct but studied French, "Non, non, it's not what you think. "*Vous parlez anglais?* Let me explain..."

But Marie-Christine was back, picking up pace again. "I tell you what. I have no clue who let you in here, but I am not looking at that wound of yours. I don't cater to Germans!"

As M-C was refusing medical help, Agnès could do nothing else but step in as her superior. She approached the nurse and the patient carefully, with a friendly smile on her face.

"Listen M-C, Major Hamilton has interrogated this man, and

apparently he's a spy. He may be in a German uniform, but he has British nationality. Don't ask me how this change of uniforms has taken place because I have no clue either." Her voice was calm, and she put a gentle arm around the overwrought nurse, whose shift had already ended and who was as wasted as the rest of them.

But M-C, who had seen too much of the ugliness of war, especially during all her ambulance trips to the front, was not that easily mollified. "So, you want me to believe that this despicable character is one of us?" she thundered. "And why would I believe that? This guy looks as German as all the other Krauts I've seen lying in the ditches."

"It's true, though, what the lady doctor says," the soldier murmured meekly, putting his hopes on Agnès's support. "I was on my way to get behind the front line to collect information when I got shot. It was dark. I don't even know if it was us or the Germans who injured me."

This last remark seemed to calm M-C to some extent, but she said in a gruff voice, "Well, if you all put your bet on it that he's an Allied soldier, let's inspect him, doctor, and get him to the ward as quickly as possible. He has plenty of mouth, so I don't think he's wounded badly."

It was indeed a grazing shot in his left thigh, so they cleaned and dressed the wound and gave him some painkillers for the night. When they left him, the guards came in to carry him to the nearest ward.

When he was out of earshot, Agnès said, "Don't upset yourself over him, M-C. I understand that that uniform works like a red flag on you, but please calm down. He's really an Allied soldier. These things happen in the war, you know. It's just that we haven't come across it yet."

"You're right, I suppose," M-C said more calmly, as she turned off the light in the operating room. As they companionably ascended the stairs to their bedrooms on the top floor, the nurse added, "With the enemy so close, we just get suspicious and go barmy."

"It'll be all right. Good night!"

"Good night."

When she finally lay in her bed, sleep evaded Agnès despite her exhaustion. She kept hearing strange noises, as if the walls were whispering, and when she finally did fall asleep, she dreamt the Germans were crawling through the castle's corridors. There was no stopping them.

The next morning, Agnès woke with a start. She heard the roar of engines outside and coarse voices shouting. A quick check of her clock told her she had slept ten hours and that it was already past nine. She still felt drained of all energy and had a hard time focusing her thoughts. She wanted to get up, but her body refused her brain, so she just lay there listening to the commotion outside and closed her eyelids again. Had the evacuation of the patients started, or had the enemy arrived on their doorstep? That thought made her sit up abruptly, rubbing her sore neck and stretching her tired muscles. She dragged her body out of bed and moved to the window. On opening the shutters, she let out a sigh of relief. It was the evacuation of the patients, not a German invasion. At least, not yet.

After a quick wash, she dressed in one of the only two dresses she had brought, a simple taffeta silk dress in dark burgundy with a white lace collar and cuffs. The once fashionable and expensive dress now was crumpled and stained, having lost all its former shape and allure, but Agnès could not care less. She was not even aware what she put on her body in the morning, apart from noticing that her dresses had become too big around her waist.

Whatever she wore underneath her white doctor's coat had long ceased to interest her. *Poor Petipat would be appalled the way I look these days, and pull the gray hairs from her scalp over my diminishing options for a splendid marital catch*, Agnès thought, grimacing at the idea of her beloved housekeeper's disappointment in her, but then she said out loud, "I do this all for you, Petipat! To avenge your needless death. So please forgive my appearance."

Strengthened by her vow to her surrogate mother, Agnès made her way downstairs to breakfast and another interminable day standing at the operating table. As she was later than usual, only

Jacques was seated at the dinner table, enjoying a moment of solitude, reading an old newspaper.

"Hi," she said. "Sorry to interrupt you. Am I too late for breakfast?"

"Of course not, Aggie!" Jacques sprang to his feet. "What can I get you? Toast? Croissant, scrambled eggs?"

"Coffee mostly," she grinned, "and a glass of water. I seem parched all the time."

"But you need to eat something as well!"

"You sound just like Alan. Do me a favor – one of you looking after my food intake is quite enough."

"Oh, sorry," Jacques mumbled, blowing the lock of hair from his face and taking her in through his round metal spectacles. "It's just that you seem so... even more ethereal than when you arrived. But coffee it is then. Sit down and be waited on, Baroness!"

They smiled at each other.

"Those days seem to be over for good," she observed softly, "and to be honest, I don't know if I'm sad about it. You do know that I'm not a Baroness by birth? I am... was adopted."

Jacques turned around on his heels, the cup and saucer balancing on his palm. "No, I didn't. I just always assumed you looked more like your deceased mother than your dark-haired, dark-skinned father."

"No, Papa is not my biological father. And that was the main reason he objected to me working at the front. My mother... my parents were German."

Jacques looked even more puzzled now. "But my father told me that your parents were married before you were born. My father was your father's best man. You know they've been pals forever; each other's best man. Does my father know this?"

"I don't know what your father knows. But I can't tell you any more right now. I just thought I ought to tell somebody that I'm German by blood, in case... you know... But I'm totally French by heart, and should they invade us, the Germans won't find out because I have a French passport and my father's legal name. They can only see in my passport that my mother was German, but I don't think that matters. More important is my stance in this war, and that lies totally with the Allies."

Jacques seemed to ponder this for a moment. "No, I don't think it matters at all, Aggie. I'm half British; we're all part this or part that. But thank you for telling me." They sat down and Agnès gratefully sipped her coffee. Real coffee was such a treat these days. As they got their supplies from the Americans now, they were well-stocked for the first time in the war, but her enjoyment was also increased by the relief she felt of having told her secret – at least partially – to Jacques, as he was the one most likely to not lose his mind over this disclosure and accept her bloodlines on face value. Just as he had done.

Her secret had weighed heavily on her conscience ever since the first German set foot on French soil, but certainly since she had been at Château de Dragoncourt, so close to the front and where – in case of an attack – she might be the one jeopardizing everyone's safety. Chances were small, but still. It was best Jacques knew. Papa had fretted about this so much as well.

With her gaze fixed on her cup, she felt that Jacques studying her in that peculiar way of his, half untamed, half restrained, and for some reason she blushed. After she had drained her first cup and put it back on the saucer, she met his eyes, a dark, unfathomable gaze.

"I'd like some breakfast now, if I may, please." She smiled warmly at him; he was such a deep thinker at times, and then again light as a feather.

Jacques kept studying her and momentarily ignoring her request for breakfast. Slowly, deliberately he observed,

"Something has just fallen right into place, Agnès de Saint-Aubin. Ever since we first met... what were we, you five, I eight? I've always subconsciously wondered where these ethereal, light features of yours originated from. The white skin, the blue eyes clear as a lake in summer... but now it makes sense that you're more a Northern type, not Gallic like the French." He nodded his dark head and added, "I love it. I know it's totally inappropriate and the worst of times, but I think you're heavenly beautiful, Agnès. If we lived in other times and you weren't Alan's girl, I'd court you without a second thought!" He seemed utterly serious.

Agnès's mouth fell open. She did not know whether to laugh or to stay serious. It was all so muddled.

"For Heaven's sake, Jacques, what are you saying? Alan's married. And what is everybody thinking? Your little sister also said something about him being my boyfriend. No! We're just colleagues. He was my professor. We get on well, but he's married!"

Jacques held up his hands as if to defend himself against the torrent of her words. "Sorry, Aggie! I didn't mean to upset you." Then he grinned. "So I might have a chance after all?" He ran to the kitchen shouting, "What do you want? More coffee? Tell me!"

And Agnès had to laugh despite herself. Now he was like a puppy, overexcited and ready to play with anything. "Just make me anything, dear Jacques! I will trust my stomach to you, but not my heart."

When he came back from the kitchen with a plate loaded with freshly baked bread thick with butter and jam and more fresh coffee, she did not know what was bigger, his smile or the plate.

"There you go, my phony baroness. I'm your eternal slave from now on. You know what is funniest of all?"

She shook her head, taking the plate that made her mouth water.

"You may be a phony baroness, but your net worth is at least ten or twenty times this earldom."

"I know," she said solemnly. "I know Papa is awfully rich, but I've never really cared about money or worldly possessions. All I always wanted was to study and have a profession. First, I wanted to be a lecturer, but when the war started, I immediately knew I wanted to be a doctor. I don't know; maybe it's my German blood, wanting to be a scientist?"

She finished eating in no time, and after a third coffee, faced Jacques again. He was playing with the chain of his watch, seemingly in thought.

Interrupting his thoughts, she ventured, "I wonder what today is going to look like for us. Alan and I aren't supposed to take part in the tunnel expedition, are we? Patients may still be brought in, and we have the remaining sick men to look after."

Jacques pulled himself away from wherever his thoughts were and shook himself. "Sorry, Aggie. You were saying?"

"What's up, Jacques?"

"Nothing! Nothing important. I sometimes catch myself thinking what will become of us, of me, when the war is over, and for some reason that makes me uncertain. It sounds crazy, I know, but this as it is now – he made a swiping gesture around him – "somehow makes sense to me; gives me a reason to be."

"I know," Agnès replied. "I sometimes feel the same. The war's been going on for so long, we don't know what life without it will look like anymore. We're totally caught up in it. It's consumed the best of our young years."

"But you were asking something?" Jacques' dark features had resumed their regular expression.

"Yes, about my day. Should I stay here and tend to the patients, or do I go on the expedition with you all?"

"I guess you stay here, as Gerald suggested last night," Jacques answered. "Makes sense to me. It's just a preliminary exercise, so you, Alan, Bridget, and M-C stay here. I suppose Gerald will leave some of his men here as well. We don't expect the Krauts to be barging in today."

"I'd better get to the hospital then and start my day." Agnès got up. "Thanks so much for looking after me, Jacques."

"So, there's still hope for me?" He gave her a lopsided grin.

"There's always hope," she retorted, also with a grin. "Just don't bet your heart on it."

He gave her an amorous look, but cheerfully whistling *I'm always chasing rainbows*, he turned his back on her and started to clear the breakfast table.

In the operating room, Agnès saw Alan was already hard at work with a patient, and she felt guilty at arriving so late. He was concentrating on stitching an intricate belly wound with a deep frown, and she supposed it was because of her tardy arrival.

"You okay?" she asked hesitantly.

"Not really." The reply was gruff. "But it's personal, and I have no time for it right now. Let's get to work."

"How's the pilot?"

"He came through the night all right and seems a bit revived. Only nineteen and most likely crippled for life. Damn shame."

Alan seemed in a sour mood, and Agnès thought it wise to stick strictly to work related issues. "And how's the man in the German uniform?"

"Him?" Alan looked at her in surprise. "I haven't seen him at all. Suppose he's gone. Thought you'd given him his leave?"

"I did no such thing." Agnès raced to the ward where the guards had left him the night before. On storming in, she saw what she already been dreading: his bed was empty. The unusual haste of her arrival made some of the patients in the other beds stare at her in bewilderment, their eyes moving behind bandaged faces or some with hardly any eyes at all, just turning white bandages. But most did not even stir, deep in morphine-induced sleep.

"Sorry," she muttered, about to leave with the same haste as she had entered. This was bad – the spy having sneaked out. Had he been a German after all, contrary to what he'd claimed to be? She needed to go and find Major Hamilton at once to tell him to go after the guy, whoever he was.

But at that moment she heard a soft voice in French calling out to her, "*Docteur, s'il vous plait.*" It was the young pilot, who apparently was in great pain and trying to get her attention.

She went over to his bedside, and he seemed relieved to see her. "How are you, Capitaine Heurtier?" It was a superfluous question, but it was meant to calm him, to take away some of the fear and agony that shone in his feverish eyes while her professional glance studied his condition. The suffering of this young flight sergeant, no more than a boy really, with faint traces of a beard and round, inno-cent eyes, moved Agnès deeply, not only because he was so young and fragile looking, but also because he was the first pilot she ever seen in the flesh. His profession seemed almost magical and other-worldly to her.

They had heard these fighter pilots racing overhead, but they were like a new evolution of mankind, fighting air battles in their flying machines. Agnès could not grasp how this was possible, but she admired it greatly. The pilot was meanwhile gazing at her in his turn, and it flashed through her mind that he probably also thought a female surgeon rather out of the ordinary. He most likely had not ever encountered a female doctor in *his* life.

While checking his intravenous drip and seeing she could just slightly increase his already extremely high dose of morphine, she addressed him in a soft voice, "We met yesterday, but you were in no fit shape to be introduced to me. I'm Doctor Agnès de Saint-Aubin. Can you tell me a little about yourself while I give you a medical check?"

He smiled weakly at her with bloodless lips. "I'm from Marseilles, Docteur. My father owns a grocery store on the rue Paradis, and I always helped in the shop until I enlisted with the 2nd Infantry Division in 1914. I've always been mad about airplanes, ever since I heard about Louis Blériot flying across the Channel, so when I was given the chance to be transferred to the aerial service, I was ever so glad."

Agnès nodded, encouraging him to keep talking while she checked his legs and tried not to gasp. In between the splints, the flesh of his right leg was red and swollen despite debridement. The infection was worse. But she did not want to alarm him in any way.

"Go on," she said, meanwhile trying to catch the attention of Bridget, who had come in to dress the wound of a patient further down the ward who was moaning loudly.

"I went through my pilot's training at Issoudun Aerodrome and was assigned to MS38, a Morane-Saulnier squadron, as an observer. In 1916 I transferred to a fighter squadron, N3, to fly Nieuports. And that's when my aerial fighting career really took off. And I was good. I had fifteen victories to my name, bringing down four zeppelins and eleven German flying machines. Once I almost managed to hit the Red Baron, but my luck turned against me yesterday when a Gotha G V, one of these long-range German bombers, brought me down." He blinked, flushed with feebleness and disappointment.

Bridget had come to stand next to Agnès and her face, never giving away any concern to patients, declared in her usual optimistic voice, "We're so proud of you, Capitaine Heurtier. We want to hear the stories of all your victories, but may I steal Madame Docteur away from you just for a short consultation?" She did not wait for his answer but pulled Agnès aside and out of earshot.

"Are you thinking what I'm thinking?" It was said in the same breezy tone but with a grave undertone.

"Yes," Agnès sighed. "We have to take the splints away and start from scratch again after disinfection. It will be an arduous job and very exhausting for him, but we have no choice."

"Nah!" Bridget agreed. "Let's get on with it as fast as we can. I reckon we'll have to wheel the poor fellow in ourselves, as everybody else is gone on that exciting tunnel expedition."

Agnès nodded. "I'll make a quick round to see if any of the other patients need me and then we'll start again on the pilot."

They did not tell the pilot what was going to happen, so as not to frighten him further; just told him it was a routine check-up and they would give him some extra sedation, in effect putting him to sleep so he would not needlessly suffer more than he had already done. Together with Bridget, Agnès was concentrating on carrying out the complicated steps of the Thomas splints on the young pilot when Alan came over to their side.

"Need a hand?"

"Oh, would you?" Agnès looked up at him gratefully, as it was her first time struggling with the Thomas splints on her own, and she was fighting both her fear of making a mistake and her sudden relapse into tiredness.

Soon everything went much more smoothly. The young pilot was half awake at times, and when he opened his eyes, he smiled at the doctors and nurse around him but peacefully dozed off again under heavy sedation. So Agnès was surprised to see him suddenly shift on the operation table and blink in the strong lights above him. He turned his head towards Agnès.

"You know what, *docteur*," he said in a slurry voice. "If I survive this ordeal and the war is over, I'll take you up in my airplane. Would you like that?"

Although he could not see her mouth smile behind her cap, she beamed, and she nodded enthusiastically. "Now that's a promise I'll keep you to, Capitaine Heurtier. An extra reason to get you fit and on your feet again!"

He sank back into oblivion, and for some reason, his promise made Agnès feel as if she literally had wings. She was happy having Alan by her side, feeling once more how well they worked as a team. It was quiet in the operating room and it was quiet outside. She had totally forgotten about Charles Green. All the other inhabitants of the castle had either gone to Paris or were making their way through the tunnel. A serene peace fell over Agnès, and despite the arduous situation, she was happy.

She did not know how long they had been working on getting the splints in place when the door to the operation room burst open and one of the guards that Hamilton had left behind came in with an anxious look on his face.

Apologetically he whispered, "I'm sorry, doctors, but... but I'm afraid we're surrounded by Germans. They are... they are... all around the castle and on the driveway. I don't know what we should do."

Alan looked up, and after a quick worried glance at Agnès, growled, "There's little we *can* do, sergeant. Don't put up any resistance. It would be futile, and Major Hamilton would not want unnecessary casualties. Surrender for now and wait for the garrison and the commander to return. We'll continue here. We're doctors; we don't take sides."

Agnès felt as if her legs had been pulled from underneath her, and she started shaking all over. She tried to stop the tremor, but her body refused her brain. Seeing her struggle, Alan was by her side in no time and, in his surgeon's apron with his mouthpiece and cap still on, put an arm around her as she began to sob without control.

"Don't panic, Agnès." His voice was unnaturally calm, as if he had known all along that this would happen. "There's nothing they can do to us. We're medical staff, not soldiers. I'm sure they'll treat us with respect."

She felt his warmth and leaned into it, needing his physical support. She briefly closed her eyes and smelled his personal, musky scent even through the disinfectants and hospital odors. It was a welcoming, soothing smell in all her turmoil and anxiety. But the tears kept coming; she had no control over them. Just when she thought she had found a sense of balance, the tables were turned again. What now? And Alan did not even fathom the danger she was in.

"Try to keep working as usual, Agnès," he said in her hair. "That's your power – our only power – and it's what this young man on the table deserves."

He let her go after a small squeeze of his hand on her hip and returned to his side of the table, picking up the last part of the Thomas splint to place high on the inside of the pilot's thigh. The young man had awakened again when the alarmed British soldier burst in.

In a wavering voice he asked, "What will happen to the patients... to us... if... when the Germans occupy the hospital?"

With the same strange calm that Agnès so much admired and drew strength from, Alan looked down on the young pilot and, putting a comforting hand on his operation jacket, said in a reassuring tone, "Military conquests are outside my power, Capitaine Heurtier, but I will do everything that is in *my* power to protect you and keep you safe. As seriously as I take my profession, I take my patients. They are mine. No one else's."

9

AN UNWELCOME GUEST

<p>

t that moment, the door to the operating room was pushed open once more, and M-C, wringing her hands in despair, walked in, followed on her heels by a tall, slender German in full uniform. Apparently high-ranking, he absolutely looked the part, wearing a long belted *feldgrau* coat with the German cross pinned onto it and shining, knee-length black boots that he clicked together ostentatiously. Under his peaked cap he had a haughty face with laser-blue eyes that showed no emotion and tight white skin over high cheekbones. His lips were almost covered completely by a well-groomed ash-blond mustache.

It was not so much his impressive height or the foreign uniform that startled Agnès but his demeanor, as if he'd stepped inside a place that already belonged to *him,* had been his since the beginning of mankind; the attitude of the invincible conqueror. Both she and Alan stopped working, although Alan put a protective hand on his patient, whose eyes fluttered nervously towards the newcomer.

All eyes were fastened on the German, who stood looking around for what seemed an interminable time before shouting in coarse, staccato German, "*Korporal Spitzel, komm mal hier.*"

And in stepped the German soldier who had turned up at Dragoncourt the day before as the so-called British spy pretending to need medical treatment. Spitzel gave them a prideful smile, now showing great comfort in his German outfit and nodding jovially at the medical staff as if meeting a couple of old friends. Agnès had to suppress the urge to hurl herself at him and scratch that smile off his face. She had been right after all, and so had been Madeleine and M-C. He was a spy, a traitor, and he had given their vulnerable situation at Dragoncourt away, knowing they were at their weakest today with the patients being transported to other hospitals and most of the military staff and the castle owners testing the tunnel escape route. How vile, and how cunning!

A quick glance at Alan told her he had not recognized Spitzel, alias Charles Green, and despite her own anger Agnès was relieved he'd only had a glimpse of this despicable individual the evening before. She had no idea what Alan might have done had he understood the man's treason. But Alan was just biding his time, calm and composed as ever, certainly as tall as the imposing general, with the last part of the Thomas splint in one slender surgeon hand and the other resting on the pilot's exposed thigh.

Agnès bit her lip behind her mouthpiece until she tasted blood, unable to stop her hands from trembling while she waited for the German commander's verdict. After having taken in the green operating room at a leisurely pace, as if inspecting their equipment and supplies, the army officer finally turned to the two surgeons with a curt nod, his blue gaze unwavering, not a quiver of emotion.

"*Ich bin Major-General Eberhard Graf von Spiegler*, the Prussian commander of the 17th Imperial German Army, and my orders are to seize Château de Dragoncourt. From this day forward, the castle and its grounds are considered German property. As Château de Dragoncourt lies on the vital crossroad to Amiens, it will function as my headquarters for the region. Everyone still present in the castle, military, medical or civil, is forbidden to leave the grounds unless with my personal permission. Medical staff is not considered to be prisoners of war, but you *are* under German command. To put up resistance would be futile."

Agnès had not even heard his last words; she had been swaying on her legs from a couple of moments while his booming voice rang through her territory, *la grande salle verte,* feeling increasingly unwell, as the world began to spin. Vaguely she registered Alan's thumb pressing in the flesh of her arm and his alarm as he watched her slip to the floor. Then everything turned black with a soft swooshing sound.

AGNÈS AWOKE IN AN UNFAMILIAR, darkened room, unable to orient herself. The room did not give a clue as to whether it was dark because the curtains were drawn or because it was night. She was lying flat on her back, feeling physically feeble, while her legs were numb and heavy as lead. She tried to turn her head to see if she could identify the shady objects around her, and then it hit her like a boomerang as it all came back. She was at Dragoncourt; she had fainted, and she remembered why – the horrible realization of who was in charge of the castle now, and of her. She swallowed, wanting to get up and flee the place as fast as she could, as far as she could, but her body lay limp and defenseless.

Then she heard Alan whisper in the dark next to her, "Are you awake, Agnès?"

She must have stirred. She wanted to answer, but her tongue failed her. Where was he? She stretched out her arm in the direction his voice had come from but then saw his face like a white oval looming over her in the dusk. She could make out the contours of his face but not his expression.

"We'll be okay," he said soothingly. "Von Spiegler told me the medical staff has to stay at Dragoncourt to look after the wounded but that we're not prisoners. I don't think we have a choice right now, Agnès. It's a rotten situation, I know, and I feel terrible that you have to do this, but just remember we have an obligation to our patients. He ensured me that they too will not be taken prisoner of war as long as they are recovering. I'm just not sure Hamilton's men will share their fate, but that's outside our power."

He stopped talking, sighed in the dark, and then flicked on the lamp on the bedside table. The diffused golden light lit up his face. He looked so normal and familiar that she relaxed a little, and the wild beating of her heart slowed down. She wanted to nod and smile, but then the terrifying fear washed over her again and involuntary tears welled up in her eyes, spilling over her lashes and rolling down her cheeks. Her throat constricted, and she had to sit upright not to choke on her own anguish. Alan handed her his handkerchief, and she rubbed her face taking in his scent, trying to make it comfort her.

"Would you like some water?"

Before she could answer, he handed her a glass and she sipped gratefully. She wanted to tell him what was going on, needed to tell him, but her throat was completely blocked. Even the water had difficulty going down. Yet it was ever so urgent that she told him the truth. She had to.

"Take it easy, Agnès. We have time. The German considers us vital to this *Operation Michael*, as he calls it. He won't harm us. And just think of it as temporary. The Americans and Australians are so close that the Germans – strong as they now may seem – will be defeated in time. Mark my words."

"Alan," Agnès managed to say finally, "have you... have you... told that German general my name?"

"No, I haven't. Why? I just told him you were overworked, and that you had to rest and I had to take care of you. Only gave him my name. He didn't even bother to ask for my papers. Well, I guess I sound American enough." He smiled, obviously to lighten her heart, but Agnès was pacified more by the fact she was still anonymous to the German.

Then the tears welled up again and she sobbed, adding in a scared voice while raising herself to a sitting position, "Where is my bag? My papers?"

"Don't worry, they're here. I brought our medical bags upstairs, just in case."

"Oh, thank you." She gave him a small, relieved smile. "But Alan, you have to do something for me. You have to help me!" She looked exceedingly small and afraid, her blue eyes big with terror.

"Anything, Agnès," Alan vowed, an earnest expression on his handsome face.

Agnès sniffled, shifted on the bed, unsure how to begin, until Alan ordered, "Out with it. Tell me what's bothering you."

"Would you... would you... be willing to pretend you're married to me and that my name is Agnès Bell, just... just for the time being?"

"If you tell me why."

She sensed his worry, how he was trying to fathom the deep anguish and despair that were inwardly ripping her apart. Never before had she shown real fear for the enemy, not in Paris and not here in the weeks at Dragoncourt; contempt, yes, and hatred and determination to save as many Allied lives as she could, but never fear. He must think her a weakling after all, but there was so much more to it. Agnès supposed that all the contradictory emotions were showing on her face because Alan kept his full attention on her and had become very still, waiting patiently.

"It's a long story," she finally muttered.

"Try me."

"I best start at the end. Von Spiegler is my biological father." If she had ever taken her former professor off guard, it was now. Alan's gaze was one of total astonishment, which turned to disbelief as he slowly shook his head, but he did not say anything, so after another quick glance at his face, Agnès continued, her voice aquiver.

"My father went to work as a young music teacher in the Von Spiegler family in Prussia in the early 1890s. He had fled to Frederick's Schloss in Holstein after his then-fiancée broke off their high-profile engagement, leaving my father heart-broken and in need of recuperation from Paris society. In the Von Spiegler family, my romantic father fell in love once again, this time with one of the light-haired German maids. She was called Ingrid Gescke."

Agnès paused her account, feeling embarrassed and terribly exposed to be telling Alan – in essence a stranger to her life – all these intimate and difficult details about her family, but his earnest attention demanded she continue her tale.

"Ingrid, in her turn, was in love with the twenty-two-year-old son of the family, Eberhard von Spiegler, who probably only saw her as one of his playthings, as the family was high-class Prussian aristocracy and there was no way he would ever marry below his rank. He had no scruples, though, and Ingrid became pregnant with his child. But as he was serving in the *Deutsches Heer,* Germany's Imperial Army, he was hardly ever at home and at this time – the winter of 1894 – he had been gone for months.

"Ingrid's condition was quickly becoming impossible to conceal from her employers and being at her wits' end and feeling my father's kind disposition towards her, she confided in him. My father, who has never had any regard for status or titles, and in love as he was, persuaded my mother to go with him to Paris. He promised to marry her and raise Eberhard's child as his own. For the shame of it, my mother, believing Eberhard would never look at her again if he found out her state, and knowing the family would soon throw her out on the streets, consented to my father's plan. My father defied his parents' disapproval about this sudden and graceless marriage, and went ahead with it.

"So, he made Ingrid Gescke the Baroness de Saint-Aubin. She might not have loved my father, but she was certainly fond of him, and eternally grateful that he'd saved her reputation. But... but... then she died shortly after giving birth to me, and they... we never had a chance to find out if we could have been a loving family together. So, that's why I grew up in Paris with Max de Saint-Aubin as my legal father, never knowing my mother, what she was like, and of my biological father, only knowing his name.

"My father, honest and upright as he is, never shielded the truth from me. The sad conclusion is that I'm half-aristocratic after all, but that's the parental part, which I would ditch with pleasure if I could." Agnès stopped talking, not knowing how to go on and hoping Alan would somehow come to her aid, interrupt her, but he just stared at her, clearly having a hard time to take in the contents of her long, strange monologue.

So she sighed, folded her hands together, and proceeded, "Von Spiegler doesn't know who I am – he probably doesn't even know my mother was pregnant with his child – but if he hears my last name, he may put two and two together and start asking questions. You know, because of my white skin and blonde hair. As I have no idea how much he knows or remembers, I can't take the risk of him hearing there is a de Saint-Aubin at Dragoncourt." She sighed again, taking another sip of water and carefully putting the glass back on the bedside table.

"Anyway, you can imagine the shock when I realized my biological father was standing before me, after twenty-three years of not knowing what he looked like and then under these circumstances. I've always hated him as much as Papa hated him, and now, he suddenly has total control over my life, as my enemy, both on a personal and a territorial level. It was too much, it happened too quickly, and it was too raw on my nerves. But if I can pretend that I am your wife, that I'm Agnès Bell, I think I could manage to go on with this charade. It would at least make me feel safer."

Her voice trailed off, and then Alan whistled between his teeth. "Holy Moses! I honestly don't know what to say, Agnès. But I'll support you in whatever way I can. It's a grim turn of fate, that's for sure. I promised your father – Max, I mean – to protect you, so I will. If necessary, with my own body."

He looked at her with ardor, but for once Agnès was not thinking of what she felt for him but how she would have to go through her days facing her biological father as the occupier, the enemy, meanwhile pretending that the man she had such tender feelings for was her husband, married though he was to someone else.

And then Alan did something she least expected. He took her into his arms and embraced her. His voice in her hair, he murmured, "What a strange turn of events. I never would have imagined it to be this way." His voice was deep, not at all like the clear, practical surgical voice she was used to, but full of emotion and with a tinge of sadness.

She unlocked herself from his embrace to look at him. "What's going on, Alan? Are you all right?"

"Never better, apart from the pickle we're in," he said with a grimace. "You confided in me, so I'll confide in you."

Agnès waited, not sure how everything could become even more muddled than it already was.

"My marriage is definitely over," Alan said, his voice flat and broken.

"What?!" This turn in the conversation was so abrupt that she thought she'd heard it wrongly, but Alan continued.

"Suzanne sent me a letter that she has fallen in love with some art director in New York and is filing for divorce."

"But you were so happy." Momentarily forgetting her biological father being under the same roof, she stared at Alan in puzzlement. "How could this happen?"

Alan shrugged. "I thought we were happy, at least in the beginning. But it takes two to tango. Suppose I've always been quite blind when it came to Madame Blanchard. Wonder if she ever cared a fig for me."

Agnès was at a loss for words. She wanted to console him, but also felt a weird sense of relief. The whole world seemed to have become surreal in the past hour. At any other point, she would have had a glimmer of hope that there was a future for her and Alan, but right now she just felt deflated, for herself and for him.

They sat in silence for a couple of minutes when Alan declared, "I guess I have to go down to the operating room again. See what's going on there."

"I'll come with you," Agnès said, swinging her legs over the edge of the bed, but Alan pressed her back down with a firm hand on her shoulder.

"You'll do nothing of the sort. Stay here for a while. I'll tell that awful Von Spiegler that my wife is still feeling unwell." He grinned, but not very heartily.

"But what will I do here, Alan? I'll just worry myself sick. Who's going to look after us now? And what will happen to Jacques and Elle and the rest? Do you think they can come back to us?"

For a moment, Alan looked beaten too, but then his voice returned to its normal calm and controlled tone. "I have no idea. I just hope this madness will be over soon. I actually long to go back to Paris."

"So do I," Agnès agreed in a small voice. "I miss Papa. I hope he's all right, but he hasn't written to me in over two weeks."

"He probably has, but the mail system isn't working, and it will be out of order for a while longer now."

"I still want to come downstairs with you, Alan. I'll have to face the facts some time, and then I'd rather have you by my side, especially coming eye to eye with that... man again."

Alan consented to her plea but with reluctance. "Stay close to me at all time and do not hesitate to give me a signal when you can't cope with a situation. Promise?"

"Yes, husband." It was a weak attempt at a joke.

They found the operating room strangely quiet and deserted on their return.

"Let's check on our patients. they must be scared out of their wits now that the Huns have marched in." Alan scowled. In the only small ward they had kept operational after the other patients and staff had left for Paris, they met with a handful of Allied soldiers, most of them awake and lying with a helpless and anxious expression on their battered faces. They had obviously heard of the enemy's invasion.

"What will happen to us? Are we going to be taken to a German camp?" It was young pilot Heurtier who addressed them first.

"Not if we can help it," Alan said resolutely. "The German commander-in-chief has assured us that you can all stay here as long as you're recovering, and Doctor Agnès and myself will extend that period as long as we can. Meanwhile, for safety reasons, just call us Doctor Agnès and Doctor Alan; no last names. Understood?"

The men nodded in unison.

"We're on our way to discuss the future of the hospital with the

German commander, and as soon as we have more details about what is expected of us – and of you – we'll let you know. So, for now, I order you to just focus on getting better."

"I can't be transported," an older French soldier grumbled wearily, his head and hands invisible in their white bandages. "I'm very weak as it is. I'll die if they transport me."

Others chimed in, but now it was Agnès to cut in with her high, female voice.

"As Doctor Alan said, don't worry unnecessarily. We'll do everything we can to have special arrangements made for you. Okay?"

It was clear that the general feeling was still one of great uncertainty and concern, but the patients also understood that they had no other option.

As they retreated from the ward, Alan said, "Let's check if Bridget and M-C are in the garden room. We haven't spoken to the girls yet, and they must be in crisis. I want to know how they are faring under this, and I could do with a coffee. How about you?"

Agnès nodded and observed, "We also have to inform them of our secret arrangement."

Over the garden room hung an icy silence, with Bridget and M-C perched on the straight-backed chairs at the dinner table in the corner and Eberhard von Spiegler and Corporal Spitzel lounging in the armchairs in the middle of the room.

"Ah, there you are," the tall general exclaimed in heavily accented French. "We were waiting for you to come back. We need to discuss matters concerning the hospital, doctors."

For a moment Alan stood in front of the general towering over him and looking down on him with a forced neutral expression on his handsome face. Agnès kept standing behind him, as closely as she could, observing the man in the armchair uneasily. On the one hand, she was curious who he was, but she also feared his abrasive presence.

Her whole fate suddenly seemed to depend on this man and what he could do to her. Von Spiegler sat as if he were completely at ease, but she saw his jaw muscles tighten as he stared up into Alan's face.

He must be in his mid-forties now, strongly yet finely built and with a smooth, unwrinkled, white skin. He had removed his peaked cap, and the color of his hair was genuinely like her own, light blond but without the springiness.

She studied every feature of him for resemblances but was glad to find none except for the hair color. Papa had been right; she was the spitting image of her mother. But that was dangerous now as well. The movements of his manicured hand were slow and studied; in fact, everything about him was studied, as if he were playing the role of being important instead of really being it. He was a hard nut to crack.

"Please sit down at once, doctors. I have more things to do, and I hate being made to wait," the German said with slight irritation, gesturing to the two armchairs on the other side of the coffee table.

Alan gave the general a brief smile for a reason Agnès did not understand and did as he was told. She followed and sat down next to him. M-C had soundlessly slipped from her chair and without asking poured them a cup of coffee and put it down on the coffee table in front of them. She also refilled the general's cup, though he did not give the nurse a second look.

Agnès touched M-C's hand gratefully before she withdrew into her corner. Over her coffee cup she fixed her gaze on Von Spiegler and decided she thoroughly disliked the man, not just for being the enemy but for his whole demeanor of pretension and affectedness. He might be an aristocrat; his manners were downright boorish. Agnès could not even believe they were blood related. Papa – bless his soul – with all his eccentricities and disregard for courtesy was ten times more the aristocrat.

Still holding him in her gaze, her contempt growing, she heard him say, "My regiment has taken up its quarters in the right wing where the British battalion used to be quartered. Corporal Spitzel" – he smiled as he mentioned his name – "as you may have understood, had already informed me that four medics, ten British guards, and a couple of wounded soldiers were the only residents left in the castle. We have locked the door to the tunnel from the inside, so there's no way Major Hamilton and his regiment or the castle's owners can return through there. As from today, April 2, 1918, Château de Drag-oncourt is under German command."

"All right," Alan interrupted the general impatiently. "My wife and I already know all that, and the medical team will comply with the new rules."

Agnès saw Bridget and M-C sit up straighter and look in their direction questioningly. But then their faces became deadpan again, immediately guessing that for some reason this was the plan to stick to after she had fainted when confronted with the Germans in the operation room.

"Ah, so you're a couple? I see. I must admit finding a female surgeon at the front had surprised me. That certainly would never be allowed in a German frontline hospital. But now you are here..." Von Spiegler gave Agnès a thin, false smile under his thick mustache, looking her straight in the face.

It took a lot of courage to return his gaze. Her hands trembled in her lap, but she managed to keep her focus steady, all the while comforted by Alan's nearness and that only he knew who she really was.

"Madame, I hope you have sufficiently recovered from your.... weakness?" The general continued, trying to sound friendly, but his voice never lost its cold ring. "There is no reason to fear the situation as long as you do what I tell you to."

She nodded with the slightest movement of her head. There seemed no need to reply. Alan put a warm hand over hers and squeezed it lightly.

He spoke on her behalf. "I would like to know what is going to happen to our own patients. They're all severely wounded. That's the only reason they are still here."

"I am aware of that," Von Spiegler said coldly. "Spitzel told me so much. You have transported all the other patients to Paris, which suits me just fine. It means there will be ample space for my own men now. Your order is to tend to German casualties from now on, and you're expected to give them the same level of treatment as you gave to the Allied patients."

Agnès felt Alan's grip tighten, his whole body going rigid. He hesitated a moment, but then said in a slightly superior voice, "We *are* physicians, General Von Spiegler, not military staff. We are trained to help the sick and wounded of whatever side or rank. But you haven't answered my question."

Von Spiegler looked as if he would leap from his chair in rancor, his white neck above his stiff gray jacket turning red and blotchy and his blue eyes blazing, but apparently he thought the better of it and sank back in his chair.

"Herr Doctor, I am in no way obliged to answer any of your questions. I told you already that for the time being, your patients can stay where they are. Do not make me repeat myself. That should be enough of an answer."

Alan remained unruffled by the general's biting words and just shrugged his shoulders. "I only asked it on behalf of our patients, and I wanted my wife to hear these words from your mouth so she would be reassured."

"All right," the German said, more placated, "I will order medical supplies and if necessary, extra medics from our field hospital near Albert. I'll also order provisions for the kitchen and a cook. That will be all for now."

Alan glanced at Agnès, his hand still on hers. She twitched her lips in a vague resemblance of a smile, as if saying, *What choice do we have?* Alan got up before the general had a chance to rise and walked over to the table where a very subdued Bridget and M-C were sitting perched on their chairs like two forlorn birds.

"Nurse Bridget and Nurse M-C," he said warmly, "we *are* the medical team at Château de Dragoncourt, and we'll continue to be just that under my supervision. We'll support and help each other at any time, and despite these difficult circumstances, we'll perform our jobs as best as we can. Is that agreed?" His leadership and apparent fearlessness made them slightly relax their tight postures against the straight-backed chairs and the nurses nodded, sadness and despair etched on their tired faces.

While the general got to his feet, Agnès ventured to ask, "When do you expect the first... uh... German patients to arrive at Dragoncourt, General Von Spiegler?" She was surprised to hear her own voice; it sounded quite normal and matter of fact, even as she uttered his vile name.

"Probably tonight," he replied, moving with rigid steps in his creaking black boots to the door. "There's been heavy fighting early this morning south of the Somme River, but we had to set up camp here first before we could bring them in."

Heavens, no, Agnès thought but she said nothing, just grateful the commandant left the garden room to go to his own quarters and with him that crony, Spitzel. The remaining four breathed a sigh of relief but no one spoke for a while. There was so much to digest, but at least they had each other.

THE FIRST GERMAN soldiers were brought in that evening. Most had suffered bullet wounds; some had inhaled gas. It was all just a repetition of what they had seen before, the only difference being that these men wore different uniforms and spoke in an unfamiliar tongue. The four Allied medics set about doing what they had been doing for months and tried not to think in terms of sides. The patients, at least, seemed to be as grateful to be relieved of their pain and suffering. Some moments, Agnès felt a force from within blocking her to keep on working, but she suppressed it as best she could.

As doctors, they had sworn to treat patients no matter which religion or race, and that was what she was now expected to do. But she had a hard time concentrating on the simplest actions, like dressing a wound or removing a bullet from an arm or a leg. Her mind kept slipping away to Jacques and Elle and Madeleine – where they were now and how they must feel being trapped in Amiens or wherever they

had ended up. She knew they would be worried about the team at
Dragoncourt. It was hard and conflicting to suddenly be in that green
room and performing the tasks she'd been trained to do without their
support and without the protection of the British army. Afraid for her
fate, the only steadying force was Alan's presence.

"Focus, Agnès," she heard Alan say next to her, as he cut open the
gray tunic of an unconscious German infantry soldier who was
having trouble breathing.

"Sorry," she said, shaking herself out of her stupor and reaching
for the antiseptics to clean the area around the bullet wound in the
young man's stomach.

She managed to get through the next two patients without her
mind drifting to the absurd situation they now found themselves in,
but then it happened again. They were working on a high-ranking
officer, although she had no idea how high as she had never studied
military insignia, certainly not of the German army. But he had
stripes, and his uniform was of better quality than those of the
ground troops, and like Von Spiegler he had been brought in
wearing one of those ridiculous peaked caps. They had difficulty
getting it off his swollen head as one of the bullets had grazed the
side of his face. The man was older than most of the other soldiers,
with gray grizzly hair and a sunken shallow face under a disheveled
mustache.

They all have these same mustaches, Agnès thought. Maybe they think
they look powerful that way.

The man shivered uncontrollably as he was laid out on the operation table, but Bridget had already sedated him with such a high dose
of chloroform that he had passed out. When Agnès cut open his
tunic, she saw his midriff had been dangerously perforated by one or
more bullets that had hit him full on.

Bridget was putting him on extra oxygen because he had a hard
time breathing himself. He was one of these hopeless cases, but it
suddenly struck Agnès that she did not know what would happen to
them if he died on the operation table. Would they get disciplined for
letting a high-ranking German die? That sobering thought helped

her to stand up straight up and focus with all her might only on the job at hand.

"Completely impossible," Alan said at some point. "Bridget, more oxygen."

Agnès managed to finger out the bullet from his diaphragm, but then they discovered a second one almost directly behind the first.

"Impossible to get that one out as well. He won't make it." Alan threw his surgeon's knife down on the tray.

"But you know we have to get it out," Agnès said, trying to sound more confident than she felt. "He'll certainly die if we don't try."

"Okay, if you say so," Alan said dully. He knew what she was thinking – their own lives could depend on it if this man died.

They worked on, and after what seemed like an eternity, managed to remove the second bullet.

"Blood transfusion, now!" Agnès cried out, and Bridget immediately fulfilled the order.

"God save us all," Alan grumbled, as after the long and emotional day, they decided to take a break in the garden room, munching on a supper of hard black German bread and drinking a cup of lukewarm coffee. They were toil-worn, but at least it was quiet and warm in the room. Agnès was lying on the couch with her eyelids closed, and Alan lay sprawled in one of the chairs. They were too tired to talk. Agnès felt even too tired to think and only squinted when Bridget stormed in.

"Sorry to disturb you, but one of you have to come and see to that last patient," she said, out of breath from running the long way through the castle's corridors. "It's critical, I'm afraid."

"I'll go," Alan said, already getting up. "You stay here and rest for a bit, Agnès."

"No," she said, also getting up, "I go where you go."

On arrival in the recovery room, it was obvious they were too late. The German was as dead as a brick, his whole display of insignia lying in neat rows next to his body.

"Will Von Spiegler hold it against us?" Agnès's voice was small from fear.

"He might," Alan pondered. "But we'll know that he's wrong. We did what we could to save that bastard's life."

"Shhhh..." Agnès and Bridget hushed in unison.

Difficult as it was, Agnès knew that from a medical standpoint they had indeed done their utmost. She had even pushed it further than Alan had wanted to go. Or had her decision to continue caused the man's death?

She had no more time to consider her musings as behind them the gruff voice of Von Spiegler boomed, "What have you done? The German Emperor is not going to be pleased with the two Allied doctors that let Graf Hausenhoffer die. I thought you promised that you would act as neutral professionals?"

"But General Von Spiegler..." Alan started, but the German cut him short.

"No buts, Doctor. This is a grave matter, very grave! I cannot dispense of you two for the moment, but you are under arrest. As soon as my German doctors arrive here, you'll be taken to Germany to face a court martial."

Agnès gasped. How unfair this was! And so far from the truth. But she thought it wise not to say anything. Alan looked sideways at her and saw her struggle.

Then he said softly, "Herr General, I assure you that my wife and I and Nurse Bridget did everything in our power to save Graf Hausenhoffer's life. I could give you the medical details of what we were facing, if you want."

"*Nein!*" Von Spiegler exploded, "I don't trust you at all. From now on, you'll be operating with two of my guards present in the operating room to keep a close watch on the pair of you."

Agnès swallowed hard. What was going to become of them now? Sent to Germany as criminals, when all they'd wanted to do was help men survive this atrocious war? But the fear was soon replaced with ice-cold rage. The unfairness of it all. They were all innocent. They were working around the clock to save as many lives as they could, and now this horrible man – this man who had fathered her but done nothing else for her in his entire life – was threatening to take her prisoner.

It was on the tip of her tongue to tell him who she was, but she decided against it. He was unworthy of the truth. He was just part of a terrible war machine that had disrupted her adopted country and mutilated it to a degree that was beyond repair. At some point he would have to pay for it, one way or the other. Meanwhile she let her shoulders hang and returned to the garden room with Alan to await the new batch of wounded Germans that would soon be arriving on their doorstep.

"I am so sorry," Alan said in the unlit room. The evening light was temporarily soothing, absorbing the fighting, the blood, the unfairness of it all for one glorious moment of peace and quiet.

"It's nothing you could have changed," Agnès said flatly, but then with more passion in her voice, "He's going to pay for it! I tell you; I'm not done with him yet!"

"Be careful, Agnès," Alan warned. "He's dangerous, and you know it."

"I don't care," she cried out. "What he just threatened us with is against all human rights. He should be grateful to us, not insult us. Who does he think he is? What right does he have to court martial us? We're doctors, for Heaven's sake!" But her voice died down when the general marched into the kitchen with a sour expression on his face.

He interrupted their conversation abruptly. "Madame, can I have a word with you alone?" It was not even a question; it was a command.

Alan looked up from stirring his coffee. "Do you want me to leave, Herr General?"

"Yes. Please do."

Agnès looked pleadingly at Alan. "Please stay," she whispered, afraid to be alone in a room with that unpleasant man.

"I'll be right outside," he said. "Don't worry. You'll be okay."

But she felt far from okay. Not only did it annoy her that the German continued to address her as *Madame* instead of *doctor*, she had a strong inkling he was going to blame her for Haussenhoffer's death. She remained seated, outwardly perfectly calm, as Von Spiegler sat himself opposite her and placed one long uniformed leg over the other.

He remained silent for a while, studying her, and she felt the queasiness settle in her stomach she had felt the first time she found out who he was. Did he suspect something? Why was he not talking? She hoped by God that Alan was outside the door as he had promised and would rush in if something went wrong.

Finally, the general cleared his throat, while still scanning her whole being with his arctic gaze. "Am I to believe that you and Doctor Bell are married?" The question was meant to sound neutral, but she did not miss the threat underneath it, and her throat constricted.

"Of course," she said, hoping it sounded chirpy enough. "We married last summer. In Paris."

"So, you want to make me believe he's a bigamist?" There was a sardonic smile under the dull blond mustache, and Agnès wrung her hands in her lap.

"What... what do you mean, Herr General?"

"What I mean," he said slowly in his studied, affected manner, "is that Alan Bell is married to Suzanne Blanchard, and that you are colleagues but not husband and wife."

Agnès felt her face go red, and her eyes darted to the door. *Please come in, Alan*, she begged silently, *please rescue me from this bully.* She remained quiet, hanging her head.

"Look at me, Madame, and please explain yourself!" He really seemed to be enjoying his game, and it cost Agnès all her power not to burst into tears. She looked up briefly at him but could not stand the cruel blue eyes and looked down at her hands again.

"Nothing." It was no more than a whisper. Through her cast-down eyelashes she could see the German untwisting his long legs and placing the other knee on top. The studied attitude was unbearable; it choked her and simultaneously made her rage inside but there was truly little she could do. He held all the power and she was his plaything, probably as her mother had been once upon a time.

"Your name – as you know very well yourself – is Agnès de Saint-Aubin. And now enlighten me. What was your reason to keep that from me, Madame, and pretend you were married to the American?"

She cast him a sidelong glance, aware how trapped she was. He had adopted an expression as if he honestly wanted to know the answer, but Agnès saw he was still acting his part. He had probably known all along who they were, even before he had captured Château de Dragoncourt, gaining all the information he needed from his intelligence services. But why he had made them believe he bought their story was puzzling to her. She had to answer and decided to keep it vague.

"No particular reason at all, Herr General. I just... felt safer pretending Alan was my husband. It was all so sudden – the enemy... uh... the Germans taking over."

"Liar!" It was said with a force that shook her, and Agnès cringed in the big armchair, "I want to hear the truth from your own mouth."

"Because... because you might know who my father is." There seemed no point in hiding the facts any further. Her mind clung desperately to the slight hope that he did not know her mother had been pregnant with his child.

"Oh, him?" the General said with disdain. "I remember him vaguely. Short, dark fellow, gypsy type. All talk and no substance."

"That's not fair!" Despite herself, she heard herself raise her voice. "My father is a very good and decent man!"

"Ha!" The general gave a short, cheerless laugh. "Decent indeed. Leaving my parents' house in the middle of the night like a thief when they had been so good to him. And only to marry one of the maids. Decent indeed for an aristocrat!"

Agnès pricked up her ears. She might still be safe; he might not know. A little more spirited, she glanced at him through her eyelashes, feeling with all her heart how much she loved her adopted father; and this man, whose blood might be running through her veins, was nothing to her at all, nothing but a cold-hearted bully she despised.

"And you are the produce of that fated marriage, I presume?" He looked at her as if she had spent her whole life in the Paris gutters, but his words hurt her less now. Agnès felt the air stream back into her lungs. Papa was by her side, giving her strength with his love, and she *was* safe with the horrible truth only known to her and to Alan.

With a sigh of relief, she said, "You are correct, Herr General. I was afraid you and your family would not have a positive remembrance of my father and that was the reason to hide my last name from you." He was still looking at her in disgust, but something changed in his face, a small crack in the veneer he had so arduously polished for himself. Had he started hating women because her mother had left him? Without warning the actor reappeared.

"And tell me, Madame, how did the Prussian maid fare in the French Baron's arms?" It was meant to be as sardonic as he could muster.

Agnès hesitated, but as she had no remembrance at all of her mother and she wanted to get out of this evil man's presence as quickly as she could, she said with little emotion, "My mother, Ingrid Gescke de Saint-Aubin, died shortly after giving birth to me."

She saw the crack in the veneer of his façade again, and it made her wonder if her mother had meant more to him than he was willing to admit, even to himself. Her mother must have been a special lady to have kindled an attraction in two noblemen. She thought of the framed photograph of her mother on the grand piano in her father's music room, taken a short while after their marriage.

Ingrid was dressed in a beautiful but quite outmoded pink dress of a soft-looking material with lace lining and embroidered with tiny pink and white roses with red hearts. Her blonde hair was also styled in an old-fashioned way, all heaviness at the front in thick rolls of springy light hair, making her look too old for her young age.

Her eyes were striking, and although it was a black and white photograph, the clear light in them sprang at you; there was zest for life and mockery in equal doses in the gaze and the mouth, with its soft, full lips, smiling bountifully, showing two rows of perfect, strong teeth.

The photograph had become full of color for young Agnès,

because Papa Max had ordered the French symbolist painter Edgar Maxence to paint a portrait from the photo, and this large painting was hanging over the mantelpiece in the dining room. The two images had melted into one in Agnès's vision, and as they were the only visual image she had of her poor mama. She had studied them often, as if that way she could connect with a missing piece in her heart.

Agnès's attention was so deeply on the photograph and her memories that it was only from the distance she heard the general address her in his commanding voice.

"You are dismissed, Madame. And for all I care, you can share Bell's bed. But I warn you to be very careful what you say to your patients, as they will be interrogated by my men. You are *all* under close inspection."

Agnès fixed him again in her blue gaze, but something had shifted in the energy between them. She was no longer afraid of him.

She remained seated, unwilling to leave the garden room because he was still in it. It was *their* room, not his. This room, just like the operating room, would never be the property of General Graf Von Spiegler, whatever he thought himself. He had revealed his weakness to her, and he did not know who she was, but tried to get his inside information from her patients. No matter his pretensions, this man was not all powerful and he never would be. It was her turn to cross her legs and relax back into the armchair. She was Papa's daughter, and she would do him proud.

"Thank you, Herr General," she said evenly, and then called out, "Alan, please come back in."

The general's face darkened for a moment, but then he raised himself to his full length and went over to the bay window, his back towards her.

When Alan's dark-curled head peeked around the door, a smile of relief glided over her face. Apparently he had not overheard their conversation because he came to sit on the arm of her chair and put his arm around her.

"You're okay, honey?" Agnès's smile broadened. She was going to enjoy this fantasy for as long as it lasted.

"I am, sweetie. Let's check on the patients one more time and then head for bed." Alan winked at her conspiratorially, and hand in hand they left the garden room and the surprised Von Spiegler behind. *Ha,* Agnès thought, *he isn't the only one here who can play a role.*

10

TIME TO ACT

Madeleine

Hotel L'Europe, Amiens, 2 April 1918

Madeleine sat fidgeting with a piece of French bread, pushing the crumbs around on the white damask table-cloth with her index finger as she listened intently to the conversation. Gerald Hamilton was consulting with Elle, Jacques, and Philip. Her heart was as heavy as the weight of her worries and she was searching inside herself for a glimmer of strength in this bleak situation; something that would help her change this awful truth.

"We have to put our hopes on the Australian Corps led by General John Monash and the Canadian Corps under the command of General Arthur Currie. They're preparing a major counterattack, together with the Brits, the French, and the Americans, but it may take a couple of weeks or even months to regroup and plan the attack. The Germans are excessively strong this spring," Gerald explained. "Really, my British division is far too small to carry out a counterattack right now. It would be sheer suicide."

"But we can't wait for weeks, Major! We don't have that amount of time. Think about Agnès and Alan and the nurses, who are in grave danger this very minute. What will happen to them? And to our château?" Elle's voice was an anguished plea for action.

"I know what's at stake, Countess Elle," Gerald said in a clipped voice, but Madeleine could hear his concern as well. "I'm afraid this is the consequence of warfare. You can't save the few and imperil the many."

"Oh, God," Elle whimpered, "what a hellish situation!"

"Look at it this way." Gerald made an effort to calm her. "The medics at Dragoncourt face the least risk just because they are medics. My own men and the patients still there are another case since they will most certainly become prisoners of war."

Madeleine immediately thought about the round, innocent face of Sergeant Cooper, with whom she'd had such a light-hearted, flirtatious conversation on the day after her arrival and who was one of Hamilton's men trapped in their German occupied castle. Her heart went out to him. Suddenly, she could not take one minute of the gloom and doom anymore and briskly got up from the breakfast table, overthrowing her porcelain coffee cup, which crashed onto the linoleum floor and broke into four pieces.

All eyes were on her as she picked up the white scraps and mopped the brown stain with her serviette. With a flushed face and mumbling a "Sorry," she grabbed Loulou, who had been sitting opposite her munching a banana, and made her way from the breakfast room through the bay windows onto the hotel balcony. She breathed in deeply the crisp morning air, stared down at the deserted Boulevard de Bapaume, and tried to calm herself, but even the open air failed to qualm her skittishness. She went back inside, up to her room to fetch her coat.

"You stay here, Loulou," she ordered sternly. "Mistress will be back soon."

The little monkey did not look all that happy being abandoned to a strange room on her own but obeyed, taking a seat on the double bed and continuing to tear down the banana peel and taking small bites, grinning and showing Madeleine her yellow teeth.

Despite strict orders not to leave the hotel, Madeleine soon found herself marching down the boulevard, ignoring French guards that asked for her papers, her hands deep in her pockets and her flaming hair freely behind her in the morning breeze.

It was a mild early April day, and billowing white clouds, interspersed with patches of blue sky, moved swiftly overhead. Most people stayed indoors, per instructions, but there was the occasional housewife rushing by on felt slippers on her way to the bakery or butcher, and a bent, white-haired man shuffled slowly through a patch of greenery dragging a ratty white dog on a string. Two blue-uniformed soldiers, their bayonets crossed over their breasts, stood talking and smoking on the corner of the street, eyeing Madeleine with interest as she sped by. But Madeleine had no eye for any of them; she just stamped her walking shoes hard and rhythmically on the pavement – how fortunate she had been to put on sturdy shoes for their expedition through the tunnel – and tried to form a coherent plan in her head.

How could she – a lone, upper-class girl without money or training – be of any use in this wide scheme of nations, where men, hung heavy with medals and blood-thirsty minds, were in charge, moving their own soldiers around like pawns on a board, sending them to their death as stock for slaughter? She was handcuffed by her sex and her inexperience. Then Agnès came for her mind's eye, as clearly as if she was actually standing in front of her – the frail, blonde beauty with eyes as blue as a robin's egg, young and fragile as early spring; the epitaph of femininity, but those eyes spoke of a quiet determination, an unbreakable spirit, and Madeleine felt ashamed of herself.

"If you can do it, Doctor Agnès, without loud speech and self-importance, I can do it too."

Madeleine breathed a little more freely, drawing from Agnès's invisible strength, but it did not solve the problem of what she could do for Dragoncourt, where the enemy now reigned. But not doing anything was not an option either. She would go and inspect the lay of the land, one way or another.

Feeling less fettered and reenergized from her brisk morning walk, Madeleine strode back to Hotel L'Europe and took the stone steps up to the gilded entrance two at a time. She ignored the doorman who came rushing to her aid and pushed the stained-glass panel of the revolving door herself to step into the luxurious entrance hall of the old family hotel, where the thick deep-red carpet subdued footsteps and voices alike to a hushed tone.

Before the war, Hotel L'Europe had been one of Amiens' jewels of French heritage, a refuge for the upper classes, whether to arrange a secret *rendez-vous* with their mistresses or to entertain foreign princes and ambassadors. Though still full of splendor, and the owners, la Famille Archambeau, still as formally hospitable and confidentially strict as they had always been, there was no denying that Hotel L'Europe had been quite ravaged by the war, and its former sophisticated elegance was now only a vague memory.

In 1918, it was a coming and going of coarse-voiced, grim-looking military men, clumping about in mud-caked boots without any concern for the precious Persian rugs, tipping cigar or cigarette ash into potted plants, and talking as loudly and freely in whatever native tongue they possessed as if no one had a delicate soul anymore. The mistresses were of another caliber as well, less soft-spoken and demure, leaving lipstick stains on the lace pillowcases and the remnants of powder all over the marble bathrooms.

It made no difference to Madeleine who stayed at the hotel or what they were up to. Without looking left or right, she marched over to the bar and ordered a Side-car. She watched how the bartender, a lanky, timid young man in a white cocktail jacket, with a skinny neck above his white shirt and his black bowtie askew, mixed the Grand Marnier, lemon juice, and triple sec and poured it with great concentration into a wide-rimmed, crystal glass, decorating it with a thin curl of orange peel. It was clear that he was hoping to impress his attractive customer with his cocktail skills. She threw a couple of francs on the counter and had just taken a grateful sip when she heard a familiar voice behind her.

"Care if I join you for a morning drink, Countess Madeleine?"

She turned to see Gerald Hamilton standing behind her, all smiles under his sandy mustache, his cap under his left arm and dressed to the nines. He clearly took great pride in wearing his Major uniform with all his decorations, even more so it seemed now they were cornered by the Germans. *A uniform is something to draw strength from* passed through Madeleine's mind, and she wondered why women could not wear military uniforms or become commanders in the army.

"Sure," she grinned. "We need it."

"What is it you're drinking?" Gerald sniffed her glass.

"A Side-car – cognac and triple sec. Have you not heard of it? It's the latest fashion in Paris."

"Do me one as well," Gerald ordered the lanky waiter. "Though it's a funny name for a drink."

"Named after the sidecar of a motorcycle, I'm told," Madeleine explained, but then dispensing with the chitchat about drinks, she looked him straight in the eye and inquired, "So what's the plan, Major?"

He sighed deeply. "We wait, that's all. We *wait*."

"What?!" Madeleine pushed her glass away so roughly that she spilled half its contents. "You can't be serious?"

"Little else we can do; we don't have enough troops ready in formation to push the Germans back behind the Hindenburg line again. We can only hope they don't push us further west and south because – by God – they are trying. It would mean we might have to retreat even further."

Madeleine saw the pain these overwhelming odds caused him, knowing that he blamed himself dearly for miscalculating their expedition through the escape route, which had left the medics and his men at Dragoncourt defenseless and at the mercy of the Germans.

Almost inaudibly she whispered, hanging her head, "I think it's as much my fault, Ger...Major. What if I let a German in after all?"

"Nonsense, Madeleine! The Boches would have taken Drag-oncourt anyway, spy or no spy. It's their timing that has taken me off guard. It's actually my spies who haven't done their job properly, or I would have been warned. Ah, it's all such a muddle! But" – he reined in his frustration and added more companionably – "do call me Gerald or Gerry, please. I may be Major Hamilton to my men, but I'd rather be Gerry to you and your family. You, the Dragoncourts, have almost become my next of kin these past two years."

He smiled sadly as he fixed his Celtic eyes on her, and she felt so sorry for him that a surge of compassion washed over her. She wished there were a way to take his self-reproach and wretchedness away from him. If she had dared it, she would have kissed him on the mouth right where they stood, but instead she pulled a cigarette from her case, and he hastened to offer her a light.

Through a whirl of smoke, she said, "I'm going to find a way to remedy this situation. You see, I'm not terribly good at being stuck in a place where I don't want to be."

He laughed heartedly at this. "You can say that again, Miss Madeleine. Escaping from your finishing school in Lausanne. Hah! Nothing keeps you down if you can help it, but I'm afraid you're as trapped in this situation as we all are. So, don't you try anything!" His tone was breezy, but his expression commanded her not to be reckless.

She shrugged as if dispatching his concerns but at the same time gave him her most endearing smile, pouting her red lips. Major Gerry Hamilton might want to rein her in, but she was not ready for that yet. But let him try. It would be fun.

Apart from the veiled flirting, which she greatly enjoyed, Madeleine's brain was still in overdrive and deeply focused on serious matters. Inwardly discontented with herself that she had failed to strike a plan that would change their situation for the better, she was throwing some vague ideas against her canvas of heroism and female ingenuity, but nothing concrete manifested. And Madeleine loved concrete manifestations.

"I'm hungry. Let's have lunch," she announced impulsively, realizing she'd interrupted something Gerald was saying and that she had no idea what it was. Rueful and honest as was her nature, she quickly added, "Forgive me, Gerry, I was preoccupied. Please, repeat that last part."

Giving him her arm, they walked companionably to the sunny, pastel-blue *salle à manger* that formerly had only been the breakfast room but now also served as lunch and dinner space now that the other, larger *salles* of the hotel had been transformed into headquarters for the military.

"I was commenting on your all-too-clever brain that might work against you if you lose sight of the danger around you." Gerald gave her arm a light squeeze but did not look at her. '

And you're not that dumb yourself, Madeleine thought, but aloud she said, "Don't worry about me, Gerry dear, I'm a cat with nine lives. You'll see."

He sighed and pulled out a chair for her.

The de Dragoncourt twins and Philip Lane were seated at a table in the alcove near the bay windows, drinking aperitifs and smoking cigarettes. They looked more like a morose trio of traveling salesmen than young sprouts of old aristocratic lineages. The oval dinner table, draped with a white damask cloth that was blotched with red wine stains and smears of gray ash, was the place assigned to the Dragoncourt family during their stay at Hotel L'Europe.

The Archambeau family, who had known the Dragoncourt for decades, had come to their aid. As all of them, including Elle and Jacques and Madeleine, had left their château the day before without sufficient money or spare clothes, the hoteliers had kindly supplied them with the necessities of life, extra clothes, toothbrushes and other toiletries, as far as available in war-time Amiens, and assured them they could stay as long as they needed.

Gerald Hamilton was not a guest at the hotel, as he was stationed with the other Royal West Kent battalions near Amiens, but Monsieur Archambeau, who read his customers like an easy novel, had quickly grasped the importance the Major had for the bewildered Dragoncourt siblings and an extra plate was invariably placed at the young Count's table for him.

Seeing her elder brother and sister so disheveled and disheartened made Madeleine bite her lip and vow once more to herself that she would do everything in her power to get them out of this pickle and back in their castle where they belonged.

"Jacques," she ventured casually, pretending to be fully concentrated on cutting her veal steak into small cubes, "do you have any idea if the lock on the tunnel door is the original one? I mean is it 16th century?" She felt Gerald's intense gaze on her but innocently popped a piece of meat in her mouth and cocked her head sideways to look at her brother.

Jacques seemed to come back from some form of coma, muttering a confused, "What... what was that again, Mad-Maddy?" He pushed his round spectacles higher on his nose and tipped the ash from his cigarette, apparently forgetting he was eating and smoking at the same time.

Madeleine remained fully composed and asked again, "The lock on the tunnel door, you know, that the Germans seemed to have locked or barricaded from the inside, is that the original lock? And do we only have one key to it?"

Jacques seemed to revive a little at her probing questions and jabbing the stub of his cigarette in the overflowing ashtray, reflected in a slow voice,

"Now you ask me, I seem to remember Papa telling me that the lock was replaced somewhere in the 1880s. That Grandpa lost the old key."

"But is there a spare key?" Madeleine was adamant to get her answer, aware all eyes were on her now.

"Thinking of bribing the Boches into letting you back in their midst as the fair maiden of the castle?" It was Philip's attempt at a weak joke, but Madeleine ignored his remark.

"Please think. Jacques, is there but one key?"

"There was one key in the door, and there might be another key in Papa's old secretary. But what good is that to us now, Maddy? Let it rest; we're done." The sadness of that reflection made him push his uneaten plate away and light another Gauloise.

Elle, who had also eaten very little and had been silently listening to the faltering conversation between her ardent sister and deflated brother, now asked, "Darling, what are you getting at?"

Madeleine looked at her sister through her eyelashes, not wanting to give anything away. She shrugged her shoulders as if dismissing the subject herself. "Nothing. Just wondered. It seems silly that we can't use the door we came out through to go back in. You know, in case the Boches lose this futile battle, which eventually they will."

The conversation then turned to nonessential things, while she brooded further. There was hope if there was another key. It was something; very little, but something.

After lunch Madeleine went outside to smoke a cigarette in the hotel's garden, and resting her back against the wooden balustrade that surrounded the porch, she listened to the chatter of the cook and the kitchen maids, who were sitting a little further on the porch, enjoying a break after lunch before having to go back into the hot kitchen for the preparation of dinner. Suddenly she pricked up her ears. The cook was talking about his hazardous daily cycle trip from Blangy-Tronville to Amiens and back.

"It feels like a cannon ball will hit my behind any minute of that ride. I take the footpath through the forest along the river, but a man's life is never safe these days. I run into scouts all the time, armed to the teeth. They can't judge which side they're on in the pit of the night. Bloody business it is."

"Why aren't you moving into the hotel, like us? That would save you the trip back and forth," one of the kitchen maids inquired.

Madeleine stealthily gazed up at the little group seated in dilapidated wicker chairs around a wicker coffee table with a glass top. The cook, a plump man in his mid-thirties with a friendly but not very smart demeanor, scratched the sparse black hairs under his white chef's hat and drained the remains of his coffee in the geraniums at his side. A cigarette, unlit, hung from the corner of his thick lips.

Putting the cup down, he folded his white hands over his protruding belly, the buttons of his chef's coat tearing at the buttonholes.

"The missus doesn't want to move to Amiens. She has to look after her old mother, who lives with us. It's not that I don't get that." He sounded defeated, lost for options, but Madeleine had discovered enough and leisurely strolled back inside. This was exactly what she had been looking for.

That evening at dinner, she was unusually quiet, and when asked what the matter was, complained of a headache. In reality she was battling fierce emotions that took her back to that other escape, only a week earlier – which now seemed years ago – when she had also left another beloved person, her friend Carolina, in the dark whereto she had vanished. But this time it was even more heart-wrenching because Jacques and Elle were her next of kin; they would be deadly worried about her, and then there was Gerry to consider. What would he do?

She shuddered at the idea he would send out a search party to try to bring her back to Amiens. And there was another aspect that made *this* escape much more gruesome and perilous than the first one. Escaping from a school on the shores of idyllic Lake Geneva in peaceful Switzerland was a whole different ballgame from romping through the fields around Dragoncourt, which was full of enemies, while devising a plan to get inside. It was sheer madness, she knew, but she would forge reality as a blacksmith forges a clump of iron.

"Psst..." Madeleine whispered, when the cook appeared with his bike from the shed at the hotel's back gate. The poor man jumped in the air with fright, but she quickly shushed him. "Don't be alarmed. It's me, Madeleine de Dragoncourt, the Count's daughter. Please, can I ask you something?"

As she was dressed in a dark long cloak, with Loulou wrapped on the inside, and a pair of man's pants, she was hardly visible against the wall overgrown with dark-green ivy, but she took a step towards him so the cook could see her contours in the dim moonlight.

"Mademoiselle," he protested, "you gave me such a shock! What is it? Was the dinner not to your satisfaction? I can't help it, you know

– the ingredients are so inferior these days, and the Count and Countesses don't seem to have much appetite anyway…"

"No, no." She raised her hand to stop his apologies, "Nothing of the sort, dear man! Your food is excellent. I have another favor to ask you."

"But, Mademoiselle, could it not wait until tomorrow morning? It is late and I need to get back home."

"I need to go with you to Blangy-Tronville, cook." She decided to not beat around the bush any longer. She heard him draw in his breath, not knowing how to reply to this sudden revelation. *Damn class distinctions*, she thought grimly. *He can't refuse but feels forced. Well, I don't have a choice either.*

"But Mademoiselle," the cook began again, his voice hesitant, "what do you mean, go to Blangy-Tronville? I have but this one bicycle and only a two-room cottage. My wife…"

"I don't mean go to your house with you. I just mean go to the village. I've got some business to tend to there, but I have no transport. Can I ride along on the back of your bicycle" It's just me and my pet Loulou." Despite the dim light, she could see he looked skeptical and terribly ill at ease.

Before he could reply, she continued, "I'm sorry, but it is rather urgent. I can't tell you more about it, but I promise to be silent during the ride, and as soon as we reach Blangy-Tronville, you will no longer be bothered by me. Only one more thing. Do not tell a soul about this. Understood?"

"Of course… Mademoiselle," he stammered. "Will you… will you be needing a ride back to Amiens tomorrow morning… or the day after?"

"No," she said curtly. "Now shut up and let's go."

Two hours later, she watched the broad, white back of the cook disappear into his tiny roadside cottage with relief and inhaled a guzzle of fresh night air. So far, so good. Eight miles to go albeit without a plan. It was long after midnight, and she was alone with the little monkey under the starlit sky and surrounded by belligerent Boches. No food, nothing to drink. What a party! But in all the uncertainty that enveloped her like her thick cloak, Madeleine knew one thing.

She had to cover most of the distance that separated her from Dragoncourt during the night. The closer she could get there before dawn, the better she would be able to find a hiding place from where she could observe what was going on. So, she retraced her steps towards the Somme, deciding to follow the winding river for another four miles until she reached the western border of her father's estate.

"Thank God, I've always been such an ardent horse rider," she whispered to Loulou, who was fast asleep against her bosom. "At least I know every track and every path around here like the back of my hand. Seems I've been preparing for this job for a long time."

When she saw the surface of the river glint through the foliage, she stepped forwards with more confidence. Not only was there more protection from possible undesired company from the bushes and trees that hung low over the footpath, the faint light of the quarter moon shining on the inky-black water also gave her a degree of light and direction. She felt safer than in the village here, sensing she could trust her instinct syncing with nature on a deeper level and sharpening her senses.

Despite her determination, Madeleine made slow progress as more and more wet soil of the riverbank clung to the soles of her walking shoes and tiredness began to set in. The little monkey even started to feel like a dead weight. She had to concentrate not to stumble and fall. How she missed Paradise, her Arabian mare! She would have given her title or her inheritance to be riding her fast, loyal horse right now, but all the Dragoncourt racehorses had been transported to the Versailles stables in 1914. Nobody rode Paradise or any of the other horses these days, as Antoinette was afraid of horses and her flaccid husband Maurice only ever sat his portly behind on the leather upholstery of his car seat, never in a proper saddle.

Soundlessly humming the refrain of *La Madelon* to herself, she tried to keep her spirits up, imagining she was the fair Madelon herself.

La Madelon pour nous n'est pas sévère
Quand on lui prend la taille ou le menton
Elle rit, c'est tout le mal qu'elle sait faire
Madelon, Madelon, Madelon!

HAD ONE HOUR PASSED? Two? Sometimes a night bird, a tawny owl or a wood pigeon, would suddenly make a rustling flutter to wrestle free from the branches and seconds later skim soundlessly over the river, a dark silhouette, the feathers of its wings stretched wide as a delicate fan. The night was still but for the soft lapping of the water against the banks. Still, Madeleine halted regularly to listen with all her might for other sounds; human sounds. There were none.

As she came further west, the landscape changed and she was forced to leave the seclusion of trees and bushes to enter more open territory – sloping fields that before the war had been rich cornfields and lush meadows but now lay barren despite the fact it was spring. Years of fighting and famine had driven the farmers from their fertile lands to join the army for an income, and their wives and young children were too feeble or too afraid to plant large crops, instead creating small plots of vegetable gardens close to home at the most. And what was left of the livestock had been eaten.

When Madeleine finally discerned the dark contours of Mme Denis's small cottage against the deep purple gray of the approaching dawn, she sighed with relief. She had entered Dragoncourt territory. Home! Her thoughts drifted to the elderly, white-haired Mme Denis, almost toothless and as withered as birch wood in winter and her middle-aged hunched backed son, Patrick. Her father had insisted on taking his children in turn to visit the tenants on his estate, "to get a better understanding of how ordinary people lived," as he had explained.

Madeleine had been ten when Papa had taken her to the Denis family, and although the miniature farmhouse had looked like those in her fairy-tale picture books from the outside, with whitewashed walls, red-tiled roofs, and tiny wooden windows, she had been appalled by the primitive circumstances in which mother and son lived: in two tiny rooms and a small kitchen, earthen floors everywhere, and no sanitary provisions. Yet the old widow had been ever so generous and seemingly content with her little house. Madeleine had had to force herself not to pinch her nose when offered a cup of the lukewarm milk that came straight from Mme Denis's cow, and very unladylike had burped afterwards in her lace-gloved hand.

The homestead was still shrouded in darkness, either due to the blackout in front of the tiny windows or because the inhabitants were still asleep. Yet, exhausted as she was and with no clear idea how to proceed further, eerily exposed in this open terrain with day fast approaching, Madeleine set foot towards the farmhouse. Maybe, just maybe, she would knock on the door and see what happened. Loulou stirred, intuitively waking up to the dawn and the prospect of something to eat.

Something whizzed through the air, and then there was a sharp, cutting pain that cracked her head open, hard and merciless. The shock was so sudden that her lungs could no longer draw in air, and she toppled headlong, tripping over her own cloak to land face down in the tall, wet grass. Loulou shrieked and escaped from underneath her. It momentarily became black before Madeleine's eyes, and she fought not to lose consciousness.

She was struggling with all her might to turn around to see what had hit her, but she could not move. Then she heard a male voice hovering above her, and instinctively she lay very still, feeling her warm blood trickle down the side of her head, then alongside her neck. The back of her head throbbed with intense pain and was so overwhelming she almost vomited.

"*Verdammt noch mal! Es ist eine Frau. Nicht die elender Verräter Denis.*"

Another voice replied hurriedly, "*Lass uns gehen.*"

Madeleine understood German and anxiously hoped the men would indeed disappear and let her be, at the same time wondering why these men thought that either Mme Denis or her invalid son were traitors. Even in her agonized state, that seemed a preposterous thought, but her bruised brain could no longer think coherently, so she gave up trying to concentrate on understanding anything. The excruciating headache and the fear that the Germans would return to finish what they had started kept her where she was, lying helplessly in the grass and feeling her whole body go limp and prostrate in the cold grass.

With great difficulty, she lifted one arm and tentatively felt the back of her head, but drew her fingers back immediately. In the tangle of her hair she felt a gaping wound. The shock of it was so great that she wanted to scream out, but her voice failed her. She knew this was a serious injury and that she needed help – and soon. If she stayed where she was, she would most likely die, the wound being that deep. With all her might, she dragged herself on hands and shaking knees and managed to utter a thin wheezing "Help!" To no avail.

She sat up in the grass, her upper body swaying, and retched. The remains of last night's dinner rose in her throat and landed next to her, half on her cloak, half on the grass. The turning of her stomach aggravated the pain in her head to a pounding hell, and tears streamed down her cheeks. *I have to get to Mme Denis* was the only thought that kept her sane, and again she turned on hands and knees and started crawling towards the farmhouse with no idea how far in the distance it lay.

Vaguely she remembered she had been with someone, but who was it? Swallowing the foul taste in her mouth and ignoring the blood that dripped down the sides on her face onto her hands, Madeleine moved forward at a snail's pace, regularly sinking down and resting because she felt too weak to go on. The sun was just about to rise above the horizon when she could go on no further. She fainted, accepting oblivion with a shallow sigh. Sleep was merciful.

"MADEMOISELLE MADELEINE, RÉVEILLEZ-VOUS!"

The gentle voice came from far away, singsong, light as a breeze, while she was lying in a garden full of summer flowers. She stirred on the mossy ground, her body exquisitely languid and relaxed. She did not want to open her eyelids, but the voice floated back to her: "*Réveillez-vous, s'il vous* plaît!" Wake up! But she was awake; how silly was it to ask her to wake up. Was it Mummy calling her? No, Mummy spoke mostly English and sometimes French with a strong accent, not this singsong dialect that was so soothing, soft as the feathers of a baby bird. Something wet was pressing against her mouth and she breathed, "Fie, Paradise, you know you're not allowed in the gardens, you silly horse."

"*Elle parle!* She's talking!"

Madeleine frowned. A male voice? Was it one of the stable boys coming to fetch Paradise from the lawn?

"She's a naughty horse," Madeleine told the boy, "but I love her!"

Now something was put in between her lips, and she wanted to blow it away, but it was pressed down, and water dribbled through the tube into her mouth and made her swallow. She wanted to see what was going on and squinted, but immediately closed her eyes again as the light, though shaded, hurt as if an electric bolt had flashed to the back of her eyeballs.

The pain in her skull hit her anew, sharp like a hammer clanging on a red-hot anvil, and then she remembered it all: the blow to her head, the Germans, and the crawling through wet grass, injured and desperate. Her hands went to her face and she felt around tentatively, realizing it was bandaged completely but for the slit for her eyes, mouth, and nose. Her hands fell back on the covers, shaking.

"It is me, Marie Denis," the gentle voice said next to her. "You're safe here, Mademoiselle Madeleine. I've dressed your wound. You'll be okay."

She felt a hand put softly against the outside of the bandage on her cheek and wanted to lean into it, but the coarse material made real touch impossible.

The voice continued, "I suppose that little monkey is yours? Your Papa always said you kept the most peculiar pets. Well, the dear little thing has saved your life. Made a racket on our doorstep until we woke up and would not stop screaming until Patrick went out to have a look. She led him straight to where you were lying unconscious in the grass."

"Am I really here with you, Madame Denis?" Madeleine's voice was a raspy whisper, hardly audible, and although she turned her head slightly towards the kind, singsong voice, she kept her eyes tightly closed. "And is Loulou alive as well?"

"Yes, yes," Mme Denis affirmed. "The little dear has already had a slice of bread with strawberry jam. Poor thing was famished and numb with cold. I put her next to the fire, where she's dozing now."

"Maman, I'm going outside to see if I can find evidence of how Mademoiselle got injured."

Madeleine now understood that the male voice was Patrick's. She raised a hand to stop him. "Wait, Patrick. I know what happened. I was mistakenly attacked by two Germans. They thought I was you. I heard them say they were looking for you, but when they saw I was a woman they quickly ran away. I didn't see their faces because it was still dark, and they ambushed me from behind."

"*Mon Dieu*," Mme Denis swore under her breath. "Why would they want to attack you, Patrick?"

"Never mind, *Maman*," he answered hastily, "you don't have to worry about it." Madeleine heard Mme Denis grumble some more about those ghastly Boches needing to bugger off to their Heimat before she said in her kindly voice, "I'm going to make you a light breakfast, my dear, and then you're going to sleep for as long as you need. When you wake again, you can tell me why you were traipsing around here in the middle of the night. Last thing I heard about you was that you were safely tucked away in neutral Switzerland, so my old head is in a spin what this is all about."

11

THE MASTER PLAN

Madeleine stayed with the Denis family for more than a week. Every day she expected one of her family members to knock on the door and drag her back to Amiens, but nothing of the sort happened. They would be out of their minds with worry, there was no doubt about it, but Madeleine told herself she had no time to think of that now. She could only imagine how delighted they eventually would be if her mission succeeded. Until then, they would just have to learn to live with their worries.

Quickly getting stronger on Marie Denis's nutritious soups and stews while her head wound healed and the calm, uneventful days in the small cottage unruffled her frayed nerves, Madeleine was actually enjoying a lull in both her personal and the bigger war. In reply to Mme Denis's probing questions, she remained vague about her presence in the fields near their house – not completely untruthful, as she was still pondering how to enter Château de Dragoncourt without drawing attention to herself.

Marie Denis turned out to be a lively and clever old lady with a ready tongue and a wise, practical approach to life. She nursed Madeleine not only back to health but made the rather spoilt daughter of Count Horace make good use of her surplus of energy by letting her do all sorts of physical chores, such as milking the cow, fetching buckets of water from the well, and digging over the kitchen garden to prepare the soil for sowing lettuce and radish.

Madeleine loved all this stomping about in her oversized-male pants and sturdy shoes, being in the fresh air from dawn till dusk. There was nothing more rewarding in the evenings than stretching out her stockinged feet contentedly towards the fireplace, her tired muscles relaxing from the arduous labor, and sipping Mme Denis's home-made brandy while nibbling on a macaron.

For the first time since the beginning of the war, Madeleine felt thoroughly alive, the more because she was deeply grateful to still *be* alive and having escaped the stifling, depressed atmosphere in Hotel L'Europe together with Loulou. In the aftermath of the attack, Loulou behaved frightened and jittery but soon gained confidence in the wake of her mistress's recovery and started to follow Madeleine everywhere, making her glottal *hoe-hoe-hoe* sounds to show her happiness, while the dark, round eyes shone with mischief.

Mme Denis's chicken coop, in particular, seemed to delight the little ape; she could not get enough of peeking her little black head around the wire netting of the hen house just to see the brown laying hens scatter in all directions, cackling wildly ending in long-drawn squawks. To Loulou this was a fascinating game of peekaboo, and she even attempted to mimic the chuckling of the hens while grinning to herself.

If Madeleine caught her scaring the chickens, she scolded her firmly, "Loulou, no! The poor hens won't lay eggs anymore if you frighten them, so stop it."

It would work for a little while until Loulou found another source of mischief, such as snacking on the winter carrots she dug up from the garden or staring too deeply at her own reflection in the drinking bowl for the cows and toppling in, screaming out and splashing wildly to get back on dry land. For both Madeleine and Loulou, life at the Denis farm was a welcome interruption from the war, no matter how close the ugly beast continued to growl and roar.

The only thing that kept annoying Madeleine was that the Denis homestead – like the rest of the Dragoncourt estate – was under German occupation. It not only meant defeat – more practically, it meant staying close to house and barn all day and making sure to be inside when the chickens went to roost, apply the blackout, and use the bucket in the kitchen instead of the outdoor toilet when curfew applied. It also meant being on the alert all the time, keeping an eye out for patrolling German guards, and staying out of their sight whenever she heard the rumble of their motorcycles on the dirt roads that led to the scattered homesteads on the Dragoncourt lands.

The Germans were not averse to coming to the farms to collect eggs, vegetables, and milk, and even sometimes live poultry and cattle for their own use, their harsh, guttural voices commanding in a strange gibberish of French and German.

"*Gib mal... donnez zes oeufs, Kartoffeln! Vite! Voulons essen maintenant. Hunger!*" And off they would ride with their saddle sacks full, sometimes even towing a cow or sheep behind a wagon piled with confiscated food. It was a disheartening and cruel sight, as the Picardy people themselves could hardly make ends meet, but refusing such an order was usually answered with a cold, calculated shot between the eyes so nobody dared to refuse.

The Krauts had also knocked on Mme Denis's door that week to order fresh meat, and Madeleine had seen, from the top of the haystack where she was hiding with her hand over Loulou's mouth to prevent the little primate from making but the faintest noise, how the family's last goat had been stolen. The poor beast had been roughly dragged away, bleating and struggling against her captors, while Mme Denis stood forlorn next to the empty goat pen, her knotted fingers clamped over her mouth and her eyes moist but with her back straight. Madeleine had felt her own body go rigid with rage and resentment, and she had clenched her teeth not to shout some stiff German expletives but had instead cursed them under her breath. "*Abschaum! Drecksack! Scheisskerl!* Scum of the earth!"

She knew she could not risk being recognized by her attackers and was glad Patrick was not at home either, as there was always that ringing in her ears of Patrick being labeled a traitor.

She had not had the opportunity to ask Mme Denis's middle-aged son why the Germans would be looking for him and why they would attempt to kill an invalid. She was eager to get hold of him alone and confront him with this strange predicament, but he never showed himself during the day, staying hidden in the barn where she had the idea that he slept during the day in a straw bed behind a wooden partition. He only showed up in the house at dinner time, when his mother was also present, and Madeleine did not want to upset the kind old woman by asking unsettling questions.

It was unclear to her why Patrick stayed away during the day and why he left the kitchen again immediately after dinner, going God knows where. Despite many protests, Madeleine had been given Patrick's box bed in a corner of the living room, after which he had moved out. Both mother and son had insisted that the arrangements stay as they were. It made her feel guilty, but there was nothing she could do except find a way of talking to him some time soon.

Madeleine had seen how Mme Denis gave her son worried, side-long glances when he was bent over his plate with potato soup and how she sighed noiselessly, but she never referred to his personal whereabouts. They would talk of crops to plant or the affairs of other tenants, sometimes the weather; but the war and their own situation was not a topic of conversation. Because Madeleine could not piece together why invalid, introverted Patrick would be a German target, she had begun to wonder if she had misheard the German attackers due to the debilitating blow on her head.

But suddenly, unexpectedly, her much-sought-after opportunity arose. One Sunday morning, a week after Madeleine's arrival, Mme Denis, who was also something of a local herbalist, had been summoned to the LeMaître family, who lived a few kilometers away, to see to one of their children who had caught chickenpox.

"I'll be back in time to make lunch," the frail, white-haired lady announced, pulling her crocheted black stole tight around her shoulders and putting her wicker basket, filled with lemon balm and St.

John's wort and a pot of strawberry jam, decisively on her arm. "Can you peel the potatoes and salt the chicken, Miss Madeleine? And don't you dare escape while I'm gone, little lady!" She wagged her gnarled finger at Madeleine and grinned, showing the remains of two brown tooth stubs in her lower jaw.

"I won't. I promise." Madeleine grinned back, inwardly excited at the idea she finally might be able to interrogate Patrick, who had surprisingly stayed indoors for the Sunday morning. Expecting him to evade her as soon as his mother was gone, Madeleine was bracing herself to bar the door to demand an explanation from him. But this was unnecessary because to her surprise Patrick stayed leisurely in the kitchen and even poured himself another cup of coffee from the softly gurgling percolator. He sat down at the simple wooden table and lit a Gitane Maïs. Had he been looking for an opportunity to talk to her alone as well?

Through her eyelashes, Madeleine studied him while busying herself with peeling an oversized potato and cutting it, letting the pieces plop into a water-filled cooking pot. She observed that Patrick Denis was actually not an unattractive man despite the misshapen back, the huge bulge between his shoulder blades that forced his bent spine to push his head forward in a strange, birdlike way. His belly also protruded because his ribs were pointing downwards instead of being straight.

On closer inspection, only his torso was deformed; his arms and legs were normally shaped, and he had a kind, almost delicate face, very like his mother's, albeit with black hair and a stubbly beard, but with the same friendly fowl-brown eyes with thick black eyelashes, a firm mouth, and a well-proportioned Gallic nose. Not a person to be afraid of, or someone harboring criminal intentions.

"I guess you want to know why the Germans are looking for me."

Aha, just as well! He was not going to beat around the bush. Madeleine stopped her manual tasks at the sink, nodded, and putting down the potato peeler and half-peeled Agata potato, dried her hands on her borrowed apron and moved to the table. She sat down opposite him, her hands folded in her lap, and looked straight at him.

He hesitated, his dark lashes blinking as he sat brooding, but then he cleared his throat and after taking another long drag on his yellow cigarette, he said slowly but deliberately, "Your father, Count Horace, has always been very kind to me, when other people – old and young – shunned me or bullied me. He would come here and talk to my mother and me about my father, whom I never really knew as he died when I was only a year old. Your father would say that my father was the best tenant he'd ever had and that as young men, they would occasionally go fishing together or shoot pheasants. It was always very pleasant when he came to pay us a visit. Maman and I would talk about it for days."

Patrick smiled at the memory. "Anyway, did you know that your father sent Master Jacques' personal tutor over here to teach me to read and write?"

Madeleine shook her head but did not want to interrupt the flow of his story by saying something herself. She was mesmerized.

"I could have gone to the school in the village, of course, but I was so sensitive to the people always staring at me and saying ugly things that I begged Maman to keep me at home. One day your father asked me if I was ill, because I wasn't at school, and then in her honesty Maman told him that I never went to school. He was dismayed, protesting that I was much too bright not to learn the things other children learn in the classroom, so that's when he suggested that Master Jacques' tutor could teach me three afternoons per week, and that he would pay for the expense as a tribute to my deceased father. Count Horace is such a kind and thoughtful man. But of course, you know that yourself."

Madeleine nodded, glad about the praise for her father but wanting him to hurry up with his long-winded story.

"Because of what your father has done for me, I'm devoted to him for the rest of my life and would do anything in my power to protect him and his family. But what could a poor sod like me do? I can't fight as a soldier, and I can't work in a factory. Yet I didn't want to just sit around and idle away while the Germans destroy our beautiful

France, certainly now they've come to capture Château de Drag-oncourt.

"Anyway, through the grapevine, I heard that Martin Jules, the registrar clerk in Blangy-Tronville, was a staunch anti-German and that he was looking for men willing to sabotage enemy provisions or spy on them. I didn't think he'd be interested in me, you know, because of my humped back, but Martin said that not all the obstructing they undertake involves man-to-man fights. They need scouts, too. To make a long story short, the Boches found out about Martin's small anti-German cell – someone in Blangy-Tronville must have blabbed. He was arrested last week, and knowing how inhu-mane these brutes are, they probably tortured him, and he might have given away other names, although I doubt it because Martin's a bloody decent and courageous man."

Madeleine could not help interjecting. "But why are you sitting here right now, Patrick? You're not safe. They could barge in any minute and arrest you too."

"They could," Patrick observed calmly, "but they won't."

"Why not?" Madeleine was puzzled.

"Because your father made a special stipulation for me that I cannot work or fight in this war and should be left here at the farm at all times to help my mother. Your father has given me his legal protection, and since he's the French ambassador in London and knows not only the French government but also the Kaiser – diplomat as he is – they will refrain from arresting me openly. But they can try to kill me in a so-called accident, and that's what they were trying to do when they attacked you by mistake."

Madeleine looked incredulous. She could not believe that the power of her father's arm reached that far, certainly in these times of war and when even his own castle was sieged; but Patrick seemed to believe it, and maybe he *was* right, what did she know?

"So, what do you do?" she asked. "I mean, how do you obstruct the Germans?" She liked the idea and already imagined herself joining this movement.

"Not much," Patrick sighed. "I go to Blangy-Tronville late at night, always via a different route. We are three now – Blaise and André and me. We meet in the wine cellar underneath Le Bistro, where we just sit together and discuss plans. We're really at a loss right now because Martin was the one who had the contacts with the Allies; he gave the orders, told us what... uh... we were supposed to do. Blaise and André would carry out the more dangerous stuff, and I would be standing on watch. My sign for danger is the hoot of a night owl, which I learned as a kid: two short, deep *hoo* sounds followed by a long *hooooooo*. It's fortunate that I have very good sight and hearing, despite... you know..." He gestured to his infirmity, a grim yet apologetic expression on his face.

Raising one hunched shoulder, he added sorrowfully, "We're really very worried about Martin Jules. We have no idea where the Krauts took him. We went to his house, but his wife didn't answer the door. So, since his arrest, we've been at a bit of a loss as how to proceed with our... um... actions, now that we no longer have our contact person. Feels weird. Bloody useless." He fell silent and lit another cigarette.

"Can I have one?" Madeleine asked, pointing to the blue packet.

"Of course," he said, shoving the cigarette packet over the table in her direction. "Help yourself."

"So, what now?" Madeleine asked, trying not to cough as the distinctive, hearty flavor of the Gitane hit her lungs. She much preferred her lighter Lucky Strikes but had run out of them.

Patrick shrugged his one shoulder again. "There's little we *can* do."

"Do you know how we got from Dragoncourt to Amiens last week?" Her voice was as casual as if suggesting a slice of cake with their coffee, while she stubbed out the yellow stump with a concentrated frown between her dark brows. She stared fixedly at the smoldering stalk, standing straight among the smaller stubs and ashes in the ashtray. Invisibly she held her breath. This was her chance. At last.

"What do you mean, got from Dragoncourt to Amiens?"

From his puzzled tone, it was clear he did not understand

what she was talking about. Still not looking back at him, she explained, "There's an eight-mile tunnel that runs from Dragoncourt's cellar to Blangy-Tronville. That's how we got out. It was supposed to be like a dress rehearsal in case the Germans suddenly turned up at Dragoncourt, but we were betrayed, and they invaded the castle while we were in the tunnel and locked the door from the inside. That's why we can't go back. My brother and sister and most of the English garrison are biding their time in Amiens now with not really any perspective. We don't know how long these Krauts will stay at Dragoncourt. A month, a year, a decade?" She sounded bitter but glancing up, she saw she had his complete attention.

"Interesting," Patrick observed. "I didn't know anything about that tunnel. Pity the Germans know it too, though."

Madeleine observed his reaction minutely, gauging if she could trust him with her own secret, and decided she had no other alternative but to involve this man in her plans.

"I don't think we've met by accident," she declared slowly. "I need your help." She folded her hands back in her lap.

He whistled through his teeth. "What are you getting at, Mademoiselle Madeleine?"

"Can you get me a German uniform, not too large?"

It was silent at the other side of the table. The percolator gurgled softly on the stove, and outside, the last Denis sheep bleated loudly, mourning her miserable state. Loulou awoke from her nap near the fireplace and, stretching and yawning, jumped on Madeleine's shoulder, where she coquettishly fanned out her little pink dress over her small thighs before starting to scratch her cheek with long black nails.

Madeleine wondered if Patrick would reply at all, and she was beginning to give up hope when he finally said softly, "If you tell me what for. I can't have you endanger yourself in any way. I would not be able to ever see eye to eye with your father again if something happened to you."

Madeleine hesitated. He was right, of course: *if* something happened to her and her father found out Patrick had been involved, the poor man would be scorned for life, if not worse.

"All right," she said, "I'll tell you my plan. But after that, you have to promise me you'll help me. It's my decision, and mine only. Papa will never be involved in it."

Patrick listened to her intently as she explained, and she saw his admiration for her rise with every sentence she spoke.

"By God, Mademoiselle Madeleine, you're an asset to the Resistance. I'd never in a thousand years have thought you could pull this off, but it's a magnificent plan! My comrades and I will be honored to help you. Welcome to the movement!"

Madeleine's heart swelled with pride. "I won't disappoint you!"

SHE FELT MORTALLY uncomfortable in her Prussian infantry uniform, the stiff *feldgrau* tunic buttoned tightly over her bust and a pair of wide-legged trousers in the same color and rough texture. Although the long johns she was wearing underneath were grubby and hung loose, she was rather glad to have those, as the fabric of the outer garment was so coarse and itchy it made her tender skin sore. The trousers were way too wide at her waist, so she had downsized them with the help of some safety pins. On the outside, a brass and silver belt buckle helped hold the whole ensemble together.

Her thick hair had been cut short like a boy's and she wore a regular *feldmütze,* with a canvas camouflage strip on her cropped head. She sported a fake mustache above her full lips and her eyebrows had been darkened with charcoal. On her feet were a pair of laced-up ankle boots at least two sizes too big, filled up with wads of newspaper, while puttees were bound around her calves and shins.

She had to bolster her confidence to pick up the long bayonet, thankfully in its leather holster, the trench dagger and the gasmask in an airtight metal tin. As this was all part of the guise, she had no choice but to lug them along, although she had no intention of using them. Or would she? The ribbon pinned onto her tunic was the

Prussian *Eiserne Kreuz II Klasse*, and her ID stated she was *Gefreiter* Ernst Höbel of the 4th West-Prussian Infantry.

It was a black, starless night, with the sky overcast with thick rain clouds. Madeleine descended the stone steps to the wine cellar at the back of Le Bistro in Blangy-Tronville and sat down uncomfortably on a wooden crate. Her heels had already blistered in the oversized boots, and she was jerky and nervous.

Impatiently waiting for Patrick and his comrades, who had gone out to explore the best route along which to approach Dragoncourt, she lit a cigarette and poured herself a generous glass of brandy from the bottle that stood on the ramshackle table in the middle of the crates that served as stools. Not finding a clean glass, she hopped up and poured the liquor into one of the empty jam jars that stood on a shelf along the wall.

It was not that she was terribly afraid of what lay before her – she tried to block all thoughts and feelings thereof – what gnawed at her was that she was wearing the uniform of a recently killed man, an unknown man who had been lynched by Blaise the night before. It felt uncomfortable, to say the least, to be clad in a dead man's outfit, a man who had been specifically killed for her. But taking another stiff swig from the jar, she also blocked that ghastly thought. It was his death or hers; simple as that. No regrets. War was supposed to make one hard as nails.

"Watch out, you Boches! What you did, you despicable *Abschaum*, I can do better!" She said it aloud to boost her morale, clenching her fist and raising it defiantly.

But the stark reality was that she felt ridiculously small and alone, facing an almost insurmountable task ahead. Would she succeed? So far she had been helped along by Patrick, Blaise, and André, but soon she would be completely on her own, in enemy territory wearing enemy clothes and having to navigate by her own instincts while staying alert as she had never done before in her life. If Patrick had not acquiesced to her plan, she would not be sitting here like this, dressed up as one fictitious Ernst Höbel; at least not this fast.

For Madeleine, his help had come just in time, restless and testy as she had been, having left Hotel l'Europe almost two weeks earlier while her family most likely was incredibly worried about her and her still no closer to Dragoncourt. But now the moment of her approach had arrived, she felt weak in her stomach. The strong liquor made her simultaneously nauseous and want to drink more.

How had this come about that she, Madeleine Liliane Virginia de Dragoncourt, big-idea-thinker, the bold *je ne sais quoi* Benjamin of the family, was to rescue the entire Dragoncourt clan from the precipice? All she was and all she would ever be lay encapsulated in this endeavor, where it presently hung suspended in mid-air, like a rope between two mountain ridges and she the tightrope dancer. She suddenly thought of Gerry, his freckled, handsome face angrily reprimanding her, a mixture of concern and admiration in his all-seeing gaze. *You leave military matters to military men!* She gently shook her head, a shadow of a smile under her fake mustache.

"I'm doing this for you too, Gerry, and for Elle and Jacques. I hope you will see that. If I'm to survive this." Then she thought of Loulou, who had been left with Mme Denis with the excuse she had an errand to take care of. As if that was plausible in the middle of the night! First, Madeleine had wanted to take the little monkey with her, since Loulou was after all her lucky mascot, but the risk of attracting attention as an ordinary soldier with a monkey on her shoulder was too great. Ernst Höbel kept a low profile.

Madeleine roused herself from her musings when she heard Patrick's sign, the hooting of the night owl, and she got up, stretched stiffly in the awkward uniform, and slowly went up the stone steps, her boots dragging and her weaponry clattering against her thighs.

The three men were dressed entirely in black, their heads covered with balaclavas, all of them armed with knives and rifles. She could only recognize them by their postures: the bent, misshapen Patrick, the short, stubby Blaise, and the slightly taller and slimmer André. They looked like sinister ghosts with eyes gleaming through small slits, their personalities like their disguise covered in a somber, ominous silence. Their anonymous appearance was more unnerving to Madeleine than she dared to admit. They could have been anyone, friend of foe, there on *her* side or to kill her.

"Are you ready?" It was the form of Patrick addressing her in whispered tones, and when she nodded, he added, "Take the straightest route you know from here to the castle. We'll accompany you until you reach the beginning of Dragoncourt's main driveway. You won't see us, but we'll be there to" – he hesitated a moment – "you know, to intervene if necessary. Until you come to the driveway, draw as little attention to yourself as you can. Move stealthily, stay low, don't make unnecessary sounds. When you're on the driveway, change your attitude, walk leisurely, saunter – so to say – without a care in the world towards the Château and visibly light a cigarette. We'll take the light of your cigarette as a sign you're among your so-called fellow compatriots, and then we'll leave. I'll give one more night owl hoot. You make sure to act jovially and nonchalant, but do not enter conversation with the guards unless you can't avoid it. Just do your thing, quick and dirty."

She saw Patrick's dark eyes from behind the black cover staring into hers. "From that point, it's up to you, Mademoiselle Madeleine. We wish you all the luck in the world. And do send word to us when... if... you get back to Blangy-Tronville or Amiens in one piece."

Madeleine swallowed hard; her voice caught in her throat when she finally managed to speak out. "Thank you, Patrick, I will. And thank you Blaise and André... uh... for everything. I won't forget."

"One more thing," Patrick uttered. "Maman knows. Of course, she disagrees ardently with your foolhardiness – her words, not mine." She saw the half-grin behind his balaclava. "She wants to let you know she'll look after Loulou for as long as needed; she said that with all the livestock the Germans have recently stolen from us, she's happy to have an animal they'll most likely find too rubbery to chew on."

With those last words, the four dispersed and Madeleine directed her feet... home. Though the sounds of the night startled her a few times, she could retrace them all to animals: a night bird taking off, a hedgehog scurrying away, a fox rustling in the tall grass. No human sounds could be detected, no matter how she strained her ears to get some form of evidence that the three men following her were close by. They must have learned to move quietly as statues, prepared yet invisible. It was eerie, but the simple fact she knew that they were by her side propelled her forward.

The sky was dark with rain clouds – no moon, no stars – and when she had almost covered half of the distance, it started to rain, first softly and then more incessantly.

"Oh, my luck," she muttered to herself. Now she had to walk even more carefully in her sagging boots as the undergrowth became slippery with wet mud. She was also very aware of the noises she was making – the sucking soles at every step, the clanging of bayonet against the case of her gas mask. At some point she was sure she could even hear her own breathing as it became more laborious the more tired and soaked-through she became. She drew the cap deeper over her forehead to keep the charcoal eyebrows from smearing, and gingerly felt the mustache to see if it was still glued in place.

There was no telling what time it was but as they had set out past midnight, she guessed it was about three in the morning when she finally saw the contours of the stately walls and the many turrets of Château de Dragoncourt loom up through the drizzle, as the rain had lessened. The castle stood tall and majestic among the sloping hills, the outstretched wings as arms that wanted to embrace her.

Her heart started to beat more rapidly in her chest; her home was intact, not burnt down or bombarded into a ruin. For some reason, she had half expected to chance upon a big heap of rubble instead of the home she had left, frightened as she had been to be the witness of the end of everything. Madeleine revived as the contours of her beloved Château came closer, but she realized it also meant she was soon having to say goodbye to her stealthy companions.

"I can do this," she encouraged herself. "This place is nobody's but the de Dragoncourts'. I've come to show who the real master is and who are the ones who have no business being there!"

It was noticeably quiet around the castle; she had still not seen any soldiers or guards, but all her senses were heightened. Finally, the driveway came in sight, and she saw the first trucks and cars with German license plates parked along the gravel path with its unclipped box-trees. She pulled the packet of Lucky Strikes from her pocket. Her hands, cold and wet, trembled as she struck a match, and she had to make another attempt before she succeeded.

Not knowing where her helpers were, she stood still and slowly turned to all four sides while she took deep drags on her cigarette, her boots crunching on the gravel. The cigarette steadied her nerves; the taste was delicious although the hot smoke burned in her lungs. There it was: *Hoo-Hoo-Hoooooooo.* She felt an urge to salute, not knowing where that came from.

"Time to shine, Ernst Höbel," she said through her teeth, and walked decisively up the lane towards the big entrance doors. Only two guards were standing outside on each side of the oak doors that were firmly closed.

Confidently she ascended the steps and said in a deep baritone voice in perfect German, "*Machen Sie auf, bitte!* Open up, please! I have an urgent message from the hospital in Roye for the doctor here."

"*Papiere, bitte!*" Madeleine flicked her cigarette away with a practiced movement of thumb and forefinger and fished her ID from her wet tunic pocket.

One of the guards yawned and stamped from one foot to the other while the other, an unhealthy looking man with a tired expression, grabbed her papers and glanced at them under the electric lamp that hung over the door.

Handing them back to her, he said rather irritably, "The doctors are asleep right now, but you can go to the canteen to dry yourself and get something to drink. They'll get up in an hour or so. Corporal Hansen will show you the way."

And with that Madeleine was inside, following the guard who was still yawning loudly and staggering like a sleepwalker. They had not even asked how she had gotten from Roye to Dragoncourt, who she was, or what message she had to deliver. Round one was for her!

The canteen was quiet and empty. The Germans apparently felt no outside threat right now so no need to be on guard against assaults. This was what Madeleine had been hoping for; that they were still lingering in their victorious mood considered themselves unbeatable, unchallenged. Strike the iron when it's hot.

She turned to the corporal who was resting his back against the wall, half asleep. "Where can I find a drink?" she asked in friendly but decisive manner.

"What do you want?"

"Schnapps, what else?" It was curt; to the point.

The guard pointed to a mahogany cupboard with a broken glass-paneled door that had been shoved roughly against a corner wall, and Madeleine marched straight towards it, stretched out her arm through the broken glass to grab the bottle, popped off the cork with her teeth, and tipping the bottle to her lips, drank thirstily. Then she burped.

The guard shrugged, and with an "I'll come back for you at five 'o clock when the doctor is awake," turned on his heels and with that same trance-like gait left the canteen.

Madeleine sank onto one of the hard wooden chairs and eyed the space around her.

It was a large square room, barely furnished now but for an assortment of mismatched chairs and tables strewn about. In front of the large windows, which had supplanted the small, fortress-like pigeonholes her father had set out to replace with such candor wher-ever architectonic values mattered less, hung floor-to-ceiling, deep-green velvet drapes, a sure touch of her mother Lady Virginia. They looked moldy and dust-ridden now, but their lush, heavy folds were still a cry to happier times when this grimy atmosphere of neglect and the ravages of war had seemed unthinkable to twentieth century civilization.

She recognized the room as one of her father's reception rooms, not a room she had often been in, but she still vividly remembered her Papa standing in it in his expensive, tailored suit, white "chemise", and silk cravat, tall, straight-backed, dark-haired like Jacques, with hands clasped at his back, the fingers of one hand playing with the signet ring on the other. She had watched him closely, conversing amicably with an array of foreign ambassadors and ministers of all plumage, fluidly changing from this language to that, looking alternatingly serious when he had to drive a hard bargain and relaxed and cheerful when his diplomacy had worked.

All her life, she had been the keyhole watcher of this impeccable behavior that could crack the hardest deal. She hoped desperately she was cut from the same cloth, but how she missed her strong, righteous Papa at this moment! What would he make of his little girl if he saw her now, prancing about his own centerpiece in a dead man's German uniform, drinking schnapps from a bottle, inwardly shivering from damp clothes and fear, but set on turning this whole bloody war machine one hundred and eighty degrees? Would he be proud of her, or declare her mad? Both, possibly.

"At least I have your courage, Papa," she whispered to his oil portrait that hung over the mantelpiece, showing some bullet holes in his distinguished face and scarlet coat. "Please, let me succeed. And forgive Patrick. He adores you, as do I!"

At that moment, the door was brusquely pushed open, and the most fair-haired and white-skinned man Madeleine had ever seen in her life strode in. He had laser-blue eyes and a long, straight nose over a mustache that made her own modest one shrivel in comparison. He was wearing an impressive uniform, hung heavily with a row of medals neatly aligned, and boots that shone and creaked as if they had just come from of the shop.

She instantly understood that this was the man responsible for the degradation of her family's estate, and she straightened her back and gazed frankly up at him, amber cat eyes meeting cold fisheyes.

"*Korporal* Höbel!" He clicked his boots, and despite her tense body and heightened awareness, she had difficulty not to snigger. *You bet!*

He continued in his snappish German, "*Du kommst von General Von Spitzenburg in Roye*? What brings you here?"

Thank you, Madeleine thought, *for giving me the right name in my mouth*. Aloud she said, also clicking her boots and saluting with the tips of her fingers tightly together against her *feldmütze*, "*Es freut*

General Von Spitzenburg Ihnen die besten Wünsche zu übermitteln." Well, if that did not sound posh, what would?

But this general, who had not had the decency to introduce himself to her by name, although he was standing on *her* carpet, was not that easily tricked.

"Was bringt dich hierher!" It was a command, not a question.

"Aha," Madeleine said, smiling wryly, and remembering all her father's lessons, and added in a friendly yet resolute voice, "Could you please tell me, sir, whom I have the honor of talking with? General Von Spitzenburg has given me the strictest instructions to only disclose my message to the commander in charge here or to the Dragoncourt medical staff."

The German general eyed her as if he wanted to skin her alive, and Madeleine felt her knees become wobbly in their stiff trousers. He kept staring at her for a long moment, not at all in a friendly manner, and then very studiously sat down on the chair Madeleine had abandoned only moments earlier.

"Ich bin Major-General Eberhard Graf von Spiegler, the Prussian commander of the 17th Imperial German Army, as I am sure General Von Spitzenburg has informed you."

The disdain in his voice would have been laughable had this man not held such extreme power over her. She was aware how easily she could lose the cards she had been dealt to this high representative of the race she despised, but she could and would bluff, poker face and all.

"Pleased to meet you, Graf Von Spiegler." She nodded, knowing how intensely she was offending him by not using his military title. "Then it was you that General Von Spitzenburg extended his good wishes to."

"Enough!" he barked. "Show your manners, Corporal! How long have you served under Von Spitzenburg to still be such an ignoramus?"

Madeleine adopted a correct servile expression on her mustached face and with head bent to the carpet, replied,

"Only four months, *Herr General.*"

"And now answer me: what message do you bring?"

"It's a verbal message, *Herr General*. The telephone line seems to have been disrupted yesterday evening, so there was no communication possible between the hospitals. The doctors in the field hospital in Roye are in need of an X-ray machine, and they were told there are two such machines here at Dragoncourt, so they wondered whether they could borrow one."

"And you want me to believe one word of that gibberish?" It was shouted so loudly that Madeleine startled and jumped back.

"It's true," she whispered. "Why would it not be?"

"Well, for one thing," General Von Spiegler now spoke very slowly, articulating every syllable in an exaggerated way, "how did it come that you arrived here in the middle of the night, you good-for-nothing? Did you decide to visit a brothel first, or take a detour to enjoy the countryside?" He laughed a joyless, snickering smile.

Madeleine thought fast and responded in a polite manner that demonstrated *she* would not stoop to his level of conversing.

"*Herr General*, you are right. Let me apologize for my tardiness. It is entirely my fault. I volunteered to make the trip from Roye to Dragoncourt because the rest of my battalion was celebrating the birthday of one of our men. So, I set out on a borrowed bicycle around ten in the evening, as I am still too young to drive or ride a motorized vehicle. However, when I had covered about half of the twenty-five kilometers, I incidentally got a flat tire and was greatly incapacitated as a result. It had meanwhile also started to rain, which explains the wetness of my attire, for which I also apologize, but I assure you that I walked the rest of the distance as fas..."

"Halt!" Von Spiegler cried in uncontrolled rage, the white skin on his neck above his *feldgrau* tunic turning to a blotchy red, while the medals on his chest clanked against each other as he sprang up from his chair. "What do you take me for, you babbling idiot? You may have a ready mouth, but you're a disgrace to the Kaiser's Imperial Army!"

"Exactly what my mother said when I had to enlist, *Herr General*, and sadly I agree with both of you. I'd be much more useful to this world as the great novelist I intend to be, but there is unfortunately no need for fiction in the army."

Madeleine, who could not help but push the buttons of this volatile, narrow-minded man, expected he would now throw her in the dungeons or pin her to the wall, pierced through by his bayonet; but before the general could decide what he was going to do with this thorn in his flesh, there was a soft knock on the door. He seemed displeased by this interruption, as it was clear that anger was a great aphrodisiac for him.

"In!" he barked, and around the corner showed Agnès's sweet face, looking exceedingly tired and fragile.

Madeleine was so pleased to see her that she almost fell out of her role and was about to throw her arms around the lovely doctor before she checked herself and remained stock-still where she was. *Heaven-sent*, she thought. *God is merciful!*

"Sorry, am I interrupting?" Agnès asked hesitantly in her lovely, melodious voice. "I was asked to…"

"*Nein!*" the General bellowed, "this good-for-nothing corporal has come with a message from the hospital in Roye. I'll leave you two to it but report to my office before you leave, Corporal Höbel! I am not finished with you, and will report your negligence to General Von Spitzenburg."

Madeleine nodded. "You *will* see me again as soon as possible, *Herr General!* And thank you for your understanding." She waited until she heard his footsteps die out in the corridor and quickly went over to Agnès, who was standing forlorn in the corner of the room, a shadow of her former self. Madeleine wanted so much to grab both her hands in hers but knew that would shock the living daylights out of Agnès, so she said in a soft voice that was her own and taking off only her cap, "It's me, Agnès – Madeleine de Dragoncourt."

Agnès blinked, stared, and blinked again but said nothing, her mouth falling open with wonder.

"It's a long story, and I don't have much time, so please listen carefully, Agnès. But first, do you believe I'm Madeleine de Dragoncourt and not a German soldier?"

Agnès was fighting to find her voice but finally managed to bring out in a raspy hiss, "You are in *so* much danger, Madeleine. For Heaven's sake, what are you doing here? And dressed up like this? Have you gone mad? This is no joke!"

"I know," Madeleine replied hastily, "but the most important thing is that you believe who I am. So, listen carefully." Now she did grab Agnès's hands and felt the slender fingers, warm and comforting, in her own cold ones.

"We, the family and the Allies, are stuck in Amiens, but a great force is building up with the aid of the Australian and Canadian forces. A counterattack will be set in motion very soon. We *will* come and liberate you, rest assured! So please hold on a little longer. I'm here because the Germans locked the tunnel from the inside, and that's why we couldn't come back to Dragoncourt, but perhaps that was just as well, because we would have been outnumbered anyway.

"According to Jacques, there might be a second key in my father's old secretary, which stands in what you now use as your recovery room, next to *la grande salle verte*. Agnès, we have to find that key, and we also have to find out if the Germans took the key out of the cellar door and whether it is guarded or not, so we can open it with that second key and I can escape back through the tunnel to Blangy-Tronville, where I have friends who will help me back to Amiens. Do you understand?" Madeleine's plea was so urgent and spoken so fast that she almost tripped over her words.

"There's one more thing. You must get me civilian clothes so I can discard this uniform before I leave the tunnel on the other side. All I'm here for is to make sure the Allied forces can use the tunnel for their surprise counterattack. Access to Dragoncourt that way is vital for the final victory. But Gerry knows nothing about this yet." She finally stopped talking and scanned Agnès's face for understanding and support.

Agnès had listened with a concentrated crease between her light eyebrows, her quick brain grasping it all. "How incredibly brave you are, Madeleine," she whispered. "But it's also incredibly crazy. Of course I'll help you, but how are you going to deal with General Von Spiegler? He's not going to let you go."

"That's why we have to do this in under fifteen minutes. I'll come with you for the key and the check of the tunnel door. We'll stroll through the corridors as casually as we can. You also grab me some clothes – anything, it doesn't matter. I have no intention of seeing Von Spiegler again today. My *au revoir* will be under totally different circumstances, which he's going to like even less, but I don't give a fig. It will be my revenge. If he asks you where I went, tell him you have no clue. You brought me back here to the canteen to wait to be called for. I hope it won't get you into any trouble."

And Madeleine told her the fake story of the X-ray machine as an excuse. Of course, they would find out that there was no request for such a thing and no Ernst Höbel in General Von Spitzenburg's battalion, but Agnès could hardly be blamed for that treason.

"All right, let's do it. But what if there is no key?" Agnès sounded doubtful and afraid.

Madeleine took her by the elbow and led her out of the canteen. In the doorway, she turned and threw her father's portrait a last kiss.

"Thank you, Papa," and to Agnès she said, "Come on, dear, there's not a minute to waste."

The doctor in her white coat and the young soldier in his Prussian uniform strolled through the familiar corridors of Dragoncourt as leisurely as they could. They did not talk with one another and only nodded to the few early risers they met on their way. There was no time to go to the bedrooms on the upper floors, so Agnès grabbed one of the doctor's coats and a random shawl with a big hole in it that was hanging on a peg in one of the wards. Madeleine instinctively understood this brilliant insight – the white coat with the long johns underneath it would make people believe she was a nurse and thus out of danger when emerging from the tunnel.

They both held their breath as they approached the bulky old secretary, laden with dust and some of the small drawers broken. Madeleine quickly opened one drawer after another, feeling through the contents with her fingers, but without avail. Despair creased her forehead, and Agnès, who was standing on guard at the entrance to the door, motioned her to hurry.

Then Madeleine's fingers touched something like a little pouch in the back of the last drawer and drew it towards her. It was made of faded red velvet, moldy and falling apart, tied closed with a ribbon. In her haste, she tore the fabric apart and held an old-fashioned metal key in her hand. Something else fell to the floor. She stooped to pick it up, and unfolding it, saw it was a miniature but detailed plan of the tunnel. She stuffed both the key and the plan back in the pouch and was already moving to the door as she tucked it in the inside pocket of her tunic.

"Round one," she mouthed to Agnès, who was white as a sheet and slightly trembling. Madeleine, on the contrary, felt energized by this catch and would have given everything to give the frightened woman at her side a big hug and tell her they would be all right, something she was getting increasingly more hopeful about. Still marching towards the former servant's centers, where the kitchen and the sculleries were, with the cellar beyond, Madeleine also tucked the white coat and shawl underneath her tunic, walking now as if she were a rather stout German soldier with a fat belly.

"Wait," Agnès suddenly whispered. "You'll need a good flashlight to get through that dark tunnel." She turned on her heels and quickly ran back to the operating room, from where she reappeared holding a boxlike brown leather flashlight, with a metal handle and a miniature incandescent light bulb at the front. "I checked it yesterday, so it should work. We have several in case the electricity falls out." Agnès pressed the flashlight into Madeleine's hand, who decided to hang it on her belt with her other paraphernalia.

"Thank you," she replied in a low voice. "How wise of you!" In a dusky corner of one of the corridors, she briefly squeezed Agnès's hand, who reacted by clasping her hand tighter before she let go.

Without trouble, they reached the cellar, and even their last obstacle seemed to have been removed. There was no key in the door. Tentatively, Madeleine pushed the big key in the lock, but it would not turn. She tried with both hands, a small trail of sweat dripping down her temples.

"Here, let me try," Agnès suggested. "I've got strong hands." Madeleine thought she was right, despite Agnès's overall frailty – her hands were strong and capable; surgeon's hands.

The lock gave a nasty, screeching sound, which made both women jump and prick up their ears, waiting motionless. Were there footsteps coming towards the cellar? They stood for what seemed an interminable time, listening to the pounding of their own hearts, but nothing happened. Then Madeleine checked the round iron door latch, and the door slowly opened, heavy and creaking. Again, they waited; again silence.

"Here," Agnès said, searching in her coat pocket and retrieving a mini flask. "I always carry some brandy for my patients, but it will serve you better right now."

Tears sprang into Madeleine's eyes at this kindness, and the two women embraced, both sniffling now.

"Give my love to Alan and Bridget and M-C," Madeleine sniffed in Agnès's curls. "And stay safe, darling. I'll be back; we'll be back! Have faith!"

"You too, brave Madeleine! And thank you. Please make sure you lock the door from the other side. I'll wait here to listen if you manage. May God be with you!" Agnès waved a sad goodbye, her face contorted with emotion and exhaustion.

"Till we meet again here at Dragoncourt, dear Agnès!"

Madeleine switched on the flashlight and stepped into the dark tunnel, closing the door behind her. She fumbled with the key, her hands refusing to hold still, but eventually she managed to put it in the lock and turn it. Trying the latch one more time to make sure it was properly locked, she pressed her lips against the door and shouted a muffled, "Goodbye, Agnès!" But she did not hear anything from the other side, so she quickly turned around, carefully making her way through the dark, moist tunnel.

Suddenly the whole heavy weight of the situation fell on her like a roof collapsing, and she was extremely exhausted, afraid her legs would double under her any moment. She stopped to take a firm drag from Agnès's flask and spoke sternly to herself, *Now is not a time to become a weak ninny, Mad-Maddy! You can get rid of weakling Ernst Höbel soon, just drag him along a little longer.*

SHE AWOKE with something prodding softly against her rib cage and her name being called, "Mademoiselle Madeleine, wake up!"

She was coming from somewhere very far away, feeling dreadfully sleepy and out of sorts, but the voice calling her did not give up, so she eventually opened her eyelids a little to find herself in a dark place where there was nothing to see.

"Mademoiselle Madeleine, are you awake?" The voice kept insisting, and it sounded vaguely familiar.

Her throat was so parched that she had to cough a couple of times, a dry, painful tickle in the back of her throat before she could speak.

"Where am I?" It did not sound like her own voice, but then everything was weird. Her arms and legs did not feel like part of her body, her head throbbed like an over-temped engine, and she was ice-cold while at the same time feverishly hot.

"You're in the wine cellar underneath Le Bistro. You made it!"

So, it was Patrick's voice? She realized she was lying stretched out on a bench wrapped in a foul-smelling blanket, her damp clothes sticking to her shivering body. Slowly she raised herself on one arm, blinking as he lit a gas lamp and a ray of filtered light spread through the stone cave. He was but a mere shadow among shadows, so she blinked to focus her sight, but there was something wrong with her eyes. Trying harder, she could just make out his deformed posture, sitting on the other side hunched on a crate. He was smoking, and the smoke hit her lungs, so she coughed again, which was painful. She tried to make out the expression on his face, but it was half turned away from her and dancing in the flickering light. Unexpectedly, an immense gulf of gratitude washed through her spent body, and tears started to flow again. She *had* made it!

"What did you do with the German uniform?" Patrick asked with apparent urgency.

With some effort, Madeleine heaved herself to an upright position, dizzy and – as she suddenly realized – weak with hunger. She drew the blanket tighter around herself, and steadying herself with both hands on the bench, replied, "Don't worry. I've buried everything, weapons and all. Close by. We can dig it up and burn the clothes, and use the weapons."

Patrick breathed out, seemingly relieved at this. "I guess you were successful?"

"I was," she nodded, "very, but now I'm terribly cold and dirty and hungry. I must have fallen asleep. I hardly remember arriving here. Do you think you can get me back to Amiens? My family will be…"

"Sure, sure," – he waved a hand – "but I promised Maman that I would bring you to her first."

"No, sorry." Madeleine made a weak gesture. "It's too dangerous. The Boches may come looking for you or for me there. I'll have more protection when I'm with the Allied forces in Amiens, and besides, I really can't keep my family worrying about me any longer. Can you bring Loulou later?"

"Sure!" Patrick agreed. "I'll take care of the uniform. I've got Blaise waiting with a car outside. You'll be in Amiens before lunch. Here are your real papers." He handed her own ID to her, and then smiling, added, "You will tell me everything later, won't you?"

"Of course!" Madeleine replied with as much energy as she could muster. "And thank you for everything, Patrick. You're my hero!"

He chuckled at that. "There's only one heroine here, Mademoiselle Madeleine, and that is *you*. I've never met anyone in my life – man or woman – as courageous as you." The admiration in his dark gaze was so formidable that it made Madeleine blush.

"Nonsense," she muttered defensively. "My family wouldn't call it courageous; rather reckless. Well, whatever! As long as it helps our cause!"

An hour later, a bone-weary, cropped-haired Madeleine, dressed in a white coat with a dilapidated stole around her thin shoulders, saggy long underwear, and a pair of oversized army boots staggered up the steps of the Hotel L'Europe. The doorman did not recognize her and asked authoritatively for her ID. Her grubby hand reached into the pocket of her coat and gave it to him. On seeing her name, the young man reddened and immediately corrected himself, muttered an *"Excusez-moi, Comtesse Madeleine,"* and swung the door wide open for her.

Madeleine was aware that the few guests in the hotel were staring at her wide-eyed and immediately started talking in hushed tones behind their hands. She could not care less but went, with as much straightness as her tired body could muster and her cropped head held high, straight for her family's table in the bay window. They were all there – Jacques, Elle, Philip, and Gerry – smoking, drinking wine, biding their time.

Four pairs of eyes looked up at her in astonishment, mouths gaping wide open, as she deposited the pouch on the table and declared ostentatiously, "My kingdom for a bath!"

12

THE HARD SUMMER

Agnès

Chateau de Dragoncourt, 8 August 1918

It was midday; a pleasant, sun-laden summer's day in early August as can only be enjoyed in Picardy; not the scorching hot of the Mediterranean that makes one flee indoors from the sun's most powerful rays, nor the humid, hazy temperature of the more Northern countries, where a sunny day more often than not leads to clamminess and respiratory problems.

The pre-war French, especially that privileged class of wealthy and aristocratic Parisians, used to cherish their long summers in their summerhouses and chateaus scattered over the large region of Picardy; this northern French pearl, with its diversity of landscapes, broad rivers, sloping hills, and fertile fields, stretched from north of Noyon to Calais, via the whole of the Somme Département and the north of the Aisne Département. Shaped more or less like a flattened horseshoe, curving its ends towards the Belgian border, it was – with hindsight – no wonder it had become a hotbed of persistent warfare, with the almost uncrossable meandering Somme River in its midst, westwards giving access to the open waters of the English Channel and southwards to that trophy of all trophies: the French capital, Paris.

Yet never in their worst nightmares would the Picardian inhabitants, permanently or seasonal, have fathomed this fate four years earlier. If there was one landscape that breathed peacefulness and tranquility, it was Picardy, consisting of endless acres of lush countryside interspersed with farmland and forests but hardly any industry, the typical non-violent habitat where mankind and beast lived in peaceful coexistence, a rare heaven on earth.

Agnès sat with her back against the warm stone wall of the kitchen garden outside Château de Dragoncourt, her eyelids closed, for a few fleeting moments enjoying that energizing sunshine of her youth. On a day like this, before the war, the afternoon would have stretched endlessly into a lazy, peaceful retreat under her favorite chestnut tree in the garden of Château de Saint-Aubin, sipping Petipat's freshly made Earl Grey tea, an earmarked novel in her lap and Papa playing Chopin's *Nocturne in C Sharp* on his violin with the windows wide open. A tender breeze rustling the leaves overhead and an eternity of life to be lived before her. The Halcyon days.

I will not cry, she thought. Someday some form of peace will return to this once beautiful land, even if its soil is stained with the blood of millions of able-bodied young men and we can never really return to normal again. I will then cherish a different peace; a peace that means the absence of warfare and maimed soldiers.

Someone's weight dropped down beside her, and the rickety wooden bench protested with an alarming creak and sigh. Agnès opened her eyes and saw the familiar shape of Alan Bell sitting next to her, his tall frame now underweight in his white doctor's coat and his profile too sharp. He had aged so much. His whiskers were graying, and there were permanent grooves etched on his high forehead and around the firm mouth. The only thing that looked boyish and out of place on him was his mop of dark hair, now lacking any form of cut, as a barber's visit was something they vaguely remembered from another era. Alan had just turned thirty-four the week before, but he looked at least ten years older, a much grimmer and more studious doctor than the one Agnès had first encountered – and become instantly captivated by – in that airy, light-filled Sorbonne lecture room way back in 1914.

He was so intimately known to her, both in that first dashing form of his and in this more somber one, almost like he was a close family member with whom she had grown up, beloved and revered, a steady presence in their absurd life, held hostage by Germans and healing enemy soldiers. But it was only at moments like this, when she had been ruminating about the past and he suddenly popped into view again, that it struck her how much he had changed, and how much dearer he had become.

"You okay?"

She heard the question even before it was posed; always his "You okay?" with that probing look on his face, as if he wanted to peer deep inside her soul and be reassured it was still there, inside of her, and had not flown off with all the hardship and death they had encountered together. Whenever they had been apart for some time, and every morning at breakfast, every night before she went to bed, there was his question, and she needed to answer it, or he would ask again.

To anyone else's ears, it could have sounded like a habitual, rhetorical question, a matter of habit, but Alan never said anything that he did not mean to say. She knew that he cared so much for her that it pained him. So she nodded, giving him the reassurance he needed. She was well, under the circumstances.

In her turn, it pained Agnès that she knew that some of Alan's wrinkles were due to her, to his worries about her welfare and his feeling of guilt over having consented to her accompanying him to the front. It did not help that she tried to convince him time after time that she had decided to go herself. He was not to blame for their fate, and neither was she. The Germans were! But his concern for her was a constant factor between them, and it made them both desperate for a change in their situation.

Because all Alan could feel for her was worry and care, it was plain to Agnès that it would never transform into anything else, anything resembling a romantic connection. He kept his distance, wielding the protective sword of caring concern deftly between them, accepting her close only as a colleague and his protégé, and not... more. Their encounter four months earlier, when she had requested to pass as his wife because her biological father, General Eberhard von Spiegler, had marched in, had not been brought up between them again, nor had she dared to ask Alan what had happened to his relationship with his wife, the artist Suzanne Blanchard.

The time since the German occupation of Dragoncourt in the beginning of April felt like it had been years ago; they were together every day, hour after hour, yet alone in their own emotional world, unable to express what they really felt inside for fear of treading on the other's frayed nerves or for fear of saying something out of line. How Agnès missed her loquacious, extroverted father; he would have filled this pit of agonizing longing inside of her, this forced silent distance in the midst of the cacophony of war. He would have lifted her spirits with his stories and plans and music.

Papa was vibrant color and extravagant exuberance, all the things her life was lacking right now and that she craved with every cell of her body. She did not even know where her father was or whether he was well. Mail was disrupted and the telephone lines strictly reserved for German calls. Without Papa in her life, and only the aloof Alan at her side, Agnès felt like the most important part of her – her soul – had been cut out of her, and she was only functioning mechanically; the responsible doctor. So why was Alan accepting it when she told him she was all right, when really, she was not? But she could not give him her honest answer because he would not be able to bear it. And neither would she.

"We're awfully silent." She felt a strong urge to break the silence between them, if only by just saying something, but also because in some way she feared that Alan could read her thoughts and that that would make him even more worried. She did not want him to worry; she wanted him as he had been before, strong and confident and so funnily American, not grim and cast down and snappy all the time.

"I know, we are!" he replied, leaning his back against the warm wall and stretching his long legs in dull khaki corduroy pants that had seen better days, crossing them at the ankles. "The closer the turn in the war comes, the more silent we become inside, as if we're baiting our breath. There's so much at stake."

As always, Alan turned the subject of their conversation away from them personally to the war, to work, to the general state of affairs. Agnès sighed and listened for a moment to the rumbling, growling war that was indeed coming closer every day, though now from a different direction, as if the wind had changed from northeast to southwest. Better winds, hopeful winds, but at what price? They both knew that chances were slim that they, the doctors, together with the nurses Bridget and M-C, would survive a counterassault by the Allied forces.

The Germans had even taken down the Red Cross flag from the rooftop and replaced it with the German imperial flag, so how could Allied bombers know Dragoncourt was also a hospital, not just a German headquarters, and that there were still non-Germans inside? Only Major Gerald Hamilton knew; but how long did his arm reach within the Allied Alliance? One Royal Air Force bomb dropped on top of them and they were all gone, vanished from the earth, friend and foe: just collateral damage of war.

Dragoncourt had already been a frenzied beehive in the past weeks, the Germans digging themselves in in trenches around the castle, uprooting trees and flower beds, and turning the castle into a fortress from the inside, machine guns sticking out of every turret window. But Agnès thought that it was most likely all those efforts would be in vain, that the war – should it end – would be decided from above, by brave air fighters such as Capitaine Heurtier. And the medics would be trapped inside, alongside their enemies; and worst of all, she would die in the same breath as her biological father.

The wounded French and Commonwealth soldiers that had stayed at Dragoncourt during the Spring Offensive in April had long been taken prisoner of war, among them Capitaine Heurtier. They had no idea where they had been taken or if they were still alive.

Agnès felt terribly sad, thinking of the young pilot's promise to take her up in the air in his flying machine when the war ended. It was unlikely now that that would ever come to pass.

"Alan," Agnès said suddenly, urgency in her voice, "I keep falling into reveries of the past, and then in the next thought I find myself thinking how awful the future is going to be. It feels like I can't stay in the here and now. Only when we're operating can I focus on the here and now. Do you think that my mind is out of control? I mean from a physiological standpoint. Like... uh... a form of loss of control of mental functions?"

She turned to him, her face honest and young, the blue eyes wide, her unruly curls tucked inside a faded silk scarf. Alan sat upright and studied her with his intense gaze, the crease between his eyes deepening. She immediately regretted her question, but it had seemed so urgent that she had blurted it out before she'd had time to check herself. Still, it was true – also in the still of the night when she lay tossing and turning in her narrow bed in the servants' quarters, she'd had times she *was* afraid of the roaming of her mind. Was it possible she could lose control over herself at some point?

Alan dropped his gaze from her face, clicked open his horn cigarette holder, and chose another Lucky Strike. He lit it and inhaled the smoke deeply. She could see that he was contemplating her question. As he exhaled two long plumes of gray-blue smoke through his nostrils, he shook his head.

"I think it's actually normal, Agnès; just part of all the stress. I never really studied my own disoriented thought processes much up till now, but I believe I do the same. The past feels like a pleasant dream to which you long to go back all the time and just linger there, and the future is a dark and unsure place, that we're trying to get to grips with creating all sorts of scenarios, mostly negative ones. The present is so empty and desolate that our mind tries to escape from it whenever it can. When we're working, we have to concentrate, so then there's no space for past or future, but the mind will be busy again going both back and forth as soon as we leave the operating room or our patients. But as long as you can focus normally during your work, there's nothing wrong psychologically, I think."

"Thank you. I needed that. I was suddenly afraid of my own mind."

"It isn't often we can take a break from work in the middle of the day and just sit here for a bit in the sun. It's unsettling, as well," Alan observed, "like too much calm before the storm."

"Yes, I *was* enjoying the sunshine, so it *was* something good in the here and now." Agnès closed her eyelids for a moment again and let the sunrays warm her face. Gently she added, "It seems like a luxury these days – a moment of peace and quiet, not being bossed around in coarse German. *Mach das, schnell!*" She sighed. "I wish I never had to hear another word of German in my life."

Alan put his beautiful, long fingers over hers, his thumb rubbing the stretch marks of the surgical gloves still visible on her wrists.

"Hopefully, it won't be for long anymore," he said, blowing the smoke from his cigarette away from her face. "Let me give you a reverie for the future: can you imagine *un café au lait et des petit fours* at La Petit Chaisse with a view of La Notre Dame?"

Agnès gazed at him sideways, a rueful smile on her lips, and exclaimed, "Ah, that I can! Is it a promise?"

"It is, dear Agnès! That will be the day!" He smiled back at her, flicked his cigarette away, and getting up from the unstable bench, offered her his hand to pull her up.

"But come on now, Doctor de Saint-Aubin, first work and then play!"

"How much longer?" she said, but her heart was suddenly much lighter, as if she'd glimpsed the old Alan again and that gave her the power to endure. What if they would survive after all?

That night at the dinner table, the atmosphere was somber and oppressive. Bridget, who in the time when the Dragoncourt twins and Philip and Gerry had still been present, had kept up a lively conversation and cracked one Scottish joke after the other, often on the verge of indecency, had since their departure lost all her vigor and spiritedness, and sat evening after evening withdrawn, spooning the food inside, whatever happened to be on her plate. She still did her job as punctually and precisely as ever, but her heart was not in it, and she simply could not care anymore to keep up appearances. If she spoke it was work-related, factual, cold.

M-C, who had always been quiet as a mouse and preferred books to people, had become a thin, wandering ghost, all black hair and dark eyebrows in a pinched white face and with a desperate look in her charcoal eyes. Mostly she wandered around muttering *Our Father* or *Hail Mary*s to herself while clutching her crucifix as if it were the Lord Jesus himself. At times she would even forget to tend to the German patients, so Bridget and Agnès – anxious about German reprisals – would double check her work and if necessary, correct her mistakes.

Everybody was silent because it had become second nature to listen for German boots coming in the direction of their dining room, interrupting their short moment of rest with this command or that. And besides that, there was really nothing to say. What could they talk about that would not be anti-German and could be overheard?

But Agnès, having taken heart from her short moment in the sunshine that afternoon with Alan, felt she needed to cut the tongue-tied oppression that hung in the room like a heavy sack of bricks.

"There's something I have to tell you," she said, addressing no one in particular. Three heads turned and looked at her with some surprise, but no one said, *Go on* or *What, then?* like in a normal conversation among friends.

Agnès continued, "It's something I think you need to know, but it would be best if we kept the door ajar and one of us stood near it to check for undesired German ears."

"I'll do it." Bridget had already risen and made sure she was close enough to listen in to both sides.

Agnès smiled broadly, and for a moment her face shone with youthful radiance, erasing the traces of hardship and fear.

"I don't know why I didn't tell you earlier, but I think for a long time I thought I had dreamt it. But I didn't. It was real. About a week after the German invasion, Madeleine was here."

Now there was a muffled gasp from the girls, and Alan raised his brows.

"She was wearing a German uniform – I have no idea where and how she got that – her hair was very short, and she was wearing a fake mustache. She came to fetch an extra key to the tunnel door. I spoke with her briefly and helped her escape through the tunnel again. She had a nasty encounter with Von Spiegler while she was here. That's why he was so abominable for weeks after she was gone because he didn't understand how she had escaped and was hell-bent on arresting her again. Of course, he also interrogated me, but I kept saying I didn't know who that person was and where he had gone – Madeleine was a so-called Ernst Höbel from the regiment in Roye – and Von Spiegler had no proof I could know of her whereabouts. But that's the reason he usually singles me out for harsh criticism." Agnès swallowed, remembering all the cruel and unfair treatment she'd had to endure from him.

It was still silent, but a different silence now, one where you could hear a pin fall, suspenseful but also electrifying. Madeleine was a symbol of their liberty; she represented a world they wanted to return to so much that they did not even dare to think of it.

Agnès said quickly, for fear she'd been talking too long and there would be ears somewhere that were not supposed to hear this, "I'm telling you this now because I think that if the Allies come back, they may rescue us via the tunnel. I think it would be a good idea to regularly check that that door is unobstructed and unguarded. I guess it will be, because the Germans consider it their secret escape route, thinking there can only be one-way traffic through it."

"Be quiet," Bridget whispered, gliding back to the table as fast as a snake on its way to prey. She was just seated when the door was flung open further, and Corporal Spitzel barged in and without greeting them, snapped at Agnès, "Herr General wishes to speak with you. *Komm mit. Nun!*"

Not again, Agnès thought. What fault has he found with me now? Can he never give it a rest?

She saw Alan rise from his chair as well but motioned him to sit down. "I'll be back in a minute. Save a cup of coffee for me, please." She made an attempt at a smile.

Following the hated back of Spitzel, she dragged her feet to Von Spiegler's office – the best room in the château, of course, Countess Virginia's private quarters, in the south wing overlooking the French gardens. It was still light outside at ten o'clock, but all the windows and doors were shut and covered with blackout. The General was sitting at his desk, or rather the Countess' desk, a rather feminine inlaid rosewood table with thin curved legs ending in small lions' heads.

The general did not look up when Spitzel announced Agnès's entry but mumbled a hardly audible *"Danke"* and kept writing in a big ledger, a cigarette smoldering between the fore and middle finger of his left hand, a diamond studded ring on his right hand glittering under the electric table lamp as his fountain pen scratched over the yellow page.

Spitzel withdrew from the room where he had been scanning the Picardy fields with his binoculars. Agnès stood alone on the thick carpet that was lavishly adorned with green leaves and red roses, her hands in the pockets of her doctor's coat. As usual she fiddled with her stethoscope that she kept in her pocket and not around her neck when she was not working.

Her gaze was fixed on Von Spiegler. She took in all his details, as if needing to etch them in her memory: the slick ash-blond hair that was combed backwards very neatly, a ruler-straight parting on the left; the white, almost translucent skin with the pronounced features that communicated authority and dominance but nothing rounded or benevolent; the straight, rather thin nose with the full mustache underneath, always clipped in such a way that it hid most of his mouth; the shoulders, rather slim in his *feldgrau* uniform with the high collar, the German cross in the middle and the gold epaulettes on his shoulders. She could go on and on to describe his features and his dress, but not the man – the man behind those features was like a fortress to her, impenetrable and inhospitable.

Yet this was the man who had fathered her – her, Agnès, alive and full of emotions. She simply could not bridge that gap between that stranger and herself. As if he felt her scrutiny and her scorn, General Graf Eberhard von Spiegler looked up from his writing and gazed back at her.

"Aha," he said in his toneless voice, "if it isn't the Parisian Doctor de Saint-Aubin!" He did not invite her to sit – he never did – but he got up himself and marched around the desk in his creaking boots, pacing back and forth in the room.

As a lion in a cage, Agnès thought. She knew he always did that for a couple of minutes, probably to frighten her, before telling her where and how he had found fault with her, so she bided her time and sought comfort in touching her stethoscope.

"I had a phone call from your father today."

Agnès could not help herself, so she exclaimed excitedly, "Papa! How is he? Is he all right?" before realizing who had just spoken and what the possible implication of Von Spiegler's announcement was. She mumbled a soft "*Excusez-moi*."

Von Spiegler sneered. "Well, I was not really interested in the well-being of your father, and that is not the reason I have summoned you here."

Agnès said nothing, biting her lower lip. At least Papa was alive. That was the most important thing. But what had he said? He had not revealed...

"The Baron seemed rather taken aback when he found out I am in charge here now." Von Spiegler grimaced while he continued to march, ten steps one way, turn on heels, ten steps the other way. Agnès's nerves were on edge now, and the pacing unsettled her even more, but she had to keep quiet. She had no idea where this conversation was leading.

"Your dear Papa kept yammering that I should let you go, that he could not stand the idea that you were still here as a... doctor." – the German sniggered – "that for old times' sake, him having served in my father's household, etc. etc., that I should consider that, and more of that jabber. Pah!"

Suddenly he came to a halt right in front of her and looking down on her, his eyebrows raised in his studied actor's way, demanded, "Well, should I?"

"I don't know, *Herr General*," Agnès stammered, confused and frightened.

"You know what, I might consider it. But that American stays here. He's too good. I need him."

"Alan?" Agnès said in a tiny voice. "But I can't leave without him."

"Ha, it would be my pleasure to break up the love birds!" Von Spiegler said in contempt.

At that moment, there was an enormous crash. Half the outer wall came down, windows shattered, and windowpanes snapped like firewood. Agnès screamed out and instinctively ducked away from the window in the direction of the door, her hands over her ears. The enormous bang resonated through the whole wing of the castle.

"*Herr Gott!*" Von Spiegler cried out, more surprised than angry, and immediately forgot all about Agnès. He marched to the door and bellowed to Spitzel, who was standing on guard, to gather his men. "*Beeil dich! Nun!*"

Strangely enough, the telephone on his desk started to ring, as if everything was still completely under control and half of the façade had not just been shot to smithereens. Agnès stood frozen in the middle of the carpet, eyeing the rubble with a terrified expression, half expecting another attack and knowing she had to move away but hoping against hope it was her father on the phone again.

"*Was ist?*" Von Spiegler's voice had a high-pitched screeching tone that it had not had before, his veneer cracking. In rapid German, he explained the attack on part of the castle and said that he immediately needed reinforcements.

Agnès moved stealthily to the door, half expecting him to call her back, but he did not. All she wanted was to find Alan and the nurses. As long as they were together, they would sit out this madness. She scrambled over the debris to the door, skinning her knee and feeling the blood trickle down her shin, but when she got in the passage, she was relieved to see Alan running towards her with a handkerchief over his mouth. This time his question, "Are you all right?" was even more weighty.

"Take off your headscarf and put it over your mouth," he ordered. "Not that it will be much good if it's a gas attack but breathing in debris isn't good for your lungs either." He grabbed her hand, and together they ran towards the servants' centers.

"We heard the explosion come from this wing," he said, keeping her close to him, "but we had no idea what it was. It is frustrating that we're not getting any knowledge of the front lines anymore. Was this the beginning of the Allied attack or just a random mistake?'

"Is the rest of the castle undamaged?" Agnès asked, still half-dazed from shock and her knee pricking more painfully with every step. She tried not to limp, but her whole leg was swiftly becoming stiff and swollen. She needed to take a look at it.

"Seems intact as far as I know. But what's wrong with you? Are you wounded?" Alan slowed down his fast pace to accommodate her.

"Nothing important – just grazed my knee. It could have been much worse. A large part of the wall came down. Do you think the Allies know that Von Spiegler uses that room as his headquarters? Was it an attempt to kill him?"

"I could not care less about that, but it could have killed you," Alan observed grimly. "Thank God it didn't! I'll have a look at that knee as soon as we're back in our quarters."

It was the first time that Agnès felt Alan's skilled hands on an injury of her own, and she enjoyed his fingers touching her knee. Even disinfecting the wound and putting a bandage around it was pleasurable, and she was ashamed to admit she wished the treatment would go on for a little longer, the way his fingers moved, as if with a life of their own, touching, diagnosing, then healing. It was such a strong desire to feel his touch on her skin, she almost closed her eyes to feel her skin aglow. But the doctor in her won – as always – and she forced herself to watch him work and then it was over.

"All done!" Alan announced, briskly getting up from his kneeling position in front of her, already on his way to disinfect his tweezers and scissors. "You must have gotten caught on a piece of stone with iron in it. Good thing we treated it straight away because that wound, so harmless now, would have become infected. Can you bend your knee? But make sure you do it carefully. Bandage not too tight?"

"Yes... uh... no, it's fine. Thank you, Doctor Bell!"

"You're welcome, Doctor de Saint-Aubin," he mimicked, drying his hands on a towel and grinning at her. "Let's go and find Bridget and M-C and make a plan for the night. To be honest, I don't expect this sudden attack to be the last one, so we'd better prepare ourselves."

Bridget and M-C were waiting for them in their living room and were relieved to see them back in one piece.

"What happened?" they asked in chorus. When they understood that the Allies were most likely preparing the recapture of Drag- oncourt, the four medics decided to check the tunnel door in turns, just to be sure. That evening, their own quarters remained relatively quiet, and there was no further upheaval. Sitting around the dinner table while Bridget served them a cup of strong Ceylon tea, none of them expressed a wish to go to their respective bedrooms despite being at the limits of their endurance.

As they sipped their tea and nibbled on a dry German biscuit, Alan observed, "Now that the Germans are tangled up in their defense tactics, they'll probably pay less attention to us, so it's our best time to be as prepared for escape as we can." The expression on his face was gloomy but composed.

Agnès listened attentively. The tea was hot and comforting in her stomach, and the idea that they were not the Germans' target for the first time in months a pleasant thought. With just the four of them, it felt almost intimate, a closed circle of like-minded souls, better than it had been in ages.

Alan continued, "As you know, we've got twenty German patients in our care right now, eight of whom are in a bad shape. It's a blessing in disguise that there's been little fighting of late, so our hospital beds aren't crowded, and the work is doable. We'll tend to them as usual, but I suggest that we do it together, that we stay together, both inside and outside the hospital. It's our best chance to survive." He looked around at his three female companions, and they nodded in unison.

"Good idea," Bridget agreed. "I actually think we should make our beds here in this room. We'll be safest down here, in th' dungeons as it were, close to food supplies – and to that cellar door."

"I agree," Agnès assented. "Whatever happens, if we stick together night and day, we have more chance of helping each other if needed and getting away together."

"But what do we do if Von Spiegler summons just one of us, as he sometimes does?" M-C inquired in her soft, uncertain voice.

"We'll deal with that if it happens," Alan answered, "but he's probably too busy saving his own skin right now."

"We'll have to bring as much of our medical kits and supplies into this room as well," Bridget said, with more enthusiasm she had shown in a long time. "That way we'll be prepared for everythin'."

"Sounds like a plan. But we'll have to do that in stages and secretly," Alan observed cautiously. "If they find out we're creating our headquarters here, they'll thwart our plans. They think the hospital and its contents are theirs."

"We can do it!" Agnès said defiantly. "I like it!"

A little later, their living room and kitchen were a beehive of activity, with mattresses being dragged down from the upstairs bedrooms, clothes stacked in valises in the corner of the storage room, and medical bags in a neat row of four next to the cupboard with their most important clinical equipment and supplies. Alan had even moved one of the mobile X-ray machines into the scullery behind the kitchen. The place was overfull now and rather hot and stuffy because of all the action that had been stirred up.

"I'll open one of the windows just a crack," Agnès declared. "We can't sleep in a hothouse like this with the four of us squeezed in tight." Her knee was throbbing painfully, but she had worked as hard as the others, and now felt flustered and out of breath. She sank in a chair close to the window, gratefully inhaling the fresh air through a gap in the curtain.

"Be careful with the blackout. Don't tear it," Bridget warned.

An hour later, they were lying side by side on the stone floor, their bodies only supported by thin kapok mattresses that had once belonged to the Dragoncourt kitchen maids. Agnès, still quite hot and glad the floor offered some much-needed coolness, had wrapped herself fully dressed in no more than a sheet. Alan was on her left and M-C on her right. Although her body was heavy with fatigue, her mind was wide awake, and she sensed all four of them were vigilant. Nobody talked or stirred, wanting to give one another the chance to catch some vitally needed sleep, but there was an alertness in the room as only medics are prone to, ready at the slightest sound.

Agnès was keenly aware of Alan's presence so close to hers, his long body stretched only inches away. It was something she had not dared to imagine in her wildest dreams. She lay listening to his even breathing, knowing he was also awake, for it did not sound like the deep breaths of a sleeping person. She longed to stretch out her arm and snuggle her hand into his, but she knew she would never attempt anything like that, nor would he accept it.

He was probably thinking of Suzanne Blanchard, how he missed lying next to his absent wife. Agnès silently scolded herself for her selfishness. She never gave much thought to how heart-broken he must be and how apprehensive of what was to happen should they be able to leave Dragoncourt in one piece. Return to Paris without Suzanne, or immediately go back to the States and resume his life there, with or without her?

'It's none of my business,' Agnès reminded herself, as she turned on her side away from Alan so as not to be so conscious of his presence.

She was still unable to fall asleep, and the whole day flashed by, from sitting in the sunshine and talking with Alan to the encounter with Von Spiegler, the bomb attack, and reorganizing the kitchen. She loved best the part in the sun, so in her mind she returned there, when suddenly her father popped back into her thoughts and she concentrated on him, on her love for her Papa. She imagined his dark, bohemian face, his wide gestures, the flowery language, his music, his erratic and sometimes annoying presence, and his over-bearing personality.

What would it be like to see Papa again? To feel his kiss on top of her head, to stroll through Paris on his arm and listen to his endless stories as she had done ever since she was a little girl, his little girl? But something was wrong. Papa was the same, but she was no longer the little girl. The war had changed her, robbed her of her innocence, made her hard and full of spite. A survivor, perhaps even ready to be a murderer to save her own skin. And Alan had also changed her: made her grow up, face challenges, stand up for herself.

A sudden cold shiver ran down Agnès' spine. What if Papa were on his way to her? After all, he now knew who was in charge of Drag-oncourt, and given his protectiveness, he might want to shield her from Von Spiegler. And that vile man would not shrink from killing her Papa in cold-blooded hatred, thus settling an old bill. She had to get a message out to her father; tell him not to endeavor such folly. The occupation of Dragoncourt would hopefully be over soon, and then they could meet in freedom and forget all about Graf Von Spiegler and that sordid common history. Because one thing was clear to Agnès, if she escaped Dragoncourt alive: she was not going to work as a doctor on the front again. She would go back to Paris, or any other place where there was no war, with... or yes... even without Alan!

13

THE ABYSS

At some point, Agnès had fallen asleep, but she was woken up soon after by the deafening roar of airplanes racing overhead. Alan shot upright and was out of bed to switch on the light in a blink of a second. It was a relief to see the living room bathed in a soft golden glow that kept the darkness and the frightening sound in check. The three women sat up in bed, dressed in their white uniforms, long braids in disarray and looking aghast.

The air above them vibrated with the sonorous roar of what sounded like a thousand machines, which made everything rattle and tinkle from the windows to the lamps to the porcelain in the cupboard. It was no use trying to shout over the noise as they quickly rose and fled to the cellar. The roll of wave after wave of planes deafened and muted everything. They were all expecting that one thing: the crash of explosions, nearby or further off. *Please God, let it be further*. They listened, holding their breath, but the booms did not come until later, further to the east... Roye perhaps, or Péronne. Not here; not yet.

To Agnès this brought back the nightly attacks on Paris, and she shuddered in the damp basement. There was something so indefinitely eerie and unpredictable about air raids. So far, this part of

Picardy had been spared them, at least since she had been here, but she now realized that that deep angst had been with her all the time.

"Holy Mary!" Bridget exclaimed. "That was near! I really thought I was goin' to meet mah maker."

"What time is it?" Agnès asked, her teeth rattling from shock.

"It's half past three," Alan said, checking his clock. "Best try and get some more sleep here, ladies."

They looked around the cellar in the beam of a small flashlight. It did not look like a good place to sleep.

"I don't think I can sleep anymore," Agnès uttered, peeling the sheet she had been dragging with her off her body and folding it up. "I'm going to check on the patients. They may have wakened, too."

"You're doing no such thing," Alan commanded sternly. "Remember we promised to stay together? Unless the Germans force us to tend to them during the night, we stay here. These planes may be returning any minute, and who knows if they intend to drop off some extra cargo on their way back."

They *had* slept on the cellar floor, fitful and waking every half an hour, until the clock on the mantelpiece upstairs chimed six and it was time to start their morning routine. Everyone was silent, white-faced, and hollow-eyed from lack of sleep and absorbed in their own recollections of nightly attacks. Agnès moved like a sleepwalker, staying close to Alan wherever he went, and constantly checking if Bridget and M-C were on her heels. It felt more like a four-person unit than four individuals, but it worked, and after a while the proximity of one another's bodily presence became so natural that it almost felt irregular if one component started moving in another direction.

They spent the morning in the hospital, tending to the patients and getting emergency treatments ready. Nothing out of the ordinary happened, except that they did not see one of the Germans, not even the ones who usually stood on guard near the hospital's entry door.

"Do you think they've gone and left us here?" Agnès whispered to Alan, as she was storing the used scalpels, scissors, and needles in liquid antiseptics while he was inspecting their medical cabinet.

"Don't suppose so, but let us check as soon as we're done here. I'm actually quite interested how *Herr General* is liking his new outdoor office." Alan grinned, and his gaze included Bridget and M-C, who were collecting the dirty laundry and stacking the gauze material away. The nurses drew closer, and Agnès leaned against the operating table and took off her surgical gloves and massaged her stiff fingers. When together in their own hospital, their habitat, it seemed easier to talk about work than when they were huddled together in the kitchen. Some form of normality. A work planning.

"It all depends on how fast the Allies will strike and where," Alan explained. "If we become part of a siege – and I think that's what the Germans intend – we'll probably be forced to deal with the German wounded for as long they can hold off capitulation. There may come a time that we've got to provide medical care for both sides, which will be extremely awkward and against our nature. But remember, we're medics, not military. We're here to save lives and keep our personal preferences to ourselves. Unless," He hesitated a moment, scratching his one-day dark stubble. "Unless it's the choice between an Allied life and a German life. Then it's up to your own conscience."

"But we said we'd stay close together at all times," M-C said in her hushed voice, rubbing the crucifix intently between her fingers. "So difficult choices we'll make together, right?"

"I don't think that will always be possible when it becomes really chaotic," Agnès observed, "but we must try, I agree."

"Hopefully, it'll be quick and dirty with few or no casualties on the Allied side, and we'll be immediately evacuated. The Germans can look after their own wounded then, who by the way will be prisoners of war." Alan almost spit out these last words, losing some of his usual composure, and Agnès understood that despite his oath and the words he spoke, it fell as hard on him to tend to Germans as it did to her.

"All understood," Bridget said with her usual breeziness, as if she already saw herself discarding her German ward and back in the

Scottish Highlands. "Let's check where our Herr General is havin' his lunch these days."

"But..." M-C interjected. "What happens if the Allies lose, or they're not coming for us after all?" Her thin shoulders drooped, and her narrow face seemed even more pinched and unhappy.

Alan went over to her and grabbed her by the shoulders. "Don't worry, M-C," he said almost tenderly, "they will, I promise you. They will. Just you pray for that!"

She sighed, but a small quiver of a smile slid over her features when she mouthed a *Thank you*.

Two by two, they made their way through the corridors to the canteen, where the German soldiers usually gathered and where Agnès had met Madeleine on that hit-and-run visit in the spring. They found the large room in great agitation, with coarse, staccato German sentences filling the air that was thick with smoke. It seemed like most of the battalion was present there, but the leaders, Von Spiegler and Corporal Spitzel were not among them. It was clear from the confused shouting that they found themselves in complete chaos.

Agnès thought it was necessary to find out what the Germans had heard that made them all so worked up. With her excellent knowledge of the Germanic language – despite her father's disgust of everything German, he'd had his daughter trained in all the modern European languages, and even in some dead ones such as Latin and Greek – she inched forward with her ears open.

"They call it the 4th Battle of Amiens!" one yelled.

"Australians nearby," another exclaimed.

"Devastating attack on the *Luftstreitkräfte*." Yet another.

"We should capitulate! We stand no chance! Even the Americans and the Canadians are in it now!"

It went on and on. Agnès translated as best as she could. It was all music to the ears of the four medics, who stood unseen in the midst of this *feldgrau* sea of sweating and swearing German soldiers. But in the end, they were still none the wiser. The Germans might be in a state of uproar, but unless they would surrender without bloodshed, it was going to be a bloody battle after all, with them sandwiched in between.

"Let's go and have some lunch," Bridget suggested. "I guess at some point Von Spiegler will come and give some form of explanation, unless he's willin' to put up with a rebellion from his own men."

"Good idea," Agnès agreed. "I can't make much sense out of all that hubbub anyway."

They were just about to sink their teeth into ham sandwiches and freshly brewed coffee when there was a gigantic explosion at the castle's main entrance, as if a cannon had blasted out the front. For a short spell, the entire 16th century castle seemed to sway from one side to the other as if gripped by seismic forces too powerful for its foundations, but it soon corrected itself, yielding to the collapse of its magnificent front façade and the shattering of all the front windows. The sound waves that followed the explosion tore eardrums to shreds and led to temporary deafness.

Immediately the *rat-tat-tat* from the German anti-aircraft guns answered the attack from the rooftops, but they seemed to clack like toy guns in comparison to the mammoth enemy opposite them. The medics gazed at each other in a state of perturbation, unable to speak, but all thinking the same thought: *Should we go and look and do our duty, or run away as fast as we can?*

At that moment, the kitchen door burst open, and a German officer, his face red and his eyes bulging, panted, "Quickly – the general is wounded. Bring a stretcher. *Schnell!*"

As if woken from their trance, they sped towards the hospital for the stretcher and first aid kit, and then followed the German to the main entrance.

"Alan, where's your white coat?" Agnès shouted, running beside him.

"Never mind, Agnès, I'll put it on when we're back in the operating room." And turning to the bewildered soldier, he asked, "What happened, sergeant?"

"I don't know, Doc, it was a major attack that came out of nowhere. The General was standing outside, scanning the surroundings with his binoculars, when he was just blown over like a reed. It's awful, just awful."

"Was he on his own? Are there any other casualties?" Alan remained in control even under these hazardous situations. Agnès, who was following him with the medical kit, while Bridget and M-C pursued with the stretcher, was as always filled with admiration for him. Even in his civilian clothes, he was every inch the physician. How well he did it, every time. She still had so much to learn.

"Not that I know of, Doc. Maybe the two guards who are always posted at the door."

"We'll see."

They had to make a detour because a large part of the inner wall close to the entrance had also collapsed, and they had to climb over a pile of debris to get to the wounded man. They left the interior of the castle to be hit by a blaze of yellow sunlight filtered by millions of dust particles slowly whirling down from the sky and settling as a thick layer on all and everything.

Agnès blinked against the harsh light and pulled her scarf around her mouth against the dust, thinking that it was an idiosyncrasy that nature refused to bend for war and the sun shone as if it were a merry day. Standing on top of the stone rubble next to Alan, she inspected with him how they could best reach the man lying underneath. He was moaning, so he was alive, but there was no saying what condition he was in. They would have to remove the stones from his body, one by one, while one of the nurses applied a temporary drain to keep his vital functions going and to sedate him.

She wanted to turn to Alan to see if he agreed with that plan when she heard a whizzing sound and automatically ducked sideways. What happened in the next few instances was like life-size photographs projected in slow motion on a vast screen with no sound, just vision. She stretched her hand towards Alan, who doubled and fell head down on the huge clumps of stone. He seemed to say something that she could not hear, and then she was on top of him, putting her arms around him.

Bridget and M-C grabbed her forcefully from behind and tore her away from his bleeding body, with Bridget's voice sharply in her ear: "Emergency, Agnès! Pull yerself together!"

But she kept clawing at them to let her near him, crying, "Alan, no! Alan!"

Then Bridget slapped her cheek. It stung; the slideshow of photographs stopped, and she became Agnès again, Doctor de Saint-Aubin. While Bridget and M-C rolled him on his side, she took his pulse, already noting he was breathing, although shallowly.

"How's his pulse?" Bridget demanded, all business-like and strong.

Agnès drew strength from her resolute behavior.

"Still breathing, but unconscious. It's a shot wound, in the belly. Better get him inside. Who knows what else might happen if we treat him here? No time for that."

While they hoisted Alan's limp body on the stretcher, Agnès shouted to the German soldier who had been accompanying them outside.

"You, sergeant, and the nurse – start uncovering the General's body. M-C, apply a drip immediately. Sergeant, you get rid of the stones on top of him; but do it carefully! Make sure you don't squash him any further. Get two other soldiers to collect a stretcher bed for the General. And stay alert to more attacks." And then she ran inside, carrying the head-side of Alan's stretcher, not thinking ahead."

Bridget and Agnès carefully deposited Alan's body on the green sheet of the operation table. Agnès was briefly lost in his beautiful, still features and she almost pushed a strand of dark hair that had fallen forward over his face away from his brow but then she recalled herself and slipping into her operation gear, only thought of all the lessons he had ever given her: no emotions, Agnès! Focus, be alert, watch for irregularities, check vital functions, eye-hand coordination... on and on. But she knew what was most important now and that was to forget who was lying there. This was to be her ultimate test. *She* had to save *his* life.

She worked quickly, glad to remember all the earlier shot wounds in the stomach area that she'd treated; they usually were not mortally dangerous, like they could be in the chest or head. Gruesome, and difficult to heal, but doable – and a complete recovery was possible. She was grateful also to have Bridget by her side, so experienced and calm, and they worked well as a team. But then they gasped at the same moment when Agnès cut close to the hole to remove the bullet. It had not just gone through below his stomach – the bullet had hit his spinal cord and was stuck there, right at the place where it should *not* have been.

"Spinal injury," they said at the same time, and pushing away the horror, Bridget began to prepare for a much longer operation, getting the Shipway apparatus ready to anesthetize Alan for a longer and deeper sedation, while Agnès prepared her X-ray machine to diagnose the damage. She was surprised to see that her hands were not shaking, and her mind was clear. With her peripheral vision, she observed that Von Spiegler, still croaking like a parched cowboy, had also been brought in and was placed on the other operation table. M-C was busy cutting open his military tunic while the German sergeant stood by stock-still and in apparent shock.

"What are the General's injuries?" Agnès asked, meanwhile studying the X-ray of Alan's backbone and vertebrae and making up her mind how she would remove the bullet with as little risk as possible to his spine.

"Concussion, broken leg, and possibly damage to his chest – a large block fell on top of him. Doesn't look like he's in mortal danger, though. Shall I just give him a stiff dose of morphine for the time being?"

"Yes," Agnès affirmed. "Shut him up, but do keep an eye on him while Bridget and I extricate this bullet. Sergeant, I need you to hand me the instruments on this tray when I ask for them."

The next ten hours were, in hindsight, possibly the longest of Agnès's young life, yet she had no recollection of time or place. She worked as if she had wings, listening to Alan's instructions as if he were standing beside her as usual. She saved both men's lives, and only when they were lying side by side in the ward, still blacked out from sleep-induced medication, did she become aware of herself again, both the weariness of her body and the triumph of her victory.

"You stay with them while the nurses and I clean the operating room and take a short break," Agnès instructed the young German sergeant, who had actually proved to be a great help once his apprehension had subsided. "Come and get us if anything changes in their condition. Understood?"

He nodded, taking his cap off his tousled blond hair and placing it over his kneecap as he sat statuesquely between the two sleeping man.

"Let's finish this quickly, girls," Agnès said, impatiently getting out of her blood-stained operating coat and tossing it in the laundry basket. "We desperately need a break and a chat." It did not even amaze her how simply and naturally she took the lead; it just happened, and again she felt Alan so close by her side it was as if he were almost under her skin.

"You're sure we shouldn't take an X-ray of the General's lungs before we go?" M-C, who had done the major part of getting Von Spiegler back into shape, asked in her hesitant mousy way.

"No, we'll do it later tonight, if necessary," Agnès decided. "There's no need for concern; he doesn't even need extra oxygen, so no worries before there's a reason for them."

"It's really strange that nothin' happened th' rest of th' day," Bridget observed, while she folded the last of the gauze material and stacked it away in a drawer. "I wonder how th' night is goin' to pass now there are two holes in th' castle's walls, one on th' south and one on th' north."

"That's what I want to discuss with you," Agnès remarked, bringing the volume of her voice down, "but not here where there are wrong ears that can hear." After switching off the last lamps in the operating room, she went to make one last check on Alan. Standing next to his bed, watching the pallid, still frame under the hospital blanket, she had to fight back her tears. Only hours ago, he had been her rock, the one she thought she could not live one day without, and now the tables were turned, and his life was in her hands. He would live, of that she was sure; but would he ever be able to walk again? His chances of a full recovery were slim, yet she had done her utmost, her absolute utmost, and he had taught her well. She lay a soft hand on his motionless wrist, once more feeling the feeble but steady pulse.

"Come on, Agnès," Bridget urged her, but there was deep compassion in the gentle turquoise eyes, clear as a Scottish glen. "Yer break, remember?"

She put an arm around Agnès's shoulders and drew her softly away from the bed. "Let him have his beauty sleep," she nudged. "Ye've done a hell of a job, Doctor de Saint-Aubin, and I hope ye realize it."

"I do," Agnès affirmed, "but I couldn't have done it without you. Still, I'm afr..."

"Hush," Bridget silenced her, "don't invoke th' evil spirits with yer fears!"

And to M-C, who was still scrubbing the operating table with ferocious intent, her crucifix dangling to and forth on her apron, she said, "Come on, darling, it *is* clean already."

M-C hung her sad head, but seeing the two women waiting for her, she dried her hands on her apron and followed them.

"Thank you for your trust in me," she said simply. "I've never before done so much on my own. It was quite scary, but also quite liberating."

"It's just us girls now," Agnès said wistfully, "but we're stronger than we think."

As soon as they sat around the table, they unwrapped their former lunch packets of sandwiches and sipped cups of fresh coffee, grateful for the food entering empty stomachs and the warm liquid filling the spaces in between.

While she ate and drank, it struck Agnès how quiet the castle was – no coarse shouts from the courtyard, no rumbling of truck engines on the gravel outside, no heavy footsteps in the corridors. It was as if the complete castle including its inhabitants was hanging in limbo. It was unsettling, this ghostlike atmosphere where anything could happen anytime, and yet she felt calm and collected inside. What else was there to fear now that she had conquered the worst?

"I want us to think how we could transport Alan through the tunnel should the occasion arrive," she remarked. "Any ideas?"

"I know one thing," Bridget said with her usual assertiveness, "and that's that I hope that it doesn't come to pass tonight! It would be absolute torture to the old chap unless we kept him knocked out all through it."

"That's what I was considering as well," Agnès acknowledged. "For his recovery, it would be much better if he lay still for a couple of days. But what if we don't get that time?"

"Then we'll strap him as tightly as we dare to th' stretcher and give him such a high dose of morphine that he'll only see th' light of day again in a week or so." Bridget planted her elbows on the table, her red locks and turquoise eyes aflame, as if she were the mythical Queen Scathach of Skye herself, ready to go into battle.

M-C, conscientious as ever, dabbed the corners of her mouth with her serviette and, whispering her prayer of thanks, pushed back her chair. "I'm going to look in on the patients."

"Wait," Agnès and Bridget said as of one accord. "We'll all go."

They found the two men still fast asleep, oblivious to their wounds and the long recovery ahead. Alan was sleeping peacefully, but Von Spiegler grimaced even in his induced coma-like condition.

"We have to wait with that lung X-ray," Agnès stated, checking that the cast around his leg was not too tight and the angle it was suspended in not too high, "but I'm not sure what's wrong with him. Look out for symptoms of septicemia, but for the time being just give him a higher dose of morphine, M-C."

There was only a handful of German soldiers in the ward, and they seemed to be all recovering well, either asleep or reading or writing letters.

After their final round, Agnès gave voice to what all three of them were thinking: "We'll sleep in the operating room tonight. That way we'll be at Alan's bedside should he wake up."

They looked at each other, wondering and calculating. It would not be as safe as sleeping in the living quarters and close to the cellar door, but Alan's life was momentarily more important.

"I suppose we won't sleep a wink," Bridget vocalized, "but th' same boilin' water that softens th' potatoes, hardens th' egg, as mah dear *Mamaidh* used to say. We'll get through it."

"For how long?" Agnès wondered. "This situation can't continue for much longer. It's sheer madness."

She was greatly concerned about her own safety and that of the two nurses, realizing all too well that – with their rock fallen – the well-being of those still in the castle fell on her slender shoulders. And then there was the extra complexity of the castle walls being blown apart, which meant that the night wind could freely sweep from front to back, bringing friendly or unfriendly visitors in its wake.

"Do you suppose we have to find out who of the Germans is in charge now?" M-C, asked, phrasing what they had all thought but had been able to put off due to their work. It seemed important, yet was it?

"It's eerily quiet, but I think I prefer it like this tonight. Let's just try to get some sleep and find out in the morning, okay?" Agnès made for the door, and the other two followed, relieved they could postpone facing the chaos that must reign among the German battalion.

Agnès was surprised to feel sleep descend on her mercifully within seconds of her head hitting the pillow. She was physically so drained that her brain demanded repose. No amount of mental fight could drag her from the welcome world of dreams.

She dreamt she was fighting against a merciless wind that blew right through her and used her as a plaything of the fates. She had to get somewhere, back to her people again, but she did not know how because the wind kept pushing her back. For hours she had been crossing a barren landscape on foot as dark rainclouds raced overhead as evening fell hard and fast.

Blackened tree trunks stood straight like the King's Guards in stubble fields, while clusters of soldiers in different-colored uniforms lay face down in ditches and on dirt roads, rigid as castaways, toy soldiers. A lonely cow was lowing a sad song under a corrugated iron shed. Yet Agnès knew the war had ended, and her destination was Paris. Why then was she forced to go in the wrong direction? Suddenly it dawned on her – she was heading for Germany. All the fibers of her body battled against this enterprise, but her will was not her own anymore.

She was on her way to Prussia to Graf Von Spiegler's castle with a message for his family. Only there was no message; she was the message, the message she did not want to be. All she wanted was to turn around and leave this war-torn terrain to immerse herself in the streets of Paris, where her people were rejoicing in the grand finale of the war. Tears streamed down her face, and she had never felt so desolate, not in all the horrors she had endured in the war. She tried to find God among the clouds, but there was just more blackness. Then she felt a hand over her mouth and turned to see... Alan.

Agnès tried to scream, but the hand over her mouth pressed down firmly. She wriggled to get out from underneath it when a voice whispered in her ear, "Shush, Agnès, it's me... Elle."

Blinking in the darkness and still totally submerged in her nightmare, Agnès thought for a fleeting moment she was still dreaming; that it was before the war and that Elle and she were playing hide-and-seek in a dark cupboard. But then she saw the familiar shape in the early light of the morning, and gratitude flushed through her in uncontrollable waves.

She wept and wept, her whole body shaking while Elle held her in a tight embrace, mumbling, "It's okay, darling, it's over, it's over."

"Alan," Agnès sobbed. "What about him?"

"I don't know," Elle said, raising her penciled eyebrows. "Where is he?"

"Oh, God," Agnès moaned. "He got severely wounded yesterday. I've got to check on him."

"If he's in the ward, he'll be okay," Elle shushed her. "Not a shot was fired during the recapture, thanks to some preparatory work, among others from my little sis."

Bridget and M-C had also woken up, and hugs were exchanged, and tears flowed. They wanted to know what had happened during the night and where the Germans were now. So many questions; but Agnès had only one. *How was Alan?*

So, among all the exultations of joy and relief, she quietly slipped away towards the ward. On entering the door, she saw he was awake, the whites of his eyes were wide, glistening in the half-light; the eyes of a haunted man.

Before she reached his bed, he exclaimed in a pained voice, "I can't move my legs! I'm paralyzed!" He looked at her accusingly, as if it was her fault.

She felt the tears start streaming again, but she was unable to stop them as she made her way to his bedside, hanging her head.

"I'm sorry, Alan," she said in barely more than a whisper, followed by a hiccup. "I did the best I could. The injury was at T12 where the bullet hit you, but I managed to prevent total lesion. So, there's hope. Can you let me know if your abdominal reflexes are functioning?"

She checked the medication in his drip, avoiding his gaze, and when he did not answer, she implored, "Are you in much pain?"

He did not answer, but all of a sudden reached out and drew her hand towards him, pressing his lips to the rubber glove. Now she did meet his eyes and was surprised at what she saw. It was something she could not pinpoint, but it certainly was no longer accusing or tormented. Was it appeasement, respect, devotion? Or a mixture?

"You'll be okay, Alan," she sobbed quietly. "You trained me, remember? It may take a long while before you can walk again, but one day you will. And we're free. The de Dragoncourts have returned with the Allies. The war may be over for us."

At that moment, a gasping, choking sound came from the next bed, and Agnès was forced to break eye contact with Alan and look at the patient in the other bed. The General was gasping for breath, wildly flailing his arms, with which he wrenched free the syringe in his hand.

"Lie still, I'll be back with you in a second," she promised Alan, and after sounding the copper bell on the sideboard, she hastened over to the German.

"*Hilfe,*" he wheezed. "I... can't... breathe..." but Agnès was already opening the buttons of his pajama top and listening on various places of his hairy chest through her stethoscope.

M-C, her cheeks still streaked with tears but with eyes full of joy, stormed in.

"Primary lobar pneumonia, I'm afraid," Agnès diagnosed. "Give him a dose of type I antipneumococcic serum, just to be sure. If he starts feeling better, we'll do an X-ray later today."

"Uh... are we still supposed to look after him?" M-C looked dubious and scowled at the general as if he were the worst vermin she had ever encountered.

"Yes, M-C, we are," Agnès said rather stonily. "As long as he's in *our* hospital, he's in *our* care. I assume we can hand him over to the Allies soon, but he's in no fit state to be transported right now. Now help me turn Alan on his side so he doesn't get bedsores."

In the afternoon, Eberhard von Spiegler's condition worsened rapidly, and Agnès stood by rather helplessly, seeing him float between consciousness and unconsciousness without ways to relieve his suffering. The X-ray had confirmed her suspicion that he had developed double pneumonia, and as they were already low stocked on medicine, there was little she could give him for this stage of the illness. She tried to talk with him when he was conscious, to keep him alert, but most of the time he did not seem to remember where he was and kept calling her *Masha*, whoever that was, and sometimes *Ingrid*, which she assumed was her mother.

Agnès was only glad that should he die, he would just sink deeper into oblivion without noticeable pain and remain quite unaware of his army's humiliating defeat. Why she cared about that, she was unable to tell, but she did. Seeing her biological father deteriorate like this, changing from a proud, cold, military aristocrat to a shrunken bundle of feverish flesh in a striped hospital gown, somehow changed Agnès's perspective of her profession on a dime. Von Spiegler was no longer the enemy, the man she hated even more than the enemy, but a patient needing her care. And she would give him just that. If she could save his life, she would do so, without caring about the price that might cost.

"No thinking of that right now," she admonished herself, dabbing his sweating brow with a cool cloth. Alan would be proud of her. Was this not the basics of what he had taught her? To be a doctor, not a judge of human right or wrong. While she was watching the general fall into a fitful sleep, her thoughts went back to Alan.

Bridget and M-C had moved his bed with all the contraptions to the garden room, where he would have light and space and not be confined to this ward that held nothing but bad memories for him. She would look in on him later, but he seemed to be recovering well from the operation. His greatest hurdle was going to be a mental one. She had stressed though that no visitors were allowed in his room, as he needed to gain his strength first.

Being alone in the ward with the sick general was a strange and surreal experience. The remaining German patients had been taken prisoner of war, so Von Spiegler was now the only patient in this vast rectangular room, where she had spent almost five months tending to the needs of both sides in this hideous war and where so many young men's lights had been extinguished prematurely, like that of the young Indian soldier, Revant Chopra Sehgal of the 34th Royal Sikh Pioneers.

"I don't understand it," she said aloud just to hear her own voice. "I should be celebrating with the others, and here I sit nursing a German, while his army is finally being pushed off the French land."

"Doctor de Saint-Aubin?" A weak voice was addressing her, and for a moment Agnès was disoriented and did not know where it came from. Then she realized the general was awake, trying to draw her attention. She shot upright, adopting the attitude of the conquered to the conqueror when she remembered that was no longer necessary and she relaxed. His power to control her was over – but how sneakily it had conditioned her.

"How are you?" she asked, puzzled by his sudden presence of mind.

"Not too good, but not too bad either. What am I suffering from?"

Agnès explained. "It's a good sign that you're reviving. I'll ask the nurse to come and look after you now. I have to leave."

"Wait," he said, his voice raspy but not unfriendly. "May I thank you for what you have done? I think I owe my life to you."

It was on the tip of her tongue to reply, *I owe my life to you*, but that was the one boon she was not going to grant him. Ever!

"You're not there yet, *Herr General*," she said curtly. "Now, if you'll excuse me..."

Suddenly Agnès was bone-weary and depressed. Despite the fact that the Allied forces had taken control again, and all day long she had heard a variety of English accents, from Canadian to American to Australian, in the corridors and the courtyard, she had not left the hospital; had not even been able to greet the family that was back. But she did not feel like seeing anyone at that moment, so she sneaked out the back door to the kitchen garden and sat down on the wooden bench where she had sat with Alan only two days earlier, looking out over her beloved Picardy fields.

She wanted to cry, but her eyes remained dry. It felt like her whole soul had been wrenched out of her body, and she just sat there in the late afternoon sun, unable to think, unable to feel, unable to understand, until from a source deep down inside of her a new force welled up, finding its way to the surface. *She had survived!* Then the tears came, and kept coming and coming until she understood she was free, free of it all.

14

MERCY NO MERCY

Madeleine

Château de Dragoncourt, 11 August 1918

Madeleine paced her old bedroom on the first floor of her castle with Loulou on her shoulder. Since the Allies had recaptured the castle two days earlier, she had taken possession of her own quarters and removed the reminders of both British and German soldiers in her private place as best she could. But it still did not feel like her own room. The scent was different, and she was sensitive to scent. She had kept the windows open night and day and sprinkled her *Caresse d'Amour* perfume everywhere, but it was no use. It stank of strange men and of war, and it irritated her.

Now that ownership of Dragoncourt had returned to her family, all war reminders had to be swept outside. That was what she wanted but failed to accomplish. The courtyard and castle still teemed with soldiers, albeit Allied forces, but Madeleine was done with the war. *Over is over. Go home, Boches and let us be!* Feeling her mistress's ill humor, Loulou tried to attract her attention by pulling her short hair, but Madeleine was not in the mood for pranks.

"I don't know what's wrong with me," she declared, endlessly traversing from the window to her four-poster bed and back. "I just still feel caged. I need to do something, get rid of this unrest." Then her gold-colored eyes flashed, and she clapped a hand over her mouth.

"Oh no, I can't!" she cried out, but then, "Yes, I can!"

She quickly dressed in one of Elle's ambulance uniforms and drew a camouflage cap deep over her forehead. Best disguise possible.

"You stay here, Loulou dear. I'll be back soon."

Whistling *La Madelon,* which she now considered her resistance song, Madeleine sauntered outside, smoking one of her Lucky Strikes. It was another glorious August day, the sky cloudless and free from the roar of battle. Even the acrid smell of gunpowder, which had hung over the entire area for years, was slowly evaporating. The gardens were still in a state of dishevelment and ruin after all the German digging, and the big holes in the castle walls had been provisionally repaired with huge tarpaulin shields. Dragoncourt was nothing like the beautiful castle it had been in all its centuries of undamaged glory; it stood erect and steady but battered as an old warship. Allied soldiers in blue, khaki, and dark-green uniforms busied themselves with repairs or sat around on the grass smoking and writing letters. They seemed to enjoy the lull in the war and the sunny weather.

Madeleine's keen eyes spotted a sergeant from the Royal West Kent Regiment, and on approaching him, she asked, "Have you seen Major Cooper, by any chance?"

"He's in the officer's quarters, Miss. In charge of transporting the German prisoners-of-war to Amiens today."

She flicked her cigarette stub away. Just what she wanted.

"Thanks!"

"Hi, Miss Madeleine," the young sergeant with the friendly round face greeted her. "What can I do for you?"

"How are you, mister soldier?" Madeleine asked, batting her eyelashes.

"Fine, ma'am! Much better! I guess you too, the house yours again? You did a great job. We're all in awe of you."

"Thanks, Sarge. Now I've got a question. Could you do me a favor and look the other way?"

"What do you mean, miss, 'look the other way'?"

"The German prisoners are in here?"

"Yes, they are."

"Well, could you?" He gazed at her quizzically, clearly not understanding what she was asking, but Madeleine had not counted on the wrong person. She saw understanding sink in, and his eyes became wide with bafflement but also with a deep admiration.

"For you, Miss Madeleine, I will look the other way. I know nothing." He unlocked the door for her and stepped back.

Madeleine found herself in the same square room where four months earlier she had stood in her Prussian uniform waiting for Agnès after that horrible encounter with General van Spiegler. Papa was still staring down from the wall on the group of bedraggled German soldiers who were sitting cross-legged on the floor, their hands tied behind their backs. Madeleine scanned the group, but Von Spiegler was not among them. Agnès still insisted on keeping him in the sick ward.

"The lucky bastard," Madeleine growled under her breath. She quickly checked the corners of the room, but there were no other guards. Standing among the men, towering above them, she commanded, "Charles Green, get up and meet Ernst Höbel!"

No one reacted, but the man whom she'd found lying by the side of the road eyed her with fear. Her squinted eyes fixed angrily on him, and he slowly struggled to his feet, toppling over once because he could not keep his balance.

"Come here!"

The man shuffled closer.

"What's your name?"

"Corporal Spitzel, ma'am. Who... who is Ernst Höbel?" It was almost inaudible.

"I am! As much as you are Charles Green. We're even!"

Madeleine reached within the tunic of her ambulance uniform and pulled out a Smith and Wesson Colt. A ripple of hushed fear went through the room, and Spitzel swayed on his legs, begging her with his weak blue eyes.

"Please don't, Miss, please don't shoot me."

She pointed the gun straight at his chest, cocked it, and put her finger on the trigger. Looking straight at him, she said in an even voice, "You swore your name was Charles Green, and I believed you and consequently brought the enemy into my father's room. You rat, you betrayed me, and I don't forgive."

The man in front of her started to shake over his whole body, but still Madeleine kept the barrel pointing at him.

"What do you have to say for yourself?"

"No... nothing, Ma'am. I fo... followed orders, that was all. Please, I have a family in *Köln*."

Madeleine squinted, thinking hard; could she do it? Should she? But the moment had passed, and she let the gun sink. Spitzel collapsed at her feet. She kicked him hard.

"You're lucky today. But don't praise the day yet. I'll see to it that you get a long, awfully long prison sentence." She marched out of the door.

"Wise decision, Miss Madeleine," Sergeant Cooper shouted after her. "And I'll pass on your orders. You're one of us now. Keep your head cool."

Madeleine shrugged her shoulders. It was not the satisfying end she had envisioned, but it was a lot less messy. Perhaps killing another human really *was* another league.

She found Elle and Jacques rearranging *la grande salle verte* into some of its former role. She could see how tired her brother and sister were, but the recapture of the castle had given them new energy. Madeleine hurried over to help them carry the heavy oak dinner table back to the center.

"It will be so special to eat here again tonight," Elle beamed. "Gosh, it's been four years!"

"Don't you think it's a bit morbid to eat here? Where all these men have been operated on and even died?" Madeleine wrinkled her nose.

"We'll clean every bit of furniture, and the windows have been open all the time," Bridget chimed in, who was just about to wheel the X-ray machine outside.

"Still it smells of chloride and stained blood."

"You with your dog's nose, Mad-Maddy," Jacques laughed. "Who cares? It's our dining room, and we'll eat in it if we want."

"When are Papa and Mummy arriving?" Madeleine fingered Agnès's surgeon knives that lay on a tray in the window.

"Not until next week," Elle observed. "But Agnès's father arrives tonight. There was no stopping the Baron de Saint-Aubin anymore."

"Oh golly," Madeleine exclaimed. "But that German general is still here – her other Papa."

"Hush, Maddy!" Elle hissed. "Von Spiegler's unaware of that, and Agnès doesn't want him to know, so hold your blab."

"Sorry, but *we* all know now! Where is Agnès, anyway?"

"Where do you think?" Jacques' voice did not hide his disappointment.

"With Alan?" Madeleine dropped the delicate, sharp knives back on the tray. "I'm going to see her. Unless you need me here?"

"On your way out, catch Phil and ask him to instruct cook to make something special tonight! Entertaining our first guest since the occupation." Elle's eyes had some of their former shine, and Madeleine just had to go over and give her elder sister a big hug. But then she looked puzzled.

"Cook, you said? Isn't our lovely Earl the one stringing the onions and the rhyme words together into a spicy casserole?"

"No, he's been able to snare Madame Denis into preparing us a meal tonight."

"You should marry Phil," Madeleine remarked, as she walked out the door, shaking her head. "Times change, and they don't change."

She was happy she would see Marie Denis again but not sure she wanted to go back to a life where servants were servants again.

Alan was asleep on a chaise lounge, his long, thin body in dark-blue pajamas with white piping, resting comfortably on the cushions. But his deep frown betrayed his unhappy situation. Agnès was sitting in a chair next to him, reading a book. She had drawn the shades, so the light of the afternoon sun was diffused. It was very still in the room, and Madeleine treaded in softly. Agnès lifted her angelic face and smiled that endearing smile of hers. Madeleine hesitated for a moment, not knowing whether to approach further or to halt.

There was always this tentative energy between the two young women, a combination of respect and awe for each other, but also a slight discomfort at being so completely opposite in character. Agnès made Madeleine softer, but Madeleine felt she had no influence on the accomplished, determined young surgeon, who was not a great speaker but a formidable doer. Yet she sensed that Agnès liked her and was always pleased to see her.

With a thin, white finger to her lips, Agnès rose from her chair and went outside the door, beckoning her.

"I know it's none of my business," Madeleine blurted out, "but I was worried about you. You know, your Papa coming and Von Spiegler still here. What are you going to do?" She gauged Agnès anxiously and was surprised to see a flicker of doubt in the otherwise cloudless gaze.

For a while Agnès said nothing. Then she swallowed hard. "Thank you, for asking, Madeleine. I've not wanted to burden anyone with this personal matter, but it's been on my mind constantly since my father said he was coming to Dragoncourt. Knowing him, there's no doubt he's going to make a racket, especially after the general's treatment of me." Agnès sighed. "I don't know what to do."

"Do you want me to handle it for you?"

"You? How?" Agnès stared at her in disbelief.

"Well, I don't know. I never know what's going to come out of my mouth when I'm under pressure, but it usually works out perfectly. As you've seen. And I would never do anything to harm you."

"Gosh," Agnès shook her head slowly. "It would take a lot of tension away from me if Von Spiegler knew before my father arrives, but it's ridiculous to expect you to cut my meat for me."

"Don't forget I still have my own bone to pick with him. It would be a double-edged sword."

"But what if he freaks out? He's still not in good shape."

"Let him work himself up! Oh, Agnès, you're too good for this world. After all he's put you through and all you've done for him. You know what? You listen behind the door, and if I say anything you don't want me to say, you just come in and shut me up. Is that an idea?"

Agnès thought about that and then nodded. "It has to be done straightaway, then. Alan will wake up soon, and he's always in a bad mood when he finds out he can't get up."

"That guy doesn't know the gold he's got right under his nose." It sounded harsher than she'd intended, but Agnès did not seem to notice.

Together they went to the small alcove that had been turned into a convalescent room for the general. Although Von Spiegler could not rise from his bed, there was a guard outside his door night and day.

Agnès motioned for Madeleine to go in, obviously eager to have it over and done with.

"I'll be right here," she whispered.

As Madeleine strode in, she saw the German was awake, although drowsy from the sedation he was on. He turned his eyes in her direction and observed her without recognizing her as impudent and phony German soldier.

Madeleine sat down on the chair that stood next to his bed and gazed straight back at him. "I came here as Ernst Höbel a couple of weeks ago, but my real name is Madeleine de Dragoncourt."

He blinked, and she saw his brain clicked, but it did not seem to impress him much.

"I must say," she continued, "it was a great triumph to pay you back with the same trump card that you had used on us with your

damned Corporal Spitzel. In fact, I have to thank you for that ingenuity because it helped me prepare my plan – which was ultimately
more successful than yours, *n'est-ce pas*?" She waited to see if he
would say anything, but he did not.

"By the way, I've had a word with Spitzel earlier this afternoon,
and I can assure you he'll be under lock and key for a long time
coming. Just like you!" Still no response.

"Well, as you seem to have little words left after all your barking
and commanding around *my* castle, I have another surprise coming
for you." Madeleine folded her hands in her lap and pressed her lips
together. She wanted a reaction from him, not this limp surrender. It
was too cowardly; too easy.

The general coughed, a raspy, unhealthy rattle, and shifted on the
bed. Then he raised his hand as if wanting to say something.
Madeleine waited. He took his time.

"I've been in the army since I was sixteen. All in all, it's been
thirty-five years. I do not remember a life outside the army, and I
thought I had seen it all, until this war. No man was prepared for
this." His face contorted, and Madeleine braced herself, not
wanting to be taken on the sympathy trail. He had another
coughing attack.

"When I was injured and this female doctor, who is supposed to
be my enemy, took care of me, it set me thinking. What is my life?
What am I fighting for? What is right, or wrong? I've just been
following the Kaiser's orders like everybody else in my army, in this
war and in all the other wars I've fought. I've forsaken a family life, a
cozy home, put Kaiser and country always before myself, gave everything up for my career and my rank. I sent men to their death – not
one, not ten, but thousands, men much younger, much more intelligent, much more qualified than me. And yet I lie here in this bed and
live."

Madeleine did not like where this was going so interrupted him,
"I'm not here to listen to your philosophical chatter, Von Spiegler.
Keep that for your memoirs, in which you can glorify yourself and
your *Deutschland*."

"You misunderstand me, Miss de Dragoncourt!" There was some of the old commander in the voice.

Madeleine lifted an eyebrow. "Oh, do I? I may be a lot younger than you, but I know the sort. You're trying to wriggle yourself out of this pickle you're in. Trying to get a shorter sentence by showing pathetic regret. I don't buy it. Not from you!"

"And I don't blame you." The general was reviving, and Madeleine, feeling the battle begin, sat up straighter to enjoy herself.

"Why are you telling me this?"

"Because I finally realize that I made the wrong choices in life, or rather, I didn't make choices at all but let family privileges do that for me. I was never an army man. But being a Prussian, from a long line of proud military men, I did what I was supposed to do."

Madeleine was still not satisfied. "You're not answering my question! Why do you tell me?"

"So that you, fiery young man Ernst Höbel, when I am well and truly rotting away in a French prison, can tell that wonderful Doctor de Saint-Aubin that *she* changed my life. I'm too much of a coward – as you've correctly observed – to tell her myself."

Now Madeleine gaped at him, temporarily forgetting her role. "What do you mean?"

"It's probably a combination of the drugs I'm on and her resemblance to the only woman I ever really loved and whom I lost – oh, irony – to that doctor's father by an act of my own stupidity."

"Ho, ho, ho!" Madeleine shouted. "You mean to say you loved Agnès' mother?"

"I've only loved two women in my life: my mother Masha and Ingrid Gescke. And I've managed to alienate both from me." It was said as an observation, not a plea for pity.

"Hell!" Madeleine swore under her breath. This conversation was going in quite a different direction than she had anticipated. How to get it back on track? She was aware poor Agnès was hearing every word of it on the other side of the door.

"Listen," she said firmly, "it's all well and good, but this is not bringing us any further. Why cry over spilled milk?"

"I agree. I just wanted to let someone know before I'm gone from here, and you happened to walk in. I couldn't tell one of the guards, and the only other person I see is Doctor de Saint-Aubin."

"Then I might as well tell you the truth." Madeleine sighed deeply. "Agnès is your biological daughter. Ingrid was pregnant with your child when she left your family. Baron Max de Dragoncourt married her and adopted your child as his own. Agnès has known all along that you were her biological father."

It was as if she could hear Agnès hold her breath on the other side of the door. Madeleine kept her attention fixed on the general, ready to react to whichever angle he would take.

For a moment he did nothing. He blinked; he coughed. And then it happened faster than daylight, and even later Madeleine would not understand how this could have happened in an instant.

With one quick tug, Eberhard von Spiegler tore the syringe from his arm, grabbed the razor knife that lay on his bedside table, and had cut the main artery in his throat before Madeleine even had time to do anything. Blood spurted on the bedclothes and against the walls. Agnès ran into the room and instantly pressed a towel on the gaping wound. Madeleine screamed at the top of her lungs, and the general fixed his dying gaze on Agnès. With a "Sorry" on his cold, white lips, he let out his last breath.

THE EVENING MEAL that was supposed to be a reunion of regained peace and renewed hospitality was overshadowed by the German general's sudden suicide. Madeleine in particular felt responsible for the ugliness that had happened that afternoon, and she kept glancing across the table at Agnès's still, white face. Sitting very closely together with the Baron, she seemed to draw strength from her father's presence, and he did his utmost to cheer everyone up.

"After all, I'm the only partisan who has survived this war without even a tiny scratch," he said apologetically, drawing on his Le Roy cigar and putting a slender arm around his daughter's shoulders. "I can't tell you, my children, how proud I am to be a citizen of France, a country that bred the likes of heroes and heroines like you."

"It's not over yet, Baron," Gerald Hamilton observed, sucking on his pipe.

"Well, almost, I would say."

"If I've learned one thing from this war, it's that these Boches have tricks up their sleeves, from the Ural to dark Africa, so I wouldn't count my chickens yet."

"Don't you dare douse our convivial delight, Gerry!" Philip waved his fountain pen at him. "All we are in need of today is a Panglossian evening of toasting and chicken à la Denisoise."

"I agree." Elle smiled. "Here's to peace!"

"To peace!"

They all raised their glasses and put the past behind them – at least for the duration of the evening in *la grande salle verte*.

Madeleine glanced around the table at the faces of the people who were dearest to her now in the whole world, and she blessed each and every one of them: serious M-C, breezy Bridget, funny Philip, loyal Elle, unfathomable Jacques, strong Agnès, with in her shadow capable Alan, and finally Gerald who was looking at her with an amorous expression that made her dream of peace and dancing and having a life again.

Whatever would happen, this episode was over.

15

ARMISTICE DAY

Agnès

Paris, 11 November 1918

Agnès clapped her hands with approval. "Isn't he fantastic, Master Julien?"

Master Julien, slim, muscular, and dressed entirely in tight white overalls as if he were a fencer, rubbed his hands together with magnesium oxide. Smiling broadly, he acknowledged her enthusiasm.

"He is, Madame, but did I not tell you both to keep faith? Just some minor adjustments." Slapping the surplus powder from his hands, he took up his position between the bars.

"Madame, please stand right at the end of the bars," Julien instructed, encircling the wooden rods with his white-palmed hands. "Now Monsieur Bell, I'll show you once more how to correctly put one leg in front of the other. First, grip the bars firmly, then focus on your toes – see if you can touch that piece of paper on the floor with them, first toes of the right foot, then of the left. Don't think of the numbness in your legs, nor of the lack of coordination in your left foot. Fix your gaze on Madame, she is your carrot – so to speak."

The reconstruction aid grinned widely, showing two rows of perfect white teeth in a healthy, young face. "So, ready for your treat? Move from the hips, lift your foot, bend at the knee, hands slide along."

Master Julien slow-motioned to the other end of the bars like a man venturing out on an ice rink and at the end made a gallant bow for Agnès. Then he turned to Alan, who had let his long body sink back into his wheelchair, small drops of perspiration on his forehead, his hands folded in his lap and his beautiful eyes pensive.

"Come on, Doctor Bell, one more time. Get the prize at the end."

Alan wheeled around to the start of the contraption, and Julien helped him up. Unsteadily he gripped the bars and willed himself between them. Agnès was once again struck by how thin and fragile he looked on the outside but how much willpower he had shown in the last couple of months to rehabilitate his maimed body.

She smiled affectionately at him. "I hope you like carrots. Or we can make it chocolate?"

Alan relaxed his shoulders, and despite the concentrated frown between his dark eyebrows, he grinned. "How about a kiss?"

Now Master Julien clapped his hands, and the white powder dusted the air like a snowball pulverizing in mid-air. "Bravo!" he exclaimed. "No better reward for an accomplishment than a kiss from a fair lady. Go for it, Doctor Bell!"

It was a chaste kiss, the kiss of a friend, but it made Agnès almost as happy as Alan's progress.

"Next practice tomorrow," Master Julien announced. "Now it's party time. Are you also going to the Grand Boulevards to celebrate the Armistice?"

"Of course." Agnès beamed. "I wouldn't want to miss it for the world."

Alan shrugged but stayed silent.

"Don't be silly, Alan," she exclaimed. "I'll push you, so don't worry! You so deserve to celebrate this historic peace treaty with all of

Paris. Even more than I do. Papa will come as well, so if I'm tired of
pushing, he can do his bit. And I don't want to hear 'no'!"

"All right, if you insist on dragging an invalid along, but I tell you,
it will hamper your dancing with the handsome soldiers."

"Ha-ha," she giggled. "Don't bet on it. I'll dance to my heart's
content while I leave you in the care of some ugly, old nurse."
Winking at him mischievously, she added more seriously, "But let me
take you to your room first, so you can put on your suit. I'll ask Gaël
to prepare us some lunch, and then we're off to the festivities. Thank
you, Master Julien, see you tomorrow!"

And waving to the young man in his white outfit, who disappeared through the back entrance, she pushed Alan's wheelchair
from the basement to the elevator that Papa had especially installed
in their Boulevard mansion on the Seine.

One part of the basement was still the Baron's wine cellar, but the
other part, where the family had so often sat huddled together during
the air raids, was now refurbished as a rehabilitation room. Agnès
and Alan, under the watchful supervision of Master Julien, spent
hours there every day to improve Alan's strength and train him to
walk again.

And slowly, inch by inch, after months of many drawbacks and
violent outbursts, it was finally happening, and the once-proud
doctor seemed to be regaining some of his former *joie de vivre*. It was a
slow, painful process, and it demanded all Agnès's patience and
perseverance to keep him at it. It felt like she had to live for two; that
Alan had given up hope of ever being anything to anyone again, especially to himself.

The depression had been apparent even before they returned
from Dragoncourt to Paris in late August, and Agnès knew it was
much more than just his physical infirmity. Alan had lost his future
and would now be forced to do what he hated most: depend on
others. But it had been obvious that he could not live on his own, not
even with special care.

So, the choice had been living with the de Saint-Aubins or withering away by himself in a nursing home until he was physically fit

enough to return to the States, as Agnès supposed was his plan. To Alan it had meant his life was over; his wife was gone and his career in tatters. Often, inadvertently, he had taken a swing at Agnès, who had endured his foul moods because she understood him so well.

"Are you wearing anything special to the party?" He clearly wanted to show his good intentions and make conversation. He did not like it when she was silent. It was part of the guilt trap he sometimes fell into.

"I only have dresses from before the war, so I'll probably look really outdated," Agnès confessed, "but I'll take a proper look in my wardrobe. You're right. This is an occasion to dress up, and Papa would so like to see me in something other than a white coat." She studied the back of his head, the dark hair curling over the collar of his flannel shirt, so familiar and so beloved to her.

He craned his neck to look at her while they waited for the elevator doors to open. "Do you have a red dress? I think red would really suit you, plus it would certainly make you stand out in the crowd."

Agnès pushed aside the metal cage door with a clang, and the elevator door opened. Alan maneuvered the wheelchair inside the small square cubicle, turning it around so he could face her. She was glad to see there was a trace of happiness in his face. Today might just be a good day.

"I promise I'll try to look presentable. Isn't it funny that I have a Papa who loves nothing better than to put on fancy clothes, and I could not care less? I'd wear my doctor's coat over my day dress any day of the week and forget about it." She looked down at the white coat with the habitual stethoscope sticking out of her pocket. Even at home, even when she was not at the American Hospital where she worked two days a week, she never paid much attention to the way she dressed.

"Do it for me. Do it for what we've been through," Alan implored, and she was surprised at the urgency in his voice. He never saw her as anything but a dear friend, maybe a little sister, and alas... no longer a colleague. At least not yet – because Agnès would fight until Alan was back at the operating table where he belonged. He might not know it, but she did. So why this sudden interest in her attire? It was too late to ask because they had arrived at the second floor and each went to their separate rooms.

"See you in an hour," she called over her shoulder, as she opened the door to her bedroom. She still felt his gaze on her, and it unsettled her, so she was glad to be able to close the bedroom door behind her and be alone in her sanctuary, away from these intense eyes. She could handle it all if he did not cross the line. She would rather have him angry and upset, or normal and regular but not showing any interest in her as a woman. He was her everything – she loved him so dearly – but there were so many emotions on so many layers between them; it was so complicated, such a fragile composition.

"Don't change, Alan," she begged, watching herself in the large mirror that stood at a slight angle in the corner of her room. "Be my friend, just my friend." She studied herself intently, maybe considering what he might see, a slim girl with springy yellow hair and very blue eyes, a porcelain skin with high cheekbones and a fine nose, natural red lips, her lower lip slightly fuller. An open face; there was nothing she could hide in that face. Did he see that too?

The buttons of her wide doctor's coat were open, showing a mid-calf-length blue dress with brown low-heeled boots underneath. How many times had Papa told her to make herself more feminine if she was to ever attract a husband? But the war had mangled it all up, or maybe it had not been the war but her fear of being a woman. It was much easier to be a doctor or a friend. She disengaged from her reflection and went to her wardrobe.

Instinctively her hands reached for the red silk dress, a beautiful shade of crimson, and letting the lustrous fabric of the skirt slide through her fingers, she remembered the one time she had worn it. For her graduation, when Professor Alan Bell had handed her *Le Diplôme de l'Etat de docteur en medicine* from *l'Université de Sorbonne* in June 1914, a month before war was declared.

Removing the soft paper wrapping that diligent Petipat had used to protect the pure white of the lace collar, Agnès took the dress from its hanger and sauntered over to the mirror, holding it in front of her doctor's coat. Memories flooded through her as she watched the echo of her former, younger self.

"Please proceed, Baroness Agnès de Saint-Aubin," the chairman of the Sorbonne Medical school had announced in a booming voice, and Papa, nudging her, had whispered in her ear, "Go, *mon ange,* I'm so proud of you." And she had somehow stood up from between Papa and Madame Petit, shakily in her dainty black pumps, straightening her silk dress with sweaty palms. It had seemed as if her feet did not touch the carpeted aisle in between the rows and rows of chairs that divided the enormous hall, its walls and ceiling covered with 16th century oil paintings and its mahogany wainscoting giving the high room a rather dark demeanor.

Unaware of the presence of almost exclusively young men, Agnès had focused on the top of the three stone steps at the front of the hall where Alan was standing, flanked by Sorbonne officials, her diploma in his graceful hands. He was almost unrecognizable to her dressed as he was in a pinstriped suit instead of his doctor's attire and with his hair combed fashionably backwards over his scalp. But the steel-gray gaze that smiled down on her had been unmistakable, and his steady gaze had somehow kept her upright and not stumbling to disgrace herself in front of everybody.

His eyes had urged her forward, convincing her not to be afraid, and suddenly her heart had burst open with a tidal wave of pride and happiness. She had felt it so deeply then; she had done it! Thanks to him, to his support, she had made her own dream come true because she loved him; she had loved him right from the beginning. But he should never know.

The memory was so vivid that it brought Agnès back to the present with a jolt. She shook herself sternly.

"It's enough to have him around me every day for as long as it lasts," she reminded herself, while she slipped out of her work gear and let the red dress slip over her head, where it fell around her like a red flame of sensuous pleasure. It still fitted perfectly around her slender waist, although she could hear Petipat's voice reproach her:

The war hasn't done your pretty looks any good, my dear, you're way too skinny at the waist and no feminine bosom to speak of.

"I know, Petipat," Agnès told her mirrored image with a mock expression on her face, "but feminine bosom or not, I'm going to wear this dress tonight. I might even find myself a dashing Australian major and be scooped off my feet and planted – red dress and all – on the other side of the world." Somehow that did not sound right to her, as she could never see herself leaving her Papa or her work, but to be that far from Alan, however conflicted her feelings, sometimes seemed like an attractive option.

Unaccustomed to glitzing herself up, Agnès tossed her curls up on top of her head and fastened them with a ruby-studded pin that had belonged to her late mother. On her petite earlobes she screwed tight the pear-shaped diamond earrings that Papa had given her for her twenty-first birthday. A little rouge on her pale cheeks and a dash of coral lipstick on her full lips was all she could think of in the way of make-up. Rummaging around in the bottom of her wardrobe, she found the linen bag with her black pumps, and kicking off her booties, stepped into the patent leather heels and fastened the straps.

"Hmmm," she mused to herself, longingly eyeing the comfortable brown boots. There would be a lot of walking and dancing, and then there was pushing Alan around Paris all afternoon and evening. Nobody would have time to pay attention to her feet, Agnès decided, gratefully slipping back in the low-heeled footwear. After a last glance at herself, she giggled to herself about the mismatch of dress and shoes, but it was too late to change now. Then, taking a deep sigh, she announced herself ready to partake in the peace festivities that the Allied forces had finally acquired at such a phenomenally high price.

In one way, Agnès was still the twelve-year-old eavesdropping at the door to the parlor to overhear what Papa and Petipat were discussing, as it usually involved her, and she always wanted to know what was at stake and which side would be more advantageous to support. It had usually been Papa's. So as of custom, she halted outside the door and listened in to the humming of her father's and

Alan's voices. They got on so well, really enjoying each other's company despite their totally different backgrounds, age, and profession.

There had not been a shadow of doubt in the Baron's mind but to take the young and wounded American doctor under his roof and under his wing, seeing to it that he got the best care to be bought in Paris. But the middle-aged aristocrat with his eccentric tastes and musical passions had never fathomed how much he would enjoy the company of a new-world scientist with modern ideas and a tendency to put his own life at risk to rescue others. Yet a deep friendship had developed, and it had lessened Agnès' burden over Alan's recovery, as in the evenings the men usually took an hour or two to converse.

"I've heard from my solicitor today, and things have been settled, so I can finally sell the house in Châtelet and start paying you back for your hospitality." Alan's voice sounded relieved.

"I'm cock-a-hoop for you, old chap, but don't even dream of paying me back one centime because I would categorically refuse it," her father's much lighter voice chimed in. "By Jove, I've got plenty of the goods and chattels, I don't need it, and you'll be all too pleased to have it at your disposal in the future. Perhaps you'll want to start a family or buy an estate of your own. No, no, no talking of these platitudes. Enough!"

"I don't know if I can accept that, Max, but as you're as strong-willed as your daughter, I'll rest my case for now. I must say I *am* greatly relieved. It's been such a dark and uncertain period of my life."

"Oh, I get that much, dear fellow. It's a weight off my shoulders as well. I've been praying for this day *ad nauseam*."

Agnès put her ear to the door. Since when were Alan's worries of such great concern to her father that he would invoke a higher power to resolve them?

"So, it's okay with you?" Alan sounded doubtful.

"Okay?" her father mimicked, shouting loudly. "Oh, you prosy Americans! Of course! It's utopian!"

At that moment, she decided to make her entrance, her mind in a bit of a spin, and hoping she would not break up their conversation. She wanted to find out if her father was thinking of investing in Alan's future.

The two men were seated on both sides of the fireplace. Gaël had lit a sizeable fire, as it was a chilly November day, and thick birch logs snapped and crackled at their feet. Alan was sitting on a straight chair, smoking a Lucky Strike, while her father was lounging in his easy leather chair, a thin Le Roy cigar between his elegant fingers. A small round table with a decanter and sherry glasses stood in between them. They both looked up as her rustling skirt announced her arrival, and she blushed at their exclamations of praise.

"*Magnifique!*" her father burst out. "Ah, *ma petite,* you are the paragon of beauty! Don't you think, Alan?"

"She's amazing," Alan confirmed. "Oh, and I remember that dress. That was the one I had in mind when I asked you if you had anything in red! Perfect, simply perfect!"

"Stop it," Agnès said with mock self-consciousness, "or I'll go upstairs and put on my white coat again. After all, that's what won us the war." But she was laughing and swirled around for them, making the wide skirt swish around her slender legs.

"Come and sit here, dear, don't catch a cold in that scanty garment." Her father had hoisted his slim posture from his chair and was busy dragging an extra armchair near the fire, thereby almost knocking over the table with the drinks.

"Let me do that, Papa," Agnès berated him, saving both the chair and the table. "You're never good at moving furniture around."

"I'm never good at anything but getting in the way," the Baron replied good-humoredly, "so I'll let you young people talk for a while. Let me go and see where the devil Gaël is with our lunch."

"Papa, what's wrong with you?" Agnès demanded. "Go and sit in your chair and don't act so strange."

But her father extinguished his cigar in the ashtray and, mumbling an apology, made his way to the door. Agnès shook her head at this new folly. He never went to the kitchen to have anything to do with the maids, so what had gotten into him now was beyond her.

Time to recover was not given to her because the second after she had sat down, Alan got up with difficulty. Pushing himself up with his hands on the armrests, he stood swaying on his legs before her but looking down on her with a very strange expression on his face. Now it was Agnès's time to say, "What the devil?" as she saw him clumsily sink on one knee and, holding his balance with all his willpower, reach into the inner pocket of his jacket.

"Alan!" she cried. "Let me help you up. You're going to hurt yourself!"

"Agnès, please stop talking for a minute, will you?" His voice was hoarse, the clear eyes fixing hers. And then she saw the light break over his face, as the sun that reappeared from behind the clouds, that lopsided, boyish grin she had seen only a few times but that was sure to melt her heart to the core. Her hand instinctively covered her mouth.

"Agnès, Baroness de Saint-Aubin, will you do me the honor of becoming my wife?" He held out a tiny box with a diamond ring pinned on a white satin cushion.

"But... but..." she stammered. "You're already married."

"Not anymore, Agnès. The divorce was settled last week. I'm finally a free man, I can finally be yours. Unless you don't want me?"

Confusion was high in Agnès. This sudden change was impossible to grasp. Did he love her? He had never shown his feelings for her in that way, but she was also very aware of how uncomfortable he was on his knee on the floor in front of her, and she did not know what to do.

"Please, Alan," she begged. "Get up first and sit down. Then we'll talk."

His face fell. "I'm sorry, Agnès," he said miserably, refusing her help to scramble to his feet again and struggle to sit back on the hard, wooden chair. "I thought... well... I guess I thought wrong."

Now that he was sitting and physically safe, she could not hold back and was at his side in an instant. It was her turn to sink to her knees beside him and rest her blonde head in his lap.

"Of course I love you, Alan, I've always loved you. But you... you never gave me the slightest idea that you returned my feelings so... so... you just caught me off guard. I'm sorry. I didn't want to disappoint you."

He was softly caressing her curls, and his hands on her hair felt heavenly. But his next words were as good.

"I have also always loved you, dearest, but what right did I have to show you how I felt? I was married; I was your professor, your mentor. It was wrong in every way possible, so I had to hold back. But darling, please don't doubt my sincerity. While I couldn't tell how much I loved you, I put all my efforts in trying to protect you from all danger until... the tables were turned, and you had to save my life. Which you did, you incredible Doctor de Saint-Aubin, because humble as you are, I know full well that the operation you performed on me was a masterpiece. You are my equal in every possible way, and I love you to the galaxies and back. So, will you be my wife, Agnès?"

He lifted her head ever so tenderly from his lap to meet her eyes. And then she did not just see it in his smile but also in those lovely eyes; how he had always had that loving, yearning look but had shrouded it, replacing it forcefully with care and compassion. It *was* love, it was much more than love, it was the whole universe in those eyes – her universe.

She gave him a rather trembling right hand, and he slipped the ring on her finger.

"Your Papa told me your size," he said softly.

To Agnès this was a new bafflement. "Papa? Does he kn...?", and then she burst out laughing. "Him with his going to the kitchen to spur on Gaël! Devious men you are!"

They both laughed, and Alan got to his feet, towering a good thirty centimeters above her. But bowing down his dark head, he cupped her face in his warm hands and kissed her lightly on the lips. It was the signal of signals.

Agnès threw her arms around him and kissed him back with a

passion she had no notion she had in her. Blending into his arms, she pressed her lips against his and her body against that beloved chest, where his heart beat for her, just for her! She had no idea her small frame could sustain such overpowering happiness; it washed through her like a gigantic wave, and she had to momentarily stop kissing him to sniffle away a tear.

"Dearest," he kept saying, kissing her hair, her cheeks, her eyelids, "Oh, my dearest, my dapper life saver, my queen, you have no idea how many years I've yearned for this moment and how slim I thought my chances were it would ever come to pass. If only you knew how many nightmares I've had in which you wed another man – a younger, more accomplished aristocrat. How jealous I was of Jacques de Dragoncourt. You have no idea!

"Jacques?" Agnès giggled. "Jacques is lovely, but I could never fall in love with him. He's like a dear brother to me." She shook her head engagingly. "Oh my goodness, I'm such a goose. I could have seasoned your jealousy when I had the opportunity. But then again, it wouldn't have been fair to poor Jacques, and I'm not like that."

"No, you're not," Alan agreed. "You're my honest, upright, lovely Agnès, and I adore you for being just yourself – no games, no tricks. I've never met anyone like you. You're perfect!"

"I'm not, and I'll show you." And suiting her actions to her words, she firmly planted her lips on his and kissed him with such passion that she soon felt his body respond with an almost untamable lust and still she did not let go of his mouth, flinging her whole being in his arms with a temperament new and thrilling to him, until they both dissolved in a sensuous, enraptured embrace, from which he fought to entangle himself, panting, "Oh my God, stop, or I can't vouch for myself anymore!"

"There," she beamed, her mouth swollen and red, while she coolly pinned up a curl that had escaped. "Now forget your idea of me being perfect. Let this set the tone for what I'm also capable of."

"I surrender." Alan grinned, looking incredibly young and mischievous. "Oh, my dear, we'll be so happy. It's... well, your dad would say... utopian."

The dad, at that moment, casually sauntering into the room on his embroidered *babouches,* played his innocent man in the woods act, but the gay glint in his dark Spanish eyes betrayed his part in it all.

Agnès let go of Alan for a moment and flung herself into her father's arms. "Papa," she cried, now tears streaming down her cheeks, "Papa, I am so... so... happy! I'll leave it to you to find a posher word for it!"

"No need for posh words, my sweet," the Baron said, returning her warm embrace. "Love doesn't need poshing up with words, but it does need fire to burn. So, I suggest we dive into a hearty lunch before we head for the festivities." He smiled, then released her and, putting his arm around her waist, steered her back to Alan, who was still standing near the fire, looking rather sheepishly at his future father-in-law with Agnès' lipstick now lavishly stained around his mouth. He quickly retrieved a white handkerchief to get rid of the evidence of kissing his daughter so unashamedly.

But the Baron ignored all that and instead took both their right hands and placed them on top of each other, curling his own tanned musician fingers around theirs. "My dearest children," he said, and his voice was temporarily choked with emotion, "I wish you all the happiness in the world. Congratulations to both of you, and welcome to the family, Doctor Alan Bell. I knew Agnès had chosen you long ago, and my heart was so heavy because I knew how impossible her quest was, and yet... see... life is merciful and love still the greatest remover of obstacles."

They stood in silence for a moment, and Agnès thought that if there were a divine being, he was present at that moment and she felt blessed a hundredfold to be engaged to the love of her life on this day of all days, Armistice day. What a party!

As they sat down to lunch, Gaël, flustered but with a joyful face, raced around the table to serve them a steaming lunch of haricots verts, lamb chops and potato cakes. Agnès thought she could not recall the Saint-Aubin household in a merrier state, but then suddenly Petipat came to mind.

"Oh, how Petipat would have enjoyed this moment," she

exclaimed, her eyes suddenly moist. "It's all she could ever think of, her *bébé* getting married to a dashing suitor. I'm so glad you met her, however briefly, Alan. She was... everything a mother is to me."

Alan nodded, putting his hand briefly over hers.

"That she was," Gaël uttered, very uncustomarily interrupting the family meal. "She was like a mother to you *and* to me, Mademoiselle Agnès. May God bless her soul."

"Oh, sweet Gaël." Agnès turned to the loyal maid and, considering the special day it was, added warmly, "You and Marie take off the rest of the day and go and enjoy yourselves. We'll probably be staying out late anyway."

"Thank you, Madame, Marie and I have been talking about the procession for days. We wanted so much to see all the flags and the different soldiers. It will be such a sight."

"A historic day." Agnès nodded. "So, go, take off your apron. I've got it from here!"

When Gaël was gone, the Baron took a large sip from his Beaujolais Rouge and, putting the glass down, absent-mindedly turned it around on the tablecloth. He sighed and then looked pensive.

"*Allez,* Papa," Agnès urged. "A florin for your thoughts?"

"Ha," he said, shaking himself from his daydream. "I was pondering what the house would be like with you two gone. I think it's time for me to go and explore a new continent. What's the West like, dear chap?"

"Never been there myself, Max. Or would you prefer I call you Pa now?"

"You can call me whatever suits you. I've never been one for the rules of etiquette, as my daughter can confirm." He made a gesture with his agile hands as if saying, *Don't fuss.*

"Well, Max it is, then," Alan continued. "I was born and bred in Chicago, and then studied in Boston and Paris. Never traveled much, not even in my own country, so perhaps Agnès and I could join you?"

"Nah," the Baron observed. "You two don't want an old man on your heels all the time."

"Well." Alan looked slightly awkward. "I was meaning to ask.

Would it be okay if we kept the arrangements as they are now? I would... I would like to marry Agnès straightaway, but I've given it some thought, and..." He faltered, looking apprehensive, not his usual self. Both father and daughter gave him the space to collect his thoughts.

He turned to Agnès. "Dearest, I have one ardent wish, and that is to walk down the aisle as your husband, as a normal man, on my own two feet. But as you know, that's going to take at least a couple more months. Are you willing to wait that long?"

"Of course, Alan!" Agnès cried, but then she mischievously added, "There is one but, though."

"And that is?" He raised one eyebrow comically.

"Oh, nothing," she shrugged. "I'll let you feel it, don't worry!"

"Agnès," her father exclaimed in mock shame, "you little Siren of Anthemusa! But apart from that, I'd be happy as a lark to have my two most favorite people not flying out just yet!"

"I was thinking of taking up lecturing at the Sorbonne again," Alan mused. "What do you think, Agnès? I can't operate for maybe another year, but I want to make myself useful again."

"Excellent idea!" she replied. "There will be so many young men and women coming back from the war who now want to pursue a career in medicine!"

"I'll write that letter tomorrow!" He seemed pleased.

Max clapped his hands. "And now it's time to put on our dancing shoes. Sorry about you, old chap – you can keep on your pantoffles."

WALKING along the Seine with her father pushing Alan's wheelchair, Agnès found that a liberated Paris stretched all her senses to the extreme. Peace even had a distinct scent. When they reached the Pont de Neuilly, her nose delighted in the mélange of strong coffee, crêpes suzettes, flowery perfumes, car gas, and Seine water. It was the sounds that strained her eardrums most of all – thousands of Parisians shouting and singing as if they had landed in an cacophonic orchestra without a maestro, but the highest tone was so jubilant and exultant that she wanted to drink in this freedom with all her might.

The sight was the most awe-inspiring and chaotic she expected she'd ever see in her lifetime. Throngs of exalted citizens mingled with uniforms in all Allied colors, sailors, nurses in white aprons, and children alike crowded the boulevards and avenues, celebrating, dancing in the middle of the streets and clinking glasses with each other, throwing hats into the air, while bells pealed and military salutes boomed over their heads. Everywhere the *La Marseillaise* was sung *a fortissimo* with the whole city joining in:

Allons, enfants de la Patrie
Le jour de gloire est arrivé!
Contre nous de la tyrannie
L'étendard sanglant est levé!

BUT BRITISH AND Commonwealth troops good-humoredly set in *God Save the King*, and then everyone sang along with the British National anthem, mangling words but with great exhilaration.

The appeal of the Minister of the Interior, Jules Pams, had not been in vain: the national tricolor flapped triumphantly in the November wind, adorning embassies, official buildings, and church spires, while the people wildly waved a collection of small flags from all the victorious countries. People had climbed on statues, stood on rooftops, pressed together on balconies. The crowd surged and swung like a giant creature emerging from the depths of the earth in search of fresh air and new life. Tears streamed and laughter rang out.

Baron Maximilian de Saint-Aubin, in his capacity as senior officer of the Ministry of Food Supplies, had been ordained a special place on the tribune erected near the Arc de Triomphe, so they did not have to stand on their feet all day and were given a good view of the festivities along the Champs Elysées.

They had great difficulty getting to their places, though, as the motorcar that had picked them up at the Pont de Neuilly had taken two hours to cover the six kilometers through the dense crowds. But sitting comfortably in the car, they had enjoyed the delirious swarms of people. Watching her beloved city come to life again, Agnès had finally begun to realize she too had played her part in achieving this – maybe indirectly but at least she'd made sure that not every family was mourning the loss of a loved one today.

Her thoughts drifted to Capitaine Heurtier, and she hoped he was safe and sound with his family in Marseilles, also celebrating his incredibly brave part in the war and dreaming of a great flying career in the Armée de l'Air. She wondered if she would ever hear from him again and if she would ever fly in the clouds with him, to see for herself what the world from above looked like, which he had described so vividly. Thinking of this little victory, she grabbed Alan's hand, marveling in this simple act she had wanted to do so often in the past and had not dared. He responded with bringing her hand to his lips and kissing it.

All of Paris knew by then that in the early morning, General Foch and the Allied delegation had traveled from the Forêt de Compiègne by train and on arrival in Paris had presented the signed Armistice to President Poincaré and Prime Minister Clemenceau. Foch had spoken his immortal words: "My work is finished. Your work begins."

Everybody was waiting to congratulate the highly praised French Commander-in-Chief, but although he had been spotted at several places in Paris that day, well-wishers did not get to see more than a glimpse of him, nor of the other heroes that had steered France to its victory over Germany. Their calls for them were loud, but meanwhile the coming together of nations in the French capital was one jolly gang, with or without the dignitaries.

Agnès saw French, American, and British soldiers, arm in arm with each other or with French girls; soldiers of every color and colony marching together, waving each other's flags. Yank and Aussie,

Italian, Portuguese, British, Indian, Pulo, Nova Scotian, Czecho-Slovak paraded up and down the Champs Elysées and the other boulevards, kissing one another and kissing the girls. Italian airplanes flew overhead dropping flowers. People picked them up and blew kisses to the aviators high up in the sky.

Then Agnès saw the formidable Monsieur Aristide Briand, who had served no less than eleven times as Prime Minister of France, ascend the platform to address the crowds. His large mustache was still perfectly black, though his hair was as gray as a mule's. The elderly gentleman stood very erect, with his hands folded behind his back, while the people reverently reduced their decibels.

"*Mon peuple,*" he thundered, "at this moment, now France has achieved its most brilliant victory. You must beware of spoiling, by any undue exhibition of feeling, this sacred hour that should be lived through with becoming dignity. France who in this hour has acted as of yore the part of a champion of justice and right must not celebrate her triumph in a spirit of exultation and vain glory, but in a spirit of restraint and satisfaction at having done her duty, and in the conviction that she had labored to secure reparation for the crimes committed and for liberty of the world."

Loud applause thundered over the square, but the crowds had already had too much to drink to give one thought to restraining their spirit or dampening their exultation. His message was lost on them, but hats and cheers went up in the air for the famous statesman anyway.

"Isn't that the Red Cross nurse from Chicago?" Agnès called in Alan's ear, pointing to a young nurse on the arm of a French soldier.

"Heck, it's Elsie Gamble indeed." Alan beamed, cupped his hands at the sides of his mouth, and shouted over the noise, "Elsieeee!"

The brunette looked up and seeing them, started to wave and smile. She immediately dragged the handsome Frenchman with her and came over to their seats. But her face fell on seeing Alan in a wheelchair, and her hand flew to her mouth in shock. She brought out a muffled, "Oh no, how did that happen?"

"Sit down for a minute and don't mope. I'll be all right." Alan gestured to the seat that had been held for him next to Agnès but that he did not need.

"Jean, you sit down first, and I'll sit in your lap," Elsie commanded. "This is Alan Bell, my neighbor from Chicago that I was telling you about. And this is his colleague, Agnès. She's also a doctor." With her usual vivacity, Elsie busied herself with settling her beau and herself, extending her kindness by greeting the Baron with a handshake and introducing Jean, who apparently had been her patient at the Lycée Pasteur, where they had fallen in love head over heels."

"*Allons!*" she said impatiently, prodding Alan between the ribs. "Tell me!"

Alan, grabbing Agnès' hand in his, solemnly said, "We don't exactly know what happened, but it was at the start of the Hundred Days Offensive, when the Allies were recapturing the frontline hospital where Agnès and I were working. There was a sudden blast outside, and I made the stupid mistake of running towards it not wearing my white coat. I was hit, and it might well be that I was brought down by a friendly bullet, so to say. But this lady, my fiancée, performed a miraculous operation on me, which has saved me from complete transverse lesion. I'll be walk…"

"Wait!" cried Elsie ecstatically. "You two are a couple? No!! So, you *did* finally wake up and realize Suzanne wasn't right for you? Remember, I told you so!" She jumped off Jean's lap and first kissed Alan and then Agnès on both cheeks! "Hooray!" she cried. "Oh, my lord, Alan, what do your folks say about all this?"

"I haven't told them everything yet, Els, you know how they are." A shadow briefly darkened Alan's happy countenance, and it suddenly struck Agnès that she knew so little of Alan's family, apart from that he had lost his mother and did not like his stepmother. Elsie, who had grown up with him, knew more than she as his betrothed. But she was not to blame; Alan did not like to talk about his family, and before he had proposed, they hadn't had the kind of relationship where she could have asked him probing personal questions, like about his earlier marriage to Suzanne. That had seemed like all that mattered; but now she realized that he too had ties, and that they were to be her Chicago in-laws.

Alan just always seemed totally at ease in France and had never even mentioned going back to his home country, not even when he had been in the depths of despair, assuming he would never walk or work again. She had to find out more; but at that moment there was no more talk of Alan's folks, so Agnès did not get any insight into Alan's sudden change of mood. Elsie let the subject drop as well and instead recounted all her adventures since Agnès and Alan had exchanged the Lycée Pasteur hospital for Dragoncourt.

"We'll send you an invitation to our wedding," Alan promised, as Elsie and her beau were about to join the procession again.

"And you must come to ours," she exclaimed, kissing Jean full on the mouth, which made the young Frenchman beam from ear to ear, "Seems like us Americans have discovered Paris's *amour, n'est-ce pas?*" And then they were gone, hand in hand.

As evening fell all over Paris, the famous sights were illuminated. Bathing in golden light, the monuments proudly showed that they had stood the test of time and had not crumbled under German bombs: the Eiffel Tower, Sacré Coeur, Notre Dame, the Arc de Triomphe. Paris was once again the City of Light. Its heart had been damaged by the war, wounded deeply in places, but this was the day of resurrection and redemption. From now on, the city would never sleep again. Blackout and curfew were passé, ghosts of another era.

16

LOVE IN LONDON

Madeleine

London, 23 December 1918

"Are you sure this is a good idea?" Madeleine asked, as the black cab wove deftly through the Christmas shoppers that thronged Covent Garden.

"Of course," Elle retorted. "You've been dying to see Gerry all these months. Are you getting cold feet now?" Madeleine was sitting next to Elle on the backseat of the London cab, with Jacques opposite them.

"No, it's not that," Madeleine observed. "It'll be great to see Gerry and Phil. It's just that I want to leave the awful war behind us, and it's likely we'll be talking of nothing but the war all evening. It's what we share – the past."

"We're all war-weary," Jacques agreed, "so wouldn't it be a great idea to focus on our future? Look at all those happy shoppers. You wouldn't believe we've just come out this hell on earth if you see all the tinsel and holly and electric lights."

"I think we need a bit of both," Elle observed. "Of course, we need to get on with our lives, but we can't be expected to snap out of all we've gone through these past years. I know I can't."

The cab came to a stand-still in front of Rules, London's oldest restaurant. The girls hardly had time to wrap their fur stoles tightly around them and collect their purses as two men in liveries swung open the doors for them to step out.

Madeleine clutched the folds of her emerald evening gown and stuck one silver slipper out that tentatively found the wet pavement. An umbrella clicked open behind her and instantly protected her shoulder-length coiffure from the moist evening air. A deep, contented, *Ahhh* escaped her ruby lips as her eyes feasted on her all-time favorite place in London. When looking at Rules, there was no war, there never had been a war, and her whole fun-loving, beauty-loving heart swelled with happiness. They had survived, and it was time to party.

Rules stood as elegant and ageless as when Thomas Rule had opened his oyster bar in 1798, and at the end of 1918, upper-class London society flocked back to its cozy red booths and lavish cocktail bar as if there had never been a Great War.

"It's wonderful to be back!" Madeleine cried, and with her arm through Elle's, the tall, dark beauties entered underneath the burgundy canopy and into the golden-lit hall. Jacques, clad in his black tailcoats, followed on their heels.

"Welcome to Rules, Count and Countesses de Dragoncourt!" The head waiter bowed. "Let me escort you to your table. Or would you prefer to resort to the cocktail bar first?"

"Have our table companions already arrived?" Jacques asked.

"Yes, Earl Lane and Major Hamilton are residing at the cocktail bar."

"Then take us there."

On their way to the upstairs bar, they nodded to Virginia Woolf and her Bloomsbury Group, who were seated in an alcove near the window, smoking, drinking, and discoursing. On the other side of the gangway, Prime Minister David Lloyd George and his wife Margaret sat dining with some friends. It was all so customary, so intimately known to the half-English de Dragoncourts, whose London life was at least as important to them as the French part.

As they entered the dark wood cocktail bar, Phil and Gerry, two men so different in posture and outlook on life, rose amiably to their feet. The next couple of minutes were an exclamation of greetings, the men clapping each other on the shoulders and the women being pecked on the cheek.

"*Ravissante!*" Phil exclaimed, his deep-set eyes twinkling with merriment as he held Elle in his embrace. Madeleine saw he was already slightly under the influence of his Gin Rickey. "Elle, don't break my heart again, you bewitching Hecate! Do say you'll marry me tonight."

"Oh, you haven't changed one bit, silly Phil. Everybody knows you're engaged to Rosie Chapman, so stop it!"

"Am I?" Phil looked around him with a comical look on his face, as if Rosie would step out of the woodwork any minute, then slapped his forehead. "How could I forget. I am so sorry, Elle, I've been snapped up, I'm afraid."

With all the banter going on, Madeleine felt slightly uncomfortable, certainly with Gerry so close by again, wearing an unfamiliar civilian suit. They were the two who were less clamorous, the other three having been friends for so long and needing an outlet for their happiness at reuniting. She felt his gaze on her, studying her and her easy-going ways that had come so naturally at the end of the war in France, which seemed eons away now. Somehow the setting of Dragoncourt in need of rescue had given Madeleine Herculean power, a feeling she had been lacking since the war officially ended and the family had returned to London to recuperate.

"Can I get you all a drink?" Gerry interrupted the clatter of voices, his eyes still on Madeleine.

"Please," she said, with a smile.

"A Side-car!" they said at the same time, and the ice was broken.

A little later, with the three others still deep in conversation, Gerry lit two Lucky Strikes and offered one to Madeleine.

"How have you been?"

She sighed. "Well. I mean, I guess... It's been so different. Did you get my letter?"

"Yes, I did. I meant to phone you, but..." He hesitated, drawing on his cigarette. "It's different being back home, isn't it?"

"It is. I feel like I'm a different person," Madeleine disclosed. "I think it was that suicide of Von Spiegler's that finally made me realize I wasn't in a play of some sorts. I know it sounds naïve, but it was a bit of bravado fun for me."

"Well, your bravado fun was ultimately of great importance to our cause, Maddy."

She looked at him through the swirling smoke. He had never called her Maddy before.

"I know," she replied soberly, "I know."

"Have you considered seeing somebody?"

"What'd you mean, seeing somebody?"

"I think you're in shock, still. They have specialized doctors who can help you with that."

"Are you seeing one?"

Gerry laughed. "No, I'm not. I was trained as a soldier. That's different. You fell into the middle of a horrendous war, did something that asked all of your strength, and had no outlet afterwards to talk about it."

"Maybe I can talk with you?"

"You're always welcome, Miss Spy. I'd love that."

Somehow, that short conversation made Madeleine feel on top of the world, and she gratefully sipped her cocktail, now and then gazing at Gerry and always meeting his fair, open glance whenever she raised her eyes. Without words, a bond was formed between them, a bond that had been flirtation and protection in France but now tentatively was growing into something new, sensuous and inviting.

She remembered eating breast of Gressingham Duck with white beans, green sauce with orange and roast endive, and drinking fine Bourgogne wine, constantly aware of Gerry's protective, broad body next to hers.

There and then, Madeleine de Dragoncourt, once escapee, once brave spy, once denouncer of all society rules, decided she was in love and that she would probably do very soon what she had categorically denied to her friend Carolina Hohenzollern she would ever do: marry and set up house in the English countryside.

17

IN PICARDY'S FIELDS

Agnès

Winter 1918/1919

Max de Saint-Aubin reluctantly placed his Stradivarius in its blue cushioned case and, giving it a last caress, closed the black leather lid and fastened the closures. He placed the case closer to the fire but at a safe distance.

"It's no use," he said sadly. "It's far too cold in here to practice, but it's been eons since I played Vivaldi's *Winter*. I always play *Summer* because it lifts my spirits. What if I make a mistake?"

"Papa, you'll be all right. You know it by heart!" Agnès soothed him.

Wrapped in plaids, she and Alan sat huddled close to the big fire that the steward, Monsieur Legrand, had lit for them in the sitting room. They had arrived at the Château de Saint-Aubin near Roye the evening before and found the castle itself relatively unharmed, but vastly neglected and damp.

The elderly Legrand and his wife Sophie, who lived in a small cottage on the estate, had done what they could, but the château, built in the late Middle Ages, was gigantic, with moat and draw-bridge, and way too unpractical and old-fashioned. The family had not visited it in four years because for the larger part of the war, the estate had lain in German occupied territory.

Finding it either too drafty or too remote, the Germans had not shown any interest in using it for their own purposes, but they had clearly been wandering about the premises, because the courtyard was littered with Eckstein cigarette packages and empty Black Maria shells. Holes had been fired in the wooden drawbridge, and some of the walls had been used as practice targets. It had been a harrowing period for the Legrands, but they had stayed loyal to the Baron and had just kept their heads down.

"When are we expected at Dragoncourt?" Max asked, also sitting down, and lighting one of his Le Roy cigars. He looked haggard and dispirited, which was unusual for the flamboyant, energetic Baron.

"We can go there any time we want, Papa. You know that Horace and Virginia want nothing more than to shower us with their hospi-tality. This place is not good for you right now. I can see that. I think we should wait till summer to make this our home again."

The Baron blew a long curl of blue smoke from his lips. "Maybe you're right, *ma poupée*. What do you think, son?"

"I'd love to go back to Dragoncourt with you and Agnès," Alan said, nodding. "It's better to celebrate our engagement party there and not here. No offense, Max, but it's rather spooky at the moment."

"Done deal!" the Baron exclaimed. "Dragoncourt will probably be much more inhabitable already! And I can practice Vivaldi's *Winter*! Why not go now?"

"Will that not be an insult to the Legrands? We've only just arrived," Agnès remarked, her voice doubtful.

"I don't think so." Her father shook his head. His rather long, silver-threaded hair fell over his forehead. Pushing it back with an irritated gesture, he spilled the ash from his cigar on his waistcoat. "I'll explain it to them. The old couple got plenty to grin and bear themselves, so they'll probably be awfully relieved not to have to run after us as well."

After her father had left the room in much better spirits, Agnès grinned at Alan. "Let's get warm first before we collect our stuff. Knowing Papa, he'll be chatting to Legrand and his wife for a while, having to down at least two or three of their home-distilled glasses of brandy."

She spread the plaids on the rug before the fire, and Alan was quick to his feet. Agnès marveled again at the progress he had made in the past months, almost being his former self again, with such strength and agility in his limbs. Earlier in the week, he had even performed an appendix operation, and although he was worn out afterwards and his legs were numb, it had been the greatest triumph for them both.

As she lay in his arms, kissing him and feeling his firm, capable hands stroking the small of her back, she thanked her lucky stars for the bliss they had found together. Whatever the future held, with Alan in it, she did not fear it. And yet, ever since their brief meeting with Elsie Gamble on Armistice Day, she had felt that their future seemed an exclusively French affair, with extraordinarily little American dynamics.

"What's that busy mind of yours concocting?" Alan asked, releasing her mouth to look deep into her eyes, his hands continuing to caress her back. Agnès smiled. Somehow Alan always seemed to pick up every nuance of her moods. Or was she really that easy to read?

"You'd be a great psychiatrist," she replied, and laying her cheek against his, explained, "To be honest? I feel bad about our engagement party taking place without your parents and your sister."

Alan released her and pushed himself on his elbow, seeking his cigarettes. He seemed taken aback, and a frown creased his forehead, but after he had inhaled deeply and sent the smoke forcefully over his shoulder into the room, he shook his head.

"Don't worry about that, honey. It's the middle of winter. We'll invite them to our wedding in the summer, okay? The old man has always wanted to see Europe, and what better time to show him grand old Paris?"

"Are you sure? You never talk much about them. And I find it difficult to know what to ask." Agnès felt as if she was on uncharted
territory.

"There's nothing amiss, I promise you. They'll be on cloud nine
when they see you," Alan said, keeping his voice even, but she did not
miss the hint of irritation in it. Extinguishing his cigarette, he gave
her another kiss before jumping to his feet. "Let's get our stuff and hit
the road for Dragoncourt."

Agnès slowly raised herself to a sitting position, and while folding
the plaids, decided she would broach the subject with her father. He
would advise her. Should she just let Alan deal with it, or should she
ask him to let her write to his family in Chicago? Agnès knew the
subtleties of blood relationships; after all she had needed time to
disclose her own background and had only done so when Von
Spiegler had well and good arrived at Dragoncourt. Alan's situation
was far less compromising than hers, but the little contact he had
with his direct family bothered her.

An hour later, they were well wrapped up against the cold and
moving in the direction of Amiens, the trunk filled with suitcases and
their minds with memories. The roads they took were at once
familiar and yet totally changed. Though the winter landscape hid
most of the traces of war under a thick layer of snow, nothing could
fully camouflage the atrocities that had taken place in Picardy's fields.
They passed bombed-out churches and lake-sized craters, crumbling
walls standing forlorn in the barren landscape, and everywhere the
blackened stumps of trees, their branches powdered with white snow,
like surreal black and white skeletons pointing accusingly to the overcast skies above.

The Baron had to use all his concentration to keep the large,
scarlet Renault Torpedo on the slippery road, his Homburg hat deep
over his forehead and his lambskin gloves tightly around the steering
wheel. Alan, sitting next to him in the front seat, held a roadmap in
one hand and with the other wiped his handkerchief at regular inter-
vals across the front shield to clear Max's vision. The wind howled
around the canvas hood and blew right through it at the cracks,

sending ice-cold air inside the car that the heating could not handle. Typically Papa, Agnès mused, to buy a brand-new car on the spur of the moment, beautifully designed but meant for warm, summer rides.

Alan did his best to give directions from the roadmap, but they had to take several U-turns when roads were blocked or had simply stopped existing. Agnès sat in the back seat, pulling her fedora further over her forehead and the plaid tighter around her body. She watched the land outside the window with rising horror, wondering if France would ever recover from the magnitude of this destruction.

Paris, thankfully never conquered, had almost resumed its normal course in January 1919, but life in Picardy would need much longer to bounce back, if ever it would. Here was where all the fighting had been; here millions of men had given their lives, and for what? They had not even known themselves.

"Stop, Papa!" she suddenly cried, catching sight of a lonely rose on a long, wet stem leaning against the ruins of a wall, its red petals filled with snow. Her father braked, and she was out of the car. The rose had no reason to be there, but somehow it had withstood the elements and survived. And it was what Agnès needed right now: the comfort of something stronger than death, of indestructible nature.

The countryside stayed the same, glowing hills covered in snow, but they now passed endless graveyards on either sides, rows and rows of white tombstones everywhere, for the French, the Australian, the Brits, the Canadians, the Americans. One cross for every fallen man, lying side by side, nationality by nationality, in a place far from home.

"Stop!" she cried again, and her father grumbled, "What now?"

"Just park the car, Papa," she said. "Do you see that plaque, Alan? It says Commonwealth War Graves. I need to see if I can find the Sikh we operated on. Do you remember him?"

"Revant Chopra Sehgal?" Alan mused. "Of course. He was our first patient at Dragoncourt."

They both left the car, pushed open the iron gate, and entered the graveyard. As tiny flakes of snow began to fall from the sky, landing noiselessly on the chalky white of the upright gravestones, a deep silence settled over the secluded burial ground, where the spaces for the dead were precisely measured and positioned, so different from the chaos in which death had taken them.

The wind ceased to blow as if on command, and not a dead leaf stirred. The world had fallen into a profound silence, as if listening with devotion to the cosmic Voice, wordless, charged with tranquil emotion and the softest of touch. *I am a sacrifice to the Song which gives perpetual peace.* The doctors walked among the rows of graves, scanning the names. Some were mass graves, some anonymous, and some had name, rank, and battalion. Some were adorned with a cross, or a Jewish star, or the Islamic Moon and Star, or – very few – the crown and circle of the Sikhs.

"Here he is," Agnès finally observed. "Revant Chopra Sehgal, born Lahore, Punjab, 14 January 1900 - died Picardy, France, 30 March 1918. Oh, look! It would have been his birthday today." She bent down and swept the headstone clean, then laid the red rose on his grave.

They stood side by side, Alan's arm around her waist, deep in revered thought, until Agnès whispered, "Sorry I failed you, Revant."

"You didn't fail him, darling," Alan said, drawing her closer. "Remember how he called you his angel? Now let him be an angel for you."

Agnès let the tears stream down her cheeks in the memory of that golden boy, who should have had his whole life before him, and sniffling she promised, "I'll be back in the late spring to put poppies on your grave."

They continued their journey in silence. As they came closer to Dragoncourt, Agnès wondered what they would find there. During their phone call, Elle had told her not to worry; that Dragoncourt was almost restored to its original splendor, and that it was high time to throw the couple a small but intimate engagement party.

But it was not her engagement party that made her pluck nervously at the fringes of the tartan plaid. It was going back to the château itself. So much trauma, angst, and hardship had been endured there, and only six months had passed since. Feeling her heartbeat speed up, Agnès seriously doubted if she was ready to face the place again. Maybe this was a wrong decision. Maybe staying in Paris would have been better.

But the car moved on and she in it, and there was no more time for doubt, for Papa took the last bend and then they were on the gravel driveway lined with the clipped box-trees, green cones with a white top hat of snow. Seconds later, the château itself came into view, standing proudly amidst its snowy slopes, the walls unscathed in fresh cream-colored stucco, each turret decked with sparkling snow, and all the dorm windows illuminated, spreading a warm and inviting light from within. It was like a fairy-tale picture come to life, and Agnès immediately felt her nervousness ebb away. A pre-war sense flooded through her. Was it possible to be jolly again, to throw a party and forget? This house was proud and unconquered and as French renaissance as could be, and the national flag waved reassuringly on top.

"*Ahhhh*," the Baron exhaled. "*Mon Dieu,* is this the return to the times of yore? I sure yearn for those!"

"Jeez Louise." Alan whistled between his teeth. "So this is what you meant, Max, when you said I should visit one of Picardy's famous castles? Well, it certainly did not look this way the last time we were here. To be honest, it was a sorry mess then."

Agnès was quiet; she was just too impressed and relieved to say anything. As they arrived at the familiar parking place in front of the castle, she was surprised to see quite a number of cars with English and French number plates and even an American jeep.

Clearing her throat, she remarked, "I hope they haven't invited hordes of people. Elle promised to keep it a small affair. Well, perhaps they have other relatives staying. After all, the castle has so many wings."

At that moment, the front door opened, and a stout butler with a single tuft of black hair left in the middle of his scalp but impressive side-whiskers and a mustache stood legs apart, gauging the newcomers with shrewd, whiskey-brown eyes. He looked distinctly British in his black tailcoat, pinstriped trousers, and a high-collared white chemise. Not a person to jest with, Agnès thought. On making an impatient movement with his white gloved hand, two porters in simple black suits hastened down the steps to the car, standing ready on each side to open the doors as soon as Max brought the Renault to a halt.

Then it went all amazingly fast, in a swirl of color and motion. Elle skipped past the stiff butler in a flowery blue dress that danced around her body, with Jacques at a trot on her heels, looking dazzlingly like a pre-war polo player, and they were in one another's arms, kissing and hugging and shedding tears of joy and sorrow, with only the butler sniffing at what he considered a rather ostentatious display of emotion.

"Come quickly inside, you must be freezing," Elle cried, shivering in her own dress unsuitable for winter, and turning to Max while taking his arm in a companionable way, she continued, "Father and Mother can't wait to see you again. Is it okay if I steal Agnès and Alan away for a bit, and you catch up with my parents? They'll also show you to your quarters so you can freshen up."

"Of course, dear girl," Max said, nodding. "I'd be delighted to see Horace and Virginia again, absolutely delighted."

"Mr. Burton." Elle turned to the butler, who was still standing as if cast in wax on the platform. "Please take Baron de Saint-Aubin to my mother's drawing room. They're waiting for him there." Agnès involuntarily cringed. The room that had been Von Spiegler's office. She certainly hoped his ghost was no longer there. But there was no time to reminisce much. Elle had not exaggerated. The castle showed very few traces of what had passed there during the war. The corridors were freshly painted, and the rooms had been restored to their original function.

"I guess you want to have a quick peek at *la grande salle verte*?" Elle asked with a wink. "They're no longer your domain, Mr. and Mrs. Doctor Bell, remember."

"We had a quick meal just before we left; you know, the day..."

"Yes," Elle interrupted. "No talk of that! And that was makeshift! Come and have a look now!"

"Is it in its original splendor?" Agnès asked eagerly.

"You bet," Jacques chimed in. "No more white doctor's coats or smell of disinfectants but of roast duck and rustling silks!"

He pushed open the broad wooden door with the inlaid paneling, and around the oval dining table with the two chandeliers was sprinkled a gay light from myriad pear-shaped electric bulbs over the perfectly white damask cloth. They were welcomed by the cheers of Madeleine de Dragoncourt with Loulou on her shoulder, Gerald Hamilton at her side, and Philip Lane, Bridget McGovern, and Marie-Christine Brest.

"Well, I never," Agnès kept repeating, "Well, I never," while Alan held her tightly against him, sensing she was completely mind-blown and very emotional at seeing them all gathered. She was momentarily not even able to go over and greet them, but they understood and gave her time, meanwhile expressing their joy at seeing Alan so fit and strong.

Then there were dozens of kisses and *bonjours*, and so many stories to catch up with. One thing was clear for Agnès from the start. The audacious and charming Madeleine was having a particularly good time with the sandy-haired major Gerry, and the ring on her finger spoke volumes.

"They make a great pair," she mused, "absolute opposites but very compatible. Different from what Alan and I share, but certainly as lovely."

Agnès and Alan were also introduced to a group of three young men, one of whom was hunch-backed, and who were apparently friends of Madeleine.

Jacques had meanwhile put Irving Berlin's *That International Rag* on the phonograph and the scratchy but galvanizing sounds blasted through the room.

London dropped its dignity
So has France and Germany
All hands are dancing to a raggedy melody

Full of originality.

EVERYBODY STARTED DANCING, and Agnès marveled at sharing this new experience with Alan, seeing how fluidly he moved again and how he was enjoying himself. This was a whole new side to his normally so composed character. He threw his arms in the air, laughed out loud, and drew her into his arms, kissing her openly in front of everybody. Jacques was urged to put on new music all the time because they all wanted to dance and drink and be crazily merry. It was their first party after an awfully long and dark period, and they wanted it to go on and on.

Suddenly the door was flung open, and two impressive-looking military men with rows and rows of decorations and a high-ranking dignitary walked in, followed by the Count and Countess de Dragoncourt and the Baron de Dragoncourt and a very white-haired lady with a wrinkled face.

Jacques, mumbling an apology, rushed to the phonograph and killed the Powell brothers' *Pack Up your Troubles* mid-sentence.

"No worries, dear chap." The General in the British uniform grinned, which made his walrus mustache move sideways. "You young dogs deserve some ragtime or whatever you call it. My turn to apologize for the interruption, but I'd like to introduce you to some of *my* gang here."

He winked merrily at them, and his bushy white eyebrows danced. "On my left is General Arthur Bernard, deputy of General Ferdinand Foch, and on my right is Mr. William Graves Sharp, the American ambassador in France. And I go by the name of General Wallace Baxter, generally referred to as Uncle Wally, and I represent General Douglas Haig. Ah well, we're not as illustrious as we sound, but we like the pretense."

Despite the general's effort to downplay the importance of the military presence at Dragoncourt, the group of dancing friends huddled closer together, as they knew that in all the four years of war such high-ranking officials had never set foot in the castle – so their presence now meant something was about to happen. They all seemed to hold their breath, and Agnès seized Alan's hand and was grateful for the little squeeze he gave it.

The British general cleared his throat, and on a more serious note continued, "I can see that you're all a little anxious as to what this is all about, but there's no cause for anxiety. Not anymore. So please grab a seat. You too, Madame and sirs," he said, gesturing to the Dragoncourts and Agnès's father. Then he waited till everyone was seated.

"The procedure is as follows. I will begin, then General Bernard will address you, and finally the ambassador is here for a special purpose." He looked around the table where they were all sitting rather on the edge of their seats.

"To begin with, I want to say it is an honor to be here today with you, to present to nine young French citizens, one American citizen, and two British subjects the British War Medal 1914-1918. These nine young people have shown immense strength and courage during what has already entered history as the Great War. This silver medal is awarded to men and women of the British and Imperial Forces who either entered a theater of war or entered service overseas between the fifth of August 1914 and the eleventh of November 1918.

"Elle, Countess de Dragoncourt, would you please come forward?"

The tall girl in the flowery blue dress approached cautiously, looking from under her dark brow up into the general's fixed gaze.

He said with almost fatherly care, "You are awarded this medal for over 1100 transports of wounded military from the front to the war hospital here at Dragoncourt, numerous times descending into the trenches yourself to carry out the wounded. Many have returned to their families thanks to your actions."

Elle bent her head almost piously as he pinned the British War Medal on her dress.

The French general added, "Because you were a volunteer enlistee who served in the French army medical units, you are also awarded the *Médaille Commémorative de la Guerre 1914–1918.*"

And Elle was decorated again. She looked intensely vulnerable and shaken, and a tear slid down her cheek while she mumbled an almost inaudible "*Merci,*" and fingering the strange objects on her dress, went to sit next to her mother, where Countess Virginia, the spitting image of her youngest daughter Madeleine, kissed her eldest fondly.

General Baxter continued "Nurse Bridget McGovern, you are awarded these crosses for at least 700 ambulance rides to the front and back and for nursing some 2500 wounded soldiers here in the hospital, also during the four-month German occupation.

"Count Jacques de Dragoncourt, you are awarded these crosses for coordinating the more than 6000 wounded soldiers that were nursed here at Château de Dragoncourt and housing a battalion of the Royal West Kent Regiment.

"Nurse Marie-Christine Brest, you are awarded these medals for over 600 ambulance rides and nursing some 3500 wounded soldiers here in the hospital, also during the four-month German occupation.

"Earl Philip Lane, you are awarded these crosses for continuously assisting the hospital staff on site and making sure the hospital was well-stocked with medications and other provisions.

"Countess Madeleine de Dragoncourt, you are awarded these medals for showing enormous courage in espionage and thus providing to the Allied forces essential information during the German occupation of Dragoncourt."

Madeleine almost danced to the front to collect her medals, stating jubilantly, "I'd do it all again, Uncle Wally. So are you in need of a good spy?"

And the old man bent down and kissed her heartily on the cheek. "You'd be an asset to *my* gang, Miss Madeleine, or would you prefer to be in General Bernard's service?"

"Wherever I can be most useful. As long as it's not for the Bo..., pardon, the Germans." Madeleine walked back to the table, swinging her slender hips. She sat down between her mother and her fiancé with a broad smile on her painted red lips, and Loulou jumped onto her shoulder, chattering *Ook, ook, ook.*

"Patrick Denis, Blaise Deschamps, and André Duval, you are awarded these medals for four years of resistance against the German occupation and counterintelligence."

Madeleine sent Mme Denis a warm smile and saw the old lady almost burst with pride for her son.

"Agnès Baroness de Saint-Aubin, would you please come forward?"

Agnès let go of Alan's hand and gingerly stepped forward, but the General, so good at putting everyone at ease, gazed at her with his friendly paternal eyes and mouthed a *Don't worry* to her.

"You are awarded these crosses for carrying out more than 800 operations on wounded soldiers of the Allied forces, both in the American Hospital in Paris and here at Dragoncourt. You are the first female frontline doctor on the entire Western Front. Thanks to you, Madame Doctor, more than half of these men have been able to return to their families. You are also specifically decorated for continuing your work under German occupation, even saving the life of a German general, and thus never compromising your professional avowal to save lives."

He pinned the medal on her dress, and continued. "To honor your special services, one of your surviving patients is here to award you the *Médaille Commémorative de la Guerre 1914–1918*, together with General Bernard."

Agnès looked surprised as a young man in a blue aviation uniform entered the room, only one leg dragging slightly, but then her face broke in a wide smile as she stretched out her arms towards him.

"*Capitaine* Heurtier! Well, I never!" She did not know if it was appropriate, but she hugged him tightly as he humbly uttered, "*Madame Docteur*, it is such an honor!" He pinned the medal with trembling fingers as General Bernard looked on.

The English general took the lead again and said, "Could you please remain here for a moment, Madame, while I ask the other doctor to come forward? Please, Doctor Alan Bell?"

And Alan was by her side in no time, making her feel immediately more comfortable.

"Doctor Alan Bell, you are awarded these crosses for carrying out more than 900 operations on wounded soldiers of the Allied forces, both in Paris and here, and like Doctor de Saint-Aubin, you continued your work with the same dedication under German occupation. You are not only awarded these medals, but the American ambassador would like to address a special word to you. Please – Mr. Graves Sharp."

The portly ambassador, a frequent visitor and friend of Count de Dragoncourt, cleared his throat.

"Professor Alan Bell, even before America entered the war, you did your duty in the American Hospital in Paris, leading the medical team there. Your heroic acts during the war, in which you were severely wounded yourself, make you an outstanding American citizen, and therefore the President of the United States, Woodrow Wilson, has made the exceptional decision to award you the Medal of Honor, which very few American citizens receive."

Agnès had never seen Alan cry, not even during his own darkest hours. She had not even known if being an American meant much to him, but now she knew it did. He wept like a little boy; his beautiful surgeon's fingers curled before his face. This war had cost him so much, but it had yielded him as much. His love; his life. He was deeply moved when the third cross was pinned on his chest, and he uttered a bewildered, "God bless America," which the ambassador repeated with vigor.

General Baxter took the floor one more time.

"With the announcement that Major Gerald Hamilton will be promoted to Lieutenant-General, we have come to the end of the official ceremony. I congratulate him and the Countess Madeleine on their engagement. Allow me one final word. It pleases me immensely to note that the two brave doctors and the Lieutenant-General and Miss Spy have not only shown their professional capacities but also have found love. On behalf of all the Allied forces, the two couples will be offered a special reception at their wedding day. Long may they live!"

Agnès sought her father's eyes and saw he was quite overcome as well. She went over to him to receive his kiss and his blessing. Then she went over to hug Madeleine--both engaged to be married.

"Isn't it fantastic!" They said it in unison.

With the ceremonies over, the group of young, decorated war heroes was still rendered speechless from these words of high distinction and from being suddenly the center of all attention, when according to them all they had done was their duty.

Later, when the music had resumed and the tall champagne flutes stood bubbly and tingling in front of them, they inspected each other's medals, growing still closer together.

Together they had lost and won, and now they raised their glasses to victory and friendship, cursing and blessing the years of the Great War.

I HOPE YOU ENJOYED the two couples' stories *In Picardy's Fields?* Click here to find the original *Doctor Agnès's* story that I wrote before I embarked on *The Resistance Girl Series*. It is also an opt-in for my weekly Newsletter.

But there's more...
You will find an excerpt of the book #2, *The Diamond Courier,* on the next page.
So click through.

SNEAK PEEK THE DIAMOND COURIER

England, September 1939

Madeleine, Lili's mother, stood already in the doorway, tall and elegant in a lavender afternoon dress with a matching cardigan draped around her slim shoulders. Her coral lips curled widely though, and her amber eyes sparkled. But she would not be Madeleine to exclaim while taking Lili in her embrace,

"Oh, Liliane, we got you such lovely travelling dresses. Did you really have to wear those awful slacks?" But Lili felt forgiven by her warm kisses that landed on both her cheeks and her mother, pale and even thinner than before hugged her only child with as much strength as was femininely appropriate before leading her by the hand to the parlor where a cream tea was waiting for Lili's homecoming. Lili let herself be led like a little girl, happy to be in her mother's presence but meanwhile spied the room to see if Iain was in it too. He was not and for a moment she was disappointed. Was he not part of the little family and ought to have been present, to welcome her back? But then she corrected herself. He probably had other things to do and besides, he did not owe her anything. When she was seated on the settee with her mother close by and her father in his easy chair across from them, Lili grabbed the thin hand with the rich rings affectionately.

"Madame Paul told me a thousand times to give you her best wishes, Maman." Her mother was nibbling a thin slice of brioche and squeezed her hand back.

"Now did she?" The jest was palpable.

Lili could not stop herself,

"Now you must tell me what happened, Mummy! Stop being so secretive. I know you did something out of the ordinary when you were in Switzerland and I'm dying to know what it was and why you ran away." Her parents exchanged the same knowing look Lili had seen before and her mother raised her arms, in an expression of giving up, the bracelets tingling.

"*Eh bien*! Time to let the cat out of the bag, my girl, now you're no longer there. Well, just like you, I didn't want to go to *Le Manoir*. The Great War was everywhere, and I felt shut out and cooped up in neutral Switzerland while my sister and brother - your *Tante* Elle and *Oncle* Jacques - were having all the fun at our *château* on the front-lines. At least, that's what I thought in my *naiveté*. War is awful. Of course." Madeleine looked from her daughter to her husband, who added jokingly,

"I'm still glad you escaped that school, Maddy, or we wouldn't have met." Lili was astonished. This tone between her parents was so different from the stiff, coldish way they used to address each other. What had changed while she was gone? Had she been their obstacle? She dismissed the thought hearing her mother chuckle,

"Yes, Lili, *ma fille*, even your Maman used to have her wild days. And to be honest I sometimes miss them awfully."

"So what happened, Mummy?"

"*Ah ça*! Well, one night I just left and took the train to *Paris*. My family were outraged with me, of course. Certainly after I stole your *Oncle* Maurice's brand-new Renault and drove it all the way to Picardy."

Again, that giggle that seem to come deep from within her mother's throat. She clasped her thin beringed fingers together and her face shone with a new, natural light.

"I arrived in April 1918, just when the castle was about to be conquered by the Germans. And your dashing Papa and his battalion had to beat the retreat. There was no way for me to return to Switzerland. *Alors*...uh... I was suddenly in Amiens, with my family, biding our time in Allied territory while inside the castle our French doctors and nurses were held prisoner by the Germans. That's when I decided to win your father's heart with some tomfoolery of myself."

"Oh, Maddy, my love," Lili's father laughed, "you never told me you did it for me!"

"Men don't have to know everything." Madeleine winked at her daughter. Lili was too speechless to react. She had never seen her parents interact in so light-hearted a manner with each other. Her mother continued,

"Anyway, I became a spy, and I've got the war medal to show you, if you don't believe me."

"A spy? How?" Lili was all ears. Her posh mother, who never had one hair out of place and would not dream of going out without her coral lipstick in place.

"Easy-peasy. You have a German killed for you, you hop in his uniform, you make up a story and you walk back into your father's *château* as if you own it, without letting the temporary guests know, of course."

"Maman, you did no such thing. Not in a million years!" Lili cried out in utter disbelief.

"Gerald, can you get the little box from my *secretaire*? And the charter? The proof, *ma poupée!*" Her father was already heaving his overweight body from the chintz chair and did as his wife asked him. Meanwhile Madeleine continued in a soft voice,

"I'm only telling you all this, *ma chèrie*, so that you know that I understand your longing for a little leeway. It's partly your age, but also runs in your blood, so to say. Daddy and I have decided to give you a little more *liberté* so you can find out what you really want to do before settling down."

Lili studied her mother's war decorations in awe. Of course, she had seen all her father's medals many times before but was baffled to find out her upper-class mother was a decorated war veteran as well. From then on, Lili regarded her frail, Chanel-perfumed mother in a very different light.

DOWNLOAD The Diamond Courier.

AFTERWORD

Author's Note

Dear reader,

I hope you enjoyed *In Picardy's Fields*. I created this story with much love and care. However, I'm neither a doctor nor a historian, so I hope you'll not hold errors and impossibilities against me. It wasn't my intention to pen a truthful account of the last year of the First World War in Paris and Picardy. I wanted to write a story about brave men and women (especially women!) and what they could have been capable of and how they could have lived.

I did my medical and historic research to the best of my ability, so sometimes the story will be truthful to historic events, but I've taken the liberty to digress from history for the sake of *my* story. In case of medical mistakes, they're based on ignorance from my side.

I have honored my great-uncle Jack Westcott of the 6th Battalion, Queen's Own, Royal West Kent Regiment, by making Gerald Hamilton a major in that regiment, staying at the fictive Château de Dragoncourt. My great-uncle – my maternal grandmother's brother – fought in France in 1915-1916 and died on 3 July 1916 during the Battle of the Somme; his older brother, my great-uncle William Alexander Westcott, died eight days later when his ship *SS Calypso* was torpedoed off the coast of Norway. For more information on the history of my great-uncles, please visit my blog Historical Facts & Fiction.

I've found no evidence that female doctors went to the front lines in WWI. Nurses we all know, but I wanted to portray a female surgeon. Most likely there were also no female spies, as there was hardly any organized resistance against the Germans, but I felt the need to create a female spy *avant la lettre*.

Next to courage and honor, love is an important ingredient in my books, and I believe that great characters breed great children. So, if you liked the couples in this book, please meet the next generation doing their thing in WW2:

• Lili Hamilton, the daughter of Madeleine and Gerald, in The Diamond Courier.

• Océane Bell, the daughter of Agnès and Alan, in The Parisian Spy (Release date November 2021).

Thank you for reading!

With love,
    Hannah Byron

[Image: poppy.jpeg]

ABOUT THE AUTHOR

"Ever since I could hold a pen, I've written poems and stories and I'll write till my dying day."

Hannah Byron is the *nom de plume* of Hannah Ferguson. Born in Paris (France) in 1956, Hannah is of British/Irish/Dutch descent. She lives in The Netherlands.

Byron became a published author in 2012 and published seven books under her own name. After a forced break from writing because of family issues, she made her comeback in the fall of 2020 as a Historical Fiction author, focusing on the World Wars.

What started out as a general interest in the biggest war humanity ever endured became a passion and a drive. Byron herself is an indirect consequence of D-Day. Her uncle Tom landed on the beaches of Normandy and helped to liberate Holland. In 1949, her British mother traveled to south-west Holland, where she met Byron's Dutch father.

Studying WW 2 documents and listening to stories of (children) of active participants in the war, Byron made it her fictional duty to give a voice to those heroes and heroines who stood up against Nazism. After the war, these 'ordinary people' resumed their lives and never spoke of their heroic acts. Let future generations hear their stories and understand the devastating impact of war.

Resistance women are at the core of Byron's books. She pays tribute to a generation of women who kindled the women's lib movement, got dirty in overalls, flew planes, and did intelligence work.

Today's strong women stand on the shoulders of their (great-)grand-mothers. Byron's heroines fight for freedom, equality and... love.

  The Resistance Girl Series comprises one book on WWI *In Picardy's Fields*, and – so far - six books on WWII: *The Diamond Courier* (2020), *The Parisian Spy* (2021), *The Norwegian Assassin (2022)*, *The Highland Raven (27 Sept 2022)*, *The London Agent* (winter 2023) and *The Crystal Butterfly (Summer 2023)*.

ALSO BY HANNAH BYRON

The Resistance Girl Series

In Picardy's Fields

The Diamond Courier

The Parisian Spy

The Norwegian Assassin

The Highland Raven (preorder)

Spin-off novellas The Agnès Duet

Miss Agnes

Doctor Agnes

Printed in Great Britain
by Amazon

83261727R00181